THE OTHER SIDE OF HEAVEN

POSTWAR FICTION BY
VIETNAMESE AND AMERICAN WRITERS

EDITED BY
WAYNE KARLIN, LE MINH KHUE AND TRUONG VU

CURBSTONE PRESS

FIRST EDITION, 1995

Printed in the U.S. on acid-free paper by BookCrafters
Cover illustration: Stephanie Church
Cover design: Stone Graphics

Curbstone Press is a 501(c)(3) nonprofit publishing house whose operations are supported in part by private donations and by grants from ADCO Foundation, J. Walton Bissell Foundation, Inc., Witter Bynner Foundation for Poetry, Inc., Connecticut Commission on the Arts, Connecticut Arts Endowment Fund, Lannan Foundation, LEF Foundation, Lila Wallace-Reader's Digest Literary Publishers Marketing Development Program, administered by the Council of Literary Magazines and Presses, The Andrew W. Mellon Foundation, National Endowment for the Arts-Literature, National Endowment for the Arts International Projects Initiative and The Plumsock Fund.

Library of Congress Cataloging-in-Publication Data

The other side of heaven : postwar fiction / by Vietnamese and American
    writers ; edited by Wayne Karlin, Le Minh Khue, and Truong
    Vu. — 1st ed.
          p.   cm.
       ISBN 1-880684-31-4 (alk. paper)
       1. Short stories, Vietnamese—Translations into English. 2. War
    stories, Vietnamese—Translatlons into English. 3. Vietnam—Social
    life and customs—Fiction. 4. Vietnamese Conflict, 1961-1975-
    Fiction. 5. Short stories, American. 6. War stories, American.
    I. Karlin, Wayne. II. Le, Minh Khuê. III. Truong, Vu.
    PN6120.95.V46087 1995
    813'.0108358—dc20   95-20869

published by
CURBSTONE PRESS   321 Jackson Street   Willimantic, CT 06226

THE OTHER SIDE OF HEAVEN:
Postwar Fiction by Vietnamese and American Writers

vii ACKNOWLEDGMENTS
xi INTRODUCTION, by Wayne Karlin

PART ONE: A WALK IN THE GARDEN OF HEAVEN:
    A Walk in the Garden of Heaven, by George Evans
5   The American Blues, by Ward Just
15   Wandering Souls, by Bao Ninh

PART TWO: THE HONORED DEAD: *A Walk in the Garden of Heaven*
25   Nada, by Judith Ortiz Cofer
33   Fragment of a Man, by Ho Anh Thai
51   A Soldier's Burial, by Philip Caputo
65   Two Village Women, by Nguyen Quang Thieu
73   The Honored Dead, by Breece D'J Pancake

PART THREE: WOUNDS: *A Walk in the Garden of Heaven*
85   The House Behind the Temple of Literature, by Tran Vu
95   Helping, by Robert Stone
118   The Rucksack, by Le Luu
122   The Pugilist At Rest, by Thom Jones
137   Please Don't Knock on My Door, by Xuan Thieu
155   Speaking of Courage, by Tim O'Brien
166   The Man Who Stained His Soul, by Vu Bao
172   Dressed Like Summer Leaves, by Andre Dubus
182   The Slope of Life, by Nguyen Mong Giac
189   Waiting For Dark, by Larry Brown

PART FOUR: HAUNTINGS: *A Walk in the Garden of Heaven*
201   Waiting for a Friend, by Ngo Tu Lap
204   Paco's Dreams, by Larry Heinemann
210   Tony D, by Le Minh Khue
223   The Billion Dollar Skeleton, by Phan Huy Duong

PART FIVE: EXILES: *A Walk in the Garden of Heaven*

235   The Autobiography of a Useless Person, by Nguyen Xuan Hoang

245   Coming Down Again, by John Balaban

252   The Key, by Vo Phien

258   The Walls, the House, the Sky, by Thanhha Lai

266   Twilight, by Hoang Khoi Phong

PART SIX: LEGACIES: *A Walk in the Garden of Heaven*

279   Rashad, by John Edgar Wideman

287   The Sound of Harness Bells, by Nguyen Quang Lap

294   Point Lookout, by Wayne Karlin

300   Humping the Boonies, by Bobbie Ann Mason

308   Letters from My Father, by Robert Olen Butler

313   Above the Woman's House, by Da Ngan

322   She in a Dance of Frenzy, by Andrew Lam

327   Marine Corps Issue, by David McLean

340   Mother and Daughter, by Ma Van Khang

353   Heat, by Richard Bausch

379   The General Retires, by Nguyen Huy Thiep

PART SEVEN: *A Walk in the Garden of Heaven*

401   EPILOGUE by Gloria Emerson

404   CONTRIBUTORS/TRANSLATORS

ACKNOWLEDGMENTS

Excerpt from *Coming Down Again* by John Balaban, published by Harcourt, Brace, Jovanovich, 1985. Copyright © 1985 by John Balaban. Reprinted by permission of the author.

Excerpt from *The Sorrow of War* by Bao Ninh. Originally published as *Than Phan Cua Tinh Yeu* by Nha Xuat Ban Hoi Nha Van, Hanoi, 1991. Originally published in English as *The Sorrow of War*. Copyright © 1993 by Martin Secker & Warburg Ltd. Reprinted by permission of Martin Secker & Warburg.

"Heat" (editor's title) excerpted from *Rebel Powers* by Richard Bausch. Copyright © 1993 by Richard Bausch. Reprinted by permission of Houghton Mifflin Co./Seymour Lawrence. All rights reserved.

"Waiting For Dark" (editor's title) excerpted from *Dirty Work* by Larry Brown. Copyright © 1989 by Larry Brown. Reprinted by permission of Algonquin Books of Chapel Hill, a division of Workman Publishing Co., New York, N.Y.

Letters from My Father by Robert Olen Butler. Copyright © 1992 by Robert Olen Butler. From *A Good Scent From A Strange Mountain*. Reprinted by permission of Henry Holt, Inc.

"A Soldier's Burial" (editor's title) excerpted from *Indian Country* by Philip Caputo. Copyright © 1987 by Philip Caputo. Reprinted by permission of Bantam Publishers, Inc.

"Nada" by Judith Ortiz Cofer from *The Latin Deli* by Judith Ortiz Cofer. Copyright © 1993 by Judith Ortiz Cofer. Reprinted by permission of the University of Georgia Press.

"Above the Woman's House" by Da Ngan. Originally published as "Tren Mai Nha Nguoi Phu Nu" in *Van Nghe* (Hanoi), 1990. Translation copyright © 1994 by Bac Hoai Tran and Dana Sachs. Translated and reprinted by permission of the author.

"Dressed Like Summer Leaves" by Andre Dubus. Copyright © 1986 by Andre Dubus. From *The Last Worthless Evening* by Andre Dubus, published by Crown Publishers, Inc., by arrangment with David R. Godine Publishers, Inc. 1987. Reprinted by permission of the author.

"A Walk in the Garden of Heaven" by George Evans. Copyright © 1994 by George Evans. First published in *New Letters* 61:1. Reprinted by permission of the author.

"Twilight" by Hoang Khoi Phong. Copyright © 1991 by Hoang Khoi Phong. Originally published as "Hoang Hon" in *Thu Khong Nguoi Nhan* by Thoi Van (California), 1991. Translation © 1995 by Thai Tuyet Quan, Truong Hong Son and Wayne Karlin. Translated and reprinted by permission of the author.

The editor gratefully acknowledges the help and encouragement of the following people: Bac Hoai Tran, John Baky, Herman Beavers, Lady Borton, Chinh Huu, Renny Christopher, Dao Kim Hoa, Judy Doyle, W.D. Ehrhart, Martín Espada, George Evans, Carolyn Forché, Michael Glaser, Larry Heinemann, Ho Anh Thai, Huu Thinh, Ho Nguyen, Marc Leepson, Nguyen Nguyet Cam, Nguyen Qui Duc, Dana Sachs, Jay Scarborough, Sandy Taylor, Thoa Tham, Vu Tu Nam, Bruce Weigl, Robert Willson, and Peter Zinoman.

Special thanks to Ohnmar Thein Karlin for her patience about my astronomical telephone and fax bills and general obsessiveness, the William Joiner Center for its work bringing American and Vietnamese writers together—meetings that led to the creation of this project—and for the help and support of its director, Kevin Bowen; to Ralph Timperi for his work for the William Joiner Foundation clinic in Hue; to Dan Duffy, who through his work with *Vietnam Generation* and the *Viet Nam Forum* has worked tirelessly to bring Vietnamese literature to the United States, and who gave unselfishly of his time, knowledge and contacts to the editor. Finally, Gloria Emerson, confined to her home for over a year because of an accident, was an unending source of ideas, editorial discussion, inspiration, energy and advocacy for this book—all while undergoing physical therapy and in often great pain. The unstinting help she gave to this project under such circumstances was marked by the grace, courage and passion that have defined her entire life.

Introduction

Wayne Karlin

This book was born out of the meeting of two people who, if they had met two decades previously, would have tried to kill each other. The meeting occurred during an extraordinary program sponsored by the William Joiner Center for the Study for War and Social Consequences at the University of Massachusetts, Boston that brought together American writers, most of whom were veterans of what we called the Vietnam war, and Vietnamese writers, most of whom were veterans of what they called the American War. Over a number of years, starting in 1988, Joiner brought some of the leading writers of Vietnam to stay in the United States, and, in turn, the Vietnam Writers' Association in Hanoi hosted a delegation of visiting American writers.

In the summer of 1993, I was one of the guest writers at Joiner, teaching a writing workshop and participating in panels about the effects of war on literature and society—and getting to know the three Vietnamese writers who had been invited that year: Nguyen Quang Thieu, Huu Thinh and Le Minh Khue, with whom we shared two houses in Dorchester, hosted by the Bowen and Davidson families. A deep friendship formed between us that summer, fueled by the intensity of emotion that occurs when people who had looked at each other, first, as personifications of their most basic fears and hatreds, and, later, as figures who populated whatever mythological niches the war had settled into in their minds—suddenly become human beings to each other. "We remembered there was a time we would have killed each other," writes George Evans in the poem which serves as the structure for this book, a poem written about that meeting with the Vietnamese in Boston. The juxtaposition of that realization with the realization of how much we liked each other, how much we had in common, how terrible it would have been if we'd succeeded in killing each other, brought us to moments of what I can only describe as a grief so intense that it changed us so we could never again see each other—or ourselves—in the same way. For me, that basic emotional shift became tied to a moment when in a conversation over the breakfast table with Le Minh Khue she found I'd been a helicopter gunner for a time and I found that she, from the time she was fifteen to the time she was nineteen, had been in a North Vietnamese Army Brigade that worked, often under attack from our aircraft, clearing bombs on the Ho Chi Minh Trail. We had become friends by then and at that moment I pictured myself flying above the jungle canopy, transfixed with hate and fear and searching for her in order to shoot her, while she looked up, in hatred and fear also, searching for me—and how it would have been if I had found her then. To waste someone, we called killing in the war, and the word had never seemed more apt. I looked across the table then and saw her face, as if, after twenty years, it was at last emerging from the jungle canopy. She looked across at me and saw the same. It was that look, that sudden mutual *seeing* of the humanness we held in common—which is of course what all good stories should do—that led to this book.

What drew the Vietnamese and Americans together at Joiner was more than the historical or personal accident that we had been in the war. It also had to do with the fact that we had chosen to write about the war or its aftermath, that we shared a compulsion to use our art as an instrument of witness. The war had shown us in the most vivid way possible the kinds of choices human beings had to make and the consequences of those choices, the damage left behind. *We've destroyed too much to be sentimental. We know that those above and those below/ the jungle canopy killed anything that got in the way, and we're all guilty of something./ Wars are always lost. Even if you win*, writes American veteran George Evans, echoing the Vietnamese veteran and novelist Bao Ninh: "Justice may have won, but cruelty, death and inhuman violence have also won....Losses can be made good, damage can be repaired and wounds will heal in time. But the psychological scars of the war will remain forever." We'd become writers, like all writers, because we thought we were good at it. But we'd also become writers because we knew in the deepest sense the way in which simplifying human beings and human situations to the priorities of power or convenience or fashion could lead to death and degradation. We had become writers, in other words, for the reasons any good writers do: we wanted to tell stories that showed the complexities of the human heart, its capacity for both love and brutality; we wanted to show the human faces, under the leaves, under the noise of the rotors, under the hatred and fear that distorted those faces into configurations of hatred and fear. We knew, deeply, those of us who were in the war, that to not write about these things was the beginning of moral death and physical murder.

When the Vietnamese and American writers left Boston that summer, we felt severed, as if we were cutting ourselves off from a part of ourselves we'd just discovered. There seemed something unfinished about the meeting, a feeling something concrete should come out of it. The twentieth anniversary of the end of the war was coming up in 1995, and I began to think about another twentieth anniversary I'd had: in 1973 I'd been one of the editors of the first anthology of fiction by Vietnam veterans, *Free Fire Zone*. Why don't we do a similar anthology now, but this time with writers from both the United States and Vietnam? I wrote to Le Minh Khue in Vietnam; it seemed a fitting time to close the circle. She responded enthusiastically and we began, through the long lags of international mail, to discuss the project. What we wanted, we decided, was a work of reconciliation that came from a mutual recognition of pain and loss; what we wanted was to open in our readers' hearts the recognition that had opened in our own. We decided to collect the stories that had come out in both our countries about the aftereffects of the war—on the soldiers who fought it, on their families and on their societies, stories both by veterans and non-veterans: our criteria would only be how good they were as stories, and how well they fit into the theme of the cost of the war to both countries. In order to extend the healing we hope will be suggested by the book, we also decided that whatever royalties the book earned would go to the Joiner Foundation Pediatric Clinic in Hue, Vietnam, a facility funded by American veterans.

In Vietnam, after a request from the Joiner Center, The Vietnam Writers' Association appointed Le Minh Khue consulting editor for the anthology. In the United States, I began collecting American stories and lining up translators. As I did, my search led me to come into contact with writers and scholars in the overseas Vietnamese community—and to the realization that the anthology could not in justice be defined as a work of reconciliation unless it included voices from the other Vietnamese side of the war. I began to find some work by the younger generation of Vietnamese-Americans written in English, but I also knew that a whole body of literature was being published in Vietnamese language journals in this country. In September of 1993 I met Truong Hong Son (Truong Vu), a courageous, humane and highly civilized man who, I soon found, shared the same views about writing, about the commonality of pain and the necessity for reconciliation, about the need of literature to tell uncompromisingly painful truths—that had drawn me to Le Minh Khue. A friendship developed between me and Son that, like my friendship with Le Minh Khue and the other Vietnamese writers, has transformed and enriched my life. Son was the perfect person to help find the kind of stories suitable for the anthology. He is both the quintessential Vietnamese and the quintessential American—a stubborn survivor who dreamed impossibly and fit life to the needs of his dream, a South Vietnamese war veteran, a refugee who started with nothing and became an aerospace engineer at NASA, a lover of literature (the poetry he hated to learn in high school, he told me, helped him to get through war and exile) and a literary scholar who is the editor-in-chief and moving spirit behind the journal *Doi Thoai*, a forum that brings together both the work of intellectuals in Vietnam and that of Vietnamese overseas.

In addition to my own selections from available American fiction, Le Minh Khue, working through the Vietnam Writers' Association in Hanoi, and Truong Hong Son in the United States, had sent me over fifty stories in Vietnamese or in rough translation. I've made the final selections from that pool, adding any other work I thought appropriate, since by force of circumstance I was the editor who finally saw all of the work together and in the same language (whatever sins of omission or inclusion exist in this book are mine). Besides the stories sent to me, I also looked for work from Vietnam by writers whose work was already translated but not available in Vietnam and who may not have been in the Writers' Association, as well as work from the Vietnamese community abroad already published or written in English. I selected stories from all these groups, when I could get permission from the writers or publishers. As you read the stories, you will meet people with conflicting views about the war, characters who in some cases still hate the "enemy," still see the other side as Other—I've made no attempt to choose stories according to their politics or their characters' take on who was right and who was wrong in the war. I didn't do so because I'm pretending to be above politics or that politics don't matter. I have my own views on the war. But I wanted the anthology to reflect the many ways the war still affects us. Divisiveness, hatred and bitterness are part of the wounds of war; they are part of the cost we are still paying.

In December of 1994 I returned to Vietnam for the first time since the war. During my stay I was able to see the country the way I had come to see my friends from Vietnam: it shifted out of the morass of association, memory and imagination and became real to me, a country and a people rather than a war. In the two weeks I was there, with the cooperation of the Vietnam Writers' Association and Chinh Huu, the member of the executive committee in charge of foreign relations, I was able to work with Le Minh Khue, with my good friend the novelist Ho Anh Thai, and with the interpreter Doa Kim Hoa, and to meet and secure reprint agreements with the Vietnamese writers in the book who are members of the Association.

A note about the structure of this book: I've tried to arrange the stories so that they work like chapters in a novel, one leading into another, and the best way to read the anthology is straight through, as you would a novel. George Evans graciously allowed me to truncate his prose poem "A Walk in the Garden of Heaven"; I found its sections form introductions to the "chapters" of the book: the chapters respectively center on the need to tell the story, the grief of loss and the ways the dead continue to haunt the living, the psychologically and morally and physically wounded, the tragedy of exile, and, finally, the displaced, the lonely, the haunted, the trapped—the children of the war. There is no chapter called "the well-adjusted," and there may be some objections raised on the grounds that the stories portray only the damaged. Popular culture has stereotyped the Vietnam veteran, variously, as psychopath, loser or martyr, depending on the cultural and political needs of particular moments. These are not stereotypes I wish to encourage. Most American veterans of the war (I don't have similar statistics for Vietnam) have gone on to live normal and in many cases quite successful lives. However studies of veterans who actually were in combat show that from 27% to 65% of them, depending on which source one reads, suffer from Post-Traumatic Stress Disorder, which in its most acute forms results in "broken families, substance abuse, criminal activity, and suicide" (according to D. Michael Shafer in an article which reflects the conclusions of most of the scholars who have been concerned with PTSD—among others, Robert Lifton, Jonathan Shay and Patience Mason). Shafer maintains that "PTSD-afflicted veterans are more likely than their non-veteran peers to be divorced, separated or living alone. Their wives and lovers, too, pay an unrecognized price for their men's service in Vietnam in the form of emotional withdrawal, family disruption, and both emotional and physical abuse...many try to protect their loved ones from the latter by suicide. Thus, for example, the Center for Disease Control reported in 1987 that by five years after the war's end [1980] Vietnam veterans were dying at a rate 45% higher than those who did not serve in Vietnam, had a 72% higher suicide rate, and a higher incidence of violent deaths in general." These are the figures for the United States where we lost 59,000 killed and 270,000 wounded. We can imagine the degree of trauma among survivors in Vietnam where, according to Stanley Karnow, the Vietnamese from both sides of the war lost more than four million killed, soldiers and civilians—ten per cent of the entire population. By war's end, as reported by Marilyn B. Young, a largely rural population had been displaced, with 9000 out of 15,000 villages destroyed in the South as well as 25 million acres of farmland, 12 million acres of forest and 1.5 million farm animals. In Vietnam after the war there were "an estimated 200,000 prostitutes, 879,000 orphans, 181,000 disabled people, and 1 million widows; all six of the industrial cities of the North had been badly damaged ...Nineteen million gallons of herbicide had been sprayed in the South during the war [with]...severe birth defects and multiple miscarriages...apparent early on." "To understand my stories," Le Minh Khue wrote to me, "you have to understand their background in my country's history of suffering and war." The facts and statistics in this paragraph form some of the background of the stories you will read in this book—they form the commonality that links the individual lives you'll see illuminated.

When I sat down to decide upon an order for the stories, I found that a strange—or perhaps not so strange—synchronicity was taking place. Not only did the selections echo each other thematically, but often situations or characters would seem to leap from one story to another. Ward Just and Bao Ninh both write about writers, one in Washington, one in Hanoi, unable to let the war go, struggling to finds ways to write about it. The woman in "Nada," Judith Ortiz Cofer's powerful story of grief, loses a son named Tony in the war; in Le Minh

Khue's story "Tony D," two Hanoi hustlers find the bones of a dead American (who begins to haunt them); they identify him as Tony from his dog tags. Ngo Tu Lap's "Waiting for A Friend" is told by the ghost of a dead North Vietnamese soldier who, with his other dead squad mates, observes the life of the lone surviving member of their unit, just as the ghosts in Larry Heinemann's "Paco's Dreams" observe and comment on the life of Paco—the only survivor of their unit—as if he's living for all of them. In Nguyen Mong Giac's "The Slope of Life" we see two veterans who had grown up together in the same village, one a former soldier of the losing side, one a veteran of the winning side, one an amputee, the other blind, meeting in a Saigon cafe, just as two American veterans, one black, one white, one a quadruple amputee, the other scarred, meet in a VA hospital in Larry Brown's "Waiting for the Dark." In Richard Bausch's "Heat" a son tells the story of how he—and his mother—lost his father to the war, even though his father came home, and of his mother's need and struggle to free herself. In Ho Anh Thai's complex and whimsical "Fragment of a Man" a son tells how his mother lost her husband, his father, to the war—and how the war still clings to his life because of his mother's fear of losing him as she lost her husband, and how this has affected his need first to marry and then to stay with his wife out of pity rather than love. Many of the stories have similar threads that weave them together, and of course, in truth, that quality is not strange: a soldier's bitterness and alienation or cynicism at the way truth is twisted after the bullets no longer fly, a mother's grief, a spouse's rage at the loss of the ability to love, a child's sense of aching absence—or resentment of a war-driven possessiveness that clutches, generation to generation, like the claws of the past: these are the losses, the costs of war that echo back and forth, that unify the stories, that finally unify us.

Will any of this do any good? In the end that's the basic question any writer who writes about murderous things, whose desk sits above ditches filled with the corpses of real people who have died prematurely and in agony, has to ask. It's a question Philip Caputo tries to answer in the prologue to *A Rumor of War*, his account of his tour in Vietnam: "[This book]...might keep the next generation from being crucified in the next war," he writes, but then, in a new paragraph, a terrible pause of five spaces, he adds: "But I don't think so." He understands the fascination of war; we understand what fills in those five empty spaces: we can look around ourselves in this the last decade of the world's bloodiest century, in this time when countless works of the intellect and the imagination have endlessly analyzed and depicted the horrors of war and see that he's right.

But none of this excuses those of us who know, and who make our living by telling stories, from telling what we know. "We have to struggle against disinterest in the face of others' suffering, against greed and the baseness that corrodes heart and mind. We must teach each other to love, so that war will never happen again," said Le Minh Khue to the writer W.D. Ehrhart in Hanoi.

Each story brings us a human face. Each story brings us our own face. The stories enter us, become a part of us; afterwards we can never look at each other in the same way again. In the commonality of loss and pain, defeat and occasional triumph that make up all good stories, we see each others' human faces, emerging from the leaves of the jungle canopy, from the blankness of the sky.

PART ONE
A Walk in the Garden of Heaven

A Walk in the Garden of Heaven
George Evans

A Letter to Vietnam
for Huu Thinh, Le Minh Khue, and Nguyen Quang Thieu

1

They were talking when we entered the garden, two young people whispering with their hands, mist threads drifting from mountain tops on the raked gravel ocean. Islands afloat on the skin of infinity. The mind without its body.

"The moment I saw your face," he said, "was like walking into the Hall of A Thousand and One Bodhisattvas."

She had no idea what he meant, how it is to enter Sanjusangendo in Kyoto for even the fiftieth time and see row upon row of a thousand standing figures, carved, painted, and gold-leafed with a calm but stunned look of enlightenment, five hundred on each side of a larger, seated figure of their kind, miniature heads knotted to their scalps representing the fragments of a time when their heads exploded in dismay at the evil in this world, the way our heads exploded in the war, though we don't wear our histories where they can be seen.

Each statue has twenty pairs of arms to symbolize their actual 1,000 arms, these enlightened ones who choose to remain on earth and not end the cycle of death and rebirth some believe we go through until we get it right. They pause at the edge of nirvana to stay behind and help us all get through. It's easy to think they are foolish instead of holy.

But each hand holds twenty-five worlds it saves, and because each figure can multiply into thirty-three different figures, imagine the thirty-three thousand worlds they hold, how much distress there really is, then multiply that by a thousand and one and think of what it's like to stand in an ancient wooden temple with all that sparkling compassion, even for those of us who believe in almost nothing.

Garden of Heaven refers to Tenshin-en / 天心園 the Japanese rock garden at the Museum of Fine Arts, Boston. The three Vietnamese writers listed above came to the U.S. for the first time in the summer of 1993 as guests of the William Joiner Center of Boston. I visited the garden with Mr. Huu Thinh and Ms. Le Minh Khue, both war veterans.

It is said, and it's true, that if you search the thousand faces, you will find the face of someone lost from your life.

But the young girl in the garden was bored and looked over her lover's shoulder at a twist of flowers. Then so did he. The spell was broken.

We are older. There are so many wasted lives between us that only beauty makes sense. Yet we are like them. We are. They are the way it is between our countries. One talking, one looking away. Both talking, both looking away.

The American Blues

Ward Just

This is not a story of the war, except insofar as everything in my unsettled middle age seems to wind back to it. I know how much you dislike reading about it, all dissolution, failure, hackneyed ironies, and guilt, not to mention the facts themselves, regiments of them, *armies.* But I must risk being the bore at dinner for these few opening pages, for the life of the war is essential to the story I have to tell. And that is not about the war at all but about the peace that followed the war.

At the time the People's Army commenced its final murderous assault on Saigon I was living safely in a remote district of New England, far from the anarchy of battle and outside the circulation zones of serious newspapers. This was several years after my wife and I had quit the city for the country, having decided to go back to basics in the woods. We wanted a natural environment, clean air, safe schools, wood stoves, and a preindustrial economy. In our fervor to simplify, we went to the northern edge of the nation, thinking of it as the frontier.

In fact, we were refugees from wartime Washington. Or perhaps the more accurate term is exiles, though no one forced us to leave. Our exile was voluntary: we abandoned Washington as good soldiers might desert a ravaging army. We believed that our home for many years had become diseased—poisoned with greed, ambition, and bloodlust. My wife saw this before I did, and saw also that we had become part of it, accomplices—against our will, she insisted, though of course as a journalist I had been a willing witness to the war's progress, drawn to it for no other reason than it was there, remaining because there seemed no other place to be. In Washington my wife and I feared for what we considered our special closeness and appetite for each other. Sexual passion withered in the heat of such megalomania. My wife thought of the capital as some monstrous contagion, hence our abrupt and bravura departure for the north country— from the vicious to the chaste, from the extraneous to the basic, from the heart of America to its margins. This was in 1973.

Without newspapers to read, I followed the end of the war on television, via a single network, because my house was so situated in the mountains that I could receive only one channel. I watched the collapse on that one network, my continuity. And it was different from yours. I knew the theater of operations, its geography and ambience, and many of the American officials present at the end and most of the journalists. I knew its history as well as I knew my own, having been there for two and half years, and indeed in some respects watching the war on television was like watching a home movie, a blurred 8mm film from childhood showing the house we no longer lived in and the father who was dead, a tiresome experience unless you had been there and remembered: then it was excruciating. This was a house in which some part of you would always dwell and a father who would be on guard forever. You saw yourself skylarking, innocent, and unafraid, though entirely aware of the Kodak whirring away, seizing the moment. I wanted to call out and stop the film: *Don't Do That!* But it would speed up, the images racing, faster and faster, and there was no stopping it, then or later. Of course at the time the future was unrevealed: I could not foresee the consequences. Later, I would understand that it was predictable— even by me, one who believed that history never repeated itself. What came later was no surprise, including my own broken nerves and trepidation. The shakes came much later, when images leached from my memory like shrapnel from flesh: so many human beings, multitudes. I had watched them, now they watched me; turn, and turn about. In 1975 it was my own memory on film, and this memory was crowded with fear and ardor, hot and bittersweet as an old blues,

> *You told me that you loved me*
> *but you told me a lie.*

They were diabolical memories, hard to communicate and ever harder to share. Yet my feet beat perfect time to the music, everyone said so. The war, the war, the war, the war; for a while, we thought it would go on forever, a running story. And how fascinating that it was an American responsibility, supervised by our best minds. Surely somewhere there was consolation.

So I leaned forward toward the small screen, connected to the war by the network, my looking glass. I was alert to the most obscure detail, often smiling, frequently near tears. It was all personal. I knew their faces, mannerisms, and personal histories. A particular friend of mine was a senior diplomat in the American embassy who was routinely interviewed in the last days by my old colleague Nicholson. The interviews were near parodies of the decades-old quarrel between officials and reporters. My friend was by then a very tired and distracted official, and he gave Nicholson no satisfaction. Of course Nick was polite and sympathetic, his bedside manner never more attractive than when tending a terminally ill patient. But my friend gave at least as good as he got, and his truculence amid the ruins showed him to good advantage. On the small screen he was a formidable character.

Nicholson asked him, "What do you think, now that it's almost over?"

My friend was shrewdly silent, knowing that television cannot abide silence. He was careful not to move his eyes or dip his head or otherwise display embarrassment or disarray.

Annoyed, Nicholson began again. "It's collapsing all along the line." He named the provincial capitals that had fallen in the past twenty-four hours, even pretty little My Tho was under siege. "And now that it is, is there something we could have done differently? Or should have or might have? Or perhaps there was something we shouldn't've done at all?" Nicholson leaned over my friend's gunmetal desk, holding the microphone delicately with his thumb and forefinger, as he might a flute of champagne. He scented blood.

My friend said, "Yes," not needing to add "you son of a bitch," because it was plain in the tone of his voice. They had known and cordially disliked each other for years.

Nicholson said, "Looking back on it—"

"Looking back on it is something we'll do for a very long time," my friend said. "It'll become an industry. There are so many of us who've been here."

"Yes," Nick said. The camera moved in tight on him. "And the lessons? What will the lessons be?"

"In order to sleep soundly, Americans will believe anything. Do you know who said that?"

Nicholson, thrown on the defensive, shook his head.

"Stalin," my friend said.

"Well—"

"According to Shostakovich." Nick said nothing, wary now and alert to diplomatic nuance. But my friend only added mildly, "The composer. In his memoirs, I think."

Nick pounced: "But what will they be, the lessons?"

The diplomat's voice was soft, almost hushed. "They will be whatever makes us think well of ourselves. So that our sleep will be untroubled. But it's too early to tell, isn't it? We must wait for the after-action reports. The conferences and symposia. The publication of classified documents." I watched my friend thrust and parry, his face perfectly expressionless, though drawn. I thought he was getting the better of it.

"You've been here as long as anyone," Nicholson said, smiling as if he intended a compliment. "And now you seem to be saying that the war's ended at last." Nick wanted a confession and this was by way of reading the subject his rights. He moved the microphone in the direction of the window and cocked his head, smiling wanly. Boom boom. Gunfire, or what sounded like gunfire.

"It is lost, yes."

"That's not the same thing," Nicholson said.

"No," my friend agreed.

"Well!" Nicholson said, smiling again. I noticed that he had had his teeth capped. He looked fit, though tired. Probably it was only a hangover. "Surely you would not contend—"

"I am not contending anything," my friend said. "It's only a word. Pick the word you want. Your word isn't accurate, as a matter of fact. The war will not end when the Americans leave. One part of the war will end but the war has more than one part. However, this is not our happiest or our proudest or our most honorable hour. If that is what you want me to say, I am saying it." He opened his mouth as if to continue, then didn't. He probably figured he had said too much. There was a moment of silence. Nicholson let it run, knowing now that the advantage was his. My friend said, "One can choose his own word. That word or some other word. It depends on where one sits."

Lame, I thought. Dour, obscure, and unconvincing. But dead accurate.

"Right now," Nick said smoothly, "we're sitting in the American embassy, third floor." He smiled again and gestured at the American flag behind the big desk. It hung from a standard crowned with a fierce golden American eagle. There were framed documents on the walls, and a lithograph that I remembered from other occasions. My friend took it with him wherever he went, one of Picasso's melancholy musicians. The camera lingered on it.

"Exactly," my friend said. His voice was like flint, and now he moved to gather some papers on his desk. He ignored the microphone Nick held only inches from the end of his nose. "At least you've got that exactly right, where we are now."

I remembered his tone of voice from another occasion, early in the war. He had taken me to lunch to explain a particularly subtle turn in American war diplomacy. It was too subtle for me, I didn't get any of it, but I did not let on and let him talk himself out, thinking that sooner or later I would pick it up, understand what it was he was trying to tell me, and then I would have a story. He wound down at last and looked at me with a frigid smile. Then he said, "It's convenient for you, isn't it? Being here, listening to me, waiting for a crumb of information. Some fact, any fact at all will do, so long as it's fresh. Facts and flesh stink after a day in this heat. Isn't that right?" I protested. It was *his* lunch, undertaken at *his* invitation—Yes, he said wearily, that was true. Then he laughed, and when I asked him what was funny, he replied that his situation was too droll; now he was conducting diplomacy through the newspapers, and they were American newspapers. He explained that he was trying to reach a certain circle in Washington, and he thought he could do it through my newspaper, through me. They never read the cables, and when they did they carped and complained....Too droll, he said again, ordering cognacs for us both; it wasn't diplomacy at all, it was public relations.

There was a brief fade to black and then the camera went in tight on Nicholson. Now he was standing in the embassy driveway. He delivered a few portentous sentences, a kind of fatigued now-you-see-it-now-you-don't commentary on the interview. Artillery crashed in the background. Then he identified himself, "outside the American embassy on Thong Nhat Avenue, Saigon."

Nicholson had a reputation as television's most adroit interviewer, but that was the closest he came to cracking my friend. And he kept at it, night after night. Their little sparring match would end Nick's report, until more violent events in the streets made interviews superfluous, or perhaps they both tired of the charade. I admired my friend's tenacity but I was distressed at his appearance, his eyes tired and his hair graying and longer than I remembered it, his widow's peak pronounced and causing him to look older than he was. His shaggy hair gave him an untidy appearance. Normally he was a fastidious man and a model diplomat, the son of one ambassador and the nephew of another, the grandson of an army general and the great grandson of a secretary of the treasury. One way and another his family had been in government for a hundred years, and this fact was never very far from my friend's thoughts, certainly not then, in the last days of the war. Despite his ancestry, or because of it, he was the most "European" of the American officials I knew. His was a layered, mordant personality, the past and the present always in subtle play. He had married and divorced a Parisian and was now married to an Italian woman, a Venetian who was my wife's closest friend; my wife and the Venetian had studied history together. He had a special affection for his wife's family who had survived, by his estimate, seven centuries of criminal venery from the doges to Mussolini, in the family palazzo on the Grand Canal—and how had they survived? Indolence, he said.

I pulled for the diplomat in his struggle with Nicholson, and not only because of my friendship with him and my wife's with his languid Venetian lady. I wanted to see him come away with something. There was no equity in an agony where only the observers profited. The more bad news the better, the deeper the quagmire the more the correspondents flourished. Connoisseurs of bad news, Nicholson and I had been the most celebrated of the virtuosos, Nick with his camera and deft interrogation and I with my pencil and notebook and clear sight. We were scrupulous in our search for delusion, error, and falsehood. We worked close to the fire, give us that; and we were entranced by its light, smitten, infatuated. And it was not a schoolboy's crush but a grand passion, a *coup de foudre* that often strikes men of a certain age. However, my mordant friend was not smitten, and he distrusted romantic metaphors. He believed simply that the United States had gotten itself into a war that it could not win. It could not win against the Vietnamese Communists any more than Bonaparte could win against the Russian winter. Americans had begun the war with an excess of optimism, but what country did not? The Italians always had. Now there would be consequences and to avoid them would only make matters worse, perhaps a good deal worse. Of course he hated being a part of it, there had been so many blunders and so many dead and so much waste. And unlike the Italians, we had tried so hard.

In front of the camera my friend was still and contained and vaguely contemptuous. He approved of journalism in the abstract but disliked the kind of man who seemed attracted to it. Journalists seemed to him to be naive utopians, and they were never worse than when covering wars. They routinely violated the physicist's great rule, "Everything should be made as simple as possible, but not simpler." And Nicholson and I? We tried hard, too; no one could fault our zeal. Our enthusiasm for the fall—its blood and dark rhythms, its delusion, the inexorability of the descent, the fulfillment of all the worst prophecies—was almost religious in its intensity, and at home our dispatches were followed with the devotion that Gypsies give tarots. Of course we wanted no wider war, Nicholson and I—though I was obsessed with my friend's prediction, it seemed almost to be a curse: "Now there will be consequences and to avoid them would only make things worse, perhaps a good deal worse."

That was my own situation, appallingly real in the north country as I watched my friend on the small screen. He was a good man and an able diplomat and I felt sorry for him, distressed at his appearance and uncomfortable in his company, though we were twelve thousand miles apart; and of course disappointed that he never looked the camera in the eye, though that may have been the strategy of the cameraman, who had been with Nicholson for many years. Nick was a professional, no more but no less either.

That last week of the war I watched television every day, beginning with the morning news and ending with the wrap-up at eleven. Of course I was most attentive in the evening, my own day done; and knowing that in the Zone it was early morning. Their day was just beginning. Each day was worse than the day before, and the suspense was in wondering how much worse. How bad could it get? My wife refused to watch with me, being opposed both to the war and to television news on principle. We had always been great newspaper readers. In the evenings my son, aged seven, agreed to keep me company. That last week there was combat footage from the countryside and film also of the various landmarks in the capital, the Street of Flowers, the old JUSPAO building, Aterbea's Restaurant, the National Assembly, and the two white hotels, the Caravelle and the Continental, all places I knew well from the previous decade.

Don't you want to see this? I called to my wife.

Not especially, she said from the kitchen.

Look, I said, there's Jessel. This was another old friend, a newspaperman. A hand-held camera caught him standing in Lam Son Square at the corner of the rue Catinat, making notes. He was wearing a sort of bush suit and a side arm in a holster and a steel helmet. He was thick around the middle.

I don't know him, she said.

I said, Sure you do, don't you remember? We met him and his wife, his then-wife, in New York that time. That time we had so much fun in the bar at the Algonquin. She was very young. You liked his wife, remember?

She said, Yes. It was at some bar. And they're divorced now. And I didn't like her.

I said, I wish to hell they didn't wear those bush suits. They didn't wear them in my day, at least the newspapermen didn't. And, Christ, he's packing heat. He thinks he's Ernest Hemingway, liberating the bar of the Caravelle. Except he's not going in, he's going out.

My son squirmed on the couch next to me.

I think it's a violation of the Geneva Convention, I continued. The rules are very clear. Correspondents are not combatants, and they are not authorized to bear arms. And you have the rank of major, so if you're captured you're a field-grade officer and entitled to respect—

Your dinner's ready, she said.

In a minute, I replied. I was watching Jessel, so tubby and complacent. In the old days Jessel had never worn bush suits. The war was not a safari. He had never carried a handgun, either.

I'll go ahead then, she said.

A rooftop shot from the Caravelle restaurant provoked a cascade of reminiscence, much of it overwrought, perhaps bogus. This lunch, that dinner; who was present and what we ate and the details of the winelist, and the horror stories, the changing estimate of the situation, and the waiter whom we believed to be a VC agent. A glimpse of the adjoining building made me laugh out loud. It was the apartment window of the Indian money changer, the "mahatma"; the window was ablaze with light, and I imagined the transactions within, tortuous now no doubt. I described the look of the flares over the Mekong, the river bright as a carnival in the light of burning phosphorus, and the thump of artillery on the opposite shore. I was being cheerful for the benefit of my wife, who had convinced herself that we had all had a fine time in South Vietnam.

I thought again of Jessel. At that time he was living with a Vietnamese woman with whom he had no common language. His American girlfriend, the young woman he later married, had gone home. The Vietnamese was a well-educated woman who spoke excellent French, but Jessel had no French, so they communicated by high sign and in pigeon.

Jessel, I said. A funny son of a bitch.

Then a radio jingle came back to me, a choir:

> *Don't you get a little lonely*
> *All by yourself*
> *Out on that limb?*
> *Without Him?*

The last word was drawn out, in barbershop harmony, Himmmmmmm. Sponsored by the Army chaplain corps, it ran a dozen times a day on the Armed Forces Radio Network, inserted between the Supremes and Jimi Hendrix and exhortations to Stay Alert, Stay Alive. I sang the jingle to my son, who did not understand it. I remembered smiling every time I heard it. It was so—chaste. And the chaplains were so demoralized and broken up. They were from another world altogether, and now, thinking about them and their jingle, I moved to the other end of the couch. Tears jumped to my eyes. My wife gathered up our son and took him to bed. But I did not stop telling anecdotes, which were coming in a rush. I recited them out loud, to myself. An American official—a new man, I didn't know him—appeared on screen and gave an account in a gruff voice. He looked frightened, listening to explosions in the distance.

I waited for my friend the diplomat. I had come to depend on him. But he was not interviewed that evening, nor was Nicholson anywhere in sight. Nick had probably gone up-country. The news shifted to Washington, a correspondent standing in the great circular driveway; in the background, figures moved on the porch of the mansion. Of course, it was dusk in Washington. The correspondent had information from confidential sources, none of whom were prepared to appear on camera or permit the use of their names. But the situation in the Zone was...very grave, desperate, in fact, and they in the White House seemed courageously prepared for the inevitable. The reliable sources described the atmosphere as tense but calm. The correspondent leaned into the camera, I knew him as a bon vivant; now he was selling gravity as he would sell soap or automobiles. He despised his métier, but the camera was kind to him.

The news ended and another program replaced it. I refilled my glass but did not move to turn off the set. I had arranged a drinks tray, so everything was within easy reach. I watched a game show, noisy with hysterical contestants and a frantic master of ceremonies. My time in the Zone came back to me in bits and pieces—an exotic tapestry. It was with me part of every day in any event, but now, concentrating, I discovered forgotten material. The patterns changed according to the distance you were from it, one of Escher's devilish constructions. It was like reading a well loved novel years later and finding fresh turns of plot and character to admire. I remembered a friend saying once that if you were lucky enough to discover Trollope in middle age you'd never do without, because you could never live long enough to read all he wrote. I felt that way about the war, so remarkably dense an experience, with such treasure still buried. My Trollope war, so rich with incident and the friendships were forever. The diplomat and I had many escapades.

Upstairs, I heard my wife reading to our son.

Come on down! I shouted.

The door opened. What do you want? my wife asked.

I want to tell you about the war! On television, the master of ceremonies gestured grandly at the balcony and yelled, Come on down!

She said something I didn't hear and closed the door.

I didn't notice. I was too drunk to notice. I had been drunk for a month, since well before the final offensive of the People's Army and the collapse of the Free World Forces. So the offensive was not a cause of my drinking, or an excuse or justification for it. But it was not a reason to stop, either.

The year 1975 was turbulent and even now I have difficulty sorting it out. Public affairs seemed to loom over us, darkening the prospect. Of course Nixon was already gone. Ford was soon to go. Each day brought weird revelations. The attorney general went to jail. The disgraced vice-president was frequently photographed at Las Vegas and was said to be making a killing as a corporate consultant, import-export. There was a picture in the newspaper of him shaking hands with Joe Louis, his fingers on the Brown Bomber's shoulder as if they were friends. The vice-president's tan was so deep, he could have been the champion's brother; he was smiling, obviously enjoying himself in Vegas. Joe wore a plastic golf cap, looking old and ruined. I went on the wagon for a month.

There were changes in the north country as well. A Venezuelan bought the dairy farm down the road from my house, the purchase conducted through nominees. An article in a business paper asserted that for the rich in nations of social and political unrest, New England farmland was as desirable as Krugerrands or Old Masters. The Venezuelan was followed by an industrialist from Peru, who bought a horse farm. The columnist in the local paper complained that the lingua franca in the valley would soon be Spanish. He took to describing our selectmen as "the junta" and predicting revolution. Then he announced that he himself was emigrating to Maine, at least the Abenaki spoke English and were indisputably North American. My wife and I briefly discussed putting our house on the market, then thought better of it; we were in the north country to stay, she said. There were other confusing portents. A large New York bank failed and nearly brought down the valley bank with it. The chairman explained at a party one night that his bank had gone heavily into Eurodollars on the expert advice of the president of the New York bank, a close personal friend who owned a condominium in the ski area nearby. The president facilitated these purchases, one banker lending his expertise to another. That was the reason there was no mortgage money in the valley: it was all in Europe and disappearing fast.

The news from Indochina after the fall of Saigon was fragmentary, and weeks would pass with no reports on the evening news. No news was not good news. I thought of it as a dark and threatening silence, as unpropitious in its way as the deep restless fastness of the woods surrounding my house. When, later, the Chinese invaded north Vietnam the dominoes trembled, but held; so fathead Dulles had been at once right and wrong about the course of events in Southeast Asia.

I was writing a history of the war. I completed the book in good time, all but the final chapter. For my description of the end of the war I was obliged to depend on the recollections of others. I decided to write a simple reconstruction of the final battle. Six times I went to Washington to interview civilians from the State Department and CIA and the Pentagon, and military officers everywhere in the city. Many were friends from the previous decade and were generous with their time; we knew many of the same stories. I obtained classified documents, but these did not clarify the situation; they were secret but not very interesting, and often false or misleading. Facts piled up, but I could not fit them together in any plausible way. What had seemed so clear in front of the television set now seemed erratic and unfocused, drunken events reeling from day to day with no logic or plan. And what was the consequence, other than the obvious thing? I was unable to interview my friend the diplomat, who had been posted to another, very remote embassy; there was a rumor he was on the outs with the Department. We corresponded for a time but his letters were perfunctory, and he declined to volunteer any fresh facts or fresh interpretations of the known facts. I was disappointed but not surprised. He had always been a very discreet official.

I knew that a simple reconstruction of the final battle was not enough. Through friends who had been active in the antiwar movement I applied for a visa to Vietnam, but was put off; perhaps later, when the situation stabilized. No one was getting in then.

I told my wife, I can't end this book.

You have got to let it go, she said.

The book? I asked incredulously. She couldn't know what she was asking.

The war, she said furiously.

Wandering Souls

Bao Ninh

His room began to get colder as the winter pressed in. He stood by the window one cold night, missing Phuong as usual, as he watched the slow drizzling rain, slanting with the northeast wind. Scenes from the northern battlefront began forming before him and he saw once again the Ngoc Bo Ray peak and the woods of the Screaming Souls. Then each man in his platoon reappeared before him in the room. By what magic was this happening to him? After the horrible slaughter which had wiped out his battalion, how could he see them all again? The air in his room felt strange, vibrating with images of the past. Then it shook, shuddering under waves of hundreds of artillery shells pouring into the Screaming Souls Jungle and the walls of the room shook noisily as the jets howled in on their bombing runs. Startled, Kien jumped back from the window.

Bewildered, confused, deeply troubled, he began to pace around the room away from the window. The memories flared up, again and again. He lurched over to his desk and picked up his pen then almost mechanically began to write.

All through the night he wrote, a lone figure in this untidy, littered room where the walls peeled, where books and newspapers and rubbish packed shelves and corners of the floor, where empty bottles were strewn and where the broken wardrobe was now cockroach-infested. Even the bed with its torn mosquito net and blanket was a mess. In this derelict room he wrote frantically, nonstop, with a sort of divine inspiration, knowing this might be the only time he would feel this urge.

He wrote, cruelly reviving the images of his comrades, of the mortal combat in the jungle that became the Screaming Souls, where his battalion had met its tragic end. He wrote with hands numbed by the cold, trembling with the fury of his endeavor, his lungs suffocating with cigarette smoke, his mouth dry and his breath foul, as all around him the men fought and fell, one by one, falling with loud painful screams, amidst loud, exploding shells, among thunderclaps from the rockets pouring down from the helicopter gunships.

One by one they fell in that battle in that room, until the greatest hero of them all, a soldier who had stayed behind enemy lines to harass the enemy's withdrawal, was blown into a small tattered pile of humanity on the edge of a trench.

The next morning rays from the first day of spring shone through to the darkest corner of his room.

Kien arose, wearily trudging away from the house and out along the pavement, a lonely-looking soul wandering in the beautiful sunshine. The tensions of the tumultuous night had left him yet still he felt unbalanced, an eerie feeling identical to that which beset him after being wounded for the first time.

Coming around after losing consciousness he had found himself in the middle of the battlefield, bleeding profusely. But this was the beautiful, calm Nguyen Du Street, and there was the familiar Thuyen Quang lake from his childhood. Familiar, but not quite the same, for after that long, mystical night, everything now seemed changed. Even his own soul; he felt a stranger unto himself. Even the clouds floating in from the northeast seemed to be dyed a different color, and just below the skyline Hanoi's old gray roofs seemed to sparkle in the sunshine as though just sprinkled with water.

For that whole Sunday Kien wandered the streets in a trance, feeling a melancholy joy, like dawn mixed with dusk. He believed he had been born again, and the bitterness of his recent postwar years faded. Born again into the prewar years, to resurrect the deep past within him, and this would continue until he had relived a succession of his lives and times; the first new life was to be that of his distant past. His lost youth, before the sorrow of war.

He went to a park that afternoon, ambling along uneven rocky paths lined with grass and flowers, brushing past shrubs still wet with rain. Coming to an empty bench near a lovers' lane, he sat for hours just listening to the quiet wind blowing over the lake as he gazed into the distance, far beyond the horizons of thought to the harmonious fields of the dead and living, of unhappiness and happiness, of regret and hope. The immense sky, the pungent perfume from the beautiful new spring and a melodic sadness that seemed to play on the waves of the lake combined to conjure up within his spiritual space images of a past, previously inexplicable life.

He saw himself in a long-ago distant landscape, and from that other images and memories revived and he sat silently reviewing his past.

Memories of a midday in the dry season in beautiful sunshine, flowers in radiant blossom in the tiny forest clearing; memories also of a difficult rainy day by the flooded Sa Thay river, when he had to go into the jungle collecting bamboo-shoots and wild turnips. Memories of riverbanks, wild grass plots, deserted villages, beloved but unknown female figures who gave rise to tender nostalgia and the pain of love. An accumulation of old memories, of silent pictures as sharp as a mountain profile and as dense as deep jungle. That afternoon, not feeling the rising evening wind, he had sat and allowed his soul to take off on its flight to his eternal past.

Months passed. The novel seemed to have its own logic, its own flow. It seemed from then on to structure itself, to take its own time, to make its own detours. As for Kien, he was just the writer; the novel seemed to be in charge and he meekly accepted that, mixing his own fate with that of his heroes, passively letting the stream of his novel flow as it would, following the course of some mystical logic set by his memory or imagination.

From that winter's night when he began to write, the flames of memory led Kien deeply into a labyrinth, through circuitous paths and back out again into primitive jungles of the past. Again, seeing the Sa Thay river, Ascension Pass, the Screaming Souls Jungle, Crocodile Lake, like dim names from hell. Then the novel drifted towards the MIA team, gathering the remains, making a long trail linking the soldiers' graves scattered all over the mountains of the North and Central Highlands; this process of recalling his work in gathering remains had breathed new energy into each page of his novel.

And into the stories went also the atmosphere of the dark jungle with its noxious scents, and legends and myths about the lives of the ordinary soldiers, whose very deaths provided the rhythm for his writing.

Yet only a few of his heroes would live from the opening scenes through to the final pages, for he witnessed and then described them trapped in murderous firefights, in fighting so horrible that everyone involved prayed to heaven they'd never have to experience any such terror again. Where death lay in wait, then hunted and ambushed them. Dying and surviving were separated by a thin line; they were killed one at a time, or all together; they were killed instantly, or were wounded and bled to death in agony; they could live but suffer the nightmares of white blasts which destroyed their souls and stripped their personalities bare.

Kien had perhaps watched more killings and seen more corpses than any contemporary writer. He had seen rows of youthful American soldiers, their bodies unscathed, leaning shoulder to shoulder in trenches and dugouts, sleeping an everlasting sleep because artillery barrages had blocked their exit, sucking life from them. Parachutists still in their camouflaged uniforms lying near bushes around a landing zone in the Ko Leng forest, burning in the hot noonday sun, with only hawks above and flies below to covet their bodies. And a rain of arms and legs dropping before him onto the grass by the Sa Thay river during a night raid by B52s. Hamburger Hill, after three days of bloody fighting, looked like a dome roof built with corpses. A soldier stepping onto a mine and being blown to the top of a tree, as if he had wings. Kien's deaths had more shapes, colors and reality of atmosphere than anyone else's war stories. Kien's soldiers' stories came from beyond the grave and told of their lives beyond death.

"There is no terrible hell in death," he had once read. "Death is another life, a different kind than that we know here. Inside death one finds calm, tranquillity and real freedom..."

To Kien dead soldiers were fuzzier, yet sometimes more significant than the living. They were lonely, tranquil and hopeful, like illusions. Sometimes the dead manifested themselves as sounds rather than shadows. Others in the MIA team gathering bodies in the jungles said they'd heard the dead playing musical instruments and singing. They said at the foot of Ascension Pass, deep inside the ancient forest, the ageless trees whispered along with a song that merged into harmony with an ethereal guitar, singing, "*O victorious years and months, O endless suffering and pain...*"

A nameless song with a ghostly rhythm, simple and mysterious, that everyone had heard, yet each said they'd heard different versions. They said they listened to it every night and were finally able to follow the voice trail to where the singer was buried. They found a body wrapped in canvas in a shallow grave, its bones crumbled. Alongside the bones lay a handmade guitar, intact.

True or not? Who's to know. But the story went on to say that when the bones were lifted to be placed in a grave all those present heard the song again echoing through the forest. After the burial the song ended, and was never heard again.

The yarn became folklore. For every unknown soldier, for every collection of MIA remains, there was a story.

Kien recalled the Mo Rai valley by the Sa Thay river when his group found a half-buried coffin. It had popped up like a termite hill on a riverbank, so high even the floods hadn't reached it. Inside the coffin was a thick plastic bag, similar to those the Americans used for their dead, but this one was clear plastic. The soldier seemed to be still breathing, as though in a deep sleep. He looked so alive. His handsome, youthful face had a serious air and his body appeared to be still warm, clothed in a uniform that was still in good condition.

Then before their eyes the plastic bag discolored, whitening as though suddenly filled with smoke. The bag glowed and something seemed to escape from it, causing the bag to deflate. When the smoke cleared, only a yellowish ash remained.

Kien and his platoon were astounded and fell to their knees around it, raising their hands to heaven praying for safe flight for the departed soul. Overhead a flock of geese, flying solemnly and peacefully in formation, winged their way past.

"If you can't identify them by name we'll be burdened by their deaths for the rest of our lives," the head of the MIA team had said. He had been an insurance clerk at one time. Now his entire life was gathering corpses. He was preoccupied with this sole duty which was to locate, identify, recover then bury the dead soldiers. He used to describe his work as though it were a sacred oath, and ask others to swear their dedication.

An oath was hardly necessary for Kien or the others in the MIA team. They'd emerged from the war full of respect and mourning for the unfortunate dead, named and nameless alike.

Translated by Phan Thonh Hao
Edited by Frank Palmos

PART TWO
The Honored Dead

2

We entered the garden by chance. We were like the rocks there, plucked from some other place to be translated by circumstance into another tongue. And in the silent crashing of stone waterfalls, and rising of inanimate objects into music, we remembered there was a time we would have killed each other.

In the future we will think of it again. We might get drunk beneath a great moon and see one another's eyes in a pool of water, or remember in a glance across a Formica table in a kitchen filled with friends and noisy children, or while walking down the street. But it will not be the same.

It is called realizing you have lived, and it happens only once.

NADA

Judith Ortiz Cofer

Almost as soon as Doña Ernestina was informed about her son having been killed in Vietnam, she started giving her possessions away. At first we didn't realize what she was doing. By the time we did, it was too late.

The Army people had comforted Doña Ernestina with the news that her son's "remains" would have to be "collected and shipped" back to New Jersey at some later date, since other "personnel" had also been lost on the same day. In other words, she would have to wait until Tony's body could be processed.

Processed. Doña Ernestina spoke that word like a curse when she told us. We were all down in *El Basement*—that's what we called the cellar of our apartment building: no windows for light, boilers making such a racket that you could scream bloody murder and almost no one would hear you. Some of us had started meeting here on Saturday mornings—as much to talk as to wash our clothes—and over the years it became a sort of women's club, where we could catch up on a week's worth of gossip. That Saturday, however, I had dreaded going down the cement steps. All of us had just heard the news about Tony the night before.

I should have known the minute I saw her, holding court in her widow's costume, that something had cracked inside Doña Ernestina. She was in full *luto*—black from head to toe, including a mantilla. In contrast, Lydia and Isabelita were both in rollers and bathrobes: our customary uniform for these Saturday-morning gatherings—maybe our way of saying "No Men Allowed." As I approached them, Lydia stared at me with a scared-rabbit look in her eyes.

Doña Ernestina simply waited for me to join the other two leaning against the machines before she continued explaining what had happened when the news of Tony had arrived at her door the day before. She spoke calmly, a haughty expression on her face, looking like an offended duchess in her beautiful black dress. She was pale, pale, but she had a wild look in her eyes. The officer had told her that—when the time came—they would bury Tony with "full military honors"; for now they were sending her the medal and a flag. But she had said, "No, gracias," to the funeral, and she sent the flag and medals back marked *Ya no vive aquí*: Does not live here anymore. "Tell the Mr. President of the United States what I say: *No, gracias.*"

Then she waited for our response.

Lydia shook her head, indicating that she was speechless. And Elenita looked pointedly at me, forcing me to be the one to speak the words of sympathy for all of us, to reassure Doña Ernestina that she had done exactly what any of us would have done in her place: Yes, we would have all said *No, gracias* to any president who had actually tried to pay for a son's life with a few trinkets and a folded flag.

Doña Ernestina nodded gravely. Then she picked up the stack of neatly folded men's shirts from the sofa (a discard we had salvaged from the sidewalk) and walked regally out of El Basement.

Lydia, who had gone to high school with Tony, burst into tears as soon as Doña Ernestina was out of sight. Elenita and I sat her down between us on the sofa and held her until she had let most of it out. Lydia is still young—a woman not yet visited too often by *la muerte*. Her husband of six months had just gotten his draft notice, and they have been trying for a baby—trying very hard. The walls of El Building are thin enough so that it has become a secret joke (kept only from Lydia and Roberto) that he is far more likely to escape the draft due to acute exhaustion than by becoming a father.

"Doesn't Doña Ernestina feel *anything?*" Lydia asked in between sobs. "Did you see her, dressed up like an actress in a play—and not one tear for her son?"

"We all have different ways of grieving," I said, though I couldn't help thinking that there *was* a strangeness to Doña Ernestina, and that Lydia was right when she said that the woman seemed to be acting out a part. "I think we should wait and see what she is going to do."

"Maybe," said Elenita. "Did you get a visit from *El Padre* yesterday?"

We nodded, not surprised to learn that all of us had gotten personal calls from Padre Alvaro, our painfully shy priest, after Doña Ernestina had frightened him away. Apparently El Padre had come to her apartment immediately after hearing about Tony, expecting to comfort the woman as he had when Don Antonio died suddenly a year ago. Her grief then had been understandable in its immensity, for she had been burying not only her husband but also the dream shared by many of the barrio women her age—that of returning with her man to the Island after retirement, of buying a *casita* in the old pueblo, and of being buried on native ground alongside *la familia*. People *my* age—those of us born or raised here—have had our mothers drill this fantasy into our brains all of our lives. So when Don Antonio dropped his head on the dominoes table, scattering the ivory pieces of the best game of the year, and when he was laid out in his best black suit at Ramirez' Funeral Home, all of us knew how to talk to the grieving widow.

That was the last time we saw both her men. Tony was there—home on a two-day pass from basic training—and he cried like a little boy over his father's handsome face, calling him *Papi, Papi*. Doña Ernestina had had a full mother's duty then, taking care of the hysterical boy. It was a normal chain of grief, the strongest taking care of the weakest. We buried Don Antonio at Garden State

Memorial Park, where there are probably more Puerto Ricans than on the Island. Padre Alvaro said his sermon in a soft, trembling voice that was barely audible over the cries of the boy being supported on one side by his mother, impressive in her quiet strength and dignity, and on the other by Cheo, owner of the *bodega* where Don Antonio had played dominoes with other barrio men of his age for over twenty years.

Just about everyone from El Building had attended that funeral, and it had been done right. Doña Ernestina had sent her son off to fight for America and then had started collecting her widow's pension. Some of us asked Doña Iris (who knew how to read cards) about Doña Ernestina's future, and Doña Iris had said: "A long journey within a year"—which fit with what we had thought would happen next: Doña Ernestina would move back to the Island and wait with her relatives for Tony to come home from the war. Some older women actually went home when they started collecting social security or pensions, but that was rare. Usually, it seemed to me, somebody had to die before the island dream would come true for women like Doña Ernestina. As for my friends and me, we talked about "vacations" in the Caribbean. But we knew that if life was hard for us in this barrio, it would be worse in a pueblo where no one knew us (and had maybe only heard of our parents before they came to *los estados unidos de América,* where most of us had been brought as children).

When Padre Alvaro had knocked softly on my door, I yanked it open, thinking it was that ex-husband of mine asking for a second chance again. (That's just the way Miguel knocks when he's sorry for leaving me—about once a week—when he wants a loan.) So I was wearing my Go-to-Hell face when I threw open the door, and the poor priest nearly jumped out of his skin. I saw him take a couple of deep breaths before he asked me in his slow way—he tries to hide his stutter by dragging out his words—if I knew whether or not Doña Ernestina was ill. After I said, "No, not that I know," Padre Alvaro just stood there looking pitiful until I asked him if he cared to come in. I had been sleeping on the sofa and watching TV all afternoon, and I really didn't want him to see the mess, but I had nothing to fear. The poor man actually took one step back at my invitation. No, he was in a hurry, he had a few other parishioners to visit, etc. These were difficult times, he said, so-so-so many young people lost to drugs or dying in the wa-wa-war. I asked him if *he* thought Doña Ernestina was sick, but he just shook his head. The man looked like an orphan at my door with those sad, brown eyes. He was actually appealing in a homely way: that long nose nearly touched the tip of his chin when he smiled, and his big crooked teeth broke my heart.

"She does not want to speak to me," Padre Alvaro said as he caressed a large silver crucifix that hung on a thick chain around his neck. He seemed to be dragged down by its weight, stoop-shouldered and skinny as he was. I felt a strong impulse to feed him some of my chicken soup, still warm on the stove from my supper. Contrary to what Lydia says about me behind my back, I like living by myself. And I could not have been happier to have that mama's boy Miguel back where he belonged—with his mother who thought that he was still her baby. But this scraggly thing at my door needed home cooking and maybe even something more than a hot meal to bring a little spark into his life. (I mentally asked God to forgive me for having thoughts like these about one of his priests. *Ay bendito,* but they too are made of flesh and blood.)

"Maybe she just needs a little more time, Padre," I said in as comforting a voice as I could manage. Unlike the other women in El Building, I am not convinced that priests are truly necessary—or even much help—in times of crisis. "*Sí, hija,* perhaps you're right," he muttered sadly—calling me "daughter" even though I'm pretty sure I'm five or six years older. (Padre Alvaro seems so "untouched" that it's hard to tell *his* age. I mean, when you live, it shows. He looks hungry for love, starving himself by choice.) I promised him that I would look in on Doña Ernestina. Without another word, he made the sign of the cross in the air between us and turned away. As I heard his slow steps descending the creaky stairs, I asked myself: What do priests dream about?

When El Padre's name came up again during that Saturday meeting in El Basement, I asked my friends what *they* thought a priest dreamed about. It was a fertile subject, so much so that we spend the rest of our laundry time coming up with scenarios. Before the last dryer stopped we all agreed that we could not receive communion the next day at Mass unless we went to confession that afternoon and told another priest, not Alvaro, about our "unclean thoughts."

As for Doña Ernestina's situation, we agreed that we should be there for her if she called, but the decent thing to do, we decided, was give her a little more time alone. Lydia kept repeating, in that childish way of hers, that "something is wrong with the woman," but she didn't volunteer to go see what it was that was making Doña Ernestina act so strangely. Instead she complained that she and Roberto had heard pots and pans banging and things being moved around for hours in 4-D last night—they had hardly been able to sleep. Isabelita winked at me behind Lydia's back. Lydia and Roberto still had not caught on: if they could hear what was going on in 4-D, the rest of us could also get an earful of what went on in 4-A. They were just kids who thought they had invented sex. I tell you, a *telenovela* could be made from the stories in El Building.

On Sunday Doña Ernestina was not at the Spanish mass, and I avoided Padre Alvaro so he would not ask me about her. But I was worried. Doña Ernestina was a church *cucaracha*—a devout Catholic who, like many of us, did not always do what the priests and the pope ordered, but who knew where God lived. Only a serious illness or tragedy could keep her from attending mass, so afterward I went straight to her apartment and knocked on her door. There was no answer, although I heard scraping and dragging noises, like furniture being moved around. At least she was on her feet and active. Maybe housework was what she needed to snap out of her shock. I decided to try again the next day.

As I went by Lydia's apartment, the young woman opened her door—I knew she had been watching me through the peephole to tell me about more noises from across the hall during the night. Lydia was in her baby-doll pajamas. Although she stuck only her nose out, I could see Roberto in his jockey underwear, doing something in the kitchen. I couldn't help thinking about Miguel and me when we had first gotten together. We were an explosive combination. After a night of passionate lovemaking, I would walk around thinking: Do not light cigarettes around me. No open flames. Highly combustible materials being transported. But when his mama showed up at our door, the man of fire turned into a heap of ashes at her feet.

"Let's wait and see what happens," I told Lydia again.

We did not have to wait for long. On Monday Doña Ernestina called to invite us to a wake for Tony, a *velorio*, in her apartment. The word spread fast. Everyone wanted to do something for her. Cheo donated fresh chickens and island produce of all kinds. Several of us got together and made *arroz con pollo*, plus flan for dessert. And Doña Iris made two dozen *pasteles* and wrapped the meat pies in banana leaves that she had been saving in her freezer for her famous Christmas parties. We women carried in our steaming plates, while the men brought in their bottles of Palo Viejo rum for themselves and candy-sweet Manischewitz wine for us. We came ready to spend the night saying our rosaries and praying for Tony's soul.

Doña Ernestina met us at the door and led us into her living room, where the lights were off. A photograph of Tony and one of her deceased husband Don Antonio were sitting on top of a table, surrounded by at least a dozen candles. It was a spooky sight that caused several of the older women to cross themselves. Doña Ernestina had arranged folding chairs in front of this table and told us to sit down. She did not ask us to take our food and drinks to the kitchen. She just looked at each of us individually, as if she were taking attendance in a class, and then said: "I have asked you here to say good-bye to my husband Antonio and my son Tony. You have been my friends and neighbors for twenty years, but they were my life. Now that they are gone, I have *nada. Nada. Nada.*"

I tell you, that word is like a drain that sucks everything down. Hearing her say *nada* over and over made me feel as if I were being yanked into a dark pit. I could feel the others getting nervous too, but here was a woman deep into her pain: we had to give her a little space. She looked around the room, then walked out without saying another word.

As we sat there in silence, stealing looks at each other, we began to hear the sounds of things being moved around in other rooms. One of the older women took charge then, and soon the drinks were poured, the food served—all this while the strange sounds kept coming from different rooms in the apartment. Nobody said much, except once when we heard something like a dish fall and break. Doña Iris pointed her index finger at her ear and made a couple of circles—and out of nervousness, I guess, some of us giggled like schoolchildren.

It was a long while before Doña Ernestina came back out to us. By then we were gathering our dishes and purses, having come to the conclusion that it was time to leave. Holding two huge Sears shopping bags, one in each hand, Doña Ernestina took her place at the front door as if she were a society hostess in a receiving line. Some of us women hung back to see what was going on. But Tito, the building's super, had had enough and tried to get past her. She took his hand, putting in it a small ceramic poodle with a gold chain around its neck. Tito gave the poodle a funny look, glanced at Doña Ernestina as though he were scared, and hurried away with the dog in his hand.

We were let out of her place one by one, but not until she had forced one of her possessions on each of us. She grabbed without looking from her bags. Out came her prized *miniaturas*, knickknacks that take a woman a lifetime to collect. Out came ceramic and porcelain items of all kinds, including vases and ashtrays. Out came kitchen utensils, dishes, forks, knives, spoons. Out came old calendars and every small item that she had touched or been touched by in the last twenty years. Out came a bronzed baby shoe—and I got that.

As we left the apartment, Doña Iris said "Psst" to some of us, so we followed her down the hallway. "Doña Ernestina's faculties are temporarily out of order," she said very seriously. "It is due to the shock of her son's death."

We all said "*Sí*" and nodded our heads.

"But what can we do?" Lydia said, her voice cracking a little. "What should I do with this?" She was holding one of Tony's baseball trophies in her hand: 1968 Most Valuable Player, for the Pocos Locos, our barrio's team.

Doña Iris said, "Let us keep her things safe for her until she recovers her senses. And let her mourn in peace. These things take time. If she needs us, she will call us." Doña Iris shrugged her shoulders, "*Así es la vida, hijas:* that's the way life is."

As I passed Tito on the stairs, he shook his head while looking up at Doña Ernestina's door: "I say she needs a shrink. I think somebody should call the social worker." He did not look at me when he mumbled these things. By "somebody" he meant one of us women. He didn't want trouble in his building, and he expected one of us to get rid of the problems. I just ignored him.

In my bed I prayed to the Holy Mother that she would find peace for Doña Ernestina's troubled spirit, but things got worse. All that week Lydia saw strange things happening through the peephole on her door. Every time people came to Doña Ernestina's apartment—to deliver flowers, or telegrams from the Island, or anything—the woman would force something on them. She pleaded with them to take this or that; if they hesitated, she commanded them with those tragic eyes to accept a token of her life.

And they did, walking out of our apartment building carrying cushions, lamps, doilies, clothing, shoes, umbrellas, wastebaskets, schoolbooks, and notebooks: things of value and things of no worth at all to anyone but to the person who had owned them. Eventually winos and street people got the news of the great giveaway in 4-D, and soon there was a line down the stairs and out the door. Nobody went home empty-handed; it was like a soup kitchen. Lydia was afraid to step out of her place because of all the dangerous-looking characters hanging out on that floor. And the smell! Entering our building was like coming into a cheap bar and public urinal combined.

Isabelita, living alone with her two little children and fearing for their safety, was the one who finally called a meeting of the residents. Only the women attended, since the men were truly afraid of Doña Ernestina. It isn't unusual for men to be frightened when they see a woman go crazy. If they are not the cause of her madness, then they act as if they don't understand it, and usually leave us alone to deal with our "woman's problems." This is just as well.

Maybe I *am* just bitter because of Miguel—I know what is said behind my back. But this is a fact: When a woman is in trouble, a man calls in her mama, her sisters, or her friends, and then he makes himself scarce until it's all over. This happens again and again. At how many bedsides of women have I sat? How many times have I made the doctor's appointment, taken care of the children, and fed the husbands of my friends in the barrio? It is not that the men can't do these things; it's just that they know how much women help each other. Maybe the men even suspect that we know one another better than they know their own wives. As I said, it is just as well that they stay out of our way when there is trouble. It makes things simpler for us.

At the meeting, Isabelita said right away that we should go up to 4-D and try to reason with *la pobre* Doña Ernestina. Maybe we could get her to give us a relative's address in Puerto Rico—the woman obviously needed to be taken care of. What she was doing was putting us all in a very difficult situation. There were no dissenters this time. We voted to go as a group to talk to Doña Ernestina the next morning.

But that night we were all awakened by crashing noises down on the street. In the light of the full moon, I could see that the air was raining household goods: kitchen chairs, stools, a small TV, a nightstand, pieces of a bed frame. Everything was splintering as it landed on the pavement. People were running for cover and yelling up at our building. The problem, I knew instantly, was in Apartment 4-D.

Putting on my bathrobe and slippers, I stepped out into the hallway. Lydia and Roberto were rushing down the stairs, but on the flight above my landing I caught up with Doña Iris and Isabelita, heading toward 4-D. Out of breath, we stood in the fourth-floor hallway, listening to police sirens approaching our building in front. We could hear the slamming of car doors and yelling—in both Spanish and English. Then we tried the door to 4-D. It was unlocked.

We came into a room virtually empty. Even the pictures had been taken down from the walls; all that was left were the nail holes and the lighter places on the paint where the framed photographs had been for years. We took a few seconds to spot Doña Ernestina: she was curled up in the farthest corner of the living room, naked.

"*Como salió a éste mundo*," said Doña Iris, crossing herself. Just as she had come into the world. Wearing nothing. Nothing around her except a clean, empty room. Nada. She had left nothing behind except the bottles of pills, the ones the doctors give to ease the pain, to numb you, to make you feel nothing when someone dies.

The bottles were empty too, and the policemen took them. But we didn't let them take Doña Ernestina until we each had brought up some of our own best clothes and dressed her like the decent woman that she was. *La decencia.* Nothing can ever change that—not even *la muerte*. This is the way life is. *Así es la vida.*

Fragment of a Man

Ho Anh Thai

I heard that my mother was the most beautiful girl in the village of Yen. Every time she combed her hair, she stood on a chair and the ends of her hair would still touch the floor. Everywhere she went, the scent of grapefruit and lemon lingered discreetly in the air.

Near the village there was a military airstrip, and because it was a target for destruction by the American planes, the village of Yen was also in danger of being obliterated at any time. All the villagers understood this, but many still hesitated to evacuate the place. The responsibility of persuading them to go fell on the village beauty—Miss Tinh—the vice-chairperson of the village and commander of the militia's short-range artillery squad. In order to increase the force of their argument, the village leaders decided to send Miss Tinh to contact the air force unit and invite a youth representative to come speak about the latest news and persuade the villagers to leave.

When Tinh arrived, she saw three or four young pilots surround a young man and drag him by the collar to the mess hall bulletin board so that he could see clearly whether that day the mess hall would serve *thit trau* (water buffalo meat) or *thit chau* (the meat of a young man named Chau). When Tinh raised her voice to inquire, they all walked away, leaving behind the young man, whose hair and clothes were now a mess from the scuffle. He rearranged his uniform, then said shyly, "I am Chau."

They got to know each other very quickly, communicating easily because Chau was only 25, five years younger than Tinh. Getting permission from his commanding officer, Chau accompanied Tinh back to the village. The road ran for more than three kilometres across an empty plain and was dotted by A-shaped tunnels and manholes. Suddenly, a cluster of American planes swooped down, diving and climbing and bombing for half an hour. Chau and Tinh jumped into an A-shaped tunnel and held each other tightly throughout the convulsions of the tunnel and the earth. Tinh's heavy bun fell out, covering everything with a cascade of hair. Suddenly, they didn't hear the bombs anymore, but only the soft sounds of the cascade, carrying with it the fragrance of the wild plants and flowers of the forest. The young man's throat went dry and he felt that he was drowning in hair, like a person who has never been at sea taking his first dive into the ocean.

The two had to do this several more times on the road that crossed the empty plain, taking refuge in the tunnel of destiny, abandoning themselves in the Yen village beauty's cascade of hair.

Ultimately, Tinh had to admit all this to the village leaders. They discussed ways to punish her. Tinh found Chau just before takeoff. "Big Sister Tinh, why are you so worried?" he asked. When she was finished telling him, Chau smiled happily, sprinted into the hallway, grabbed a passing pilot, and danced in a circle. "I'm about to get married." "Marry who?" "Big Sister Tinh. She's over there." He hadn't had a chance to change the way he addressed her yet.

Tinh and Chau returned to meet the village leaders, announcing their decision to get married. However, even a wedding couldn't get her out of trouble. Discipline was discipline, and the code of conduct for a cadre did not permit a girl to get pregnant before she was married. Suddenly, Tinh lost her political status: she was expelled from the Party and removed from her position as vice-chairperson and commander of the squad.

She had to leave the village and Chau took her to Hanoi to live with his widowed mother. His mother looked dazed, as if she'd just been robbed. During the meal, Tinh used her chopsticks to place a morsel of chicken into her mother-in-law's bowl. The mother-in-law returned it to the platter and spoke through her tears: "I beg you to let my son go." The family had a cottage with a big garden in the suburbs, and so Chau had no choice but to take his pregnant wife there. A few months later, a boy was born.

Still, the young mother was secretly tortured because in an instant she had lost everything; she'd been forced to abandon her home and, like an uprooted tree, had no place to which she could cling. Unloved by her mother-in-law, she still consoled herself that the most precious things in life for a woman were her husband and children, and therefore she couldn't regard herself as having lost everything. In the end, her husband and child were all my mother had.

After 1973, because the pirates would no longer be counterattacking from the air, my mother thought that she could relax about my father, but then suddenly the news hit: the airplane carrying my father and a few army officers was lost in the border region. They searched for a month without any results. But one day when my mother had just lit three sticks of incense and put her hands together in front of the altar to my father, a middle-aged neighbor woman stepped through the door: "Stop. Snuff out the incense and stop praying. The airplane flew to Thailand. They're having fun over there. Get ready for him to send some packages home." This rumor spread everywhere and for months the relatives of the missing half-believed it and half-doubted. A few dismantled their altars. But my father never came back.

I became the only possession my mother had left.

* * *

Every time there was the sound of an airplane in the sky, my mother would shiver, not even daring to look up. But I was different. To a small boy, that tiny speck in the blue sky embodied all my boundless desire. Whirring like a plane, I would run after it with my face upturned until I tripped and fell, diving into a shrub in the garden.

My mother lifted me up. "When people want to run far, they don't look up at the sky. Instead, they look down at the ground, son."

That was an instruction only suitable for great people in their youth. But I was an ordinary boy with what was probably a very ordinary destiny. If from my childhood I only knew to look at the ground, then when I grew up my soul would be like a balloon filled with helium but tied to the ground, able to do nothing except wait until I exploded, never able to fly to the sky. It's only now that I'm able to think like that. But at that time I was a very obedient child, and therefore I listened to my mother, carefully watching my steps wherever I went. Also at that time, I could perceive the pain that grass felt when our feet tread upon it, and would cry inconsolably if I inadvertently stepped on a cricket in the road.

My mother didn't want me to look at the sky and dream about flying things, repeating the unhappy destiny of my father. She wanted to keep me by her side, not lose me for some lofty ideal or for some other person.

But an active boy cannot stay forever by his mother's side within the family garden. Eventually, I crept into the neighbors' houses and into the house of a woman named Thach. "That's a venomous snake," one of the female neighbors said to my mother about Thach. I remembered one time my mother sent me to buy some cold medicine. Thach was selling medicine in front of a glass case that had a chart of poisons on it and a drawing of a snake dropping its poison into a glass. Probably that was the reason that the woman called her a venomous snake. One night we heard the sound of Thach's voice wailing. The neighbors hurried over but her husband was dead already. People said that it was a deadly cold. The neighbor lady whispered to my mother, "That was no cold. He died when he was sleeping. In the old days, when a girl went to live at her husband's house she would carry with her a sharp hairpin, not just to keep her hair in place."* In her opinion, Thach was a slut who would be the death of any husband. But with me Thach was exceedingly gentle. Twenty-nine years old, widowed while still childless, she left the pharmacy to trade in ration coupons and after that became a traveling merchant. Every time she came back from a trip, she would invite me into her house and let me eat until I'd finished everything she'd saved especially

*Refers to folklore about a type of acupuncture performed on the husband's spine to stimulate flagging virility.

for me. Sometimes there were plums, sometimes oranges from Vinh, sometimes Gold Dragon green bean cake. In return, I read to her from various torn books saved from some unknown time.

That year I turned sixteen, still so naive that I wore shorts and sat with my legs spread wide apart when I read to her from *Two Graves on a Pine-Covered Hill*. She leaned toward me, looked at my hairy legs, and said, "You should choose your friends carefully." I stopped reading and looked at her, puzzled. "Don't make friends with boys who don't have hairy legs." I was more puzzled. "That type, every one of them are cowards." She sighed, her eyes staring off into the distance: "With all due respect to my husband, he was that type."

At that moment, my mother ran in breathlessly and saw me sitting next to Thach in my revealingly loose shorts.

"Bao, come home immediately."

"Let me finish reading first, Mother."

"No. No. Come home." She grabbed the torn book, threw it at Thach and dragged me home. If she had not come at that exact moment, my mother would have been cheated out of her last remaining possession.

Thach's torn book became extremely boring. But I still slipped out without my mother's knowledge, sometimes going to her house to watch TV. Thach had just bought a black and white TV and the tears would stream down her face whenever she watched a cai luong opera. Whenever she watched a concert and saw the face of Thach Lan with its enormous mole or Le Duyen who tried so hard to charm people that her mouth became permanently distorted, Thach would say, "If I were rich I would smash this TV into pieces."

I asked, "You aren't rich?"

"How could I be rich? I'm more miserable than you could ever know."

One time on the TV there was a play critical of illegal activities and one character loudly scolded, "You lousy merchants…" Thach went crazy: "What? Lousy merchants? They should say Mr. Merchant, Ms. Merchant. Do they think being a merchant is so easy?"

My mother put the money together to buy a TV that was used but still pretty good. I sensed that my mother wanted to entice me to stay home and avoid that *venomous snake*. But not long after that, Thach brought home a color TV with a remote control. When it reached that stage, my mother gave up, unable to compete any longer. She had to resort to radical measures and flat out forbid me, giving the explanation: You have to study for your exam.

I graduated high school but failed the university entrance exam and wanted to go work. An acquaintance tried to get me a job in a textile factory. The factory accepted me, but on one condition: I had to complete my military service first. They didn't want their operations thrown into disarray when an employee was drafted. My mother feared nothing more than this profession of guns and planes. Our acquaintance reminded her that the division commander had been a friend of my father's and in his hands I would be very safe, wouldn't have to work hard, and could come home at the end of three years. So I enlisted as an employee of the factory during that drafting period, but, by special arrangement, I joined the division of Commander Dac and worked as a clerk, safely away from the border.

Commander Dac was a strict person, but he was very fond of me because he saw in me the image of his young friend from the old days. Thanks to his occasional visits and his memories, I learned about the love between my parents. He told me that in 1972, when I was six years old, my mother brought me to the base to visit my father, hopeful that she could get pregnant. We waited in the guest house for several days but my father hadn't yet come back from an assignment and so we packed up to go back to Hanoi. The division car carrying us back to the train station had only gone a little way when we met my father's truck on the way back to the base. Commander Dac sat with me in the cabin of the truck and waved the reunited couple away: "You two get in the back to *confide* in each other, and we'll stay here."

I protested: "Let me go with Mother and Father."

He gave me a spank and said, "Behave yourself and I'll let you go in an airplane." The remainder of the distance to the station, Dac told the driver to drive slowly in order to give the couple more time for lovemaking. "If your mother had not had a miscarriage, your little sister or brother would be 12 years old by now," the commander said.

Three years in the military were about to pass uneventfully. I would return to work in the factory, an ordinary occupation with no time for me to look in the sky and dream of flying. That was my mother's wish, and she was reassured because my period of service was almost completed. But then something happened that turned everything upside down. It was the fault of my parents, who gave birth to such a soft-hearted son.

* * *

Than was a soldier belonging to the reconnaissance unit. Many times he had gone AWOL in order to go home, or, by his own decision, prolonged his leave, and so there were also many times that the military police had to send someone to bring him back and throw him into the military jail. Finally, he was granted a seven-day leave, and when he drew it out to ten days they were waiting for him to turn up at the base so they could immediately strip him of his military credentials and send him home. Only on the twelfth day, did he return to the base, and the first person he looked for was me. On his leave papers, he had erased the dates of his leave, changing the return date from March 14 to March 19. I was the person who filled out these papers for my boss to sign. Than begged me to bail him out, to say that I had made a mistake on the papers so that he could avoid being discharged and sent home, where he would face reeducation. His village was suffering from famine and when his younger siblings went to school, they would lean against the wall and fall down from hunger. He had stayed at home longer in order to search for extra rice for his family.

Although I knew that Than was not a truthful person, I was still moved by his story. I accepted the blame and prepared myself to go to jail, telling myself I was only taking a week-long rest in the mountains before returning in time to prepare my discharge papers. People asked the opinion of Commander Dac. "We have to uphold military discipline," he said firmly, simply thinking that seven days in detention would pass by peacefully.

And so I sat there in the late afternoon, almost completely worn out after a day using a pick and shovel to widen a road through a mountain village. I sank down at the foot of a kapok tree, breathing heavily and turning my face up to look at the ever-lonely evening star. Looking at stars and counting them was something that the children do, and something that my mother never wanted me to do. But put yourself in my position, finally unsupervised, my limbs exhausted, not smoking a cigarette or taking part in the dirty jokes of all the other *convicts* sitting nearby. What was there for me to do but sit looking at the stars?

At dusk of the second day, when the whistle screamed for the end of labor, I flung aside the shovel and dropped down next to the kapok tree. But before I had a chance to even look up at the sky, someone shoved some plums into my hand. The silhouette of a girl limped by, joined a group of women, then rapidly disappeared into the mist. Perhaps this is the image I will remember forever of that crippled village in the mountains, with only thirty or forty houses and several small drink shops: faceless forms in the mist.

Every day the miscreants with their shaved heads maintained a gentle and harmless appearance, standing neatly in two straight lines. They didn't dare to go into a shop if they didn't have money. When they craved a cigarette, all they could do was stand in front of the shops and pick up the littered stubs, which they called "fried fat," then light them up and suck deeply. They all wanted to appear obedient so they could return to their units as soon as possible, only to break the law later again, and then come back here again as a *convict*.

That morning, pausing in front of a few of the shops, one of them had the bright idea that one person should collect all the fried fat, open them up for the tobacco, and then use some paper to roll real cigarettes. I don't even smoke, but

I was pulled into the drawing of lots and had the misfortune to draw the short one. Reluctantly, I took my hat in my hand and ran into the drink shop in front of us, then stuck my head down to look between people's feet under the benches.

Looking through the pairs of legs, my hand deftly felt its way through all the cracked feet in order to collect all the stubs of cigarettes.

Suddenly, between all those calloused feet, those feet marked by the sorrow of daily struggle that is within every man and every woman, my eyes fell upon a girl's pretty foot. But what I saw immediately after that made me jump. That foot was matched by another that was shrivelled. Those feet would limp like a seven with a ten. One was like a young branch bursting with the sap of life. The other was dried out. One was the foot of an 18- or 20-year-old girl, while the other was that of a worn-out 60-year-old woman.

My eyes were mesmerized by the pair of feet facing me. In this position, the feet had to belong to the shop girl. I slowly stood up, my glance traveling across the backs and shoulders of the customers sipping their drinks. Everything became blurry when I looked into the face of that girl. In all the far corners of the countryside, I had never seen a face that was so beautiful and so demure. That face and that foot, a mythical flower that would blossom once in a hundred years, but blossom on a dry branch.

"Please come in and have a drink," she softly invited me, a *convict*, as if recognizing an acquaintance. I was petrified, momentarily rooted to that spot. Then, hugging the hat full of fried fat, I turned and ran. It was at exactly that moment that I realized that she was the girl who had shoved the plums into my hand the day before.

After dinner that night, Vinh, a guy who was awaiting trial for molesting a woman, proceeded with the presentation of his story for his friends. "I didn't rape that bitch. We'd known each for a while already, so obviously she wanted it. After it was over, she sat in the bushes crying so loud. Some people came by and they jumped on me and brought me in."

I asked the jailer if I could go outside to do something. The discipline in the camp was very strict, but everyone had a lot of respect for me, a military bureaucrat for the division who was rumored to be the nephew of the division commander. I sprinted for two kilometers through the misty night, occasionally catching the glimmers of stars over my head. The shop was closed. A weak light came through the cracks in the walls. "I came to buy cigarettes," I replied to the girl when she called from inside. The door opened a crack and the girl's face appeared rosy from the light of the hurricane lamp in her hand. "Is that you? What a shame. If it was daytime I could invite you into the house." It seemed like she had picked up some of my nervousness.

"Why can't I come in now?"

"No, my mother lives at the end of the road. I'm only here by myself." She was foolish enough to say it, but with a person like me, such foolishness wasn't likely to cause her any harm. "But standing here talking like this isn't convenient. Okay, please come in." I spent all the little money I had buying cigarettes, and it was only too bad I didn't have more, even though later I might throw them all away anyway. In order to appear natural, I lit a cigarette, but after only one puff I coughed and coughed. She was concerned and so she gave me something to drink. "Smoking cigarettes isn't good for you," she said.

"Then I'll give it up once and for all, immediately."

"Then let me take all these cigarettes back, okay?"

"No, let me take them back for my friends."

At that moment a child's voice called through the door: "Hey, Duyen!" In a panic, she lowered her voice: "That's my little sister. Go. Go. Whenever you're free, come back to visit me." She opened the back door, whispering the way for me to sneak out. Inside the house, in order to mask her deformity, she would either hold on to the back of a chair, the edge of a door, or a wall. But if she had to run an errand, then what could she lean on?

Every night I went to visit her, and retreated before the appearance of her spying little sister, who came from the same mother but a different father. The mother sent her to stay the night in order to chaperone Duyen. But it had to happen that one night I carried her to the bed. The happier my hands were to touch her normal foot, the more frightened and bitter they were to touch the deformed one. She told me that the foot became shrivelled after a bout of illness when she was eight years old. I took it upon myself to compensate for all her suffering. "You're not going to cry, are you?" I asked. I couldn't help being a little concerned, remembering Vinh's story. She answered, "With you by my side, I'll never cry."

We lay there for a long time, dozing off, until we heard the familiar sound of her little sister. This night was all our own. No one had a right to share a part of a sacred night like that. She called out: "Go home. I already turned out the lights and I've gone to sleep."

"No, no. I'm scared." She had used up all her courage in carrying the lamp one block down the street, believing that she'd be let inside immediately.

"If you don't go quickly, then the ghosts will come out and jump on you." Complete silence. Perhaps she was both running and crying. The destiny of spies is usually much more tragic.

Duyen's mother was lucky to have married the most resourceful and handsome man in the area, but was unlucky to have acquired as a mother-in-law an old woman who had developed at the end of her life the habit of cruelty. Every day Duyen's mother had to put up with a fit of curses, and she wasn't the only one who had to listen. The old woman would stand at the front of the house so that the neighbors could know that she was cursing her daughter-in-law. Duyen's father went with people to trade fragrant wood in Quang Binh and was attacked by a tiger. The anniversary of his death became the day that the mother-in-law would curse "the woman who was the death of her husband." When Duyen was ten years old, her mother took the next step, and was cursed: "The time of mourning isn't even over yet and she's already taking up with another man."

Duyen's mother believed that her mother-in-law was so cruel and disagreeable partly because her younger son told lies and always criticized her. Finding herself so unhappy, Duyen's mother vented her rage in revenge against that brother-in-law. After her grandmother's death, Duyen lived by herself in the house with the family altar. Her mother found out about the brother-in-law's plot to marry Duyen off early, give her a little money as dowry, then take over the house. The mother was outraged: "She's only twenty years old. Why be so crazy as to hurry up and put the yoke around her neck? Look how ugly I am, and I had no trouble finding a husband." The uncle had a decent place near Duyen's house but he never bothered to look after his niece. On the contrary, he felt that the more men she had courting her the better, so that when one of them got her pregnant, she'd have to marry him. Duyen's mother complained: "An uncle is like a father, but this one is completely irresponsible. When I first came to live with this family, if he had to pee at night he was so afraid of ghosts that he asked me to go out there with him and I had to smell his awful pee. He's really a parasite." Determined to destroy her brother-in-law's selfish plan, she had her younger daughter keep close tabs on Duyen every day so that the mother would know who came to visit often and who stayed a long time at the drink shop. Better that her daughter never marry anyone and keep the house because that would kill the uncle.

Inadvertently, the mother became the biggest hurdle in my efforts to marry Duyen and take her back to Hanoi. "I'm prepared to go anywhere with you. Wherever you go, I'll go as well," Duyen said.

My time in military prison was over. In Vinh's rape case, the victim and her family had submitted an appeal to release him because, in fact, they loved each other. He and I travelled together for a short distance. Vinh said: "She made me go to jail, and now it turns out that she loves me? Well, despite everything, at least I've found a wife." I was jealous that things were so easy for him.

Back at the base, I met Commander Dac. "I'm about to get married," I said. "Will you please certify this document for me?"

"Are you kidding? You're only 21 years old. Has your mother agreed yet?"

"It would be hard for her to agree immediately. That's why I have to seek your help," I said. He could see that I wasn't being impulsive or joking.

Commander Dac frowned. "Let me think about it."

On the night of the second day, he summoned me: "I've sent people to secretly investigate. It's an ordinary family, not landowners or reactionaries." He returned the document, already certified, and held my hand tightly, lowering his voice: "I pity you two. How can you make it with a foot like that? Your mother will curse me all her life."

I went back to find Duyen. The local committee official had a lot of affection for Duyen, so he agreed to do as we wished, taking steps to register our marriage and giving us the certificate. He also promised to keep it a secret until the wedding. Duyen and I decided to get a contract before the wedding because we were worried that something might thwart our plans in the time it took to convince our parents. Now we were reassured. That night, like every night, there wasn't a soul on the street. When we left the committee headquarters, I didn't have the heart to let Duyen limp by my side, so I lifted her up and carried her all the way through the mountain village.

* * *

When I got to my mother's house, I went straight to the point: "Mother, I'm about to take a wife."

She smiled: "Who would object? You can take as many wives as you want."

I solemnly handed her a photograph of Duyen, a face so gentle and beautiful it would break anyone's heart. "No!" She screamed as if she had just recognized that it was a picture of a hunted criminal. "No!" She held her head, collapsing onto the bed, completely unprepared for such news. Before that, her only joy was in my return, returning to become again the small child of the old days, a child with its mother, a mother with her child. Suddenly, that child was no longer completely her own. Cracks were beginning to appear that could shatter her treasure.

That was the first time I realized that people could fall ill simply because of shock and misery. She lay feverish for several days. Not a single question about the girl in that photograph, neither her name nor age nor even her family background. Bad or good, she wanted to take away a mother's only child and that was unacceptable. When my mother began to recover she stood in front of my father's altar and lit incense to pray, holding in her hand a small comb made from a piece of an American warplane. With his own hands, my father had made two combs that were exactly the same, engraved with the words: Tinh-Chau. He gave one to my mother and kept the other in his inside jacket pocket, always carrying it with him. That comb was the only remaining fragment of the life of her lost husband. She had put it on the altar and a day never passed that she forgot to dust it.

I was as restless as someone sitting on hot coals. In that remote mountain village, Duyen was waiting for me as each minute passed. I wondered if she ever doubted for a moment, if she ever thought I'd deserted her. As for me, I couldn't mope around the house forever without achieving any results.

I wandered like a lost soul, my feet taking me to Thach's house without my even being aware of it. Since the day of my return, I had noticed a handsome guy going into and out of her house. One time he was washing his feet at the public spigot in front of the gate. His legs were hairy.

Thach sat by herself silently drinking rice wine and eating roasted dried squid. That silence was rare for a person like her. Tears streamed down. She pulled and tore at the squid with the hands of a person who wanted revenge. In one gulp, I finished a bowl of wine that she gave me and saw that inside her house she already had a VCR. Finding it handy, I switched on the tape that was already in the machine. A shocking film. The porn stars were giving lessons in love. I turned it off immediately, not because I didn't want to watch it, but because it wasn't proper to watch it in front of Thach. "You're still too young. Watching this film isn't good for you," she said.

"Not so young. I'm about to get married." I recounted my circumstances in detail.

"Why didn't you tell me immediately?"

"What's the point of telling you?"

"Oh, that means you still don't understand me. When are you going to go get her? Is tomorrow morning too late?"

The next morning, we carried two heavy sacks to the station and caught the train going back up toward the mountain village. The hairy-legged guy went with us. I had to lie to my mother, telling her that I was returning to the base in order to have someone correct a mistake on my military release papers. The merchants' car was full of goods and people lying and sitting all over the place. I felt a sharp pain when one woman tried to step over me. She recognized Thach: "Who are you travelling with?"

"Well, with two younger men."

"Really? I've also got a younger man, but only one." She gave an easy smile demonstrating that she understood. Then she took the hand of her younger man, who was only about 18 years old, led him to a corner of the car, and spread out a nylon sheet for them to sit on. Night slowly fell. I could see that woman and her man discreetly rolling under the blanket. Perhaps a lot of people noticed, but everyone pretended to be dozing off.

Following Thach's plan, we first went to meet Commander Dac. "On such an important matter as this, why didn't your mother come?"

Thach cut in, "His mother was unwell, and we also needed someone at home to prepare for when we brought the new daughter home. I'm his aunt, so I'm taking care of this."

Commander Dac was surprised. "Then what do you need me for?" he asked.

"Why do you say that? You're like a father to Bao. Please participate as a sign of authority. You won't have to do a thing. I'll take care of everything."

Our registration for marriage had already been discovered by Duyen's family. A few days earlier, Duyen's uncle had proposed a family meeting, inviting everyone, including his now-remarried former sister-in-law, to announce that he had found a match for Duyen. According to him, Duyen was twenty years old already and admittedly good and beautiful, but because of her deformity she should know enough to limit her expectations and marry as soon as possible, before it was too late. "I don't want to get married yet," Duyen replied immediately.

Her mother joined in, "That's fine. Each pot will find its own lid. Why worry?"

The uncle countered, "Do you want your daughter to die old and alone in some corner of the house?"

The mother smiled sarcastically, "It's better to stay single and take care of yourself. I've been foolish enough to get married twice, so I know."

The squabble was fierce and the mother was in danger of being cornered. Therefore, Duyen reluctantly admitted, "I'm married already." She showed everyone the marriage certificate. Who's Van Ngoc Bao? What does he look like? "He's a very good person. He was a prisoner being reformed through manual labor here."

The mother held her face in her hands, screaming. After a pensive moment, the uncle said, "A prisoner but a good person. That's okay." He announced that he would give Duyen two gold leaves for her dowry. That much money proved that he wasn't an unreasonable man. But Duyen's mother continued stomping her feet.

"Your greed has made you blind," she said.

Several days went by with no movement or sign from me, and Duyen's mother began to think that I had disappeared, as slippery as an eel. Perhaps it was good that way, or would be even better if Duyen had become pregnant because then she would be content to stay home, without ever thinking of any other husband.

Duyen's mother completely lost control when a jeep pulled up in front of the house and a military official stepped majestically down. The uncle was called over and, along with Duyen's stepfather, met with Commander Dac. Thach didn't waste any time giving out candy, cookies, and toys for the children in the family and around the neighborhood. In terms of gifts there was silk for the women, flashlights and cigarettes for the men. Having carried with her a Sony cassette recorder, she now put in a cassette of cai luong opera and played it loudly.

While Thach was engaged in a lively conversation, she happened to hear the sound of voices haggling in the back of the house. She turned her head and saw the hairy-legged guy pulling things out of a burlap sack and showing them to a few of the neighbors. She waved him to the side, "As the saying goes: even a whore leaves herself a way to find a husband. So don't sell those worthless things here, okay?" She told him to put the sack away and distribute the gifts to the neighbors: a pack of cigarettes for this one, a scarf for another. Everyone was satisfied, and turned to heap praise on the groom.

There was no need to send out invitations. It was only necessary to put the word out and not a soul in the whole village was absent. Plates of cookies and candy were passed around, turning this into a modern-day wedding. In the evening, after everyone had gone, I found Thach and Duyen's mother sitting behind a closed door in the bedroom, drinking. Duyen said that whenever her mother sat by herself drinking, she had the habit of calling their yellow dog over, putting her feet on its back, and gently pushing the dog back and forth. But now she stomped her feet on the dog as if she wanted to trample it, as if she wanted to trample everything that had made her so unhappy. The two women were covered in tears. The mother took Thach's hand and sobbed, "No one understands me but you."

The next morning, with mixed feelings, the whole family saw us off. Duyen's mother called after Thach, "I'll prepare to come and visit you and the children."

I lifted Duyen into the jeep and repeated the question of that night, "You're not going to cry, are you?"

She answered, "With you by my side, I'll never cry."

When we passed by the division, Commander Dac got out and let us continue with the car to Hanoi. I went home and had to put up with a number of tension-filled days. Duyen had to remain temporarily at Thach's house, waiting until I had a proper chance to speak with my mother. But it seemed that both of us were on the defensive. My mother was afraid of the moment when I would declare again that I was going to marry that girl in the photo. As for me, I was afraid to tell my mother that I was already married and have her continue to reject it. I always found an excuse to go out and secretly visit Thach's house, staying there until late at night. Because Thach was so busy with her business, she was almost never home. It was only when we returned to Hanoi that Duyen found out that Thach and I were not actually aunt and nephew. She still showed that she was grateful to Thach, but she became somewhat suspicious. She also sensed that there was still some obstacle keeping me from taking her straight home. I understood this because she always asked about "our house" and about my mother.

Eventually the moment came when my mother asked very seriously, "You still often go to Thach's house, don't you?" I shook my head vigorously.

My mother said sharply, "Don't lie to me. She's not even home, so why do you dare to go in and out so naturally like that?" I sat quietly, trembling with fear.

"This morning I saw a girl over there. She seemed well-mannered, but she has a deformed leg. Who is that?"

I didn't dare to lie and, furthermore, my mother's question was meant to test if I was telling the truth or not. My mother already knew Duyen's face from the photograph. "Dear mother, that's my wife."

She fell silent and it was only after a long time that she was able to find her voice. "So you've become husband and wife already?"

"Dear mother, it's been a week already. She's been living at Thach's house."

The mention of Thach's name made my mother jump, bringing out the anger once again, overpowering even her sorrow. "No. No. Not over there. Bring her back here immediately."

Within half a day things changed with the speed of a whirlwind. I brought Duyen home and introduced her to my mother. Then the three of us organized the house, pulling out a bed that had for so long been pushed into a corner. My mother had compassion for a young girl who had the same disadvantages of fate that she herself had known, and that compassion proved to be stronger than her anger. She led Duyen around the house and into the kitchen, where she showed her in detail where all the saucepans, woks, fish sauce, salt, and spices were. When they were finished with all that, my mother immediately fell ill with a light but persistent fever. The neighborhood doctor came over and examined my mother very carefully then said that she hadn't come down with any particular illness, but was suffering from a physical breakdown.

In my heart I understood that this physical breakdown was caused by sorrow.

* * *

It is only now that I understand that once she accepted her daughter-in-law into the house and throughout the time that we all lived together, my mother felt that she had lost everything. Our son was born, weighing four-and-a-half kilos, and so whoever saw him had to admire him. My mother was happy, but it was the happiness of looking at someone else's treasure, not her own. After some time, I bought a sewing machine and took Duyen to some sewing classes. My mother looked after the baby. One day, people ran up and told her to take her grandson to the district's "healthy baby" contest, convinced that he would win first prize. She agreed that the child would be at the top of the chart, but she couldn't take him. Her reason was that she had not yet asked our opinion and did not know if we would agree or not. That afternoon, when Duyen and I returned, the contest was over and the prize had been presented to a boy who could not compare with our son. Hearing about it, some people couldn't understand, but I vaguely sensed something terrifying. My mother had found that she no longer had any power in this house. I once was her last remaining possession, and now I wasn't even that anymore, so the baby was only someone else's treasure that she was supposed to care for and that was that.

We were completely naive, not yet having had enough experience in life, so we didn't know what to do to change her way of thinking. In those days, she began to spend a lot of time in the garden, staring at the trees and bushes as if she were searching for something. One day, I spied on her, watching her sneak into the garden and carefully search everywhere. Her hand turned over every pile of leaves, every rock, every clod of earth around the bases of the trees, until she finally found what she was searching for. It was the metal comb made from a piece of a warplane and engraved with the names of my parents. Her eyes brightened. A look of infinite happiness infused her sad face, as if she had found the comb that my father had carried on his own body. With the happiness of a sleepwalker and walking like a sleepwalker, she cradled the comb in her hand, groped her way toward the house and reached the altar. She laid the comb on the altar, hoping to find there another comb exactly like it, her own comb lying on the altar.

The fairy tale didn't happen. The comb in her hand was the comb I had seen on the altar the day before. She had probably left it in the garden so that she could go and find it again. When she realized this, her sleepwalk ended and she slid again into a long delirium.

In the months that followed, her mind was no longer as sharp as before. She got into the habit of collecting trivial things. She wandered in the wide garden, bringing inside reels of copper wire, screws, and pieces of scrap metal. Then she would clumsily take them out and count them, looking for a way to put them together. Deep inside, I felt miserable. Only when they realize they've lost everything do people try to look again for the things they've lost and put them back together. This meant that my mother considered herself to have lost me and that she felt she was now only left with the hope of finding that missing airplane. No one said that my father had died. He was only missing with his airplane.

We lost all hope when we saw my mother's energy gradually draining, although her health had been strengthened by vitamins. One day, she said, "Last night I dreamed I saw the village chairman. He invited me to go back to the village for a meeting, and he restored everything to me." The village chairman had been dead for a long time. I assumed it was only the dream of a sick person, but two days later she passed away.

Now I knew that it was possible to die not from a real illness but from debilitating misery, from torment over lost possessions.

A widowed woman is a fragment of the man who died. Some women bear the fate of a fragment, living silently in seclusion, all the while clinging to the dream of finding and putting all those fragments back together again. Others are fragments lying here and there on the road, piercing and cutting the feet of luckier souls as a way of wreaking revenge for their own sad fates.

My mother never wanted me to look up into the sky, and counting stars was really for children, but that night, all alone in a corner of the garden, I lifted my eyes to a sky that was filled with stars. A shooting star cut open a wound in the sky. I understood then that on the face of the earth there was one more fragment.

* * *

After my mother died, there were some evenings after work when I stopped by a drink shop planning to have only a glass of tea and ended up drinking. Before, there had been times when the atmosphere in the family was gloomy, when I didn't dare show my affection for Duyen in front of my mother, and I thought to myself that without my mother perhaps my love for Duyen would have been stronger. Thinking back, I realized that I hadn't been fulfilling my duty as a son. And then, after my mother died, my love for my wife didn't become stronger. Instead, it diminished. As for my love for my mother, she had taken it with her forever.

I don't know if something was leading me there or not, but somehow I found myself going into Thach's house. "Drink up," she said. She poured me another glass, and stood up to light some incense, whispering her prayers. Then she came back and drank with me. "Your mother died too soon. I prepared her for burial and saw that her face was still young and fresh, like someone sleeping." She began to cry. "In those days, she was right. I was a worthless woman." Even in my fuzzy state, I had been rather afraid that things would turn out like this. A moment later, she dried her tears and said, "Do you want to watch a film?" I shuddered and shook my head. "No, not that kind of film," she said. "This is a love story, very happy. The ability to love always means happiness." A love that is so ideal would be true happiness. On the TV screen, the actors only loved each other in the clouds with a kind of platonic love....But Thach and I carried out the earthly aspect that was missing from the film.

As time passed, it wasn't any easier to forget the pain caused by the loss of my mother. Then one day I suddenly heard that they had found the missing airplane buried deep in a gorge within an untouched forest. The news came too late and my mother had gone too soon. I received the comb that my father had always carried with him. Both combs were finally reunited, but it was a reunion on the altar.

For many months, Thach's house was boarded up. I didn't know where she went.

One day, I happened to see the good looking guy who had once dated Thach. He was sitting with one foot up on the seat of a crimson Honda Cub 70, perhaps waiting for someone by the side of the road. I went up to him, said hello, and asked, "Do you know where Thach went?"

He brushed the question aside. "Which Thach? I don't know her. What a weird question."

I was bewildered and walked away, then turned around immediately and said firmly, "You have to tell me. If you don't, then I won't leave."

He considered it for a moment, glancing left and right, then lowered his voice, "She went to jail. Now get lost. There's nothing between you and me anymore, you understand?"

I didn't go away immediately. I stood looking at the thick thighs showing beneath his shorts. His legs were hairy.

I bought some canned food and fruit, then went to visit Thach. We sat looking at each other across a wide table. She had never thought that anyone would come to visit her, especially me. She wept softly. "Now I really am a worthless woman." When I was about to stand up, she said, "Now I don't believe that there are good people in this world." I fell silent, not knowing how to console her. "God is like that, too. If he was good, then he would have brought you and me together."

I went home. Duyen was busy in front of the house. She tripped over something and fell, but wasn't badly hurt. I lifted her up and carried her into the house. I realized now more strongly than ever that I had been right to approach her first out of pity. If it had been only love, then eventually it would have dried up. Only through pity and the bond of marriage was I able to live with her forever. Although I wasn't always faithful to her, I would never think of leaving her. Able to reach that conclusion, I only wanted to sell the house and take my wife and son away, to go to a faraway place without revealing our new address, in order to protect the happiness of our small family. Vacillating for a long time without being able to reach a decision, I asked Duyen's opinion. She said, "There's no place better than here. Why should we move?"

After that, I was constantly troubled, worrying about the day that Thach would return.

Translated by Bac Hoai Tran and Dana Sachs

A Soldier's Burial

Philip Caputo

Dreading the interview but seeing no alternative but to go through with it, Starkmann made the drive to Iron Mountain. The psychologist's office was in the Outreach Center, a converted storefront not far from the V.A. hospital, a menacing, mustard-brick building surrounded by well-kept lawns and a landscaped parking lot. The Center had two rooms in addition to Eckhardt's office: a small kitchen with a hot plate for making coffee, and a meeting room containing a cafeteria table and some folding chairs. Posters decorated the walls. One showed a photograph of a GI carrying a wounded buddy over his shoulders and bore the caption HE AIN'T HEAVY, HE'S MY BROTHER. Another displayed an artist's rendering of the Vietnam War Memorial in Washington, two huge slabs of polished black granite upon which the names of nearly sixty thousand dead were inscribed—as if, Starkmann thought, they'd been nothing more than the victims of some enormous industrial accident, like a refinery fire or a gas-plant explosion. Well, maybe that was all they had been. Modern war was an industry, soldiers mere workers on its bloody assembly line.

Eckhardt greeted him cheerfully and offered him coffee in a Styrofoam cup like the cups in Burger King. Starkmann sat in a vinyl lounger, the psychologist in a large desk chair that made him look like a boy trying on his father's office for size.

"Tastes just like mess-hall coffee," he said with his disarming smile. "Makes you feel right at home, doesn't it?"

"Yeah."

Eckhardt tried to ease into the interview with small talk about the poor fishing season this year. Such unusual heat, so little rain, the trout sluggish.

"Let's get this over with," Starkmann said, cutting off the chitchat.

"You sound like a man who's going to have his appendix out."

"I'm here because I have to be."

"I assumed you called me because you *want* to be here."

"My wife said she'd leave me if I didn't come in. I guess you gave her that idea."

"I talked to her, Chris." Eckhardt folded his hands over a file on his desk. "But I sure as hell didn't suggest that she threaten to leave you. We don't operate that way. Do you know what we do here, what this is all about?"

"No. "

"We think of ourselves as human reclamation experts. A lot of guys got messed up over there, in their heads. And messed up by the way they were treated when they got back to the States. They were made to feel like outcasts, and a lot of them think of themselves as outcasts, pariahs. We try to bring them back into the fold, so to speak, but not with the standard Freudian crap. We use rap groups, private counseling, drug-clinic referrals, the whole nine yards. Most of our people are veterans themselves, brothers helping brothers, reestablishing the bond of combat in a civilian setting. The idea is to make these guys feel good about their service, to show them that they're valuable human beings."

"That's some sales pitch, Eckhardt," Starkmann said, a little baffled by the jargon.

"This job requires some salesmanship."

"Are you saying I'm messed up?"

"Maybe we ought to start by finding out if you want to be here, regardless of what June wants."

Starkmann did not say anything, disliking Eckhardt's reference to June by her first name. His eyes ranged around the room for something to divert his attention. The office was sparsely furnished, its walls as bare as prison walls except for one small window flanked by a pair of potted ferns, a few more posters, and Eckhardt's degrees, framed in black.

"Look, if you don't feel you need to be here, you're free to walk out." Eckhardt gestured with a cock of his head. "There's the door. If you're having problems, you can stay where you are. Up to you."

"What problems am I supposed to be having?"

"I don't know. June thinks you are. Do you agree with her or is it just her imagination?"

"I wouldn't know about her imagination. Why don't you ask her? You two sound like you've gotten on pretty friendly."

"Let's forget I talked to her. Let's start from scratch. You haven't walked out of here, so maybe there's something you need to get off your chest."

"Like what, for instance?"

Eckhardt gave it some thought. "Maybe we could start with the night we ran into each other in the bar."

Starkmann crossed his legs and pulled a loose thread from the cuff of his jeans.

"I remember you passing out and mumbling something about a dust-off. I couldn't quite make it out. Do you remember why you were calling for a dust-off?"

"No. I was out."

"You were wounded over there, weren't you?"

"Yeah."

"How about elaborating?"

"Mortar fragments. It wasn't very serious. I was in the hospital only a couple of days."

"Three, to be exact." The small man opened a file and read from it: "Admitted to Fourth Field Hospital July 24, 1969; returned to full duty July 27."

"What is that?"

"It's a summary of your two-oh-one file," he answered, using the army term for a soldier's service record.

Starkmann felt as if tiny flames had begun to lick up his arms. How much did the psychologist know about his record? Did the file contain a report of his crack-up? He hadn't counted on this, and regretted not having left when he'd had the chance. He wanted to leave now, but if he bolted, Eckhardt would know he had something to hide. Control, he warned himself. Stay in control.

"Where did you get it, the two-oh-one?"

"Washington. I called for it after you phoned me."

"Why? What for?"

"Standard procedure. Unfortunately, we get our share of frauds in here— guys looking for a free lunch. You know, supply clerks who never left Saigon and cooks who dished out pizzas at the staff officers' club coming in and claiming they're emotionally shattered from all the hell they'd seen in the jungle and then hoping we'll certify them for a psychiatric disability."

"Listen, I was there."

"I know." He read from the file again. "Arrived in-country June 2, 1969. Assigned B Company, First of the Seventy-Seventh. Wounded in action July 24, then the three days at Fourth Field."

"What else does it say in there?"

"That you were in the hospital a second time, from September 25 to October 10, then reassigned to brigade headquarters. Were you wounded twice, Chris? It doesn't say so here."

"The second time in the hospital you mean."

"Yeah."

"Malaria," he lied, pleased with his quick thinking. "I had malaria. I wasn't in good shape after I got over it, so they assigned me to brigade."

"What did they have you doing there?"

"Perimeter security detail. Night watchman stuff."

Eckhardt, clasping his hands behind his head, leaned back and looked up at the ceiling. "Going back to that night you passed out. Were you dreaming about the time you were wounded? Is that why you were calling for a dust-off?"

"I don't know. I was pretty drunk."

"I'll say. You were ready to take on that big son of a bitch. What was his name?"

"Sam LaChance."

"Biggest son of a bitch I've ever seen."

"He's big, all right."

"Of course, you had that revolver in your pocket. Evened things up a bit. What were you doing with it, by the way?"

The fire again crawled up his arms and now spread to his face. "I'd left it in my pocket. I'd been exercising my bird dog, and I'd left the gun in my pocket when I went into town. I wasn't going to use it on Sam if that's what you mean."

"Hell, no. You're not here on a weapons charge, and I'm not interrogating you. I was just curious."

"Okay."

"Once more going back to what you were saying when you passed out: Do you know what a flashback is?"

"Remembering something all of a sudden."

"It's a special kind of memory. *Reexperiencing* is the professional term for it. Experiencing a past event as if it's actually happening."

The dream. Did that explain the unusual clarity of the dream? Was it a reexperience and not a journey into the past? He wanted to explore this idea, but held his tongue; if he so much as suggested that he'd thought his dream was a form of time travel, Eckhardt would lock him up for sure.

"I heard you use somebody's name," the psychologist was saying. "T.J. or P.J. Something like that."

"D.J.," Starkmann corrected, thinking: There can't be any harm in telling him that. "D.J. Fishburn."

"Do you remember calling his name?"

"I'll take your word for it."

"All right. Do that. Was he a buddy of yours?"

"Sure."

"Have any others?" Starkmann nodded.

"I don't know what kind of soldier you were, Chris," Eckhardt said, exasperation roughening his voice. "But you would have made a fine P.O.W. The bad guys would never have gotten anything out of you."

"Is that supposed to be a compliment?"

"It's a request for a little cooperation. If I'm going to do you any good, you'll have to meet me halfway. Maybe you could tell me who these buddies were and if you were tight with them. Something, for Christ's sake."

"There was D.J. and two other guys. Ramos and a medic, Hutchinson. And yeah, I guess we were tight."

"Do you still stay in touch?"

A part of him longed to cry out, Yes! I talk to them. I speak to the dead, Dr. Eckhardt! I commune with ghosts!

"They were killed. All three of them together. A booby-trapped two hundred and fifty-pound bomb. Blew them into gas."

"When was that?"

"When I was in the hospital. The second time."

"With malaria."

"Right."

Eckhardt found this information interesting enough to note it down. "How do you feel about that—their getting killed while you were in the hospital?"

Starkmann glanced around the room like a student stumped by a quiz. A bar of sunlight leaned through the window, brightening the leaves of the ferns. "How am I supposed to feel?"

"However you do feel."

"I don't think about it. I guess I don't feel anything." He paused, plucking another thread from his cuff. That answer did not sound appropriate. Eckhardt might think him unnaturally callous. "I felt bad about it when it happened is what I mean. But it was a long time ago."

The small man rose and pulled a book from the small case beside his desk. "Homer. *The Odyssey*," he said, turning the pages. "Here it is." He held the book out in front of him and read aloud: "'Would God I, too, had died there—met my end that time the Trojans made so many casts at me, when I stood by Achilles after death. I should have had a soldier's burial and praise from the Achaians, not this choking waiting for me at sea, unmarked and lonely.'"

"That's Ulysses speaking," the psychologist said, resuming his seat. "Wishing he'd died with his comrades instead of being cast adrift by Poseidon. 'I should have had a soldier's burial and praise from the Achaians.' We didn't get either, did we, Chris? We survived the war, and instead of being praised, we got cursed. We were treated like shit, weren't we?"

Starkmann heard a low roaring, as when you hold a seashell against your ear. *I should have had a soldier's burial*—the words moved him deeply.

"When I got back..." His voice broke.

"When you got back what, Chris?"

"I was hitchhiking from Travis....Never mind."

"It won't kill you to talk about it."

"Just never mind. All right?"

"All right. But you know what I mean. We had rocks thrown at us. We were spit at and called killers by undergraduate punks, but the funny thing is, some guys felt they *deserved* that kind of treatment. A man goes to war, his friends die, he lives, and he feels guilty about it."

"That's screwy."

"No, it isn't. But that kind of guilt can drive a man crazy if it goes on long enough."

"I'm not crazy, Eckhardt."

"I'm not suggesting you are. I was suggesting that possibly—"

"And I don't feel guilty that those guys got killed and I didn't."

"I wasn't trying to put thoughts into your head. You might say I was trying to prime the pump."

"I guess it came up dry."

"Maybe so. Maybe you don't need to be here, but in case you think you do, we're holding our next rap session day after tomorrow. You're welcome to come."

Starkmann went, and continued to go off and on for the next several weeks. He was puzzled by what drew him to the weekly assemblies of invisibly maimed men. It was something beyond the fear of losing June, a compulsion he could not understand, all the more so because he found the sessions an ordeal. He didn't even like the term *rap session*.

It was linguistic camouflage, a use of casual contemporary slang to give the sessions the atmosphere of friendly get-togethers, just a bunch of the boys telling war stories. In fact, the sessions were a type of group therapy. The men would talk and smoke over coffee, with Eckhardt skillfully guiding the conversation. Sometimes he would choose the topic and manipulate everyone to stay on it, at other times he would allow the men to ramble on and on, then cut in with some sage advice or psychological wisdom. At other times he would select one man and ask him to describe his experiences, or how his life had gone since coming home, and then everyone was supposed to comment on the man's revelations about himself.

Starkmann, with his reticent nature, was ashamed for the men who exposed themselves and their lives to virtual strangers. How eager they were to talk about their experiences, their relations with their families, wives, or girlfriends. He wondered what the point of all this public confessing was supposed to be. Eckhardt was always reassuring them that none of them was crazy; they had simply suffered normal reactions to abnormal experiences and he was there to help them "work through" and lead normal lives—whatever that was supposed to mean. If they weren't crazy, then what were they doing there? What good did it do anyone? None that Starkmann could see. The same men came in, night after night, and talked and talked, but their lives did not appear to change. The ones who were out of work stayed out of work; the drunks stayed drunk; the dopers kept getting stoned.

As for himself, Starkmann said very little. Quite often he spent an entire session without speaking more than a few words. The idea of spilling his guts to people whom he hardly knew disgusted him. Nor did he care much for his comrades, or whatever they were supposed to be. Except for one, an ex-Special Forces medic named Mike Flynn, they were long-haired and scruffy, and their speech, like their sloppy mode of dress, seemed frozen in the sixties. Starkmann liked Flynn because he, too, was reserved, not given to these shameful revelations. Then, one night, Flynn was maneuvered into talking. His story came out in fragments, disconnected phrases interspersed with gasps, as if he'd run ten miles at top speed.

He said he'd been on a patrol in 1969, and had cracked up after a soldier in his unit had been shot in a night ambush during a monsoon storm. It had been so dark and the rain so heavy that Flynn couldn't see where the casualty had been wounded.

He'd had to feel along the body with his hands, and discovered, when his fingers dipped into a gob of brains that the top of the soldier's head had been blown off. He couldn't pull his fingers out, he'd said. Something held them there, clutching the brains that felt like lukewarm oatmeal, and he started screaming in the middle of the jungle night, the enemy all around, firing at him as he screamed and screamed, unable to move, a man's brains in his hand.

After telling his story, the ex-medic fell into tremors, then started choking and crying as he collapsed on the floor. No one could do anything for him. He lay on the floor wheezing. Eckhardt called for an ambulance, which arrived in a short time and took Flynn to the hospital. That was the last the group saw of him. Although Eckhardt later assured them that he'd suffered a "temporary anxiety reaction," from which he'd completely recovered, Starkmann had his doubts: Mike Flynn was probably in the psychiatric ward, locked up for the rest of his life.

After that incident, he stopped attending the sessions, suspecting that their purpose might be to trick the men into saying or doing something crazy so they could be put away. America wanted to get rid of them, human refuse from an unpopular war, men indelibly stained by the muck and filth of where they'd been.

June forced him to go back with more threats and nagging making his life more miserable than it had been before. He returned after an absence of two weeks, but kept a cautious eye on Eckhardt, watching him as he'd watched the paddy farmers in Vietnam; you never knew which of them was only a farmer, which a disguised guerrilla who would set off an electrically detonated mine the moment you turned your back.

A couple of times, in his usual cordial way, the psychologist tried to pry information out of him. "Chris," he once said with an affable smile, "we haven't heard much from you. Is there anything you'd like to tell us?" Starkmann replied that there wasn't. "There must be a reason why you decided to come back," Eckhardt said. Starkmann answered as he had in their first interview: his wife had threatened to leave him if he didn't. This drew laughter from a couple of the guys, which surprised Starkmann. He'd made a joke! Except he didn't think it was very funny. "Why do you suppose she did that?" Eckhardt asked. Starkmann wanted to vanish. He wished he could reduce himself to the size of a microbe. He responded to the question with a shrug. When Eckhardt pressed him, he snapped that what went on between him and June was no one's business but his own.

"Sure, Chris, sure, we'll change the subject," Eckhardt said agreeably, but Starkmann had noticed him write something in his notebook.

The only thing he liked about attending the sessions was going to Burger King after they were over. A Burger King stood on the highway, less than a block from the hospital. He could see the hospital through the window and sometimes wondered how Mike Flynn was doing, if that's where they'd put him. He would sit, munching a Whopper and fries, and feel, in the neutral atmosphere, almost as safe as he did within his perimeter. Often, he renewed his fantasy of becoming an Interstate nomad, surviving on hamburgers and tacos. Interstate 95, Interstate 10, Interstate 65—there were dozens of them, a concrete trailwork forty thousand miles long, a country unto itself, a domain of strangers.

As much as he disliked the rap sessions, they became habitual, part of his routine, like his weekly visits to the unemployment office. At home, he put the finishing touches on his perimeter, clearing fields of fire where he could, attaching empty beer and soda cans to the wire. The gate was finished, and he was proud of his workmanship. Anchored on four-by-four posts cemented into the ground, it straddled the gravel road, solid as the gate to a frontier fort. It had a six-by-one across the back as a bar, a feature that got on June's nerves because she had to remove it when she left for work in the morning. To keep her happy, Starkmann walked down to the gate every evening about the time she returned, and did her the courtesy of opening it so she wouldn't have to honk the horn. That, too, became part of his routine.

Barring the gate after June left, opening it when she came home, going to the center and the unemployment office—these chores and activities helped him get through the depression that dropped on him like a collapsing tent-top when the perimeter was at last finished and there was nothing more to do.

To keep himself occupied and to make sure everyone was safe, he started to run regular security patrols in the early-morning hours when June and the girls were asleep. He would crawl out of bed in the predawn darkness, get his carbine and a flashlight, and then stalk along a quarter-mile section, looking and listening, alert as a cat. *Alert, alive.* The patrols did not take long; he would be back in bed within an hour.

Despite his faithful attendance of the sessions, June remained unhappy with him. If he wasn't going to look for a job, she complained, why didn't he do some of the housework, or help her get dinner ready instead of loafing around all day? And why, for God's sake, did the gate have to be barred? She felt like an inmate, and the girls, out of school for the summer, were going nuts, bored and alone out here, and if he found at least part-time work he could buy a secondhand car so he could take them to their friends' houses in town while she was at her office.

Starkmann had begun to feel toward her as he had felt toward the civilians back home when he was in Nam: aggrieved and unappreciated. He had built the fence for her protection, but she didn't realize that, nor did she seem aware of the sacrifice he was making, for her sake, by attending Eckhardt's morbid gatherings. He wondered if she thought him less than a real man because he wasn't working, bringing home the bacon. Once, to prove he could still take care of her and the girls, he went fishing in the Firedog, where he caught a mess of brook trout and a three-pound rainbow that took nearly ten minutes to land. He gutted the fish on the riverbank, stuffed them in his creel, and returned to the house, triumphant. He emptied his catch in the kitchen sink, calling June, Lisa, and Christy to come take a look. "Enough for a week," he exulted. "I can still bring home the bacon." June picked up one of the rose-speckled brookies, slapped it back into the sink, and said, "What good is this going to do? Fish. We're three months overdue on the mortgage, and you bring home fish." Then she broke into tears. Starkmann was disappointed and baffled. He couldn't understand what the matter was. Maybe she was going crazy. Or maybe his early suspicions had been on the mark: she had something going on the side, and now that he'd satisfied one of her demands, she was looking for some other excuse to leave him.

On a muggy night at the end of July, after falling asleep to the strumming of mosquitoes, Starkmann went on another journey in time, the first he'd taken in months. He relived that terrible dawn, from the moment he leaped into the foxhole with Captain Hartwell and the torso of Spec. 4 Pryce, to the instant when he saw the napalm's fire, the trees uprooted, and the smoke swallow the sun and moon.

It was still dark when he awoke, his rigid body bathed in sweat. The mosquitoes continued to hum outside the window screens. After his muscles had relaxed, he crawled out of bed and stood by the west window, through which he saw wisps of fog slithering through the meadow. Beyond was the ridge, darker than the sky, a black hole in space, a gravitational whirlpool drowning all the light in the world. The smells of where he'd been clung to him once again, smells of mud and blood, of scorched flesh and flaming gasoline. Why had the dream returned, after all this time? For every question, there was an answer, and the answer to this one came in a few minutes when Butternut let out a bark. The dream had come as a warning: trespassers, concealed by the fog, had sneaked under the wire.

Starkmann quickly dressed, got his carbine and a flashlight, and went outside, quietly locking the back door behind him. With Butternut out in front as a tracking dog, he patrolled the entire perimeter, creeping through the mists in search of footprints and breaks in the wire, but found nothing. First light had begun to gray the sky by the time he was done. Worn out, Starkmann returned to the house, cutting across the meadow, whose dew-wet ferns brushed him like clammy hands.

Inside, he found June already awake, sitting in the living room in her bathrobe. Her eyes widened when she saw him in muddy boots and wet trousers, a gun in his hand. He asked what she was doing, awake before sunrise.

"I heard you go out," she answered, her gaze fastened on the carbine. "Chris, what were you doing with *that* in the middle of the night?"

"Thought I heard something. Butternut was barking. I was checking it out. It's all right, though. You can go back to sleep."

He thought she was going to start nagging him again. Instead, as he detached the magazine from the carbine, she got up from the sofa and embraced him tightly. The smell of her body, of her nearness, repelled him.

"What's happening to you? Tell me, what's happening to you?"

He didn't answer. The question made no sense to him.

June, slipping a hand between them, undid the belt to her robe, letting it fall open so that her uncovered breasts pressed against him.

"If you can't tell me, then make love to me. Now. Right here. On the couch, on the floor. I don't care. Make love to me, Chris. Do it, Chris, now, please."

He stroked her black hair, wondering what she could be thinking. He'd just come in off a patrol, muddy, wet, and tired. How could she ask him to make love? He pulled her arms from around his waist.

"You can be one cold son of a bitch," she said, then ran upstairs. He heard her slam the bedroom door.

June was stopped at the light at Front Street and East Bay Road, her hands opening and closing on the steering wheel while Tammy Wynette wailed on the radio. June switched it off. She enjoyed listening to the blues, when she could pick up the good, gritty black stations in Detroit or Chicago, but hated the country music that monopolized the airwaves up here. Piss-and-moan music, she called it— anthems of self-pity, manufactured sorrow, and sentimental hogwash churned out by the electronic studios of Nashville. She had a special dislike of Tammy Wynette, who had made "Stand By Your Man" a hit. "Stand By Your Man," that hymn to blind feminine steadfastness. Go ahead and stand by him, Tammy, but you'd better take a look to make sure he's still there, June thought, still burning from Chris's rejection of her this morning. She had never felt so unwanted and unneeded. And what had he been up to, creeping around before dawn with that army rifle?

The light seemed unusually long. She waited, tapping her unpolished nails on the dashboard and dreading the hours ahead of her. Today was her day in the field, her day to visit the backwoods dispossessed, with whom she might soon have more in common than she'd ever feared: the last letter from the loan company had threatened foreclosure if the default on the mortgage wasn't cured in thirty days. The lawyer referred by Erickson had assured her that she had more time than that; at least six months would pass before the bank repossessed the property. The default could be paid at any time during that period, he'd said. Terrific. Before that could be done, Chris would have to get off his butt, on his feet, and find a job, which now appeared about as likely as her winning a million in a lottery. Anyone who wanted to buy his prison farm was welcome to it, as far as she was concerned; but she did not want the place sold for petty cash on the courthouse steps and have to start over from scratch.

The light was still red. It must be stuck, she decided. Ridiculous. A stoplight in a one-horse town through which a couple of dozen cars might pass in an entire day. She punched the gas and shot through the intersection, the squeal of her tires loud enough to startle two early-bird tourists sauntering toward Swanson's for breakfast. She went past the Methodist church at twenty miles over the limit. Eckhardt's therapy wasn't doing any good, none that she could see. If anything, Chris was getting worse. His personality seemed to be imploding, collapsing in on itself. He acted as if she, the girls, and the whole outside world had ceased to exist. He had become so self-absorbed that she would not have been surprised to see his eyes roll over in their sockets and turn their gaze inward.

She had phoned Eckhardt twice in the past two months to complain about the lack of results. He'd been patient with her first call, but had lost his temper the second time, when she'd shouted at him.

"Don't bully me, June," he'd answered back. "I'm a practicing professional, not some psychological private detective you've hired and who you think you can push around when he doesn't come up with any clues."

She'd deserved that rebuke, but dammit, she couldn't wait years for Dr. Eckhardt to discover the miracle vaccine or, to use his metaphor, to find the right clues and solve the mystery.

Clues, she thought, passing the sign that welcomed visitors to VIEUX DESERT, POP. 942, NATURE IN ABUNDANCE. An inspiration striking her, she touched the brakes and made a U-turn, heading back toward town. If Eckhardt did not want to play psychological private detective, she would.

At the intersection, where the light continued to cast its red at nonexistent traffic, she turned onto East Bay, then parked in front of the VFW Hall. I should have figured this out long ago, she said to herself, crossing the street to the war memorial, a large whitewashed boulder with a flag flying over it and four brass plaques bolted into its face, each inscribed with the names of the men from Raddison County who had fought in the two World Wars, Korea, and Vietnam. The names with stars after them were those who had, in the words of the legend, "sacrificed their lives in the service of their country." June, feeling she was on the threshold of a discovery, studied the Vietnam plaque like an archaeologist attempting to translate an ancient tablet. None of the names rang a bell, but then, why should they? Chris had never mentioned any of the men he'd served with, and maybe the names had nothing to do with his refusal to drive this street. Maybe the existence of the memorial alone was enough to make him panic. She read the list again. There were twelve names altogether, four punctuated with stars; but the only thing that drew her attention was that most of the surnames of the men who'd been to Vietnam matched those who'd fought in the other wars. Grandfathers, fathers, and sons—it was as if fighting in distant conflicts were a kind of legacy, passed from one generation to the next. That told her something about small-town patriotism, but nothing about what she wanted to know.

Frustrated, she debated whether or not to give Eckhardt another call. All right, it was worth a try. She cut across the street to the phone booth outside the post office.

Eckhardt wasn't in, either at the Center or at the office where he conducted his private practice. She got his home number from information and rang him there. The female voice on the other end surprised her; she didn't know he was married.

"Dr. Eckhardt, please," she said, avoiding the familiar "Jim."

"Who's calling?"

"Mrs. Starkmann. And tell him I'm sorry to call him at home, but it's important."

She waited, nestling into a corner of the booth and looking at the memorial, which resembled a giant stone that had been washed ashore. Herring gulls wheeled over the bay behind it—white, then dark, as they turned into and out of the sun.

"What is it?" Eckhardt asked. He did not sound pleased.

"Did your wife tell you I'm sorry—"

"That was my cleaning girl. My wife's in Pontiac with my kids."

"Sorry. I didn't realize you were divorced."

"Who isn't these days? What's so important?"

"This morning? Before daybreak? Chris was wandering outside with a rifle. Some kind of army rifle."

"Did he explain why?"

"He said the dog was barking and that he thought he heard a noise."

"Did you?"

"I was asleep."

"Did it ever occur to you," he said with overstrained forbearance, "that maybe he did hear something, and that, with you living out there miles from the nearest help, the rifle might have been intelligent precaution?"

"Don't talk to me like I'm an idiot. I know what I saw. Anyway, that's not the only reason I called. Do you remember my telling you how jumpy Chris got when I asked him to drive me down a street here in town? East Bay Road? That he told me he never went down that street? Drove miles out of his way to get to work?"

"Yes, vaguely."

"I think I've got an idea why."

"And what, June, has led you to this conclusion?"

Overlooking the sarcasm, she told him about the memorial. He was silent at first, but she sensed, as if telepathically, a piquing of his interest.

"Do you remember any of the names?"

"Some of them."

"Hang on. My notes are in my briefcase."

An empty logging truck, clattering down the street, almost drowned out Eckhardt when he came back on the line.

"Fishburn," June heard him say. "I don't suppose D.J. Fishburn was one of them."

"What did you say?"

"D.J. Fishburn. I don't suppose that was one of them."

"N-No," she answered, her throat catching.

"Didn't think so. Chris told me he was black, and there hasn't been a Negro up here in recorded history. How about Ramos and Hutchinson?"

"Were they friends of his?"

"Yes. They were killed over there."

"Killed? Christ."

"Are their names on the plaque?"

"No, no. Jim, he *talks* to them. My youngest daughter overheard him. I didn't tell you because all I had to go on was her word."

"I'm not following."

"He *talks* to those three guys like they're still alive. Christy heard him. D.J., Hutch, and Ramos. He talks to them, for God's sake."

Eckhardt took a while to absorb this information, then told her not to overreact. "Believe it or not, that's not all that uncommon. I caught myself doing it a few years back."

"Talking to dead people isn't uncommon? That's normal?"

"Not exactly. It's hard to explain to someone who wasn't there. But sometimes your memories can be so vivid that, yes, it's like they're still alive."

"Whatever you say," she commented wearily. "Whatever. You're the doctor."

"I've got to run. Listen, June, do me a favor. Copy down those names if you can and either phone them in to me or drop them in the mail."

He hung up. June, watching the gulls fluttering over the smooth summer blue of the bay, reflected on this assurance: it's not that uncommon. Suppose Chris started to see his trio of dead buddies? Suppose he invited them over for dinner? What would Eckhardt have to say to that? Don't be alarmed, June—it's not that uncommon.

She jerked open the folding door and rummaged in her purse for a pen and a scrap of paper, questioning why she was going through all this trouble. I'm living with a man who'd rather talk to ghosts than to me, she thought as she copied the names Allen, R.T.... Johnson, T.K.*... LeForge, P.G.... Mueller, J.L.*... St. Germaine, B.G.*... Swenson, O.R.

Two Village Women

Nguyen Quang Thieu

It started to rain as soon as the lights in the village came on. Perhaps this would be the final downpour of winter; Tet was only ten days away. Gusts of wind blew along the banks of the wide river. The rain fell like a whisper, light and soft. Perched on the river bank downhill from Chua village, was a small solitary house. The two women had lived here for decades, until their hair had turned white. They sat now in the kitchen, amid straw and banana leaves, in the warmth of a small bamboo fire. A wooden tray with a crack running down its middle lay on the rock hard kitchen floor. On it was a bowl of sour vegetable soup in which floated a few tiny steamed shrimp. The two old women sat facing each other on opposite sides of the tray, their dark, wrinkled faces resting on top of their boney knees.

"Who sold you the shrimp?" An asked, stirring the soup with her chopsticks.

"Some buffalo boys."

"For how much?"

"Twenty cents."

"You always buy too much. Half of this would have been plenty."

"Who'd buy the other half? They're already no bigger than pinches of salt."

The two women raised their rice bowls and slowly began to eat.

"Sour vegetable soup with shrimp should simmer longer," An grumbled. "These sharp shells hurt my teeth."

"What shells can such tiny shrimp have?"

"Your teeth are still good. Mine are almost gone."

So they sat, eating and bickering with each other as the rain fell outside. The sound of barking dogs drifted through the rain.

"Aha! See, I told you," An cried. "It's the shell! Ouch!"

"Try to clear your throat," said Mat worriedly.

An put down her bowl, turned away from the tray and tried to clear her throat.

"Did you get it?"

"No. You know, I could die from this shrimp."

"Nonsense," said Mat. "There's an old highland trick I know to get it out." She picked up a large pair of chopsticks, still sticky with rice and foam and approached An. "Close your eyes and keep still."

Mat held the chopsticks a hands-length from the top of An's head. Tapping them rhythmically together, she started to chant like a witch doctor: "Near out, far in, near out, far in..." After seven repetitions, she stopped.

"Is it out yet?"

An swallowed hard.

"It's out. I'm not eating any more of this. Tomorrow morning, we should re-cook it."

After dinner, the two old women placed another bamboo stick on the fire and then took out some betel nut. An chose one and handed it to Mat.

"Where did you get the fresh betel nut?" Mat asked.

"At the wedding of Phan's daughter. They stuffed it into my purse."

"Phan's daughter?"

"Yes. She wanted to bring you to the wedding feast also, but you were too sick to come. Remember?"

They chewed on the betel in silence. As the new bamboo stick caught, the image of the flames rose and flickered in their tired eyes.

"How many Tet cakes should we make this year?" An asked.

"Let's do thirty."

"That's enough for the whole village."

"So what? We can give the extras to the kids...and what if someone else comes...?"

An looked up slowly. "Who else will come?" she whispered.

In the same kitchen, decades before, on another winter night just before the new year, the two women had chatted eagerly about Tet cakes. They were young women then, no more than twenty.

"This year he'll come back," Mat had whispered. "Don't you think so, An?"

"I hope so," An said. "Last night I dreamt that a rooster was pecking my finger. It's been years..."

"I'm so sick of waiting..."

"To tell you the truth, if I had a child, I wouldn't care if they came back or not."

"Oh, An! I had a dream also, just a few nights ago. I dreamt that he came back and...then that night...."

Mat's face turned red with excitement and embarrassment.

"Yes, then that night...then what? Monkey business, huh?"

"I dreamt that I got pregnant. When I woke up, my stomach felt really strange. It's scary."

"That's crazy."

"But it's true. Today my stomach still feels different."

She grabbed An's hand and placed it on her stomach.

"What do you think? Does it feel different?"

Curious, An pressed her hand against Mat's flesh. Immediately she felt something.

"Hey," she whispered, "Your husband's away. Did you do something...?"

"What do you mean?"

"Has anyone come on to you?"

"No way. I'd die."

"I've got to keep an eye on you," An said. "If anything were to happen, we'd have to leave the village and go live in the jungle."

Both orphaned at birth, An and Mat had grown up together and gotten married at the same time. They'd settled into a peaceful life in the village alongside the river. One night, their husbands had packed their kits and joined an army unit that was crossing the river on its way to the Mieu Mon mountain. Before they'd left, they ordered their wives to move in with each other.

"At Tet, when the resistance is victorious, we'll return," they had promised.

From then on, Mat and An lived together like sisters. Each year before Tet, they would go down to the river and wash banana leaves and rice, their cheeks ruddy in the cold winds of late winter. Their laughter would echo clearly and strongly across the quiet river. On the nights they cooked their Tet cakes, the fire would caress their bodies with warmth and they would feel anxious and excited. After the cakes were done, they would pick the finest ones and set them aside for their husbands. But the days of Tet flew by like so many arrows. When the sound of firecrackers faded and they saw the blackbirds begin their return from their winter journeying, they knew another Tet had passed. Still hopeful, they would reboil the remaining Tet cakes to preserve them a little longer. When the cakes began to spoil after the second boiling, sadness would descend on the two women. At night they would lie back to back on the straw bed, trying to hide their disappointment.

"Are you asleep yet, An?" Mat would ask.

"Not yet."

"Why do you think they didn't come back this Tet?"

"God only knows," An said sadly. "Maybe the campaign isn't over."

"Maybe we should reboil the cakes again tomorrow."

"Sure. We'll reboil them until they turn into porridge."

"Still, how can we eat twenty cakes?"

In January, as the river wind turned warm and the earth took on the pleasant smell of alluvial soil, they dreamt intensely during the nights. In An's dream, a fat rooster with a scarlet comb and a hard claw pecked vigorously at her face. Mat's dreams were both happier and more worrisome. She would dream that her soldier-husband would return and on that night she would get pregnant. When she awoke, she would have the vague sensation that there was a change in her stomach.

* * *

One year, around midnight on a day near Tet, Mat had heard someone knocking rapidly on the door.

"Who's that? Who's there?"

"It's me, Bac."

"My God!" Mat cried out. "Bac?" The door opened and An's husband walked in and abruptly embraced her.

"Bac," Mat said, frightened, "I'm Mat, little sister Mat."

The soldier released her from his arms.

"Where's An?"

"She went to Kim Boi this morning to buy banana leaves and oranges from the Tet market. I stayed behind to look after the house."

"When will she be back?"

"By tomorrow, I hope. When do you have to leave?"

Bac stood quietly as the cold wind from the river blew through the walls of the house.

"Please sit. I'll start the fire."

A moment later fire blazed from a pile of dry branches.

"I'll cook some rice, okay?"

"I've already eaten. Will An be back early tomorrow?"

"She should be. Why haven't we heard anything from you for so long? How is my husband?"

"At first we were in the same unit. But after a month we were separated. I've heard that Ngu is in Bac Can now. Don't you get any word from him?"

"Nothing." Mat's voice cracked. "Every Tet An and I think that you both will be coming back. Every year we make many cakes...."

"There'll be a lot of fighting soon; my unit's being transferred to the front at Hoa Binh. Are you both okay here?"

"We can take anything. We just worry about the two of you. Why didn't you let An know you were coming?"

"How could I?"

A strong wind blew through the banana leaves out in the garden. Dew formed on the thatched roof of the house. The fire began to grow smaller.

"You should rest," Mat said. "It's way past midnight."

"Go ahead and get some sleep. I'll just sit here. It's nearly morning."

Mat didn't answer. She sat quietly, looking at the embers that flickered like winter stars.

If An were home tonight, she'd be so happy, Mat thought. And if this soldier were my husband....Her blood seemed to race through her veins and she felt her face become flushed. She remembered her recurring dream and tried to hold back the tears.

"We're miserable here," she began to sob. "If we had a child, it would be better."

"Soon there will be peace and we'll come home. With both of us here, the two of you will be too exhausted to bear children," the soldier laughed. Mat laughed with him, but tears filled her eyes. The fire turned to red embers and then died out. She sat in the darkness, whispering to herself:

"An, come home quickly. Bac is here for you. Hurry!"

The bamboo stick burned to ashes. The two old women sat quietly, their dark and wrinkled faces perched atop their boney knees. A mouse crept out from a corner of the kitchen and climbed onto the wooden tray. It jumped into the rice bowl and knocked it over.

"Are you asleep yet?" An asked Mat.

"How can I sleep?" She opened her eyes and chewed the betel. "I'm getting a little high."

"Did you remember to close the chicken coop this afternoon?"

"Yes. I even gave them some water from the pure limestone well. I'm afraid this fog will make our hens sick."

"Phan's mother said we should celebrate Tet at their house. She said we live like two ghosts by the riverside."

"We never get enough to eat or drink when we go there. She has children, guests, no time to serve us...oh God, I left the basket with a shirt still in it on the dock when I did the washing this afternoon."

"Your memory is getting worse than mine," An said.

"I was chatting with Mrs. Men and it must have slipped my mind. I'll have to go out there now and fetch it."

"Forget it: it's dark and rainy. Who's going to steal a ripped shirt and an old basket?"

But Mat insisted on going. An gave her a conical hat and warned her to be careful. The night sky seemed immense. Mat tottered towards the dock along the path that she had followed so many times that it was etched in her mind. Returning with the basket in her hand, she could hear the rippling sound of fish swimming in the river. The sound jarred her memory. She stopped and sat down to look at the river. It was here that she had said goodbye to her husband many years ago. And it was here that she had said goodbye to Bac, the time he came home but didn't meet his wife.

The memories of that night had remained vivid in her mind.

"I must go," Bac had said after dinner.

"An will definitely be here by tomorrow. You should stay at least until tomorrow night."

"I can't. I have to rejoin my unit by tonight."

He set off just before nine. Mat walked with him to the dock. He put his hands on her shoulders and held her tightly.

"I've got to go," he whispered. "You two sisters take care of each other. Ngu will return soon."

An hour after he left, An came home. Mat burst into tears.

"An! Bac came home! Bac came home!"

"Where? Where is he?"

"He left already. He waited for you all last night. He just crossed back over the river."

An dropped the bundle of leaves and the basket of oranges she had been carrying. "When did he leave?" she gasped. "Which way did he go?"

"He left from the dock."

An ran to the dock and then jumped into the river. Mat ran after her.

"He's gone far already!" she called. "Please come back!"

She sat down on the cold sand, buried her face in her hands and began to sob. Eventually she heard splashing and looked up to see An, wet and cold, climbing onto the dock. The two young women stood staring at each other. Then they fell crying into each others' arms.

The wind from the river gusted warmly up the bank. The smell of grass hung heavy in the air.

That Tet, An and Mat still made dozens of Tet cakes. But their men didn't return. When January came, they reboiled the cakes, crying each time.

Several years later, Mat received an official notice that her husband had been killed. Still, when Tet came, they cooked cakes and in her dreams Mat's soldier husband still came back and when she awoke her stomach still felt strange. Over and over, An urged Mat to get married again. Mat would smile like someone who had just woken up from a dream and say, "I'll remarry when Bac comes home."

Waiting so long for Mat to return from the dock, An grew worried. She went outside to look for her.

"Mat! Mat!" she called.

"I'm here. I'm coming."

"I told you not to go out this late. An old woman like you shouldn't be out alone at this hour."

She stood waiting until Mat got to the path. "Come on, let's go to sleep," she said. "My back hurts."

The small house seemed bigger at night. The two old women lay back to back.

"Are you still chewing betel?" An asked.

"Yes. I didn't want to waste it."

"Aren't you tired?"

They heard the sound of mice running atop the roof and then the sound of termites inside their coffins.

"Do you have the match box?" An asked.

"Why? What do you want to do?"

"I want to see the termites. They might destroy our coffins before we have time to die."

"They're inside the wood. How can you see them?"

Mat gave An the match box. An struck a match and lit the oil lamp. She cocked her head, tapped on the side of the coffin and listened intently. The sound of the termites ceased. She stood quietly for a while until she was satisfied they had stopped for the night, then blew out the lamp and went to bed.

A little before dawn, the late winter winds carried a whiff of spring's warmth into the small house. Again, Mat dreamed that a soldier had come back to her. But this time it was Bac she dreamed about, not Ngu.

Early in 1968, An had received a letter from Bac. He wrote that his unit was in Quang Binh, next to a river as beautiful as the river by his native village.

"You should go look for him immediately," urged Mat. "I'll look after things here."

An read Bac's letter over and over, crying continuously. Finally she agreed to pack up her things and go search for him.

But life is cruel. A few days later Bac again returned home.

"Bac, did you meet An? She went to Quang Binh to look for you."

"Look for me? When?"

"She left a few days ago."

Bac stood as if frozen.

"Soldiers move around all the time. How could she hope to find me?"

"This time you have to wait for her," Mat said, bursting into tears. "I won't let you leave. My husband's martyred already."

"Ngu martyred? When? Where?"

"I received news of his death three years ago."

Later that night, Bac told Mat: "I have to leave early tomorrow morning. This time I'll be going far away, perhaps for a very long time."

"You can't! You have to wait until she comes back. She'll die."

"There's nothing I can do, Mat. I have to go."

At four in the morning, Bac packed his things and left the house. Mat followed him to the river bank. She hugged him and burst into tears.

"Bac! I feel horrible for An. I feel sorry for you. And I feel sorry for myself. If only Ngu had come home one time, I'd be okay, much less miserable. Bac, why am I not An? Why are you not Ngu?"

Bac silently pulled Mat to his chest. A shiver shot through their bodies. Mat pushed him away.

"Go quickly, Bac! Go quickly."

She ran down the river bank, sobbing loudly, calling out for An and for Ngu.

"Hey Mat! Are you having a nightmare?" Mat woke up, startled. "Why are you crying so loudly?"

"I had a nightmare. Is it morning yet?"

"Still not for a long time."

"Give me the match box," Mat said. "I need to go to the toilet."

Mat struck a match and lit the oil lamp. The house glowed in its warm light.

"Do you need to go?" she asked An.

"No."

"If you have to, then you should. If not, you'll stink up the place."

"Oh God!" An clicked her tongue. "Old age."

The next morning the women awoke to the sound of roosters. Mat began chewing the piece of betel she had kept in her mouth while she slept.

"How many cakes should we make this Tet?" Mat asked.

"Tell Phan's mother to buy enough leaves for thirty. We don't eat much, but if someone comes back home..."

Mat stopped chewing her betel and turned to An. She opened her mouth to tell her something but held back.

Outside the early spring winds continued to blow through the little house.

Translated by Nguyen Nguyet Cam and Peter Zinoman
Edited by Wayne Karlin

THE HONORED DEAD

Breece D'J Pancake

Watching little Lundy go back to sleep, I wish I hadn't told her about the Mound Builders to stop her crying, but I didn't know she would see their eyes watching her in the dark. She was crying about a cat run down by a car—her cat, run down a year ago, only today poor Lundy figured it out. Lundy is turned too much like her mamma. Ellen never worries because it takes her too long to catch the point of a thing, and Ellen doesn't have any problem sleeping. I think my folks were a little too keen, but Lundy is her mamma's girl, not jumpy like my folks.

My grandfather always laid keenness on his Shawnee blood, his half-breed mother, but then he was hep on blood. He even had an oath to stop bleeding, but I don't remember the words. He was a fair to sharp woodsman, and we all tried to slip up on him at one time or another. It was Ray at the sugar mill finally caught him, but he was an old man by then, and his mind wasn't exactly right. Ray just came creeping up behind and laid a hand on his shoulder, and the old bird didn't even turn around; he just wagged his head and said, "That's Ray's hand. He's the first fellow ever slipped up on me." Ray could've done without that, because the old man never played with a full deck again, and we couldn't keep clothes on him before he died.

I turn out the lamp, see no eyes in Lundy's room, then it comes to me why she was so scared. Yesterday I told her patches of stories about scalpings and murders, mixed up the Mound Builders with the Shawnee raids, and Lundy chained that with the burial mound in the back pasture. Tomorrow I'll set her straight. The only surefire thing I know about Mound Builders is they must have believed in a God and hereafter or they never would have made such big graves.

I put on my jacket, go into the foggy night, walk toward town. Another hour till dawn, and both lanes of the Pike are empty, so I walk the yellow line running through the valley to Rock Camp. I keep thinking back to the summer me and my buddy Eddie tore that burial mound apart for arrowheads and copper beads gone green with rot. We were getting down to the good stuff, coming up with skulls galore, when of a sudden Grandad showed out of thin air and yelled, "Wah-pah-nah-te-he." He was waving his arms around, and I could see Eddie was about to shit the nest. I knew it was all part of the old man's Injun act, so I stayed put, but Eddie sat down like he was ready to surrender.

Grandad kept on: "Wah-pah-nah-te-he. You evil. Make bad medicine here. Now put the goddamned bones back or I'll take a switch to your young asses." He watched us bury the bones, then scratched a picture of a man in the dust, a bow drawn, aimed at a crude sun. "Now go home." He walked across the pasture.

Eddie said, "You Red Eagle. Me Black Hawk." I knew he had bought the game for keeps. By then I couldn't tell Eddie that if Grandad had a shot at the sixty-four-dollar question, he would have sold them on those Injun words: *Wah-pah-nah-te-he*—the fat of my ass.

So I walk and try to be like Ellen and count the pass-at-your-own-risk marks on the road. Eastbound tramples Westbound: 26-17. At home is my own darling Ellen, fast asleep, never knowing who won. Sometimes I wonder if Ellen saw Eddie on his last leave. There are lightning bugs in the fog, and I count them until I figure I'm counting the same ones over. For sure, Lundy would call them Mound Builder eyes, and see them as signals without a message, make up her own message, get scared.

I turn off the Pike onto the oxbow of Front Street, walk past some dark store windows, watch myself moving by their gloss, rippling through one pane and another. I sit on the Old Bank steps, wait for the sun to come over the hills; wait like I waited for the bus to the draft physical, only I'm not holding a bar of soap. I sat and held a bar of soap, wondering if I should shove it under my arm to hike my blood pressure into the 4-F range. My blood pressure was already high, but the bar of soap would give me an edge. I look around at Front Street and picture people and places I haven't thought of in years; I wonder if it was that way for Eddie.

I put out my hand like the bar of soap was in it and see its whiteness reflect blue from the streetlights long ago. And I remember Eddie's hand flattened on green felt, arched knuckles cradling the cue for a tough eight-ball shot, or I remember the way his hand curled around his pencil to hide answers on math tests. I remember his hand holding an arrowhead or unscrewing a lug nut, but I can't remember his face.

It was years ago, on Decoration Day, and my father and several other men wore their Ike jackets, and I was in the band. We marched through town to the cemetery in the rain; then I watched the men move sure and stiff with each command, and the timing between volleys was on the nose; the echoes rang four times above the clatter of their bolt weapons. The rain smelled from the tang of their fire, the wet wool of our uniforms. There was a pause and the band director coughed. I stepped up to play, a little off tempo, and another kid across the hills answered my taps. I finished first, snapped my bugle back. When the last tone seeped through to mist, it beat at me, and I could swear I heard the stumps of Eddie's arms beating the coffin lid for us to stop.

I look down at my hand holding the bugle, the bar of soap. I look at my hand, empty, older, tell myself there is no bar of soap in that hand. I count all five fingers with the other hand, tell myself they are going to stay there a hell of a long time. I get out a cigarette and smoke. Out on the Pike, the first car races by in the darkness, knowing no cops are out yet. I think of Eddie pouring on the gas, heading with me down the Pike toward Tin Bridge.

That day was bright, but the blink of all the dome lights showed up far ahead of us. We couldn't keep still for the excitement, couldn't wait to see what happened.

I said, "Did you hear it, man? I thought they'd dropped the Bomb."

"Hear? I felt it. The damn ground shook."

"They won't forget that much noise for a long time."

"For sure."

Cars were stopped dead-center of the road, and a crowd had built up. Eddie pulled off to the side behind a patrol car, then made his way through the crowd, holding his wallet high to show his volunteer fireman's badge. I kept back, but in the break the cops made, I saw the fire was already out, and all that was left of Beck Fuller's Chevy was the grille, the rest of the metal peeled around it from behind. I knew it was Beck's from the '51 grille, and I knew what had happened. Beck fished with dynamite and primer cord, and he was a real sport to the end. Beck could never get into his head he had to keep the cord away from the TNT.

Then a trooper yelled: "All right, make way for the wrecker."

Eddie and the other firemen put pieces of Beck the Sport into bags, and I turned away to keep from barfing, but the smell of burning hair drifted out to me. I knew it was the stuffing in old car-seats, and not Beck, but I leaned against the patrol car, tossed my cookies just the same. I wanted to stop being sick because it was silly to be sick about something like that. Under the noise of my coughings I could hear the fire chief cussing Eddie into just getting the big pieces, just letting the rest go.

Eddie didn't sit here with any bar of soap in his hand. He never had much gray matter, but he made up for it with style, so he would never sit here with any bar of soap in his hand. Eddie would never think about blowing toes away or cutting off his trigger finger. It just was not his way to think. Eddie was the kind who bought into a game early, and when the deal soured, he'd rather hold the hand a hundred years than fold. It was just his way of doing.

At Eight Ball, I chalked up while Eddie broke. The pool balls cracked, but nothing went in, and I moved around the table to pick the choice shot. "It's crazy to join," I said.

"What the hell—I know how to weld. They'll put me in welding school and I'll sit it out in Norfolk."

"With your luck the ship'll fall on you."

"Come on, Eagle, go in buddies with me."

"Me and Ellen's got plans. I'll take a chance with the lottery." I shot, and three went in.

"That's slop," Eddie said.

I ran the other four down, banked the eight ball to a side pocket, and stood back, made myself grin at him. The eight went where I called it, but I never believed I made the shot right, and I didn't look at Eddie, I just grinned.

I toss my cigarette into the gutter, and it glows back orange under the blue streetlight. I think how that glow would be just another eye for Lundy, and think that after a while she will see so many eyes in the night they won't matter anymore. The eyes will go away and never come back, and even if I tell her when she is grown, she won't remember. By then real eyes will scare her enough. She's Ellen's girl, and sometimes I want to ask Ellen if she saw Eddie on his last leave.

Time ago I stood with my father in the cool evening shadow of the barn to smoke; he stooped, picked up a handful of gravel, and flipped them away with his thumb. He studied on what I said about Canada, and each gravel falling was a little click in his thoughts; then he stood, dusted his palms. "I didn't mind it too much," he said. "Me and Howard kept pretty thick in foxhole religion— never thought of running off."

"But, Dad, when I seen Eddie in that plastic bag...."

He yelled: "Why the hell'd you look? If you can't take it, you oughtn't to look. You think I ain't seen that? That and worse, by god."

I rub my hand across my face, hang my arm tight against the back of my neck, think I ought to be home asleep with Ellen. I think, if I was asleep with Ellen, I wouldn't care who won. I wouldn't count or want to know what the signals mean, and I wouldn't be like some dog looking for something dead to drag in.

naked in the loft at midnight,
nooping through a box of old
tters tied with sea-grass string.
ped back to me, and watching
eyes, I knew she would be my
the old V-mail envelopes of my
sted her head on my thigh, and

t out."

up at me.

ldn't say that. *The way they do
tarven in the street and took him
e on the inside of my thigh and
nothin for him till I leveled off
with my gun and Howard he raised hell with me only I seen that rusky eat one
damn fine meal."* I turned off the flashlight, moved down beside Ellen. He had
never told that story.

But it's not so simple now as then, not easy to be a part of Ellen without
knowing or wanting to know the web our kisses make. It was easy to leave the
house with a bar of soap in my pocket; only the hardest part was sitting here,
looking at it, and remembering.

I went through the hall with the rest of the kids between classes, and there stood
Eddie at the top of the stairs. He grinned at me, but it was not his face anymore.
His face had changed; a face gone red because the other kids snickered at his
uniform. He stood at parade rest, his seaman's cap hanging from his belt, his
head tilting back to look down on me, then he dragged his hands around like
Jackie Gleason taking an away-we-go pool shot. We moved on down the hall to
ditch my books.

"You on leave?" I said.

"Heap bad medicine. Means I'm getting shipped."

"How long?" I fumbled with the combination of my locker.

"Ten days," he said, then squinted at the little upside-down flag on my open
locker door. "You sucker."

I watched him until he went out of sight down the steps, then got my books,
went on to class.

The butt of my palm is speckled with black spots deep under the skin: cinders
from a relay-race fall. The skin has sealed them over, and it would cost plenty to

get them out. Sometimes Ellen wants to play nurse with a needle, wants to pry them out, but I won't let her. Sometimes I want to ask Ellen if she saw Eddie on his last leave.

Coach said I couldn't run track because anyone not behind his country was not fit for a team, so I sat under the covered bridge waiting for the time I could go home. Every car passing over sprinkled a little dust between the boards, sifted it into my hair.

I watched the narrow river roll by, its waters slow but muddy like pictures I had seen of rivers on the TV news. In history class, Coach said the Confederate troops attacked this bridge, took it, but were held by a handful of Sherman's troops on Company Hill. Johnny Reb drank from this river. The handful had a spring on Company Hill. Johnny croaked with the typhoid and the Yankees moved south. So I stood and brushed the dust off me. My hair grew long after Eddie went over, and I washed it every night.

I put my fist under my arm like the bar of soap and watch the veins on the back of my hand rise with pressure. There are scars where I've barked the hide hooking the disk or the drag to my tractor; they are like my father's scars.

We walked the fields, checked the young cane for blight or bugs, and the late sun gave my father's slick hair a sparkle. He chewed the stem of his pipe, then stood with one leg across a knee and banged tobacco out against his shoe.

I worked up the guts: "You reckon I could go to college, Dad?"

"What's wrong with farming?"

"Well, sir, nothing, if that's all you ever want."

He crossed the cane rows to get me, and my left went up to guard like Eddie taught me, right kept low and to the body.

"Cute," he said. "Real cute. When's your number up?"

I dropped my guard. "When I graduate—it's the only chance I got to stay out."

He loaded his pipe, turned around in his tracks like he was looking for something, then stopped, facing the hills. "It's your damn name is what it is. Dad said when you was born, 'Call him William Haywood, and if he ever goes in a mine, I hope he chokes to death.'"

I thought that was a shitty thing for Grandad to do, but I watched Dad, hoped he'd let me go.

He started up: "Everybody's going to school to be something better. Well, when everybody's going this way, it's time to turn around and go that way, you know?" He motioned with his hands in two directions. "I don't care if they end up shitting gold nuggets, somebody's got to dig in the damn ground. Somebody's got to."

And I said, "Yessir."

The sky is dark blue and the fog is cold smoke staying low to the ground. In this first hint of light my hand seems blue, but not cold; such gets cold sooner or later, but for now my hand is warm.

Many's the time my grandfather told of the last strike before he quit the mines, moved to the valley for some peace. He would quit his Injun act when he told it, like it was real again, all before him, and pretty soon I started thinking it was me the Baldwin bulls were after. I ran through the woods till my lungs bled. I could hear the Baldwins and their dogs in the dark woods, and I could remember machine guns cutting down pickets, and all I could think was how the One Big Union was down the rathole. Then I could taste it in my mouth, taste the blood coming up from my lungs, feel the bark of a tree root where I fell, where I slept. When I opened my eyes, I felt funny in the gut, felt watched. There were no twig snaps, just the feeling that something was too close. Knowing it was a man, one man, hunting me, I took up my revolver. I could hear him breathing, aimed into the sound, knowing the only sight would come with the flash. I knew all my life I had lived to kill this man, this goddamned Baldwin man, and I couldn't do it. I heard him move away down the ridge, hunting his lost game.

I fold my arms tight like I did the morning the bus pulled up. I was thinking of my grandfather, and there was a bar of soap under my arm. At the draft physical, my blood pressure was clear out of sight, and they kept me four days. The pressure never went down, and on the fourth day a letter came by forward. I read it on the bus home.

Eddie said he was with a bunch of Jarheads in the Crotch, and he repaired radio gear in the field. He said the USMC's hated him because he was regular Navy. He said the chow was rotten, the quarters lousy, and the left side of his chest was turning yellow from holding smokes inside his shirt at night. And he said he knew how the guy felt when David sent him into the battle to get dibs on the guy's wife. Eddie said he wanted dibs on Ellen, ha, ha. He said he would get married and give me his wife if I would get him out of there. He said the beer came in Schlitz cans, but he was sure it was something else. Eddie was sure the

CO was a fag. He said he would like to get Ellen naked, but if he stayed with this outfit he would want to get me naked when he came back. He asked if I remembered him teaching me to bum off leeches with a cigarette. Eddie swore he learned that in a movie where the hero dies because he ran out of cigarettes. He said he had plenty of cigarettes. He said he could never go Oriental because they don't have any hair on their twats, and he bet me he knew what color Ellen's bush was. He said her hair might be brown, but her bush was red. He said to think about it and say Hi to Ellen for him until he came back. Sometimes I want to ask Ellen if she saw Eddie on his last leave.

When I came back, Ellen met me at the trailer door, hugged me, and started to cry. She showed pretty well with Lundy, and I told her Eddie's letter said to say Hi. She cried some more, and I knew Eddie was not coming back.

Daylight fires the ridges green, shifts the colors of the fog, touches the brick streets of Rock Camp with a reddish tone. The streetlights flicker out, and the traffic signal at the far end of Front Street's yoke snaps on; stopping nothing, warning nothing, rushing nothing on.

I stand and my joints crack from sitting too long, but the flesh of my face is warming in the early sun. I climb the steps of the Old Bank, draw a spook in the window soap. I tell myself that spook is Eddie's, and I wipe it off with my sleeve, then I see the bus coming down the Pike, tearing the morning, and I start down the street so he won't stop for me. I cannot go away, and I cannot make Eddie go away. So I go home. And walking down the street as the bus goes by, I bet myself a million that my Lundy is up and already watching cartoons, and I bet I know who won.

PART THREE
Wounds

3

During Vietnam, which we say because the name signifies more than a place—it is an epoch, a paradigm, a memory, a mistake—during Vietnam, things were the same as they are now for those who are young and poor here. We were standing around. There was no work, it was the beginning of our times as men, we were looking to prove ourselves, or looking for a way out. Some were patriots, and many were the sons of men who had gone to another war and come back admired. I don't remember any mercenaries. We were crossing thresholds, starting to lie to ourselves about things, and because we were there and ambitious or desperate, when they passed out weapons, we took them. We didn't understand the disordered nature of the universe, so disordered humans must try to arrange it, and if they get you young enough, you will help.

I'm grieved but not guilty. Sad but not ashamed.

That does not mean I lack compassion. It does not mean I sleep at night, or don't sweat at night. It does not mean it is easy to live.

In parts of my country, I'm considered insane.

The House Behind the Temple of Literature

Tran Vu

I returned to my family home for the first time after more than twenty years. Its appearance had not changed much. It was still the same three-compartment house painted plain white, its facade only disturbed by several partially opened doors. At the back was the kitchen and before the entrance was a small garden. Only a barely discernible discoloration which had changed the wall in spots from white to the golden color of tripe soup and the deep carbuncles sprouting here and there gave any indication that time had passed. The roof tiles, ordered by my father long ago before the Japanese invaded Indochina, had retained their original crimson color. And in the same spot, in the tenth row if I were to count up from the gutter, the same tile was still missing. A thin layer of green mildew had also spread over part of the exterior, running from the wall on one side of the house to the foot of the hibiscus hedge next to which my father was standing.

—Heh, is it Nu coming home? Where have you been? Come here—I can no longer see very clearly.

I was startled but anxious and excited by the prospect of seeing loved ones after so many years. Clumsily putting down my luggage, I darted into the courtyard. I wanted to clasp my father's frail frame in my arms and tell him of my abiding love and respect. But exactly at that heart-rending moment he calmly sat down on a wooden plank. His feeble hands sluggishly searched for that brown piece of felt that he kept at his side for as long as I could remember. He stooped over and raising those pale, ghastly arms gently took off his glasses for a polish. I could no longer see any vitality in those eyes that stared fixedly but failed to reflect any glitter. He sat unmoving on the plank before me with the innocent look of a child and the imperturbable demeanor of a blind man. It dawned on me that the man who just a moment ago greeted my return with so much warmth was not my father. My real father sat in the garden now, dazed and bewildered, absorbed in a world that only he knew, while his most precious possession—the decorative stone which he'd brought from China – lay ignored and exposed to the harsh sun at the end of the garden.

He sat absolutely still. His only sign of physical activity was his preoccupation with the old piece of felt, tattered even to the embroidery which spelled his family and given middle names, like the relic of an opulent past. He gently cleaned and recleaned the two thick, scratched lenses, and my voice and calls failed to reach him.

Until then, I had not been appreciative of the gravity of his illness. Now, discovering the reality in all its manifestations, actually seeing with my own eyes the picture of him sitting there and vacuously feeling those bent frames, folding and unfolding that filthy rag, lovingly caressing the cane he'd once wielded against the French, I knew that Nu—his name for me when I was little—had been gone from his life for a long time now.

When I followed my mother into the house, I saw Grandfather lying on the plank bed. The same Chinese cupboard still occupied its prized place in the corner and from the same altar that had been there when I was small a faint aroma of incense trailed across the room. In the still air, I detected the faint fragrance of eagle-wood. Grandfather dozed, breathing heavily, and something in his posture suggested that he had spent the last twenty years in this exact place, decaying. My mother opened a shutter, enlarging the square of light that had been allowed to filter into the room. The sound provoked movement: Grandfather struggled to turn his face towards me. Like my father, Grandfather had become mentally unhinged, but unlike my blurry-eyed father he still had full possession of his eyesight. Suddenly my feet were pinned to the entryway because—my God, how my grandfather's eyes flared with the fire of hatred as they finally focused upon me. The irises threatened to explode out of the two baleful eyes that dominated an otherwise pasty face. This glare that I had purposefully avoided for the last twenty years now filled the house with loathing. Grandfather's legs and lower body were paralyzed but his fingers scratched and yanked at the bed as if to will his crippled body whole again. He struggled to speak, but only incomprehensible sounds escaped from his toothless mouth. My mother pushed him down and covered him with more blankets. She caressed the wrinkled forehead while his body contorted as if his brain was undergoing convulsions. She hummed a soft melody, as though lulling a child to sleep. Transfixed at the door, I was caught by a beam of amber light that threaded its way through the panes, particles of dust glinting in its luster.

My mother gently fanned Grandfather's face and wiped it with a damp cloth. She cared for him with a patience that would have driven an ordinary person insane. The heavy air stirred around the mahogany bed. Time stopped moving on the bowl of sygyzium nervosum extract my mother fed by the spoonful to Grandfather. A very long time later, when the bowl was finally empty and Grandfather had drifted off, she stood up:

—Please don't upset him. Let him rest. He often has attacks of rage because of his paralysis. Please go inside and change while I work—I'll call you when the other relatives arrive.

That was the gist of our conversation. My mother did not express any curiosity about my life for the past twenty years. She hadn't changed much. Still the same stature, the same unyielding gestures and unwavering voice. Like my father, she had showed very little enthusiasm at my return. In silence I carried my luggage to the back of the house, taking care not to pass by my grandfather's bed. In the afternoons, the silence in Quan Than street was unbroken. A few dead leaves rustled, soulless...

Back for the first time in twenty years in the house where I spent my childhood, I could not sleep. The room in which I found myself was small and simple, the closet dusty. At the head of the bed, the curtains were teased into motion by a faint breeze. I glanced at the sparse furniture, at the climbing betel outside the window that looked into the back of the Temple of Literature, then back again. Half of me was awake and alert to each and every snore that came from my grandfather in the next room, the other half was adrift on the sea of the past. Outside in the street the arjun leaves twirled in the wind, mimicking the turbulence in my soul, torn between the two realities of past and present.

I had the middle room, between my parents and my grandfather. I felt imprisoned by the regular breathing of my loved ones. The hours ticked away. Several times during the night my father cried out in his sleep. The sound rose and coalesced into the moon floundering between two banana leaves. After each cry, everything once again became submerged in the silence of the Hanoi night, not the peaceful silence of prewar Hanoi, but the oppressive, melancholic and irredeemable gloom of thousands of years past. Once every so often I thought I saw the silhouettes of men, out late, passing the pagoda, and I heard their voices, at times clear, at times muffled. From time to time, I shivered in the silvered light of the cold moon suspended high in the sky. At one point, I heard noises in the kitchen.

That was the night I first met Nhai. When I went down to the kitchen, she was emptying large pails of coal into containers. The noises I'd heard earlier were the sounds of her dragging the bags from the garden into the house. She was very young, maybe sixteen. Noticing me, she flashed a friendly smile, as if she and I had known each other for a long time. With unaffected charm, she emptied the bags of coal and offered me a bowl of juice, while talking at the same time. I liked her. In the kitchen, smoke grew from the hot coals that Nhai lit to cook sweet rice. Deftly, she rearranged the coals, tasted the rice, split the wood, sieved rice into the big earthen jar, and adjusted her hair each time it escaped her bun. She was not beautiful in the classic sense and did not possess the grace of women from Hanoi; her two hands were coarsened from heavy work and her breasts were full compared to other women at puberty. To compensate, she had a charming face, a brilliant smile, coquettish eyes and a full figure. Her voice was also sexy, although it could be a little harsh at times:

—I'm ecstatic that you've come. I usually find myself in here at night, after spending the whole day out in the rain or in the sunlight. I'm dying of boredom.

—Where have you been all day? Why haven't I seen you since I came back?

—Where else? At Dong Xuan Market. I would have been back earlier, if it wasn't for that hare-brain Doan.

—Did you have fun at the market? There's this shop called Dao—did you go there?

—Of course I didn't have fun. I went to buy coal, not shop around. She pulled a wry face, her hands still quickly emptying the bags of coal. Her hairbun swayed back and forth every time she turned to do this or that. Looking at those large bags of coal, I was happy to see that my parents seemed to be well situated and not forced to burn wood like so many other families.

—How did you ever manage to buy so much coal? I thought it was very hard to come by here.

Nhai turned and looked at me strangely.

—Coal?

—Yes...isn't the Bureau of Energy rationing it?

—What ration? There's plenty in the market: I carry a load back here every month.

Satisfied with her answer, Nhai happily proceeded to soak sweet rice in water so that tomorrow she could make fermented rice for Grandfather. She had been living with my parents for the past ten years or maybe more. She spoke as if to herself:

—My natural father died young and my mother remarried. Father and Mother adopted me because after you left for the South, the house was too empty.

Sitting behind her, I could see each drop of sweat briefly spotting her snowy white neck, then rolling down her back. Flames from the red hot coals permeated the kitchen with heat. Nhai's thin layer of clothing clung to and revealed her robust body. Every once in a while she stopped what she was doing and turned to me, smiling, showing a row of perfect teeth. From time to time she ran her fingers through her hair, trying to keep the rebellious strands that escaped from her bun in place. In the house behind the temple, night was silent and melancholic, disturbed only by the hissing sound of the coal fire and Nhai's soft voice, shrill at times from excitement. She told me of a house filled with a negative energy generated by my parents, of Grandfather's sudden fits of madness, of my father's insanity, of my mother's growing aloofness. She also touched on her relationship with Doan, a youth who had been courting her and who tried in every way to touch her hands, feet, breasts.

—It's a sort of odd sensation, sister Nu. I don't know why, but I sort of like it. While confessing, Nhai avoided my eyes and kept her face slanted towards the stove. The glowing coals burned in her eyes like a consuming passion. Her fingers toyed with the chopstick, drew unrecognizable pictures on the floor. We stayed up late talking, until she finished her work. Then we went one after the other into the house. My room was also hers. After putting out the light, Nhai giggled and expressed a desire to sleep with me. The room had only one narrow bed and I didn't have the heart to make Nhai sleep on the floor since, after all, this was as much her room as mine. As I drifted off into a sleep full of dark images from the past, I felt her hand slipping under my clothes, her breath caressing my neck. My agitation and frequent shiftings caused her body to touch my face, my breasts, my stomach, while the door opened and closed with each gust of wind and the candle in my grandfather's room flickered weakly all night long.

When I woke up the next morning, the door had stopped creaking and the candle was out. Only the rat-tat sound of a bag tied insecurely to a bicycle that was trying to climb the hill in front threaded its way into the house, though not loudly enough to destroy the oppressive silence. The midday sun beat down on the window panes, shone on my bed and made my head swim. The short jacket that Nhai had worn the night before hung on the closet door, swaying in the wind. I lay without moving, feeling lethargic and heavy, as if someone had choked the life out of me. Only after a long while did I get up and make my descent.

I washed and combed my hair, then returned to the main hall. Grandfather still lay listlessly in the same place. His heavy breathing that sounded more like whimpering resounded at intervals. I found my father in the courtyard by the plank near the hibiscus. His two hands were weakly cleaning his glasses as if by doing this, he might regain his eyesight. He never saw me. Under the glittering sun, yesterday's plot was acted out once again, with the same actors, the same plot, the same actions. His eyes were vacant, his lips trembling. Once in a while he managed to pull a clear thought from the past:

—Where is Phu? Go get the rickshaw and fetch Mr. Phan over here for a game. He isn't there? OK, then bring the rickshaw back inside.

So it went, on and on. At times he spoke loudly to himself, then just as suddenly lapsed into silence, as if he had unexpectedly fallen into a deep chasm. I stood as if planted on the stairs, gazing with pity at this wretchedness until my mother came back from the morning market. She threw me a look of deep and ugly contempt, then went to my father. She gently caressed his shoulders and flicked away some dust before detaching herself to go in and care for Grandfather. I stood there feeling worthless, wanting to help but not daring to do anything.

There was an invisible chasm between us, one that unnerved me to the point of inaction. I didn't dare do anything unless she suggested it first herself. Again, just as I had yesterday, I watched her carry Father out for his daily toilet, then wash and feed him. That work had lasted until the afternoon. My mother went into the kitchen to reheat the food Nhai had prepared the night before.

—Father and Mother, please go ahead and eat, I said.

—Please, not at all, my mother replied.

She coldly took the chopsticks, picked up each strand of swamp cabbage and set it in my father's bowl, then added a bit of the traditional sweet and sour soup. My father ate silently, as bewildered and soulless as a trained monkey.

In the evening, after I'd returned from applying for a temporary residence, I found that my aunt and uncle had come for a visit. With them were a couple of my parents' friends who had also come when they'd learned that I'd returned from the South.

That night was again sleepless for me. The same noises, the same images that I'd experienced the night before entered the room again, their clarity pressed on me by the rays of the bright moon shining through the quivering door. I lay still, my ears straining after every wild cry uttered from my father's nightmares, blending with the heavy death rattle of my grandfather's breathing.

When I heard the familiar noises start again in the kitchen, I rose and went down to meet Nhai.

—Where have you been all day?

—I went to the market to sell betel nut for Mother, then to the train station to meet an acquaintance.

—Who?

—Phu. He was coming back from the highlands. But he'd hardly arrived when he started becoming restless.

—Is he from there?

—No, he's from Hanoi, from the district of Buom. He was sent to the mountains only after he joined the guerillas.

—Still, after all these years? I asked Nhai in surprise, for not even in Hanoi did I expect so little would change since the war of independence from the French. But Nhai was even more taken aback than I. She opened her eyes wide and looked at me as if I was completely out of it.

—What do you mean all these years? It happened only recently.

Absorbed in her work, she paid no more mind to my questions. She spilled the areca nuts on the floor and tied them into bundles of five. I helped her arrange the betal leaves into a pile and spread each with a thin layer of lime water so that they would be ready for sale at the market tomorrow.

—Tell me what you said to Phu that took so long?

Nhai blushed a deep red. Her eyes shone. For a while, she did not speak but continued to add coals to the oven as if trying to avoid the topic. Her black hair flickered in front of the fire as if flirting with it. Nhai knelt as she worked. Then, no longer able to contain her feelings, she confided excitedly to me in her Northern accent:

—Sister Nu, please don't tell Mother and Father, but I have a lover.

She stopped, then continued.

—It's not Doan; he's such a fool. It's Phu. Last night we left the vegetable flail at the train station and visited the city. He rented a rickshaw and took me to West Lake. It was wonderful. But sister, why do men like to hold our hands and caress our backs so much?

—Did you just hold hands? I teased her. Suddenly she was transformed, as if an older, more mature person had assumed her place. She asked earnestly:

—Sister, have you ever kissed anyone?

She stared at me without blinking. At this point, I realized it was more serious than I had thought—Nhai had fallen in love for the first time. She looked at me with the crazed look of a woman ready to live and if necessary to die for love. The look of a woman who had given her entire self to love.

The kitchen door was yanked ajar. A male shadow pushed inside furiously, his voice deafening me as he shrieked out:

—Where have you been, bitch? Out with men again?

My father welted her face with a swinging blow. The cane that he'd so meekly caressed in the morning now lashed with lightening speed at her body. Things were happening so quickly I didn't have time to react before she was prostrate on the floor, an easy target for even more lashes. The two arms that just that morning I'd seen as weak were now unnaturally powerful as with each motion he continued to impose his wrath on my adopted sister.

—I beg you, Father, stop.

—You whore! How dare you call me father! You've brought shame upon this whole family.

—Father, please, I beg you.

But he continued to vent his rage as if he never heard her. I drew into a corner, immobilized with fear. I wanted to jump in, take the beating for Nhai, stop my father. But my limbs felt glued to the earth. A strange thought occurred to me: my father was a mighty man and he still hadn't noticed my presence in the kitchen. He was incredibly strong that deranged night, and I, mute and helpless, could do nothing to stop him. That night he didn't wear his glasses and in his eyes I saw no insanity, only fury. His arms beat a rain of lashes onto Nhai's already battered body while I, invisible and terrified, could only shudder in horror and do nothing to stop that frightful sight. When I finally aroused myself from my pitiable condition after he left, I found Nhai twisted and contorted with pain, trembling. I embraced her and cried out along with each of her sobs of despair.

Afterwards, I brought her to our room and helped her change. We spent the night in each other's arms on her narrow bed, which had once been my narrow bed. She cried all night from sorrow and pain,—Please don't leave me, sister, I'm going to die. Phu, Phu. Her cries gradually became fainter, but her wounded body kept on twitching in pain. I drifted into an exhausted sleep. In my dreams I lashed out against each contusion on her body. I clasped her in my arms in order to know that I could still feel pain. Was it my hands or hers that massaged the wounds to reduce our mutual pain? I only remember that in my half-awake state I touched and felt each wound on her feverish body.

I awoke. The blanket at my feet revealed a comatose body, seemingly near death. In those first minutes, the thought entered my mind that Nhai was only a still life from a collective memory, that she was only an image reflected onto the bed. But in reality Nhai was still there, delirious. Her eyes were slightly closed and her breasts moved with each breath; her knees were bent towards her stomach in a fetal position. It was a long time before I could regain my composure and think about the events of the night before. I went into the living room, into the light of a troubled day. The house was still immersed in a silence which hung in the air like a sluggish, poisonous vapor. I wanted to find my mother and tell her that Nhai had grown up and that this situation could not last. I wanted to ask her about my father's strange behavior. But my mother had left early that morning, my grandfather lay breathing heavily on his deathbed and my father sat in the garden caressing his glasses. It was if he were a different man than the one who had meted out last night's punishment. From time to time he threw a bewildered glance into the house. I asked myself how Mother could endure living in a household with two such madmen, one paralyzed in his body, the other in his mind. For the first time since I'd come back, I went to light some incense at the ancestors' altar. The photos of my grandmother and other relatives glared at me with baleful eyes. I was finally called back to reality by Nhai:

—Sister Nu, I have decided to leave the family.

She stopped at the living room door, a small bag in her hands; her feet had hesitated at the prospect of walking past my grandfather's bed. She looked at me with forlorn eyes:

—I have to go. If I stay, Father will kill me. Please take care of them for me—I'll be eternally grateful.

She removed my hands and after emitting a broken sob headed determinedly for the door. The daylight caught her at the altar, followed her along the tiled floor, then stopped at Grandfather's bed. At that moment, oh God, Grandfather drew his body erect and clawed at her. The vein-broken whites of his eyes blazed. Angry, broken words escaped from his lips and enveloped her. His upper body became erect as if wanting to stand up; his long fingernails clawed blindly at her eyes and face. The horrid scene nailed me to my place. Last night's spectacle seemed on the verge of reoccurring. Overwhelmed by a sense of horror and overtaken by a weakness so complete, I could only stare at the scene unfolding before me. My brain reeled with each vengeful motion. Although within reach, Nhai and Grandfather seemed far away. At exactly that time, my father entered the room. I heard myself calling to him for help. But just like the night before, he didn't see me and instead lashed his cane without respite into Nhai's face, her back, her body. The two only stopped after she'd fallen unconscious onto the floor. Once again, I carried her into the room. Once again, I wiped her face with a damp cloth, and consoled her and cried with her.

During the next days, Nhai was kept locked in her room. In between bouts of crying, she spoke to me resolutely, her eyes full of loathing:

—Sister, I can't live without Phu. I'll have my revenge. After we take power, they'll see. Phu wouldn't forgive anyone.

At these times she bewildered me totally. The thought entered my mind that the constant abuse had robbed her of her sanity.

—You're delirious, child. Please go back to sleep. Fish without salt get tainted, disobedient children will go to the dogs. Father and Grandfather beat you because they love you.

—Love? They think I'm a servant. You'll see; soon we'll take over.

—Take over what? What government? You're talking nonsense again. A grown daughter has to obey family rules. No one here considers you a servant.

—Oh God, the whole country is in upheaval, fighting for its independence, and you still are in the dark. Oh why am I so cursed—even you don't understand. You'll see; I swear I'll denounce them, force them to beg for mercy.

She cried in hatred and desperation. Her tortured eyes fixed me with a look of pure anger, born of a woman whose first love has been violently torn from her. But Nhai couldn't maintain her anger very long, for often my father would appear at the door, his cane ready to beat her down once again. Sometimes my grandfather would also come in to help to hand out the punishment, all the while muttering abuses in the archaic language used thirty years ago. At such times, he didn't seem a bit paralyzed. Each time both men ignored me and I could only gape, motionless with horror and silence. In fact they exhibited such normalcy that I began to grapple with the shadowy fantasy that they faked paralysis only to deceive my mother. But my mother seemed not to take notice of these events. She simply continued doing her daily chores. Every time she returned my father was back on his plank in the courtyard, absorbed in wiping his glasses, dazed, an innocent smile fixed on his face. And Grandfather had once again become a cripple engaged in the process of disintegrating with the passage of time.

Since my return to the house behind the temple and my forced witness to Nhai's sufferings, the turmoil within me had grown so great that I felt myself becoming feebleminded. I wanted many times to tell Mother that she was being deceived, but each time my determination was undermined by her unyielding eyes. Each time I encountered her, I felt I was someone who had not fulfilled her duty. I knew that only she and her sanity could rescue Nhai. Finally, one morning, before my father and grandfather woke up, I approached her with trepidation and told her Nhai's story. She stared at me every time I asked her to love and treasure my adopted sister. Her already steely eyes grew icier.

—You have outstayed your welcome here. Please leave. And don't ever come back. Thus she rejected me, without saying one word about Nhai. I trembled, trying to hold on to that invisible umbilical cord that connects mother and child.

—I beg of you, let me stay and take care of you and father. He left me; I don't know where else to go. Please let me stay home to take care of all of you. I beg you, please love your daughter.

—I have no daughter and regret having adopted a traitor. Did you think that I would forget the misery your brought upon this family? How could I forget it was you who denounced this family, you who incited those men to interrogate and torture Grandfather until he lost his limbs and shock my husband with electricity until he lost his mind?

Once again, like the first time, I left Hanoi alone. Yes, you understand now that I am Nhai, the girl who ran away from her family to join her lover Phu who was with the Viet Minh. I am Nhai who returned home after the change of power and informed against my adopted father and grandfather until they were too broken even to beg for mercy—and so I fulfilled the wrathful oath I'd made after they beat me. But Phu left me also after the unification of our country. Only the house behind the Temple of Literature remains, a stain for all times.

Translated by Thai Tuyet Quan
Edited by Wayne Karlin

Helping

Robert Stone

One gray November day, Elliot went to Boston for the afternoon. The wet streets seemed cold and lonely. He sensed a broken promise in the city's elegance and verve. Old hopes tormented him like phantom limbs, but he did not drink. He had joined Alcoholics Anonymous fifteen months before.

Christmas came, childless, a festival of regret. His wife went to Mass and cooked a turkey. Sober, Elliot walked in the woods.

In January, blizzards swept down from the Arctic until the weather became too cold for snow. The Shawmut Valley grew quiet and crystalline. In the white silences, Elliot could hear the boards of his house contract and feel a shrinking in his bones. Each dusk, starveling deer came out of the wooded swamp behind the house to graze his orchard for whatever raccoons had uncovered and left behind. At night he lay beside his sleeping wife listening to the baying of dog packs running them down in the deep moon-shadowed snow.

Day in, day out, he was sober. At times it was almost stimulating. But he could not shake off the sensations he had felt in Boston. In his mind's eye he could see dead leaves rattling along brick gutters and savor that day's desperation. The brief outing had undermined him.

Sober, however, he remained, until the day a man named Blankenship came into his office at the state hospital for counseling. Blankenship had red hair, a brutal face, and a sneaking manner. He was a sponger and petty thief whom Elliot had seen a number of times before.

"I been having this dream," Blankenship announced loudly. His voice was not pleasant. His skin was unwholesome. Every time he got arrested the court sent him to the psychiatrists and the psychiatrists, who spoke little English, sent him to Elliot.

Blankenship had joined the Army after his first burglary but had never served east of the Rhine. After a few months in Wiesbaden, he had been discharged for reasons of unsuitability, but he told everyone he was a veteran of the Vietnam War. He went about in a tiger suit. Elliot had had enough of him.

"Dreams are boring," Elliot told him.

Blankenship was outraged. "Whaddaya mean?" he demanded.

During counseling sessions Elliot usually moved his chair into the middle of the room in order to seem accessible to his clients. Now he stayed securely behind his desk. He did not care to seem accessible to Blankenship. "What I said, Mr. Blankenship. Other people's dreams are boring. Didn't you ever hear that?"

"Boring?" Blankenship frowned. He seemed unable to imagine a meaning for the word.

Elliot picked up a pencil and set its point quivering on his desktop blotter. He gazed into his client's slack-jawed face. The Blankenship family made their way through life as strolling litigants, and young Blankenship's specialty was slipping on ice cubes. Hauled off the pavement, he would hassle the doctors in Emergency for pain pills and hurry to a law clinic. The Blankenships had threatened suit against half the property owners in the southern part of the state. What they could not extort at law they stole. But even the Blankenship family had abandoned Blankenship. His last visit to the hospital had been subsequent to an arrest for lifting a case of hot-dog rolls from Woolworth's. He lived in a Goodwill depository bin in Wyndham.

"Now I suppose you want to tell me your dream? Is that right, Mr. Blankenship?"

Blankenship looked left and right like a dog surrendering eye contact. "Don't you want to hear it?" he asked humbly.

Elliot was unmoved. "Tell me something, Blankenship. Was your dream about Vietnam?"

At the mention of the word "Vietnam," Blankenship customarily broke into a broad smile. Now he looked guilty and guarded. He shrugged. "Ya."

"How come you have dreams about that place, Blankenship? You were never there."

"Whaddaya mean?" Blankenship began to say, but Elliot cut him off.

"You were never there, my man. You never saw the goddam place. You have no business dreaming about it! You better cut it out!"

He had raised his voice to the extent that the secretary outside his open door paused at her word processor.

"Lemme alone," Blankenship said fearfully. "Some doctor you are."

"It's all right," Elliot assured him. "I'm not a doctor."

"Everybody's on my case," Blankenship said. His moods were volatile. He began to weep.

Elliot watched the tears roll down Blankenship's chapped, pitted cheeks. He cleared his throat. "Look, fella..." he began. He felt at a loss. He felt like telling Blankenship that things were tough all over.

Blankenship sniffed and telescoped his neck and after a moment looked at Elliot. His look was disconcertingly trustful; he was used to being counseled.

"Really, you know, it's ridiculous for you to tell me your problems have to do with Nam. You were never over there. It was me over there, Blankenship. Not you."

Blankenship leaned forward and put his forehead on his knees.

"Your troubles have to do with here and now," Elliot told his client. "Fantasies aren't helpful."

His voice sounded overripe and hypocritical in his own ears. What a dreadful business, he thought. What an awful job this is. Anger was driving him crazy.

Blankenship straightened up and spoke through his tears. "This dream..." he said. "I'm scared."

Elliot felt ready to endure a great deal in order not to hear Blankenship's dream.

"I'm not the one you see about that," he said. In the end he knew his duty. He sighed. "O.K. All right. Tell me about it."

"Yeah?" Blankenship asked with leaden sarcasm. "Yeah? You think dreams are friggin' boring!"

"No, no," Elliot said. He offered Blankenship a tissue and Blankenship took one. "That was sort of off the top of my head. I didn't really mean it."

Blankenship fixed his eyes on dreaming distance. "There's a feeling that goes with it. With the dream." Then he shook his head in revulsion and looked at Elliot as though he had only just awakened. "So what do you think? You think it's boring?"

"Of course not," Elliot said. "A physical feeling?"

"Ya. It's like I'm floating in rubber."

He watched Elliot stealthily, aware of quickened attention. Elliot had caught dengue in Vietnam and during his weeks of delirium had felt vaguely as though he were floating in rubber.

"What are you seeing in this dream?"

Blankenship only shook his head. Elliot suffered a brief but intense attack of rage.

"Hey, Blankenship," he said equably, "here I am, man. You can see I'm listening."

"What I saw was black," Blankenship said. He spoke in an odd tremolo. His behavior was quite different from anything Elliot had come to expect from him.

"Black? What was it?"

"Smoke. The sky maybe."

"The sky?" Elliot asked.

"It was all black. I was scared."

In a waking dream of his own, Elliot felt the muscles on his neck distend. He was looking up at a sky that was black, filled with smoke-swollen clouds, lit with fires, damped with blood and rain.

"What were you scared of?" he asked Blankenship.

"I don't know," Blankenship said.

Elliot could not drive the black sky from his inward eye. It was as though Blankenship's dream had infected his own mind.

"You don't know? You don't know what you were scared of?"

Blankenship's posture was rigid. Elliot, who knew the aspect of true fear, recognized it there in front of him.

"The Nam," Blankenship said.

"You're not even old enough," Elliot told him.

Blankenship sat trembling with joined palms between his thighs. His face was flushed and not in the least ennobled by pain. He had trouble with alcohol and drugs. He had trouble with everything.

"So wherever your black sky is, it isn't Vietnam."

Things were so unfair, Elliot thought. It was unfair of Blankenship to appropriate the condition of a Vietnam veteran. The trauma inducing his post-traumatic stress had been nothing more serious than his own birth, a routine procedure. Now, in addition to the poverty, anxiety, and confusion that would always be his life's lot, he had been visited with irony. It was all arbitrary and some people simply got elected. Everyone knew that, who had been where Blankenship had not.

"Because, I assure you, Mr. Blankenship, you were never there."

"Whaddaya mean?" Blankenship asked.

When Blankenship was gone Elliot leafed through his file and saw that the psychiatrists had passed him upstairs without recording a diagnosis. Disproportionately angry, he went out to the secretary's desk.

"Nobody wrote up that last patient," he said. "I'm not supposed to see people without a diagnosis. The shrinks are just passing the buck."

The secretary was a tall, solemn redhead with prominent front teeth and a slight speech disorder. "Dr. Sayyid will have kittens if he hears you call him a shrink, Chas. He's already complained. He hates being called a shrink."

"Then he came to the wrong country," Elliot said. "He can go back to his own."

The woman giggled. "He *is* the doctor, Chas."

"Hates being called a shrink!" He threw the file on the secretary's table and stormed back toward his office. "That fucking little zip couldn't give you a decent haircut. He's a prescription clerk."

The secretary looked about her guiltily and shook her head. She was used to him.

Elliot succeeded in calming himself down after a while, but the image of the black sky remained with him. At first he thought he would be able to simply shrug the whole thing off. After a few minutes, he picked up his phone and dialed Blankenship's probation officer.

"The Vietnam thing is all he has," the probation officer explained. "I guess he picked it up around."

"His descriptions are vivid," Elliot said.

"You mean they sound authentic?"

"I mean he had me going today. He was ringing my bells."

"Good for Blanky. Think he believes it himself?"

"Yes," Elliot said. "He believes it himself now."

Elliot told the probation officer about Blankenship's current arrest, which was for showering illegally at midnight in the Wyndham Regional High School. He asked what probation knew about Blankenship's present relationship with his family.

"You kiddin'?" the P.O. asked. "They're all locked down. The whole family's inside. The old man's in Bridgewater. Little Donny's in San Quentin or somewhere. Their dog's in the pound."

Elliot had lunch alone in the hospital staff cafeteria. On the far side of the double-glazed windows, the day was darkening as an expected snowstorm gathered. Along Route 7, ancient elms stood frozen against the gray sky. When he had finished his sandwich and coffee, he sat staring out at the winter afternoon. His anger had given way to an insistent anxiety.

On the way back to his office, he stopped at the hospital gift shop for a copy of *Sports Illustrated* and a candy bar. When he was inside again, he closed the door and put his feet up. It was Friday and he had no appointments for the remainder of the day, nothing to do but write a few letters and read the office mail.

Elliot's cubicle in the social services department was windowless and lined with bookshelves. When he found himself unable to concentrate on the magazine and without any heart for his paperwork, he ran his eye over the row of books beside his chair. There were volumes by Heinrich Muller and Carlos Casteneda, Jones's life of Freud, and *The Golden Bough*. The books aroused a revulsion in Elliot. Their present uselessness repelled him.

Over and over again, detail by detail, he tried to recall his conversation with Blankenship.

"You were never there," he heard himself explaining. He was trying to get the whole incident straightened out after the fact. Something was wrong. Dread crept over him like a paralysis. He ate his candy bar without tasting it. He knew that the craving for sweets was itself a bad sign.

Blankenship had misappropriated someone else's dream and made it his own. It made no difference whether you had been there, after all. The dreams had crossed the ocean. They were in the air.

He took his glasses off and put them on his desk and sat with his arms folded, looking into the well of light from his desk lamp. There seemed to be nothing but whirl inside him. Unwelcome things came and went in his mind's eye. His heart beat faster. He could not control the headlong promiscuity of his thoughts.

It was possible to imagine larval dreams traveling in suspended animation, undetectable in a host brain. They could be divided and regenerate like flatworms, hide in seams and bedding, in war stories, laughter, snapshots. They could rot your socks and turn your memory into a black-and-green blister. Green for the hills, black for the sky above. At daybreak they hung themselves up in rows like bats. At dusk they went out to look for dreamers.

Elliot put his jacket on and went into the outer office, where the secretary sat frowning into the measured sound and light of her machine. She must enjoy its sleekness and order, he thought. She was divorced. Four redheaded kids between ten and seventeen lived with her in an unpainted house across from Stop & Shop. Elliot liked her and had come to find her attractive. He managed a smile for her.

"Ethel, I think I'm going to pack it in," he declared. It seemed awkward to be leaving early without a reason.

"Jack wants to talk to you before you go, Chas."

Elliot looked at her blankly. Then his colleague, Jack Sprague, having heard his voice called from the adjoining cubicle. "Chas, what about Sunday's games? Shall I call you with the spread?"

"I don't know," Elliot said. "I'll phone you tomorrow."

"This is a big decision for him," Jack Sprague told the secretary. "He might lose twenty-five bucks."

At present, Elliot drew a slightly higher salary than Jack Sprague, although Jack had a Ph.D. and Elliot was simply an M.S.W. Different branches of the state government employed them.

"Twenty-five bucks," said the woman. "If you guys have no better use for twenty-five bucks, give it to me."

"Where are you off to, by the way?" Sprague asked.

Elliot began to answer, but for a moment no reply occurred to him. He shrugged. "I have to get back," he finally stammered. "I promised Grace."

"Was that Blankenship I saw leaving?"

Elliot nodded.

"It's February," Jack said. "How come he's not in Florida?"

"I don't know," Elliot said. He put on his coat and walked to the door. "I'll see you."

"Have a nice weekend," the secretary said. She and Sprague looked after him indulgently as he walked toward the main corridor.

"Are Chas and Grace going out on the town?" she said to Sprague. "What do you think?"

"That would be the day," Sprague said. "Tomorrow he'll come back over here and read all day. He spends every weekend holed up in this goddamn office while she does something or other at the church." He shook his head. "Every night he's at A.A. and she's home alone."

Ethel savored her overbite. "Jack," she said teasingly, "are you thinking what I think you're thinking? Shame on you."

"I'm thinking I'm glad I'm not him, that's what I'm thinking. That's as much as I'll say."

"Yeah, well, I don't care," Ethel said. "Two salaries and no kids, that's the way to go, boy."

Elliot went out through the automatic doors of the emergency bay and the cold closed over him. He walked across the hospital parking lot with his eyes on the pavement, his hands thrust deep in his overcoat pockets, skirting patches of shattered ice. There was no wind, but the motionless air stung; the metal frames of his glasses burned his skin. Curlicues of mud-brown ice coated the soiled snowbanks along the street. Although it was still afternoon, the street lights had come on.

The lock on his car door had frozen and he had to breathe on the keyhole to fit the key. When the engine turned over, Jussi Björling's recording of the Handel Largo filled the car interior. He snapped it off at once.

Halted at the first stoplight, he began to feel the want of a destination. The fear and impulse to flight that had got him out of the office faded, and he had no desire to go home. He was troubled by a peculiar impatience that might have been with time itself. It was as though he were waiting for something. The sensation made him feel anxious; it was unfamiliar but not altogether unpleasant. When the light changed he drove on, past the Gulf station and the firehouse and between the greens of Ilford Common. At the far end of the common he swung into the parking lot of the Packard Conway Library and stopped with the engine running. What he was experiencing, he thought, was the principle of possibility.

He turned off the engine and went out again into the cold. Behind the leaded library windows he could see the librarian pouring coffee in her tiny private office. The librarian was a Quaker of socialist principles named Candace Music, who was Elliot's cousin.

The Conway Library was all dark wood and etched mirrors, a Gothic saloon. Years before, out of work and booze-whipped, Elliot had gone to hide there.

Because Candace was a classicist's widow and knew some Greek, she was one of the few people in the valley with whom Elliot had cared to speak in those days. Eventually, it had seemed to him that all their conversations tended toward Vietnam, so he had gone less and less often. Elliot was the only Vietnam veteran Candace knew well enough to chat with, and he had come to suspect that he was being probed for the edification of the East Ilford Friends Meeting. At that time he had still pretended to talk easily about his war and had prepared little discourses and picaresque anecdotes to recite on demand. Earnest seekers like Candace had caused him great secret distress.

Candace came out of her office to find him at the checkout desk. He watched her brow furrow with concern as she composed a smile. "Chas, what a surprise. You haven't been in for an age."

"Sure I have, Candace. I went to all the Wednesday films last fall. I work just across the road."

"I know, dear," Candace said. "I always seem to miss you."

A cozy fire burned in the hearth, an antique brass clock ticked along on the marble mantel above it. On a couch near the fireplace an old man sat upright, his mouth open, asleep among half a dozen soiled plastic bags. Two teenage girls whispered over their homework at a table under the largest window.

"Now that I'm here," he said, laughing, "I can't remember what I came to get."

"Stay and get warm," Candace told him. "Got a minute? Have a cup of coffee."

Elliot had nothing but time, but he quickly realized that he did not want to stay and pass it with Candace. He had no clear idea of why he had come to the library. Standing at the checkout desk, he accepted coffee. She attended him with an air of benign supervision, as though he were a Chinese peasant and she a medical missionary, like her father. Candace was tall and plain, more handsome in her middle sixties than she had ever been.

"Why don't we sit down?"

He allowed her to gentle him into a chair by the fire. They made a threesome with the sleeping old man.

"Have you given up translating, Chas? I hope not."

"Not at all," he said. Together they had once rendered a few fragments of Sophocles into verse. She was good at clever rhymes.

"You come in so rarely, Chas. Ted's books go to waste."

After her husband's death, Candace had donated his books to the Conway, where they reposed in a reading room inscribed to his memory, untouched among foreign-language volumes, local genealogies, and books in large type for the elderly.

"I have a study in the barn," he told Candace. "I work there. When I have time." The lie was absurd, but he felt the need of it.

"And you're working with Vietnam veterans," Candace declared.

"Supposedly," Elliot said. He was growing impatient with her nodding solicitude.

"Actually," he said, "I came in for the new Oxford *Classical World*. I thought you'd get it for the library and I could have a look before I spent my hard-earned cash."

Candace beamed. "You've come to the right place, Chas, I'm happy to say." He thought she looked disproportionately happy. "I have it."

"Good," Elliot said, standing. "I'll just take it, then. I can't really stay."

Candace took his cup and saucer and stood as he did. When the library telephone rang, she ignored it, reluctant to let him go. "How's Grace?" she asked.

"Fine," Elliot said. "Grace is well."

At the third ring she went to the desk. When her back was turned, he hesitated for a moment and then went outside.

The gray afternoon had softened into night, and it was snowing. The falling snow whirled like a furious mist in the headlight beams on Route 7 and settled implacably on Elliot's cheeks and eyelids. His heart, for no good reason, leaped up in childlike expectation. He had run away from a dream and encountered possibility. He felt in possession of a promise. He began to walk toward the roadside lights.

Only gradually did he begin to understand what had brought him there and what the happy anticipation was that fluttered in his breast. Drinking, he had started his evening from the Conway Library. He would arrive hung over in the early afternoon to browse and read. When the old pain rolled in with dusk, he would walk down to the Midway Tavern for a remedy. Standing in the snow outside the library, he realized that he had contrived to promise himself a drink.

Ahead, through the storm, he could see the beer signs in the Midway's window warm and welcoming. Snowflakes spun around his head like an excitement.

Outside the Midway's package store, he paused with his hand on the doorknob. There was an old man behind the counter whom Elliot remembered from his drinking days. When he was inside, he realized that the old man neither knew nor cared who he was. The package store was thick with dust; it was on the counter, the shelves, the bottles themselves. The old counterman looked dusty. Elliot bought a bottle of King William Scotch and put it in the inside pocket of his overcoat.

Passing the windows of the Midway Tavern, Elliot could see the ranks of bottles aglow behind the bar. The place was crowded with men leaving the afternoon shifts at the shoe and felt factories. No one turned to note him when he passed inside. There was a single stool vacant at the bar and he took it. His heart beat faster. Bruce Springsteen was on the jukebox.

The bartender was a club fighter from Pittsfield called Jackie G., with whom Elliot had often gossiped. Jackie G. greeted him as though he had been in the previous evening. "Say, babe?"

"How do," Elliot said.

A couple of men at the bar eyed his shirt and tie. Confronted with the bartender, he felt impelled to explain his presence. "Just thought I'd stop by," he told Jackie G. "Just thought I'd have one. Saw the light. The snow..." He chuckled expansively.

"Good move," the bartender said. "Scotch?"

"Double," Elliot said.

When he shoved two dollars forward along the bar, Jackie G. pushed one of the bills back to him. "Happy hour, babe."

"Ah," Elliot said. He watched Jackie pour the double. "Not a moment too soon."

For five minutes or so, Elliot sat in his car in the barn with the engine running and his Handel tape on full volume. He had driven over from East Ilford in a baroque ecstasy, swinging and swaying and singing along. When the tape ended, he turned off the engine and poured some Scotch into an apple juice container to store providentially beneath the car seat. Then he took the tape and the Scotch into the house with him. He was lying on the sofa in the dark living room, listening to the Largo, when he heard his wife's car in the driveway. By the time Grace had made her way up the icy back-porch steps, he was able to hide the Scotch and rinse his glass clean in the kitchen sink. The drinking life, he thought, was lived moment by moment.

Soon she was in the tiny cloakroom struggling off with her overcoat. In the process she knocked over a cross-country ski, which stood propped against the cloakroom wall. It had been more than a year since Elliot had used the skis.

She came into the kitchen and sat down at the table to take off her boots. Her lean, freckled face was flushed with the cold, but her eyes looked weary. "I wish you'd put those skis down in the barn," she told him. "You never use them."

"I always like to think," Elliot said, "that I'll start the morning off skiing."

"Well, you never do," she said. "How long have you been home?"

"Practically just walked in," he said. Her pointing out that he no longer skied in the morning enraged him. "I stopped at the Conway Library to get the new Oxford *Classical World*. Candace ordered it."

Her look grew troubled. She had caught something in his voice. With dread and bitter satisfaction, Elliot watched his wife detect the smell of whiskey.

"Oh God," she said. "I don't believe it."

Let's get it over with, he thought. Let's have the song and dance.

She sat up straight in her chair and looked at him in fear.

"Oh, Chas," she said, "how could you?"

For a moment he was tempted to try to explain it all.

"The fact is," Elliot told his wife, "I hate people who start the day cross-country skiing."

She shook her head in denial and leaned her forehead on her palm and cried.

He looked into the kitchen window and saw his own distorted image. "The fact is I think I'll start tomorrow morning by stringing head-high razor wire across Anderson's trail."

The Andersons were the Elliots' nearest neighbors. Loyall Anderson was a full professor of government at the state university, thirty miles away. Anderson and his wife were blond and both of them were over six feet tall. They had two blond children, who qualified for the gifted class in the local school but attended regular classes in token of the Andersons' opposition to elitism.

"Sure," Elliot said. "Stringing wire's good exercise. It's life-affirming in its own way."

The Andersons started each and every day with a brisk morning glide along a trail that they partly maintained. They skied well and presented a pleasing, wholesome sight. If, in the course of their adventure, they encountered a snowmobile, Darlene Anderson would affect to choke and cough, indicating her displeasure. If the snowmobile approached them from behind and the trail was narrow, the Andersons would decline to let it pass, asserting their statutory right-of-way.

"I don't want to hear your violent fantasies," Grace said.

Elliot was picturing razor wire, the Army kind. He was picturing the decapitated Andersons, their blood and jaunty ski caps bright on the white trail. He was picturing their severed heads, their earnest blue eyes and large white teeth reflecting the virginal morning snow. Although Elliot hated snowmobiles, he hated the Andersons far more.

He looked at his wife and saw that she had stopped crying. Her long, elegant face was rigid and lipless.

"Know what I mean? One string at Mommy and Daddy level for Loyall and Darlene. And a bitty wee string at kiddie level for Skippy and Samantha, those cunning little whizzes."

"Stop it," she said to him.

"Sorry," Elliot told her.

Stiff with shame, he went and took his bottle out of the cabinet into which he had thrust it and poured a drink. He was aware of her eyes on him. As he drank, a fragment from old Music's translation of *Medea* came into his mind. "Old friend, I have to weep. The gods and I went mad together and made things as they are." It was such a waste; eighteen months of struggle thrown away. But there was no way to get the stuff back in the bottle.

"I'm very sorry," he said. "You know I'm very sorry, don't you, Grace?"

The delectable Handel arias spun on in the next room.

"You must stop," she said. "You must make yourself stop before it takes over."

"It's out of my hands," Elliot said. He showed her his empty hands. "It's beyond me."

"You'll lose your job, Chas." She stood up at the table and leaned on it, staring wide-eyed at him. Drunk as he was, the panic in her voice frightened him. "You'll end up in jail again."

"One engages," Elliot said, "and then one sees."

"How can you have done it?" she demanded. "You promised me."

"First the promises," Elliot said, "and then the rest."

"Last time was supposed to be the last time," she said.

"Yes," he said, "I remember."

"I can't stand it," she said. "You reduce me to hysterics."

She wrung her hands for him to see.

"See? Here I am, I'm in hysterics."

"What can I say?" Elliot asked. He went to the bottle and refilled his glass. "Maybe you shouldn't watch."

"You want me to be forbearing, Chas? I'm not going to be."

"The last thing I want," Elliot said, "is an argument."

"I'll give you a fucking argument. You didn't have to drink. All you had to do was come home."

"That must have been the problem," he said.

Then he ducked, alert at the last possible second to the missile that came for him at hairline level. Covering up, he heard the shattering of glass, and a fine rain of crystals enveloped him. She had sailed the sugar bowl at him; it had smashed against the wall above his head and there was sugar and glass in his hair.

"You bastard!" she screamed. "You are undermining me!"

"You ought not to throw things at me," Elliot said. "I don't throw things at you."

He left her frozen into her follow-through and went into the living room to turn the music off. When he returned she was leaning back against the wall, rubbing her right elbow with her left hand. Her eyes were bright. She had picked up one of her boots from the middle of the kitchen floor and stood holding it.

"What the hell do you mean, that must have been the problem?"

He set his glass on the edge of the sink with an unsteady hand and turned to her. "What do I mean? I mean that most of the time I'm putting one foot in front of the other like a good soldier and I'm out of it from the neck up. But there are times when I don't think I will ever be dead enough—or dead long enough—to get the taste of this life off my teeth. That's what I mean!"

She looked at him dry-eyed. "Poor fella," she said.

"What you have to understand, Grace, is that this drink I'm having"—he raised the glass toward her in a gesture of salute—"is the only worthwhile thing I've done in the last year and a half. It's the only thing in my life that means jack shit, the closest thing to satisfaction I've had. Now how can you begrudge me that? It's the best I'm capable of."

"You'll go too far," she said to him. "You'll see."

"What's that, Grace? A threat to walk?" He was grinding his teeth. "Don't make me laugh. You, walk? You, the friend of the unfortunate?"

"Don't you hit me," she said when she looked at his face. "Don't you dare."

"You, the Christian Queen of Calvary, walk? Why, I don't believe that for a minute."

She ran a hand through her hair and bit her lip. "No, we stay," she said. Anger and distraction made her look young. Her cheeks blazed rosy against the general pallor of her skin. "In my family we stay until the fella dies. That's the tradition. We stay and pour it for them and they die."

He put his drink down and shook his head.

"I thought we'd come through," Grace said. "I was sure."

"No," Elliot said. "Not altogether."

They stood in silence for a minute. Elliot sat down at the oilcloth-covered table. Grace walked around it and poured herself a whiskey.

"You are undermining me, Chas. You are making things impossible for me and I just don't know." She drank and winced "I'm not going to stay through another drunk. I'm telling you right now. I haven't got it in me. I'll die."

He did not want to look at her. He watched the flakes settle against the glass of the kitchen door. "Do what you feel the need of," he said.

"I just can't take it," she said. Her voice was not scolding but measured and reasonable. "It's February. And I went to court this morning and lost Vopotik."

Once again, he thought, my troubles are going to be obviated by those of the deserving poor. He said, "Which one was that?"

"Don't you remember them? The three-year-old with the broken fingers?" He shrugged. Grace sipped her whiskey.

"I told you. I said I had a three-year-old with broken fingers, and you said, 'Maybe he owed somebody money.'"

"Yes," he said, "I remember now."

"You ought to see the Vopotiks, Chas. The woman is young and obese. She's so young that for a while I thought I could get to her as a juvenile. The guy is a biker. They believe the kid came from another planet to control their lives. They believe this literally, both of them."

"You shouldn't get involved that way," Elliot said. "You should leave it to the caseworkers."

"They scared their first caseworker all the way to California. They were following me to work."

"You didn't tell me."

"Are you kidding?" she asked. "Of course I didn't." To Elliot's surprise, his wife poured herself a second whiskey. "You know how they address the child? As 'dude.' She says to it, 'Hey, dude.'" Grace shuddered with loathing. "You can't imagine! The woman munching Twinkies. The kid smelling of shit. They're high morning, noon, and night, but you can't get anybody for that these days."

"People must really hate it," Elliot said, "when somebody tells them they're not treating their kids right."

"They definitely don't want to hear it," Grace said. "You're right." She sat stirring her drink, frowning into the glass. "The Vopotik child will die, I think."

"Surely not," Elliot said.

"This one I think will die," Grace said. She took a deep breath and puffed out her cheeks and looked at him forlornly. "The situation's extreme. Of course, sometimes you wonder whether it makes any difference. That's the big question, isn't it?"

"I would think," Elliot said, "that would be the one question you didn't ask."

"But you do," she said. "You wonder: Ought they to live at all? To continue the cycle?" She put a hand to her hair and shook her head as if in confusion. "Some of these folks, my God, the poor things cannot put Wednesday on top of Tuesday to save their lives."

"It's a trick," Elliot agreed, "a lot of them can't manage."

"And kids are small, they're handy and underfoot. They make noise. They can't hurt you back."

"I suppose child abuse is something people can do together," Elliot said.

"Some kids are obnoxious. No question about it."

"I wouldn't know," Elliot said.

"Maybe you should stop complaining. Maybe you're better off. Maybe your kids are better off unborn."

"Better off or not," Elliot said, "it looks like they'll stay that way."

"I mean our kids, of course," Grace said. "I'm not blaming you, understand? It's just that here we are with you drunk again and me losing Vopotik, so I thought why not get into the big unaskable questions." She got up and folded her arms and began to pace up and down the kitchen. "Oh," she said when her eye fell upon the bottle, "that's good stuff, Chas. You won't mind if I have another? I'll leave you enough to get loaded on."

Elliot watched her pour. So much pain, he thought; such anger and confusion; they were what had got him in trouble that very morning.

The liquor seemed to be giving him a perverse lucidity when all he now required was oblivion. His rage, especially, was intact in its salting of alcohol. Its contours were palpable and bleeding at the borders. Booze was good for rage. Booze could keep it burning through the darkest night.

"What happened in court?" he asked his wife.

She was leaning on one arm against the wall, her long strong body flexed at the hip. Holding her glass, she stared angrily toward the invisible fields outside. "I lost the child," she said.

Elliot thought that a peculiar way of putting it. He said nothing.

"The court convened in an atmosphere of high hilarity. It may be Hate Month around here but it was buddy-buddy over at Ilford Courthouse. The room was full of bikers and bikers' lawyers. A colorful crowd. There was a lot of bonding." She drank and shivered. "They didn't think too well of me. They don't think too well of broads as lawyers. Neither does the judge. The judge has the common touch. He's one of the boys."

"Which judge?" Elliot asked.

"Buckley. A man of about sixty. Know him? Lots of veins on his nose?" Elliot shrugged.

"I thought I had done my homework," Grace told him. "But suddenly I had nothing but paper. No witnesses. It was Margolis at Valley Hospital who spotted the radiator burns. He called us in the first place. Suddenly he's got to keep his reservation for a campsite in St. John. So Buckley threw his deposition out." She began to chew on a fingernail. "The caseworkers have vanished—one's in L.A., the other's in Nepal. I went in there and got run over. I lost the child."

"It happens all the time," Elliot said. "Doesn't it?"

"This one shouldn't have been lost, Chas. These people aren't simply confused. They're weird. They stink."

"You go messing into anybody's life," Elliot said, "that's what you'll find."

"If the child stays in that house," she said, "he's going to die."

"You did your best," he told his wife. "Forget it."

She pushed the bottle away. She was holding a water glass that was almost a third full of whiskey.

"That's what the commissioner said."

Elliot was thinking of how she must have looked in court to the cherry-faced judge and the bikers and their lawyers. Like the schoolteachers who had tormented their childhoods, earnest and tight-assed, humorless and self-righteous. It was not surprising that things had gone against her.

He walked over to the window and faced his reflection again.

"Your optimism always surprises me."

"My optimism? Where I grew up our principal cultural expression was the funeral. Whatever keeps me going, it isn't optimism."

"No?" he asked. "What is it?"

"I forget," she said.

"Maybe it's your religious perspective. Your sense of the divine plan."

She sighed in exasperation. "Look, I don't think I want to fight anymore. I'm sorry I threw the sugar at you. I'm not your keeper. Pick on someone your own size."

"Sometimes," Elliot said, "I try to imagine what it's like to believe that the sky is full of care and concern."

"You want to take everything from me, do you?" She stood leaning against the back of her chair. "That you can't take. It's the only part of my life you can't mess up."

He was thinking that if it had not been for her he might not have survived. There could be no forgiveness for that. "Your life? You've got all this piety strung out between Monadnock and Central America. And look at yourself. Look at your life."

"Yes," she said, "look at it."

"You should have been a nun. You don't know how to live."

"I know that," she said. "That's why I stopped doing counseling. Because I'd rather talk the law than life." She turned to him. "You got everything I had, Chas. What's left I absolutely require."

"I swear I would rather be a drunk," Elliot said, "than force myself to believe such trivial horseshit."

"Well, you're going to have to do it without a straight man," she said, "because this time I'm not going to be here for you. Believe it or not."

"I don't believe it," Elliot said. "Not my Grace."

"You're really good at this," she told him. "You make me feel ashamed of my own name."

"I love your name," he said.

The telephone rang. They let it ring three times, and then Elliot went over and answered it.

"Hey, who's that?" a good-humored voice on the phone demanded.

Elliot recited their phone number.

"Hey, I want to talk to your woman, man. Put her on."

"I'll give her a message," Elliot said.

"You put your woman on, man. Run and get her."

Elliot looked at the receiver. He shook his head. "Mr. Vopotik?"

"Never you fuckin' mind, man. I don't want to talk to you. I want to talk to the skinny bitch."

Elliot hung up.

"Is it him?" she asked.

"I guess so."

They waited for the phone to ring again and it shortly did.

"I'll talk to him," Grace said. But Elliot already had the phone.

"Who are you, asshole?" the voice inquired. "What's your fuckin' name, man?"

"Elliot," Elliot said.

"Hey, don't hang up on me, Elliot. I won't put up with that. I told you go get that skinny bitch, man. You go do it."

There were sounds of festivity in the background on the other end of the line—a stereo and drunken voices.

"Hey," the voice declared. "Hey, don't keep me waiting, man."

"What do you want to say to her?" Elliot asked.

"That's none of your fucking business, fool. Do what I told you."

"My wife is resting," Elliot said. "I'm taking her calls."

He was answered by a shout of rage. He put the phone aside for a moment and finished his glass of whiskey. When he picked it up again the man on the line was screaming at him. "That bitch tried to break up my family, man! She almost got away with it. You know what kind of pain my wife went through?"

"What kind?" Elliot asked.

For a few seconds he heard only the noise of the party. "Hey, you're not drunk, are you, fella?"

"Certainly not," Elliot insisted.

"You tell that skinny bitch she's gonna pay for what she did to my family, man. You tell her she can run but she can't hide. I don't care where you go—California, anywhere—I'll get to you."

"Now that I have you on the phone," Elliot said, "I'd like to ask you a couple of questions. Promise you won't get mad?"

"Stop it!" Grace said to him. She tried to wrench the phone from his grasp, but he clutched it to his chest.

"Do you keep a journal?" Elliot asked the man on the phone. "What's your hat size?"

"Maybe you think I can't get to you," the man said. "But l can get to you, man. I don't care who you are, I'll get to you. The brothers will get to you."

"Well, there's no need to go to California. You know where we live."

"For God's sake," Grace said.

"Fuckin' right," the man on the telephone said. "Fuckin' right I know."

"Come on over," Elliot said.

"How's that?" the man on the phone asked.

"I said come on over. We'll talk about space travel. Comets and stuff. We'll talk astral projection. The moons of Jupiter."

"You're making a mistake, fucker."

"Come on over," Elliot insisted. "Bring your fat wife and your beat-up kid. Don't be embarrassed if your head's a little small."

The telephone was full of music and shouting. Elliot held it away from his ear.

"Good work," Grace said to him when he had replaced the receiver.

"I hope he comes," Elliot said. "I'll pop him." He went carefully down the cellar stairs, switched on the overhead light, and began searching among the spiderwebbed shadows and fouled fishing line for his shotgun. It took him fifteen minutes to find it and his cleaning case. While he was still downstairs, he heard the telephone ring again and his wife answer it. He came upstairs and spread his shooting gear across the kitchen table. "Was that him?"

She nodded wearily. "He called back to play us the chain saw."

"I've heard that melody before," Elliot said. He assembled his cleaning rod and swabbed out the shotgun barrel. Grace watched him, a hand to her forehead. "God," she said. "What have I done? I'm so drunk."

"Most of the time," Elliot said, sighting down the barrel, "I'm helpless in the face of human misery. Tonight I'm ready to reach out."

"I'm finished," Grace said. "I'm through, Chas. I mean it."

Elliot rammed three red shells into the shotgun and pumped one forward into the breech with a satisfying report. "Me, I'm ready for some radical problem solving. I'm going to spray that no-neck Slovak all over the yard."

"He isn't a Slovak," Grace said. She stood in the middle of the kitchen with her eyes closed. Her face was chalk white.

"What do you mean?" Elliot demanded. "Certainly he's a Slovak."

"No he's not," Grace said.

"Fuck him anyway. I don't care what he is. I'll grease his ass." He took a handful of deer shells from the box and stuffed them in his jacket pockets.

"I'm not going to stay with you. Chas. Do you understand me?"

Elliot walked to the window and peered out at his driveway. "He won't be alone. They travel in packs."

"For God's sake!" Grace cried, and in the next instant bolted for the downstairs bathroom. Elliot went out, turned off the porch light and switched on a spotlight over the barn door. Back inside, he could hear Grace in the toilet being sick. He turned off the light in the kitchen.

He was still standing by the window when she came up behind him. It seemed strange and fateful to be standing in the dark near her, holding the shotgun. He felt ready for anything.

"I can't leave you alone down here drunk with a loaded shotgun," she said. "How can I?"

"Go upstairs," he said.

"If l went upstairs it would mean I didn't care what happened. Do you understand? If I go it means I don't care anymore. Understand?"

"Stop asking me if I understand," Elliot said. "I understand fine."

"I can't think," she said in a sick voice. "Maybe I don't care. I don't know. I'm going upstairs."

"Good," Elliot said.

When she was upstairs, Elliot took his shotgun and the whiskey into the dark living room and sat down in an armchair beside one of the lace-curtained windows. The powerful barn light illuminated the length of his driveway and the whole of the back yard. From the window at which he sat, he commanded a view of several miles in the direction of East Ilford. The two-lane blacktop road that ran there was the only one along which an enemy could pass.

He drank and watched the snow, toying with the safety of his 12-gauge Remington. He felt neither anxious nor angry now but only impatient to be done with whatever the night would bring. Drunkenness and the silent rhythm of the falling snow combined to make him feel outside of time and syntax.

Sitting in the dark room, he found himself confronting Blankenship's dream. He saw the bunkers and wire of some long lost perimeter. The rank smell of night came back to him, the dread evening and quick dusk, the mysteries of outer darkness: fear, combat, and death. Enervated by liquor, he began to cry. Elliot was sympathetic with other people's tears but ashamed of his own. He thought of his own tears as childish and excremental. He stifled whatever it was that had started them.

Now his whiskey tasted thin as water. Beyond the lightly frosted glass, illuminated snowflakes spun and settled sleepily on weighted pine boughs. He had found a life beyond the war after all, but in it he was still sitting in darkness, armed, enraged, waiting.

His eyes grew heavy as the snow came down. He felt as though he could be drawn up into the storm and he began to imagine that. He imagined his life with all its artifacts and appetites easing up the spout into white oblivion, everything obviated and foreclosed. He thought maybe he could go for that.

When he awakened, his left hand had gone numb against the trigger guard of his shotgun. The living room was full of pale, delicate light. He looked outside and saw that the storm was done with and the sky radiant and cloudless. The sun was still below the horizon.

Slowly Elliot got to his feet. The throbbing poison in his limbs served to remind him of the state of things. He finished the glass of whiskey on the windowsill beside his easy chair. Then he went to the hall closet to get a ski jacket, shouldered his shotgun, and went outside.

There were two cleared acres behind his house; beyond them a trail descended into a hollow of pine forest and frozen swamp. Across the hollow, white pastures stretched to the ridge line, lambent under the lightening sky. A line of skeletal elms weighted with snow marked the course of frozen Shawmut Brook.

He found a pair of ski goggles in a jacket pocket and put them on and set out toward the tree line, gripping the shotgun, step by careful step in the knee-deep snow. Two raucous crows wheeled high overhead, their cries exploding the morning's silence. When the sun came over the ridge, he stood where he was and took in a deep breath. The risen sun warmed his face and he closed his eyes. It was windless and very cold.

Only after he had stood there for a while did he realize how tired he had become. The weight of the gun taxed him. It seemed infinitely wearying to contemplate another single step in the snow. He opened his eyes and closed them again. With sunup the world had gone blazing blue and white, and even with his tinted goggles its whiteness dazzled him and made his head ache. Behind his eyes, the hypnagogic patterns formed a monsoon-heavy tropical sky. He yawned. More than anything, he wanted to lie down in the soft, pure snow. If he could do that, he was certain he could go to sleep at once.

He stood in the middle of the field and listened to the crows. Fear, anger, and sleep were the three primary conditions of life. He had learned that over there. Once he had thought fear the worst, but he had learned that the worst was anger. Nothing could fix it; neither alcohol nor medicine. It was a worm. It left him no peace. Sleep was the best.

He opened his eyes and pushed on until he came to the brow that overlooked the swamp. Just below, gliding along among the frozen cattails and bare scrub maple, was a man on skis. Elliot stopped to watch the man approach.

The skier's face was concealed by a red-and-blue ski mask. He wore snow goggles, a blue jumpsuit, and a red woolen Norwegian hat. As he came, he leaned into the turns of the trail, moving silently and gracefully along. At the foot of the slope on which Elliot stood, the man looked up, saw him, and slid to a halt. The man stood staring at him for a moment and then began to herringbone up the slope. In no time at all the skier stood no more than ten feet away, removing his goggles, and inside the woolen mask Elliot recognized the clear blue eyes of his neighbor, Professor Loyall Anderson. The shotgun Elliot was carrying seemed to grow heavier. He yawned and shook his head, trying unsuccessfully to clear it. The sight of Anderson's eyes gave him a little thrill of revulsion.

"What are you after?" the young professor asked him, nodding toward the shotgun Elliot was cradling.

"Whatever there is," Elliot said.

Anderson took a quick look at the distant pasture behind him and then turned back to Elliot. The mouth hole of the professor's mask filled with teeth. Elliot thought that Anderson's teeth were quite as he had imagined them earlier. "Well, Polonski's cows are locked up," the professor said. "So they at least are safe."

Elliot realized that the professor had made a joke and was smiling. "Yes," he agreed.

Professor Anderson and his wife had been the moving force behind an initiative to outlaw the discharge of firearms within the boundaries of East Ilford Township. The initiative had been defeated, because East Ilford was not that kind of town.

"I think I'll go over by the river," Elliot said.

He said it only to have something to say, to fill the silence before Anderson spoke again. He was afraid of what Anderson might say to him and of what might happen.

"You know," Anderson said, "that's all bird sanctuary over there now."

"Sure," Elliot agreed.

Outfitted as he was, the professor attracted Elliot's anger in an elemental manner. The mask made him appear a kind of doll, a kachina figure or a marionette. His eyes and mouth, all on their own, were disagreeable.

Elliot began to wonder if Anderson could smell the whiskey on his breath. He pushed the little red bull's-eye safety button on his gun to Off.

"Seriously," Anderson said, "I'm always having to run hunters out of there. Some people don't understand the word 'posted.'"

"I would never do that," Elliot said, "I would be afraid."

Anderson nodded his head. He seemed to be laughing.

"Would you?" he asked Elliot merrily. In imagination, Elliot rested the tip of his shotgun barrel against Anderson's smiling teeth. If he fired a load of deer shot into them, he thought, they might make a noise like broken china. "Yes," Elliot said. "I wouldn't know who they were or where they'd been. They might resent my being alive. Telling them where they could shoot and where not."

Anderson's teeth remained in place. "That's pretty strange," he said. "I mean, to talk about resenting someone for being alive."

"It's all relative," Elliot said. "They might think, 'Why should he be alive when some brother of mine isn't?' Or they might think, 'Why should he be alive when I'm not?'"

"Oh," Anderson said.

"You see?" Elliot said. Facing Anderson, he took a long step backward. "All relative."

"Yes," Anderson said.

"That's so often true, isn't it?" Elliot asked. "Values are often relative."

"Yes," Anderson said.

Elliot was relieved to see that he had stopped smiling.

"I've hardly slept, you know," Elliot told Professor Anderson. "Hardly at all. All night. I've been drinking."

"Oh," Anderson said. He licked his lips in the mouth of the mask. "You should get some rest."

"You're right," Elliot said.

"Well," Anderson said, "got to go now."

Elliot thought he sounded a little thick in the tongue. A little slow in the jaw. "It's a nice day," Elliot said, wanting now to be agreeable.

"It's great," Anderson said, shuffling on his skis.

"Have a nice day," Elliot said.

"Yes," Anderson said, and pushed off.

Elliot rested the shotgun across his shoulders and watched Anderson withdraw through the frozen swamp. It was in fact a nice day, but Elliot took no comfort in the weather. He missed night and the falling snow.

As he walked back toward his house, he realized that now there would be whole days to get through, running before the antic energy of whiskey. The whiskey would drive him until he dropped. He shook his head in regret. "It's a revolution," he said aloud. He imagined himself talking to his wife.

Getting drunk was an insurrection, a revolution—a bad one. There would be outsized bogus emotions. There would be petty moral blackmail and cheap remorse. He had said dreadful things to his wife. He had bullied Anderson with his violence and unhappiness, and Anderson would not forgive him. There would be damn little justice and no mercy.

Nearly to the house, he was startled by the desperate feathered drumming of a pheasant's rush. He froze, and out of instinct brought the gun up in the direction of the sound. When he saw the bird break from its cover and take wing, he tracked it, took a breath, and fired once. The bird was a little flash of opulent color against the bright-blue sky. Elliot felt himself flying for a moment. The shot missed.

Lowering the gun, he remembered the deer shells he had loaded. A hit with the concentrated shot would have pulverized the bird, and he was glad he had missed. He wished no harm to any creature. Then he thought of himself wishing no harm to any creature and began to feel fond and sorry for himself. As soon as he grew aware of the emotion he was indulging, he suppressed it. Pissing and moaning, mourning and weeping, that was the nature of the drug.

The shot echoed from the distant hills. Smoke hung in the air. He turned and looked behind him and saw, far away across the pasture, the tiny blue-and-red figure of Professor Anderson motionless against the snow. Then Elliot turned again toward his house and took a few labored steps and looked up to see his wife at the bedroom window. She stood perfectly still, and the morning sun lit her nakedness. He stopped where he was. She had heard the shot and run to the window. What had she thought to see? Burnt rags and blood on the snow. How relieved was she now? How disappointed?

Elliot thought he could feel his wife trembling at the window. She was hugging herself. Her hands clasped her shoulders. Elliot took his snow goggles off and shaded his eyes with his hand. He stood in the field staring.

The length of the gun was between them, he thought. Somehow she had got out in front of it, to the wrong side of the wire. If he looked long enough he would find everything out there. He would find himself down the sight.

How beautiful she is, he thought. The effect was striking. The window was so clear because he had washed it himself, with vinegar. At the best of times he was a difficult, fussy man.

Elliot began to hope for forgiveness. He leaned the shotgun on his forearm and raised his left hand and waved to her. Show a hand, he thought. Please just show a hand.

He was cold, but it had got light. He wanted no more than the gesture. It seemed to him that he could build another day on it. Another day was all you needed. He raised his hand higher and waited.

The Rucksack

Le Luu

"Would you say that again?"

Annoyed, Sai said, "I did what you told me to do."

"You put in the whole rose?"

"Yes."

Chau wanted to scream, spew out the suppressed anger swelling in her chest. "I asked you to use about ten petals. You threw in the whole rose. No wonder we have problems. Whatever! Watch the baby so I can go get him some medicine."

She hurried to the door, afraid that in a few more seconds she wouldn't be able to hold back the words she wanted to hurl like a bowl of dirty water into the face of this careless simpleton.

For the last few days, Sai had been taking the baby outside to show him off while he was talking to his acquaintances; now the child had a cold. This morning, Chau had been able to obtain a white rose that was as big as a "*chen vai*" cup and a few *quat hong bi*—wampee fruits. But then she'd had to go back to the office, so she'd told Sai to put one wampee fruit, ten rose petals and a few drops of honey into a cup, steam it in the double boiler and then let the baby drink the mixture a few drops at a time. "I know, I know," Sai had said impatiently, then threw all three wampee fruits and the whole rose—over a hundred petals—into the bowl and let the baby drink it all. Now the child had diarrhea. Just over seven months old and the infant was dehydrating! It was just what her mother and sister had warned her against—diarrhea, they'd told her, could easily become a recurring disease, almost impossible to cure.

Tears welled up in Chau's eyes. There were so many men of good family and position she could have loved. Instead she fell for this coarse peasant, an ignorant man always afraid that others might consider him inferior, yet at the same time so arrogant about having won on the battlefield, facing up to the Americans, that he thought he would survive anywhere, do anything. Even with his limited education—he'd only finished one year of college before going into the army—her husband didn't think he needed to listen to anyone or to enlarge his understanding of anything. The only reason he picked up a newspaper or a book was to cover his face and snore. From the day of their wedding, she'd never seen him pondering anything, studying anything thoroughly. And yes, she felt mortified when people in the neighborhood scolded her because she forced him to wait on her. But since both of them had to work, why shouldn't she ask him to help her out if she found him just sitting around, doing nothing? Besides, he seemed to enjoy doing physical rather than mental work. Had he devoted his efforts to some worthy project, some objective, Chau would have been willing to do everything herself; more, she would have felt proud of him, not have a second thought about putting in an extra effort to create the conditions for him to advance. She couldn't believe the mistake she'd made.

By the time she came back with the medicine, the baby had already discharged seven times within the span of an hour. He'd gone sixteen times altogether, in less than half a day! Bewildered, Chau inserted the pill into the baked lime and put it on a bed of charcoal until it cooked to white ashes. Then she mixed the ashes with lukewarm water. With this method, passed down from age-old family tradition, hundreds of babies had been cured. Usually it only took a dose of three pills. But after six pills, her child was still discharging profusely. People from all over the housing complex came by to give advice. Some offered blades of *la phen da*, iron sulfate, or guava buds roasted until yellow and then liquefied. Others suggested *cay co sua*, young wild grass, or *ha tho sac*, purslane roasted until it was yellow; or roasted, burned rice boiled into a drink, all to no avail. The more fluids the baby took in, the more he passed out. All the medicines, the herbs touted by the best known healers of Hanoi to be the most effective, did nothing. Chau's mother, sister and nieces came by and exhorted her to take the baby to the hospital. Her brother offered her use of the office car from his department. Amid all the confusion, Chau saw support coming only from her side of the family. As for Sai, he only did what she angrily ordered him to do: from his actions, someone would think him an indifferent stranger with no sense of responsibility towards her baby. It made her all the more resentful that he was the one who had brought about the disaster in the first place. And why, with their house right in the middle of the city, did he allow the baby to get so dehydrated before taking it to the hospital?

In the emergency room, the baby's pulse became very faint and his blood pressure dropped to a dangerous level. His eyes took on a vacant stare; his lips became dry as stones; his temperature reached 41.2 degrees. Still he wasn't allowed to take water. Even as she worried frantically, in another part of the pediatric emergency room a three month old baby died on the table because of too much loss of liquid. When she saw the child being carried away, Chau screamed and fainted. Her relatives stared at Sai as if he was a criminal. If something happened, he would be responsible for snuffing out two lives. Sai felt numb. He ran here and there like a puppet, following the commands or accepting the scolding of anyone who yelled at him. He was relieved to be ordered to do something, even when he really didn't understand the reasons for doing it.

Drawing from his own experience, Chau's brother sent a car to pick up his friend, the vice director of the city's best children's hospital. The vice director put together a team of doctors and medical students to take charge of the case. Despite some objections and his own uncertainty, he decided to go ahead with the team's procedures to bring down the baby's temperature and prevent the child from going into convulsion.

For twelve days and nights Sai sat and pressed the needle, keeping it securely attached to the vein, watching every drop of water, every drop of fluid, fall slowly from the inverted IV bottle into the conduit line. He knew if he let the flow go too fast, it would back up; too slow and it would cause either blockage or insufficient nutrients. Drop by drop, tens of liters of water and blood entered his baby's veins and Sai did not allow one drop to fall faster or slower than the initial adjustment made by the nurse. Years later he would still feel the pain in his own flesh that he felt when the nurses stuck a needle into the baby's temple or forehead or ankle. Whenever the vein was not found, the needle was pulled out, drawing a spurt of blood. The nurse cringed, her face falling like a popped bag, but her fingers kept jabbing the needle into the baby's head, time and again, breaking all the veins while she muttered, "I still can't find one." His heart breaking, Sai blurted, "Please..."

"If you're afraid your child is being hurt here, why don't you take him home and treat him yourself?" the nurse snapped.

Although Chau fainted that first night, during the following days she sat by her husband next to the transfusion table, securing the needle for Sai when he went out to eat or to relieve himself in the back yard or, when he could no longer abstain, had a smoke on the water pipe. At night, he insisted she rest and leave the baby to him. If not for these times during the emergency, he thought he probably would never be able to mollify the anger of his wife's family. Before, they'd been taken with him because he was hard-working and artless—people felt he was cunning but charming—his cunning that of a peasant, not of a charlatan. He was loved because he was seen as naive and simple, in contrast to his wife's seasoned shrewdness. But now he'd managed to create an impression of incompetence. Everybody has the right to show disdain for an ignoramus.

After moving from the emergency room, Chau stayed at the hospital to be with the baby while every day Sai brought clothing and diapers home to wash and took back meals for his wife. He tried to prepare the dishes Chau liked, to atone for his dereliction, and Chau was pleased when everyone in the ward remarked how much her husband pampered her. But even so, something inside her refused to release her anger. She grew more indifferent to Sai, only communicating with him when it was unavoidable and even then speaking to him as if he was a stranger. When they had first fallen in love, her whole family had been cold to Sai. But he'd thought that as long as Chau loved him, that would be enough. Then, after the wedding, when Chau nagged or criticized him, her family had shifted its sympathy to him and he'd thought he'd found in them a source of love and support. But now, feeling contempt from both Chau and her relatives, he felt like a man who had been climbing up a tree, believing he was within arm's reach of the fruit, only to discover that the distance was still immense and he was exhausted. He had not the strength left to go any further—and yet to stop trying now would be too humiliating. For the first time since he'd gotten married he felt totally alone and totally ineffectual. For the first time he was afraid of the coldness he could feel in the looks and words of his wife and her family, a coldness that made it impossible to find a foundation for happiness. Looking at himself, he couldn't find the man he'd set out to be...

...His old army rucksack had at first been put on top of the cabinet, then squeezed under the bed, then hung behind the door; finally, it was tied to the rafters under the roof where it wouldn't get in the way. In the morning, when Chau climbed up on a chair to hang up the quilt, her head accidentally bumped against the sack's "hang-go." She immediately took a knife, cut off the straps, and threw the rucksack on the single bed where Sai slept. Only that night, while trying to lay his head on what seemed a very bumpy pillow, did Sai realize it was there. Stunned, he noticed the stumps of the severed straps and saw the quilt hanging under the roof and realized what had happened. He could even picture the look on his wife's face when she flung the rucksack aside.

It was as if something was lodged in his throat. He could barely breathe. Although he was ready to drop from fatigue, he couldn't even close his eyes. He lay perfectly still, trying not to even utter a sigh. After his wife switched off the light, he lay in bed and fingered every item in his beloved rucksack. Touching these things he had forgotten about, he was at once short of breath, as if reliving the violent hardships of the past, the fits of high fever, the bombing attacks, the times when he'd had to piss into the canteen and drink it, that night when his friend Them had lain wounded on the bank of the brook and he'd carried this canteen, this rucksack pressed into his back, and Them as well. He could understand after a time that Them could not feel any pain, but he could still not understand why he hadn't felt anything either, even after knowing that the friend he was carrying had stopped breathing. This very metal bowl! It seemed just the other night that he'd poured water into it for Them so the wounded man could swallow his dried provisions, and Them had cried out, "Let me have a little more. Don't be so stingy, brother." Just the other night. "Oh, Them," he whispered, "I haven't gone to see your mother and brothers these last few years—I don't have any time and I'm not in any condition, any frame of mind to think about you. And now, I don't even have a place. There is no place for me here—this is not my place..."

Translated by Nguyen Ba Chung
Edited by Wayne Karlin

The Pugilist at Rest

Thom Jones

HEY BABY got caught writing a letter to his girl when he was supposed to be taking notes on the specs of the M-14 rifle. We were sitting in a stifling hot Quonset hut during the first weeks of boot camp, August 1966, at the Marine Corps Recruit Depot in San Diego. Sergeant Wright snatched the letter out of Hey Baby's hand, and later that night in the squad bay he read the letter to the Marine recruits of Platoon 263, his voice laden with sarcasm. *"Hey Baby!"* he began, and then as he went into the body of the letter he worked himself into a state of outrage and disgust. It was a letter to *Rosie Rottencrotch*, he said at the end, and what really mattered, what was really at issue and what was of utter importance was not *Rosie Rottencrotch* and her steaming-hot panties but rather the muzzle velocity of the M-14 rifle.

Hey Baby paid for the letter by doing a hundred squat thrusts on the concrete floor of the squad bay, but the main prize he won that night was that he became forever known as Hey Baby to the recruits of Platoon 263—in addition to being a shitbird, a faggot, a turd, a maggot, and other such standard appellations. To top it all off, shortly after the incident, Hey Baby got a Dear John from his girl back in Chicago, of whom Sergeant Wright, myself, and seventy-eight other Marine recruits had come to know just a little.

Hey Baby was not in the Marine Corps for very long. The reason for this was that he started in on my buddy, Jorgeson. Jorgeson was my main man, and Hey Baby started calling him Jorgepussy and began harassing him and pushing him around. He was down on Jorgeson because whenever we were taught some sort of combat maneuver or tactic, Jorgeson would say, under his breath, "You could get *killed* if you try that." Or, "Your ass is *had,* if you do that." You got the feeling that Jorgeson didn't think loving the American flag and defending democratic ideals in Southeast Asia were all that important. He told me that what he really wanted to do was have an artist's loft in the SoHo district of New York City, wear a beret, eat liver-sausage sandwiches made with stale baguettes, drink Tokay wine, smoke dope, paint pictures, and listen to the wailing, sorrowful songs of that French singer Edith Piaf, otherwise known as "The Little Sparrow."

After the first half hour of boot camp most of the other recruits wanted to get out, too, but they nourished dreams of surfboards, Corvettes, and blond babes. Jorgeson wanted to be a beatnik and hang out with Jack Kerouac and Neal Cassady, slam down burning shots of amber whiskey, and hear Charles Mingus play real cool jazz on the bass fiddle. He wanted to practice Zen

Buddhism, throw the I Ching, eat couscous, and study astrology charts. All of this was foreign territory to me. I had grown up in Aurora, Illinois, and had never heard of such things. Jorgeson had a sharp tongue and was so supercilious in his remarks that I didn't know quite how seriously I should take this talk, but I enjoyed his humor and I did believe he had the sensibilities of an artist. It was not some vague yearning. I believed very much that he could become a painter of pictures. At that point he wasn't putting his heart and soul into becoming a Marine. He wasn't a true believer like me.

Some weeks after Hey Baby began hassling Jorgeson, Sergeant Wright gave us his best speech: "You men are going off to war, and it's not a pretty thing," etc. & etc., "and if Luke the Gook knocks down one of your buddies, a fellow Marine, you are going to risk your life and go in and get that Marine and you are going to bring him out. Not because I said so. No! You are going after that Marine because *you* are a Marine, a member of the most elite fighting force in the world, and that man out there who's gone down is a Marine, and he's your *buddy*. He is your brother! Once you are a Marine, you are *always* a Marine and you will never let another Marine down." Etc. & etc. "You can take a Marine out of the Corps but you can't take the Corps out of a Marine." Etc. & etc. At the time it seemed to me a very good speech, and it stirred me deeply. Sergeant Wright was no candy ass. He was one squared-away dude, and he could call cadence. Man, it puts a lump in my throat when I remember how that man could sing cadence. Apart from Jorgeson, I think all of the recruits in Platoon 263 were proud of Sergeant Wright. He was the real thing, the genuine article. He was a crackerjack Marine.

In the course of training, lots of the recruits dropped out of the original platoon. Some couldn't pass the physical-fitness tests and had to go to a special camp for pussies. This was a particularly shameful shortcoming, the most humiliating apart from bed-wetting. Other recruits would get pneumonia, strep throat, infected foot blisters, or whatever, and lose time that way. Some didn't qualify at the rifle range. One would break a leg. Another would have a nervous breakdown (and this was also deplorable). People dropped out right and left. When the recruit corrected whatever deficiency he had, or when he got better, he would be picked up by another platoon that was in the stage of basic training that he had been in when his training was interrupted. Platoon 263 picked up dozens of recruits in this fashion. If everything went well, however, you got through with the whole business in twelve weeks. That's not a long time, but it seemed like a long time. You did not see a female in all that time. You did not see a newspaper or a television set. You did not eat a candy bar. Another thing was the fact that you had someone on top of you, watching every move you made. When it was time to "shit, shower, and shave," you were given just ten minutes, and had to confront lines and so on to complete the entire affair. Head calls were so infrequent that I spent a lot of time that might otherwise have been neutral or painless in the eye-watering anxiety that I was going to piss my pants. We *ran* to chow, where we were faced with enormous steam vents that spewed out a sickening smell of rancid, super-heated grease. Still, we entered the mess hall with ravenous appetites, ate a huge tray of food in just a few minutes, and then *ran* back to our company area in formation, choking back the burning bile of a meal too big to be eaten so fast. God forbid that you would lose control and vomit.

If all had gone well in the preceding hours, Sergeant Wright would permit us to smoke one cigarette after each meal. Jorgeson had shown me the wisdom of switching from Camels to Pall Malls—they were much longer, packed a pretty good jolt, and when we snapped open our brushed-chrome Zippos, torched up, and inhaled the first few drags, we shared the overmastering pleasure that tobacco can bring if you use it seldom and judiciously. These were always the best moments of the day—brief respites from the tyrannical repression of recruit training. As we got close to the end of it all Jorgeson liked to play a little game. He used to say to me (with fragrant blue smoke curling out of his nostrils), "If someone said, 'I'll give you ten thousand dollars to do all of this again,' what would you say?" "No way, Jack!" He would keep on upping it until he had John Beresford Tipton, the guy from "The Millionaire," offering me a check for a million bucks. "Not for any money," I'd say.

While they were all smoldering under various pressures, the recruits were also getting pretty "salty"—they were beginning to believe. They were beginning to think of themselves as Marines. If you could make it through this, the reasoning went, you wouldn't crack in combat. So I remember that I had tears in my eyes when Sergeant Wright gave us the spiel about how a Marine would charge a machine-gun nest to save his buddies, dive on a hand grenade, do whatever it takes—and yet I was ashamed when Jorgeson caught me wiping them away. All of the recruits were teary except Jorgeson. He had these very clear cobalt-blue eyes. They were so remarkable that they caused you to notice Jorgeson in a crowd. There was unusual beauty in these eyes, and there was an extraordinary power in them. Apart from having a pleasant enough face, Jorgeson was small and unassuming except for these eyes. Anyhow, when he caught me getting sentimental he gave me this look that penetrated to the core of my being. It was the icy look of absolute contempt, and it caused me to doubt myself. I said, "Man! Can't you get into it? For Christ's sake!"

"I'm not like you," he said. "But I am into it, more than you could ever know. I never told you this before, but I am Kal-El, born on the planet Krypton and rocketed to Earth as an infant, moments before my world exploded.

Disguised as a mild-mannered Marine, I have resolved to use my powers for the good of mankind. Whenever danger appears on the scene, truth and justice will be served as I slip into the green U.S.M.C. utility uniform and become Earth's greatest hero."

I got highly pissed and didn't talk to him for a couple of days after this. Then, about two weeks before boot camp was over, when we were running out to the parade field for drill with our rifles at port arms, all assholes and elbows, I saw Hey Baby give Jorgeson a nasty shove with his M-14. Hey Baby was a large and fairly tough young man who liked to displace his aggressive impulses on Jorgeson, but he wasn't as big or as tough as me.

Jorgeson nearly fell down as the other recruits scrambled out to the parade field, and Hey Baby gave a short, malicious laugh. I ran past Jorgeson and caught up to Hey Baby; he picked me up in his peripheral vision, but by then it was too late. I set my body so that I could put everything into it, and with one deft stroke I hammered him in the temple with the sharp edge of the steel butt plate of my M-14. It was not exactly a premeditated crime, although I had been laying to get him. My idea before this had simply been to lay my hands on him, but now I had blood in my eye. I was a skilled boxer, and I knew the temple was a vulnerable spot; the human skull is otherwise hard and durable, except at its base. There was a sickening crunch, and Hey Baby dropped into the ice plants along the side of the company street.

The entire platoon was out on the parade field when the house mouse screamed at the assistant D.I., who rushed back to the scene of the crime to find Hey Baby crumpled in a fetal position in the ice plants with blood all over the place. There was blood from the scalp wound as well as a froth of blood emitting from his nostrils and his mouth. Blood was leaking from his right ear. Did I see skull fragments and brain tissue? It seemed that I did. To tell you the truth, I wouldn't have cared in the least if I had killed him, but like most criminals I was very much afraid of getting caught. It suddenly occurred to me that I could be headed for the brig for a long time. My heart was pounding out of my chest. Yet the larger part of me didn't care. Jorgeson was my buddy, and I wasn't going to stand still and let someone fuck him over. The platoon waited at parade rest while Sergeant Wright came out of the duty hut and took command of the situation. An ambulance was called, and it came almost immediately. A number of corpsmen squatted down alongside the fallen man for what seemed an eternity. Eventually they took Hey Baby off with a fractured skull. It would be the last we ever saw of him. Three evenings later, in the squad bay, the assistant D.I. told us rather ominously that Hey Baby had recovered consciousness. That's all he said. What did *that* mean? I was worried, because Hey Baby had seen me make my move, but, as it turned out, when he came to he had forgotten the incident and all events of the preceding two weeks. Retrograde amnesia. Lucky for me. I also knew that at least three other recruits had seen what I did, but none of them reported me. Every member of the platoon was called in and grilled by a team of hard-ass captains and a light colonel from the Criminal Investigation Detachment. It took a certain amount of balls to lie to them, yet none of my fellow-jarheads reported me. I was well liked and Hey Baby was not. Indeed, many felt that he got exactly what was coming to him.

The other day—Memorial Day, as it happened—I was cleaning some stuff out of the attic when I came upon my old dress-blue uniform. It's a beautiful uniform, easily the most handsome worn by any of the U.S. armed forces. The rich color recalled Jorgeson's eyes for me—not that the color matched, but in the sense that the color of each was so startling. The tunic does not have lapels, of course, but a high collar with red piping and the traditional golden eagle, globe, and anchor insignia on either side of the neck clasp. The tunic buttons are not brassy—although they are in fact made of brass—but are a delicate gold in color, like Florentine gold. On the sleeves of the tunic my staff sergeant's chevrons are gold on red. High on the left breast is a rainbow display of fruit salad representing my various combat citations. Just below these are my marksmanship badges; I shot Expert in rifle as well as pistol. I opened a sandalwood box and took my various medals out of the large plastic bag I had packed them in to prevent them from tarnishing. The Navy Cross and the two Silver Stars are the best; they are such pretty things they dazzle you. I found a couple of Thai sticks in the sandalwood box as well. I took a whiff of the box and smelled the smells of Saigon—the whores, the dope, the saffron, cloves, jasmine, and patchouli oil. I put the Thai sticks back, recalling the three-day hangover that particular batch of dope had given me more than twenty-three years before. Again I looked at my dress-blue tunic. My most distinctive badge, the crowning glory, and the one of which I am most proud, is the set of Airborne wings. I remember how it was, walking around Oceanside, California—the Airborne wings and the high-and-tight haircut were recognized by all the Marines; they meant you were the crème de la crème, you were a recon Marine.

Recon was all Jorgeson's idea. We had lost touch with each other after boot camp. I was sent to com school in San Diego, where I had to sit in a hot Class A wool uniform all day and learn the Morse code. I deliberately flunked out, and when I was given the perfunctory option for a second shot, I told the colonel, "Hell no, sir. I want to go 003—infantry. I want to be a ground-pounder. I didn't join the service to sit at a desk all day."

I was on a bus to Camp Pendleton three days later, and when I got there I ran into Jorgeson. I had been thinking of him a lot. He was a clerk in headquarters company. Much to my astonishment, he was fifteen pounds heavier, and had grown two inches, and he told me he was hitting the weight pile every night after running seven miles up and down the foothills of Pendleton in combat boots, carrying a rifle and a full field pack. After the usual what's-been-happening? b.s., he got down to business and said, "They need people in Force Recon, what do you think? Headquarters is one boring motherfucker."

I said, "Recon? Paratrooper? You got to be shittin' me! When did you get so gung-ho, man?"

He said, "Hey, you were the one who *bought* the program. Don't fade on me now, goddamn it! Look, we pass the physical fitness test and then they send us to jump school at Benning. If we pass that, we're in. And we'll pass. Those doggies ain't got jack. Semper fi, motherfucker! Let's do it."

There was no more talk of Neal Cassady, Edith Piaf, or the artist's loft in SoHo. I said, "If Sergeant Wright could only see you now!"

We were just three days in country when we got dropped in somewhere up north near the DMZ. It was a routine reconnaissance patrol. It was not supposed to be any kind of big deal at all—just acclimation. The morning after our drop we approached a clear field. I recall that it gave me a funny feeling, but I was too new to fully trust my instincts. *Everything* was spooky; I was fresh meat, F.N.G.— a Fucking New Guy.

Before moving into the field, our team leader sent Hanes—a lance corporal, a short-timer, with only twelve days left before his rotation was over—across the field as a point man. This was a bad omen and everyone knew it. Hanes had two Purple Hearts. He followed the order with no hesitation and crossed the field without drawing fire. The team leader signaled for us to fan out and told me to circumvent the field and hump through the jungle to investigate a small mound of loose red dirt that I had missed completely but that he had picked up with his trained eye. I remember I kept saying, "Where?" He pointed to a heap of earth about thirty yards along the tree line and about ten feet back in the bushes. Most likely it was an anthill, but you never knew—it could have been an NVA tunnel. "Over there," he hissed. "Goddamn it, do I have to draw pictures for you?"

I moved smartly in the direction of the mound while the rest of the team reconverged to discuss something. As I approached the mound I saw that it was in fact an anthill, and I looked back at the team and saw they were already halfway across the field, moving very fast.

Suddenly there were several loud hollow pops and the cry "Incoming!" Seconds later the first of a half-dozen mortar rounds landed in the loose earth surrounding the anthill. For a millisecond, everything went black. I was blown back and lifted up on a cushion of warm air. At first it was like the thrill of a carnival ride, but it was quickly followed by that stunned, jangly, electric feeling you get when you hit your crazy bone. Like that, but not confined to a small area like the elbow. I felt it shoot through my spine and into all four limbs. A thick plaster of sand and red clay plugged up my nostrils and ears. Grit was blown in between my teeth. If I hadn't been wearing a pair of Ray-Ban aviator shades, I would certainly have been blinded permanently—as it was, my eyes were loaded with grit. (I later discovered that fine red earth was somehow blown in behind the crystal of my pressure-tested Rolex Submariner, underneath my fingernails and toenails, and deep into the pores of my skin.) When I was able to, I pulled out a canteen filled with lemon-lime Kool-Aid and tried to flood my eyes clean. This helped a little, but my eyes still felt like they were on fire. I rinsed them again and blinked furiously.

I rolled over on my stomach in the prone position and leveled my field-issue M-16. A company of screaming NVA soldiers ran into the field, firing as they came—I saw their green tracer rounds blanket the position where the team had quickly congregated to lay out a perimeter, but none of our own red tracers were going out. Several of the Marines had been killed outright by the mortar rounds. Jorgeson was all right, and I saw him cast a nervous glance in my direction. Then he turned to the enemy and began to fire his M-16. I clicked my rifle on to automatic and pulled the trigger, but the gun was loaded with dirt and it wouldn't fire.

Apart from Jorgeson, the only other American putting out any fire was Second Lieutenant Milton, also a fairly new guy, a "cherry," who was down on one knee firing his .45, an exercise in almost complete futility. I assumed that Milton's 16 had jammed, like mine, and watched as AK-47 rounds, having penetrated his flak jacket and then his chest, ripped through the back of his field pack and buzzed into the jungle beyond like a deadly swarm of bees. A few seconds later, I heard the swoosh of an RPG rocket, a dud round that dinged the lieutenant's left shoulder before it flew off in the bush behind him. It took off his whole arm, and for an instant I could see the white bone and ligaments of his shoulder, and then red flesh of muscle tissue, looking very much like fresh prime beef, well marbled and encased in a thin layer of yellowish-white adipose tissue that quickly became saturated with dark-red blood. What a lot of blood there was. Still, Milton continued to fire his .45. When he emptied his clip, I watched him remove a fresh one from his web gear and attempt to load the pistol with one hand. He seemed to fumble with the fresh clip for a long time, until at last he dropped it, along with his .45. The lieutenant's head slowly sagged forward, but he stayed up on one knee with his remaining arm extended out to the enemy, palm upward in the soulful, heartrending gesture of Al Jolson doing a rendition of "Mammy."

A hail of green tracer rounds buzzed past Jorgeson, but he coolly returned fire in short, controlled bursts. The light, tinny pops from his M-16 did not sound very reassuring, but I saw several NVA go down. AK-47 fire kicked up red dust all around Jorgeson's feet. He was basically out in the open, and if ever a man was totally alone it was Jorgeson. He was dead meat and he had to know it. It was very strange that he wasn't hit immediately.

Jorgeson zigged his way over to the body of a large black Marine who carried an M-60 machine gun. Most of the recon Marines carried grease guns or Swedish Ks; an M-60 was too heavy for traveling light and fast, but this Marine had been big and he had been paranoid. I had known him least of anyone in the squad. In three days he had said nothing to me, I suppose because I was F.N.G., and had spooked him. Indeed, now he was dead. That august seeker of truth, Schopenhauer, was correct: *We are like lambs in a field, disporting themselves under the eye of the butcher, who chooses out first one and then another for his prey. So it is that in our good days we are all unconscious of the evil Fate may have presently in store for us—sickness, poverty, mutilation, loss of sight or reason.*

It was difficult to judge how quickly time was moving. Although my senses had been stunned by the concussion of the mortar rounds, they were, however paradoxical this may seem, more acute than ever before. I watched Jorgeson pick up the machine gun and begin to spread an impressive field of fire back at the enemy. *Thuk thuk, thuk thuk thuk, thuk thuk thuk!* I saw several more bodies fall, and began to think that things might turn out all right after all. The NVA dropped for cover, and many of them turned back and headed for the tree line. Jorgeson fired off a couple of bandoliers, and after he stopped to load another, he turned back and looked at me with those blue eyes and a smile like "How am I doing?" Then I heard the steel-cork pop of an M-79 launcher and saw a rocket grenade explode through Jorgeson's upper abdomen, causing him to do something like a back flip. His M-60 machine gun flew straight up into the air. The barrel was glowing red like a hot poker, and continued to fire in a "cook off" until the entire bandolier had run through.

In the meantime I had pulled a cleaning rod out of my pack and worked it through the barrel of my M-16. When I next tried to shoot, the Tonka-toy son of a bitch remained jammed, and at last I frantically broke it down to find the source of the problem. I had a dirty bolt. Fucking dirt everywhere. With numbed fingers I removed the firing pin and worked it over with a toothbrush, dropping it in the red dirt, picking it up, cleaning it, and dropping it again. My fingers felt like Novocain, and while I could see far away, I was unable to see up close. I poured some more Kool-Aid over my eyes. It was impossible for me to get my weapon clean. Lucky for me, ultimately.

Suddenly NVA soldiers were running through the field shoving bayonets into the bodies of the downed Marines. It was not until an NVA trooper kicked Lieutenant Milton out of his tripod position that he finally fell to the ground. Then the soldiers started going through the dead Marines' gear. I was still frantically struggling with my weapon when it began to dawn on me that the enemy had forgotten me in the excitement of the firefight. I wondered what had happened to Hanes and if he had gotten clear. I doubted it, and hopped on my survival radio to call in an air strike when finally a canny NVA trooper did remember me and headed in my direction most ricky-tick.

With a tight grip on the spoon, I pulled the pin on a fragmentation grenade and then unsheathed my K-bar. About this time Jorgeson let off a horrendous shriek—a gut shot is worse than anything. Or did Jorgeson scream to save my life? The NVA moving in my direction turned back to him, studied him for a moment, and then thrust a bayonet into his heart. As badly as my own eyes hurt, I was able to see Jorgeson's eyes—a final flash of glorious azure before they faded into the unfocused and glazed gray of death. I repinned the grenade, got up on my knees, and scrambled away until finally I was on my feet with a useless and incomplete handful of M-16 parts, and I was running as fast and as hard as I have ever run in my life. A pair of Phantom F-4s came in very low with delayed action high-explosive rounds and napalm. I could feel the almost unbearable heat waves of the latter, volley after volley. I can still feel it and smell it to this day.

Concerning Lance Corporal Hanes: they found him later, fried to a crisp by the napalm, but it was nonetheless ascertained that he had been mutilated while alive. He was like the rest of us—eighteen, nineteen, twenty years old. What did we know of life? Before Vietnam, Hanes didn't think he would ever die. I mean, yes, he knew that in theory he would die, but he *felt* like he was going to live forever. I know that I felt that way. Hanes was down to twelve days and a wake-up. When other Marines saw a short-timer get greased, it devastated their morale. However, when I saw them zip up the body bag on Hanes I became incensed. Why hadn't Milton sent him back to the rear to burn shit or something when he got so short? Twelve days to go and then mutilated. Fucking Milton! Fucking second lieutenant!

Theogenes was the greatest of gladiators. He was a boxer who served under the patronage of a cruel nobleman, a prince who took great delight in bloody spectacles. Although this was several hundred years before the times of those most enlightened of men Socrates, Plato, and Aristotle, and well after the Minoans of Crete, it still remains a high point in the history of Western civilization and culture. It was the approximate time of Homer, the greatest poet who ever lived. Then, as now, violence, suffering, and the cheapness of life were the rule. The sort of boxing Theogenes practiced was not like modern-day boxing with those kindergarten Queensberry Rules. The two contestants were not permitted the freedom of a ring. Instead, they were strapped to flat stones, facing each other nose-to-nose. When the signal was given, they would begin hammering each other with fists encased in heavy leather thongs. It was a fight to the death. Fourteen hundred and twenty-five times Theogenes was strapped to the stone and fourteen hundred and twenty-five times he emerged a victor.

Perhaps it is Theogenes who is depicted in the famous Roman statue (based on the earlier Greek original) of "The Pugilist at Rest." I keep a grainy black-and-white photograph of it in my room. The statue depicts a muscular athlete approaching his middle age. He has a thick beard and a full head of curly hair. In addition to the telltale broken nose and cauliflower ears of a boxer, the pugilist has the slanted, drooping brows that bespeak torn nerves. Also, the forehead is piled with scar tissue. As may be expected, the pugilist has the musculature of a fighter. His neck and trapezius muscles are well developed. His shoulders are enormous; his chest is thick and flat, without the bulging pectorals of the bodybuilder. His back, oblique, and abdominal muscles are highly pronounced, and he has that greatest asset of the modern boxer—sturdy legs. The arms are large, particularly the forearms, which are reinforced with the leather wrappings of the cestus. It is the body of a small heavyweight—lithe rather than bulky, but by no means lacking in power: a Jack Johnson or a Dempsey, say. If you see the authentic statue at the Terme Museum, in Rome, you will see that the seated boxer is really not much more than a light-heavyweight. People were small in those days. The important thing was that he was perfectly proportioned.

The pugilist is sitting on a rock with his forearms balanced on his thighs. That he is seated and not pacing implies that he has been through all this many times before. It appears that he is conserving his strength. His head is turned as if he were looking over his shoulder—as if someone had just whispered something to him. It is in this that the "art" of the sculpture is conveyed to the viewer. Could it be that someone has just summoned him to the arena? There is a slight look of befuddlement on his face, but there is no trace of fear. There is an air about him that suggests that he is eager to proceed and does not wish to cause anyone any trouble or to create a delay, even though his life will soon be on the line. Besides the deformities on his noble face, there is also the suggestion of weariness and philosophical resignation. *All the world's a stage, and all the men and women merely players.* Exactly! He knew this more than two thousand years before Shakespeare penned the line. How did he come to be at this place in space and time? Would he rather be safely removed to the countryside—an obscure, stinking peasant shoving a plow behind a mule? Would that be better?

Or does he revel in his role? Perhaps he once did, but surely not now. Is this the great Theogenes or merely a journeyman fighter, a former slave or criminal bought by one of the many contractors who for months trained the condemned for their brief moment in the arena? I wonder if Marcus Aurelius loved the "Pugilist" as I do, and came to study it and to meditate before it.

I cut and ran from that field in Southeast Asia. I've read that Davy Crockett, hero of the American frontier, was cowering under a bed when Santa Anna and his soldiers stormed into the Alamo. What is the truth? Jack Dempsey used to get so scared before his fights that he sometimes wet his pants. But look what he did to Willard and to Luis Firpo, the Wild Bull of the Pampas! It was something close to homicide. What is courage? What is cowardice? The magnificent Roberto Duran gave us *"No más,"* but who had a greater fighting heart than Duran?

I got over that first scare and saw that I was something quite other than that which I had known myself to be. Hey Baby proved only my warm-up act. There was a reservoir of malice, poison, and vicious sadism in my soul, and it poured forth freely in the jungles and rice paddies of Vietnam. I pulled three tours. I wanted some payback for Jorgeson. I grieved for Lance Corporal Hanes. I grieved for myself and what I had lost. I committed unspeakable crimes and got medals for it.

It was only fair that I got a head injury myself. I never got a scratch in Vietnam, but I got tagged in a boxing smoker at Pendleton. Fought a bad-ass light-heavyweight from artillery. Nobody would fight this guy. He could box. He had all the moves. But mainly he was a puncher—it was said that he could punch with either hand. It was said that his hand speed was superb. I had finished off at least a half rack of Hamm's before I went in with him and started getting hit with head shots I didn't even see coming. They were right. His hand speed *was* superb.

I was twenty-seven years old, smoked two packs a day, was a borderline alcoholic. I shouldn't have fought him—I knew that—but he had been making noise. A very long time before, I had been the middleweight champion of the 1st Marine Division. I had been a so-called war hero. I had been a recon Marine. But now I was a garrison Marine and in no kind of shape.

He put me down almost immediately, and when I got up I was terribly afraid. I was tight and I could not breathe. It felt like he was hitting me in the face with a ball-peen hammer. It felt like he was busting light bulbs in my face. Rather than one opponent, I saw three. I was convinced his gloves were loaded, and a wave of self-pity ran through me.

I began to move. He made a mistake by expending a lot of energy trying to put me away quickly. I had no intention of going down again, and I knew I wouldn't. My buddies were watching, and I had to give them a good show. While I was afraid, I was also exhilarated; I had not felt this alive since Vietnam. I began to score with my left jab, and because of this I was able to withstand his bull charges and divert them. I thought he would throw his bolt, but in the beginning he was tireless. I must have hit him with four hundred left jabs. It got so that I could score at will, with either hand, but he would counter, trap me on the ropes, and pound. He was the better puncher and was truly hurting me, but I was scoring, and as the fight went on the momentum shifted and I took over. I staggered him again and again. The Marines at ringside were screaming for me to put him away, but however much I tried, I could not. Although I could barely stand by the end, I was sorry that the fight was over. Who had won? The referee raised my arm in victory, but I think it was pretty much a draw. Judging a prizefight is a very subjective thing.

About an hour after the bout, when the adrenaline had subsided, I realized I had a terrible headache. It kept getting worse, and I rushed out of the NCO Club, where I had gone with my buddies to get loaded.

I stumbled outside, struggling to breathe, and I headed away from the company area toward Sheepshit Hill, one of the many low brown foothills in the vicinity. Like a dog who wants to die alone, so it was with me. Everything got swirly, and I dropped in the bushes.

I was unconscious for nearly an hour, and for the next two weeks I walked around like I was drunk, with double vision. I had constant headaches and seemed to have grown old overnight. My health was gone.

I became a very timid individual. I became introspective. I wondered what had made me act the way I had acted. Why had I killed my fellowmen in war, without any feeling, remorse, or regret? And when the war was over, why did I continue to drink and swagger around and get into fist fights? Why did I like to dish out pain, and why did I take positive delight in the suffering of others? Was I insane? Was it too much testosterone? Women don't do things like that. The rapacious Will to Power lost its hold on me. Suddenly I began to feel sympathetic to the cares and sufferings of all living creatures. You lose your health and you start thinking this way.

Has man become any better since the times of Theogenes? The world is replete with badness. I'm not talking about that old routine where you drag out the Spanish Inquisition, the Holocaust, Joseph Stalin, the Khmer Rouge, etc. It happens in our own backyard. Twentieth-century America is one of the most materially prosperous nations in history. But take a walk through an American prison, a nursing home, the slums where the homeless live in cardboard boxes, a cancer ward. Go to a Vietnam vets' meeting, or an A.A. meeting, or an Overeaters Anonymous meeting. *How hollow and unreal a thing is life, how deceitful are its pleasures, what horrible aspects it possesses.* Is the world not rather like a hell, as Schopenhauer, that clearheaded seer—who has helped me transform my suffering into an object of understanding—was so quick to point out? They called him a pessimist and dismissed him with a word, but it is peace and self-renewal that I have found in his pages.

About a year after my fight with the guy from artillery I started having seizures. I suffered from a form of left-temporal-lobe seizure which is sometimes called Dostoyevski's epilepsy. It's so rare as to be almost unknown. Freud, himself a neurologist, speculated that Dostoyevski was a hysterical epileptic, and that his fits were unrelated to brain damage—psychogenic in origin. Dostoyevski did not have his first attack until the age of twenty-five, when he was imprisoned in Siberia and received fifty lashes after complaining about the food. Freud figured that after Dostoyevski's mock execution, the four years' imprisonment in Siberia, the tormented childhood, the murder of his tyrannical father, etc. & etc.—he had all the earmarks of hysteria, of grave psychological trauma. And Dostoyevski had displayed the trademark features of the psychomotor epileptic long before his first attack. These days physicians insist there is no such thing as the "epileptic personality." I think they say this because they do not want to add to the burden of the epileptic's suffering with an extra stigma. Privately they do believe in these traits. Dostoyevski was nervous and depressed, a tormented hypochondriac, a compulsive writer obsessed with religious and philosophic themes. He was hyperloquacious, raving, etc. & etc. His gambling addiction is well known. By most accounts he was a sick soul.

The peculiar and most distinctive thing about his epilepsy was that in the split second before his fit—in the aura, which is in fact officially a part of the attack—Dostoyevski experienced a sense of felicity, of ecstatic well-being unlike anything an ordinary mortal could hope to imagine. It was the experience of satori. Not the nickel-and-dime satori of Abraham Maslow, but the Supreme. He said that he wouldn't trade ten years of life for this feeling, and I, who have had it, too, would have to agree. I can't explain it, I don't understand it—it becomes slippery and elusive when it gets any distance on you—but I have felt this down to the core of my being. Yes, God exists! But then it slides away and I lose it. I become a doubter. Even Dostoyevski, the fervent Christian, makes an almost airtight case against the possibility of the existence of God in the Grand Inquisitor digression in *The Brothers Karamazov*. It is probably the greatest passage in all of world literature, and it tilts you to the court of the atheist. This is what happens when you approach Him with the intellect.

It is thought that St. Paul had a temporal-lobe fit on the road to Damascus. Paul warns us in First Corinthians that God will confound the intellectuals. It is known that Muhammad composed the Koran after attacks of epilepsy. Black Elk experienced fits before his grand "buffalo" vision. Joan of Arc is thought to have been a left-temporal-lobe epileptic. Each of these in a terrible flash of brain lightning was able to pierce the murky veil of illusion which is spread over all things. Just so did the scales fall from my eyes. It is called the "sacred disease." But what a price. I rarely leave the house anymore. To avoid falling injuries, I always wear my old boxer's headgear, and I always carry my mouthpiece. Rather more often than the aura where "every common bush is afire with God," I have the typical epileptic aura, which is that of terror and impending doom. If I can keep my head and think of it, and if there is time, I slip the mouthpiece in and thus avoid biting my tongue. I bit it in half once, and when they sewed it back together it swelled enormously, like a huge red-and-black sausage. I was unable to close my mouth for more than two weeks. The fits are coming more and more. I'm loaded on Depakene, Phenobarbital, Legretol, Dilantin—the whole shit load. A nurse from the V.A. bought a pair of Staffordshire terriers for me and trained them to watch me as I sleep, in case I have a fit and smother face down in my bedding. What delightful companions these dogs are! One of them, Gloria, is especially intrepid and clever. Inevitably, when I come to I find that the dogs have dragged me into the kitchen, away from blankets and pillows, rugs, and objects that might suffocate me; and that they have turned me on my back. There's Gloria, barking in my face. Isn't this incredible?

My sister brought a neurosurgeon over to my place around Christmas—not some V.A. butcher but a guy from the university hospital. He was a slick dude in a nine-hundred-dollar suit. He came down on me hard, like a used-car salesman. He wants to cauterize a small spot in a nerve bundle in my brain. "It's not a lobotomy, it's a *cingulotomy,*" he said.

Reckless, desperate, last-ditch psychosurgery is still pretty much unthinkable in the conservative medical establishment. That's why he made a personal visit to my place. A house call. Drumming up some action to make himself a name. "See that bottle of Thorazine?" he said. "You can throw that poison away," he said. "All that amitriptyline. That's garbage, you can toss that, too." He said, "Tell me something. How can you take all of that shit and still walk?" He said, "You take enough drugs to drop an elephant."

He wants to cut me. He said that the feelings of guilt and worthlessness, and the heaviness of a heart blackened by sin, will go away.

"It is *not* a lobotomy," he said.

I don't like the guy. I don't trust him. I'm not convinced, but I can't go on like this. If I am not having a panic attack I am engulfed in tedious, unrelenting depression. I am overcome with a deadening sense of languor; I can't *do* anything.

I wanted to give my buddies a good show! What a goddamn fool. I am a goddamn fool!

It has taken me six months to put my thoughts in order, but I wanted to do it in case I am a vegetable after the operation. I know that my buddy Jorgeson was a real American hero. I wish that he had lived to be something else, if not a painter of pictures then even some kind of fuckup with a factory job and four divorces, bankruptcy petitions, in and out of jail. I wish he had been that. I wish he had been *anything* rather than a real American hero. So, then, if I am to feel somewhat *indifferent* to life after the operation, all the better. If not, not.

If I had a more conventional sense of morality I would shitcan those dress blues, and I'd send that Navy Cross to Jorgeson's brother. Jorgeson was the one who won it, who pulled the John Wayne number up there near Khe Sanh and saved my life, although I lied and took the credit for all of those dead NVA. He had created a stunning body count—nothing like Theogenes, but Jorgeson only had something like twelve minutes total in the theater of war.

The high command almost awarded me the Medal of Honor, but of course there were no witnesses to what I claimed I had done, and I had saved no one's life. When I think back on it, my tale probably did not sound as credible as I thought it had at the time. I was only nineteen years old and not all that practiced a liar. I figure if they *had* given me the Medal of Honor, I would have stood in the ring up at Camp Las Pulgas in Pendleton and let that light-heavyweight from artillery fucking kill me.

Now I'm thinking I might call Hey Baby and ask how he's doing. No shit, a couple of neuropsychs—we probably have a lot in common. I could apologize to him. But I learned from my fits that you don't have to do that. Good and evil are only illusions. Still, I cannot help but wonder sometimes if my vision of the Supreme Reality was any more real than the demons visited upon schizophrenics and madmen. Has it all been just a stupid neurochemical event? Is there no God at all? The human heart rebels against this.

If they fuck up the operation, I hope I get to keep my dogs somehow—maybe stay at my sister's place. If they send me to the nuthouse I lose the dogs for sure.

Please Don't Knock on the Door

Xuan Thieu

In fact, Hao was not as crazy as the bad kids in the K42 housing project made him out to be. When they ran into him, they'd whisper among themselves, "There's the crazy lieutenant colonel, crazy Hao." One child even bowed down and said, as if respectfully, "Hello, Uncle Hay" and the whole crowd would burst out laughing. It was a sort of word play: Crazy Hao would become Crazy Hay. The whole K42 knew that for some unknown reason Hao had retired when he was only 43 years old. From being an agile, loquacious, and easygoing officer, he'd suddenly transformed into a lost, reticent and suffering soul. Often he would do nothing but chuckle. It would be understandable if he chuckled when he met someone, but he also did it when he was sitting by himself. In a panic, his wife, Phuc, first ran off to find a traditional healer and after that switched to Western medicine and even visited the mental hospital in Trau Quy. They all said that he had suffered a kind of psychological shock which had damaged his nervous system and divided his psyche. Eventually, he would recover. But, Phuc wailed to the heavens, when would that be? She knew intuitively that it was a psychological disorder, but she didn't know why. Hao had not often spoken with his wife and children about what was going on at the base. She only knew that sometime before he retired his temperament had begun to change and he had often lost his temper for no particular reason. He'd be angry one moment and lethargic the next, sitting lost and staring at something outside the window. There were only a few papaya trees out there and beyond that the dirty wall of another row of houses, certainly nothing to be admired. During that time, he became jumpy. If someone yelled, he would jump and his face turned white. He was particularly afraid of a knock on the door. At night, when he heard the sound of knocking at the door, he would throw aside his blanket and sit up gasping, not only speechless but also seemingly terrified, curling into himself behind the curtain. Phuc hung a sign on the door, "Please don't knock on the door, just call out the names of the people inside." The neighbors learned to do that. Whoever came over for any reason would just call out softly. Only those who came from far away would unintentionally throw him into a panic. Every incident of being startled and panicked made him toss and turn, unable to go back to sleep. Phuc went to the military headquarters where he had worked. The personnel office received her courteously but she wasn't able to find out what she wanted to know. They said that he himself had made the decision to retire, and she saw with her own eyes the paper with his signature on it. They had not forced him to retire, and they also denied that he had suffered from any emotional shock. Everyone in the cadre at his office said that he had lived in harmony with his colleagues without ever bickering. They all came to visit him, brought him presents, and urged his wife to take him to the hospital. All she could do now was light incense at the family altar and pray to the ancestors to speed things up. Phuc was sad. It was so pitiful because, despite his illness, Hao was very gentle, never broke things, never wandered, never bullied his wife and children, never fought with anyone, even with those bad children who often followed him and teased him. He only chuckled. Sometimes when they saw him doing that, people were scared. He still labored as usual, taking care of the rows of vegetables, preparing the pig feed, sweeping the house and the yard, washing clothes, reading books. The only trouble was that almost all of his memory had vanished. When his aunt came to visit him, he didn't recognize her and asked her whom she'd come to see. This made her burst into tears. Even though he did read books, he couldn't remember them. He read up to the fifth volume of *The War Between the Three Kingdoms* and then he went back and read the third one again. His past was nothing but darkness, and during the course of several years he couldn't remember any of it. Sometimes he did have memory, but it was only for a short time, from the morning to the afternoon, for example. He would immediately forget things that had just happened the day before or, if he did remember them, it would be hazy in the way that other people might barely remember something that happened a long time in the past. One day, before leaving for work, Phuc asked him to tell Hieu to go to the market to buy some turnip-cabbage. When Hieu came home from school, he threw his book bag on the bed, and Hao put the money in his hand but could not remember the name of turnip-cabbage. He used a stick to draw on the ground the image of an oval shape with a few roots hanging off it. The ten-year-old nodded as if he got the idea, ran to the market, and came back with a bunch of onions. Another day, one of the neighbor women brought over a one-year-old boy and asked Hao to baby-sit. The baby, who'd been sleeping, suddenly woke up and started to cry. Phuc told Hao to pick up the baby and take him outside to pee. The baby squirmed and cried, refusing to pee, while Hao wet his own pants instead. Phuc shook her head, sighing. That was how it went. Looking into his eyes, it was easy to see that the soul inside had lost its way.

Late one afternoon, a staff car with a red license plate pulled to a stop in front of Phuc's house. The people in the housing project were curious sorts. The children crowded around, while the grown-ups watched from more of a distance. No one paid any attention to Major Can, the assistant chief security officer from the base where Hao had worked. Instead, they were goggling at a beautiful woman, well-dressed and wearing makeup, who had on an extremely fragrant perfume. She was carrying a handbag and wearing high heels. At the front door, Major Can introduced her to Phuc, explaining that she was an overseas Vietnamese from Canada who had come to the base in search of Hao, Mr. Phan Nhan Hao. The office had explained to her very clearly about his situation, but she had insisted on meeting him. Can had borrowed a staff car in order to bring her directly to Hao's house. The overseas Vietnamese woman politely tilted her head when greeting Phuc, which made Phuc nervous. She got even more nervous when the guests went into the shabby house, with its old wooden living room set and dirty tea set. Hao put aside his book, The *Pleasure House Fantasy,* right at the moment that Can approached him and greeted him cheerfully, "Hello, Boss" and, even though Hao may or may not have recognized him as a colleague from his former office, he still managed a limp handshake. The woman did not sit down. She stood looking Hao up and down, her face full of emotion. She took off her sunglasses and exclaimed:

"Is it you, Hao? Do you recognize me?"

Hao blinked his eyes as if trying to remember, but how could he remember when his mind was still drowning in darkness? He shook his head.

"I'm Huong! Huynh Thi My Huong from Khang Xuyen!"

If his mind had been alert, after hearing those cues he would have shouted for joy, but he still looked out of those spiritless eyes. He shook his head again.

Suddenly the woman ran to him and grabbed his hand, tears welling up in her eyes. "Oh God! Why did you come to this? You are my savior. You saved my life and gave me a chance to live like a human being while you yourself are destroyed. After the Liberation, when I learned that you were still alive, I went back to Hue to look for you. At Mang Ca I heard that you had transferred North already. The North is so big. I didn't know where to look for you. At the end of 1978, my husband and I found a sponsor so we emigrated to Canada. Living in that new land, I still had one pledge to keep. I was determined to see you again, to repay you. Now that I have met you, I'm so happy. Even if you're sick, even if you don't remember me, please accept my bows of gratitude."

The woman knelt down on the cement floor in front of him, putting her hands together and bowing her head while sobbing at the same time, shocking everyone. An atmosphere of sacred silence enveloped the whole room. No one understood a thing, and yet everyone could feel the deep emotion in the heart of the stranger. Even the curious faces outside the bars on the window became serious. Phuc, who had been preparing to make some tea, was standing rooted in one spot, the teapot in her hand. Her hands were trembling and tears filled her eyes. Their oldest daughter, Hang, who was in 11th grade, was crying.

Phuc ran to the woman and lifted her. "I beg you! I beg you! Please sit down..."

Hao had been standing and his eyes suddenly brightened, as if the gloomy curtain of fog in his mind had begun to clear and he was trying to remember.

Sitting face to face with the woman, he broke into a smile. "How did you know the address of my old office to come and find me?" he asked.

The woman, who was wiping her eyes, asked happily, "You remember my name? Good heavens! I will never forget the name Phan Nhan Hao. When I was saying good-bye to you in 1969, I reminded you that the name Phan Nhan Hao means a kindhearted member of the Phan family. I even remember that you're from the suburbs of Hanoi, right?"

No one knew whether Hao really understood or was only nodding his head out of habit. Phuc replied for her husband, "That's right! My husband is from Gia Lam."

The woman continued:

"It's a long story how I tracked you down. In 1982 I came back to Vietnam and went to Khang Xuyen to pay respects at my parents' graves and visit my relatives. Then I went to Hue and asked for news of you at the Mang Ca army camp. They said that the place was now the military headquarters of the town of Binh Tri Thien and no one knew who you were. I was so disappointed. I went back to Saigon. By chance, I met Ton. Do you still remember Ton, the tailor in Quan market in Khang Xuyen? He boasted that he was the secretary of a Communist departmental branch during the war, but then he was drafted into the South Vietnamese army. After the defeat in 1975, he was captured by his previous unit. You assigned Ton to be in charge of the prisoners of war at Cua Thuan. Today, he's the head of a clothing export company in Saigon, very wealthy and well-heeled. Actually, back in Khang Xuyen, Ton was really infatuated with me, he courted me constantly, but I couldn't...love him, because I already had a sweetheart, who is now my husband. However, when I ran into him in Saigon, I was really glad because we came from the same village. We chatted for a while and it turned out that he knew your address. Ton said he got your address from O Theo in Khang Xuyen. It seemed like when you returned to the North you still often wrote to her. So I had your address, but I didn't have enough time left to go to Hanoi. I already had my airplane ticket to Thailand. When I returned to Canada, I wrote to you immediately. There was no reply. I wrote a second letter, and then a third, but still nothing. This time, since returning to Saigon I haven't stopped by Ton's house. To be honest, something held me back. Everyone has family now, and grown children already, but still, whenever I meet him he always brings up the same old topic. Surely, you know his character. He's a very aggressive womanizer."

Hao was listening attentively, occasionally furrowing his brow as he tried to remember. And it seemed as if the woman's meandering story formed the missing and logical link that enabled him to open up all his buried feelings.

He mumbled, "Ton! Ton! Ton! Ah, I remember now. The bastard! That—"
Hao uttered a very dirty expletive, his face turning purple and his eyes burning.
Everyone was shocked and embarrassed. No one dared to look at anyone else.
Phuc broke the silence by inviting everyone to drink some water. Hang tactfully
placed a glass of boiled water in front of her father. Hao drank it in gulps. The
coldness of the water made him realize he'd gotten carried away.

"I'm so sorry! It was because I was so angry. Or, to be more precise, it was
because I understood my own anger."

"It's nothing!" The woman made light of it, but in her mind she began to
consider the possibility that Ton had had something to do with what had
happened in Hao's life.

Hao became loquacious, smiling to erase the dirty image that he had just
created. He said, "I'd forgotten…" He cheerfully introduced his wife and children
and changed the subject by asking My Huong about her husband and children
and about life abroad. Then he asked about the village of Khang Xuyen and a
certain woman there named O Theo. The conversation between the two became
vivacious and warm. His face changed according to the mood of the conversation,
and no one could believe that he was suffering from a mental illness. The spiritless
and listless look of a little while ago had disappeared. Now his eyes were sparkling
and full of life. Phuc and the children Hang and Hieu looked at each other,
thrilled and surprised. Even though they half doubted it, they could feel the
sudden change in his emotional and psychological state.

It was a while longer before Hao recognized the presence of Can. Considering
that the visitor was an overseas Vietnamese from Canada searching for a cadre
who had retired several years before, the base did not simply jot down his address,
but had lent a car and sent the assistant chief security officer along as well. They
hadn't done this purely to be sociable. Hao looked at Can as if it were the first
time they'd met. After thanking Can for bringing their cherished guest, Hao
said it was necessary for the family that she stay a while longer. He asked Can to
pass on his thanks to the base commander. Getting the message, Can took his
leave. The tiny but sensitive cassette recorder in his shirt pocket had already
served its purpose.

* * *

The people of the K42 housing project discussed heatedly the story of the well-
heeled overseas Vietnamese woman who'd come to visit the home of "crazy Hao"
and stayed all night. After breakfast the next morning, Hao and his wife called
for a cyclo and saw her to the road. Some people said that she was Hao's former
lover, from the time when he was fighting in the South. They praised Phuc for

her lack of jealousy and for the generous way she had entertained the guest. Some said, "If it were me, if I didn't give her a good beating, I would have at least kicked her out of the house and put a chain around my husband's feet!" Others objected, "That can't be true! They're only friends. When people become rich and well-heeled, they tend to become more benevolent and so when they hear a friend has a mental illness they come to visit and bring presents. And it wouldn't be a small present either. It would be at least a thousand dollars, I'm willing to bet." Only those few people who had stood outside the barred window that day knew the truth. The guest that had gone to so much trouble to return from abroad to find him had done so in order to thank him for her life. But as for the circumstances under which Hao had saved her life, no one knew. Even Phuc didn't know. The night the guest stayed, Hao asked Hieu to "evacuate" to a neighbor's, and Hang shared her bed with the guest. He himself retired to the back room. It must have been nearly four years since the wife and husband had slept together. Phuc's forty year old body was revitalized. She caressed him, hugged and kissed him, and felt happiness and satisfaction in his embrace, which was as strong as when they'd first married.

But when in their intimacy she asked him to tell her about the woman who was sleeping in the bed in the front room, he clicked his tongue. "Let's not think about it," he said. "During wartime, life and death are separated by only a hair, so the saving of a person's life is nothing out of the ordinary."

And so she didn't ask again, didn't have the heart to bother him. A great happiness was overflowing in her heart. Suddenly, her husband had become a normal person, and that was a miracle.

The people of the housing project were no less surprised than she was. They found him as happy and loquacious as he'd been in the past. When they met him, his greetings changed, and his eyes were completely different. The first clear sign was that he began to jog again in the mornings. In the past, even in the icy cold he would never abandon his habit. If he didn't jog in the street, he'd jog around the courtyard. After he became ill, though, he lay huddled in the house. Now he returned to his old habits. At daybreak, they could hear the thump of his footsteps out in the street. The children followed him in disarray. He made one circuit and then returned to the courtyard, his face bright, and joined the children in a soccer game, either playing or serving as the referee. The whistle blew. "Uncle Hao, hey!" None of them dared to call him "Crazy Hay" like before.

People began to spread rumors. The overseas Vietnamese woman had given him a very rare medicine that, after a few pills, restored his nervous system. That it was the power of love, and when the lovers saw each other again every illness was cured absolutely. That perhaps that woman was actually a fairy who'd descended from heaven. Hao and his wife had lived such a good and moral a life that it must have moved the court of heaven. Etc, etc...

As farfetched as the rumors were, it was true that Hao had been cured.

At the military headquarters, Hao's former base, the officers were also discussing the news of his cure. They didn't speak of it for long, though, because who was interested in the affairs of an officer who had retired? Only Major Can, the assistant chief security officer, kept thinking about it. He knew very clearly the story of the retirement of Lieutenant Colonel Hao, but this was a new development. Firmly shutting his office door, he played back the tape and listened again. When Hao shouted the curse it sounded like an explosion. It might have been at exactly that moment that Hao realized that the person who had harmed him was Ton. Major Can searched for the file bearing the code Y8. He reread the accusatory letter from 1982, written by someone who claimed to be Le Huy Ton, address unknown, only revealing that he was a cadre now working in Ho Chi Minh City. The letter outlined in detail the relationship between Hao and My Huong, an informer working for the enemy during the war, and asked that their movements be monitored. Perhaps evidence might be found in the letters that My Huong had written from Canada. It was true that in the six months that immediately followed Ton's accusations, the base post office turned over to the security office, one by one, the three letters that My Huong had sent to Phan Nhan Hao. The content of the letters didn't carry anything suspicious, only personal questions and reproaches as to why there had been no reply. Using a magnifying glass and chemicals to double check, they still couldn't find any invisible messages. At that time, still an aide with the rank of captain, Can was worried, because holding private letters was illegal. However, Colonel Le Hon, the vice political chairman and head of the security office, had argued rather convincingly that any private letter that might influence national security was no longer private. They had to hold onto it in order to study it more. Now, Colonel Le Hon had retired and returned to live in Quang Ngai, but the three letters were still in the office. Along with the letters were the minutes of a conversation between Colonel Le Hon and Lieutenant Colonel Phan Nhan Hao, who at that time was the vice director of the military office. It was Can himself who had transcribed the minutes, listening to the cassette tape, which was still being kept in a moisture-proof box.

"...Do you know anyone by the name of Huong?"

"No, I don't remember that name."

"Let me refresh your memory. In 1969, when you were still a first lieutenant and commander of the intelligence unit, you were assigned the duty of killing a spy in Khang Xuyen by the name of Huynh Thi My Huong."

"Oh, now I remember. Yes, there was a girl by the name of My Huong. But that was a long time ago."

"Thirteen years. You could call it long ago, but I imagined you would remember for sure."

"You can't remember everything. What's the problem?"

"It's something that happened in the past. We want to know why instead of killing her you let her go. And why didn't you report it to the authorities?"

(There was a moment of silence, and then the laughter of Phan Nhan Hao.)

"Who dug up that story to rat on me? It's making a big deal out of nothing!"

"Hao, you have to remember that this is a serious conversation between you and those who are responsible for you. You shouldn't treat it lightly. It's our job to know everything, no matter how old it is. Even if they're older incidents than this one, we would still have to investigate them. So you admit to it?"

"Yes, colonel. It's true!"

"Can you explain it in more detail?"

"Why not? It's a rather long story and you should know that it's not that simple. You've been in the this branch of the army a long time. Probably, back in 1969 you were either in Hanoi or evacuated to the countryside somewhere. I was to the south of Hue, a war zone that was full of fierce fighting and hardship, particularly after the Tet Offensive. At our base in the jungle, every day each soldier had one tenth of a kilo of rice for two meals. We would cook it with tubers. The porridge was thick and sticky, rather blue in color, and these days the pigs in my house would push it away with their snouts. We lived with that hunger in order to rebuild our base, which had been destroyed completely. It had been so different. In the past, Khang Xuyen had been a town that was liberated, a place where we were treated as friends, and so wherever we went the people would feed us. But then...(He was silent for a moment in order to recover his composure) cadres, party members, guerrillas, some of them were killed, others captured, still others either fled to Hue, Da Nang, or Saigon or else they fled to the jungle and asked for permission to return to the North. Social order was in the hands of the enemy. But, unlike other villages that had been totally wiped out, Khang Xuyen still had a nucleus of three party members living there incognito, under the leadership of Ton, the tailor in the market. We sent a group of three people to Khang Xuyen. Second Lieutenant Lan was in charge. They dug a secret tunnel directly beneath the garden of O Theo, a party member and widow who was more than fifty years old and whose daughter had already married and gone away. The illiterate old woman was really kind hearted and extremely brave. On the third night, something happened. When it had gotten completely dark, O Theo opened the tunnel and let Lan's group out. While they were eating, they looked up and saw the enemy's AR15 guns pointed at them.

As quick as lightening, Lan threw his bowl of rice at the soldier standing closest to him and shouted for everyone to run. The guns went off. Lan's two comrades died right there, their blood mixing with the rice. Only Lan escaped. Of course, O Theo was caught. In fact, she was caught in the garden while she was standing guard so that they could eat their dinner. She was tortured cruelly, but she stuck to the story that the liberation soldiers had come to her house to ask for food, and she took pity on them and let them eat. That was it. She didn't expose any of the other party members. She was exiled to Con Dao and only returned after the liberation of the South. As for Lan, who'd escaped, he spent one day lying between the rice stalks in the flooded paddy, starving, with leeches crawling all over his back. He had to wait until late the next night to go back into the village to search for Ton, but he couldn't find him. Ton had already left for a while in order to protect himself from the possibility that O Theo had exposed him. Then Lan went to look for Mr. Quan, an old party member who had arthritis. After having heard all the news and eaten his fill, Lan returned alone to the base in order to report what had happened. That fiasco really hurt our intelligence unit. We were still resolved to return to Khang Xuyen. The people of Khang Xuyen would not betray the revolution. Even under the coercion of the enemy, they would hold their breath and wait for opportunity. We had to create that opportunity for them. But before we returned to Khang Xuyen, we had to know the cause of the recent debacle. Had the enemy merely raided by chance, or was there an informer? If it was the latter, then first we had to destroy the informer."

"Can you make the story a little more brief? Please, get to the point."

"If you want to understand fully, please be patient and listen carefully. Because you have been in this branch of the army for so long, I'm afraid that you don't know enough about intelligence. The nature of our work at that time was to destroy enemy spies. Every one of us had gone through training in martial arts. After five years of working in the intelligence unit, I myself had killed no fewer than a dozen enemy spies with my bare hands. In the middle of the night I would go into the spies' houses and, in the name of the revolution, I'd invite them to "go study," and kill them right there. There was never any gunfire, because gunfire would expose us. I never used a bayonet or dagger, because I didn't want any bloodstains. I might choose to use a short club to deliver a single blow to the back of the neck , at which point the spy would collapse in a heap, gasp a couple of times, then croak. But carrying a club was too much trouble. So I stuck to my own two hands. At that time I was just over twenty years old and strong as a water buffalo. My two hands were like a pair of pliers. I'd take the ends of the collar between my fingers, pull from opposite sides until it tightened around the neck, and within two minutes the head would hang down and the spit would come drooling out of the mouth. Women were even easier. I could strangle them very quickly just with my bare hands. After I killed somebody, I'd bury them immediately and camouflage the grave so that it would look like the ground was even. Even we ourselves couldn't remember exactly where we'd buried them. In cases in which we had to deliver a warning, we'd kill them in their houses and next to the body we'd leave the message. Our line of work left us miserable, plagued by horrible memories. There was the choking sound of someone being strangled and the smell of spit gushing with the last breath out of the mouth, a stink that wouldn't fade away even after you'd washed your hands for three days with lemon-scented soap. There was the sound that came up from the grave after it had been filled, a low hiccup, sort of like the coughing of a toad. There was the look of surprise in the protruding eyes of people confronting their own death. If there was injustice, would any of those eyes ever reveal it? It was those unhappy memories, together with the peace of mind that I'd found after letting My Huong go free, that led me to request a transfer to the sabotage unit. Wearing only a pair of underwear, my face and body smeared with soot or battery powder, carrying submachine gun and hand grenade, I would sneak up on sleeping American soldiers and kill them, completely convinced that they would find repentance in God's kingdom."

"You just mentioned My Huong. You must have uncovered that she herself was a spy of the enemy in Khang Xuyen."

"We didn't discover it. The provincial committee made the orders based on a report from the base, that it is to say from the branch committee in Khang Xuyen."

"And you objected?"

"On the contrary, I was very glad. After finding a spy to destroy, we could send our people to Khang Xuyen with no trouble. However, I was very careful. Who My Huong was, I didn't know. But Lan knew. She was a student who had failed her baccalaureate exam and come back to work in her mother's sundry shop in the Quan market. Her father was an employee at the post office in Saigon. We heard that she used to take part in the student demonstrations in Hue. At that time, Khang Xuyen still had liberation soldiers, and so after she returned from Hue, she joined in the youth activities. According to Lan, she was a very beautiful and charming girl. Whether she was beautiful and charming or not, if she was a spy, then she'd have to pay for it. Before deciding for sure, I sent Lan back to Khang Xuyen so that he could double check it all with Ton. Ton provided some extra details. First, there were a couple of times that people had seen My Huong speaking with the American advisors in English. My Huong had a close relationship with a major who was also a district chief and it was rumored that they were some sort of cousins. Second, on the afternoon before the night raid on O Theo's house, My Huong had come by O Theo's for a chat and gone out into the garden and looked around. All those details were still no proof of guilt, but, having received the orders from the provincial committee, we had to do it. Forming a group of three for the job, I was directly in charge. In addition to me, there was Second Lieutenant Lan, who knew Khang Xuyen very well, and Chief Warrant Officer Nam, from the Tay minority in Cao Bang, who was extremely handsome, with white skin and lips as red as a girl's. I still remember that night. The sky was not very dark and the moon was on the wane, probably on the 17th or 18th of the lunar calendar, and covered with clouds. We safely snuck back into Khang Xuyen and met up with Ton. It was Ton himself who led us to the spy's house. After that, Ton didn't come inside. According to the principles of secret activity in occupied territory, it was right that he didn't. We knocked on the door. I had knocked on the doors of spies' houses many times already. 'Knock. Knock. Knock.' The sound of knuckles on wood was the dull sound that meant an order to kill. It's a sound that still haunts me. To be honest with you, whenever I hear the sound of knocking on the door, I still jump, still shiver."

"This story's going all over the place. Tell me, in brief, why you didn't kill the spy. Was it because you found her beautiful and charming or did some other thought crop up?"

"In my opinion, killing a spy is the fulfillment of an important duty during wartime. But at the same time, killing the wrong person is murder. I don't want to be a person who murders for no reason."

(A moment of silence.)

"So you're saying that you don't accept that My Huong was an informer?"

"That's right."

"What's your reason?"

"It's simple. Spies and informers have a look, an attitude, a demeanor, and a way of acting which is different from the way this girl was. Not one of those reactionaries would have heard the two words "go study" and misunderstood what I meant. They immediately reacted. They would tremble violently, their faces pale. Or their faces would go red and they would contradict me with anger. There was one who screamed loudly, forcing us to stick a gun in his back. There was one who shifted his eyes back and forth searching for a getaway. "Go study" was the chunk of lime we'd put in front of a leech. But when this girl heard those words, she was cheerful, even thrilled. She even asked, "For how long?" and worried that she didn't have time to get a hammock to bring with her blanket and mosquito net. She wanted to know if she was going to study "in the green" of the jungle, because, she said, she had a lot of friends there. Her mother was very worried but the girl comforted her, "One month is nothing, Mother, and whoever asks, you have to say I've gone to Saigon, okay?"

"You'd probably never met a spy who got the best of you before. Perhaps she acted thrilled and cheerful, but she'd already figured out her getaway."

"There's no way. During the night, that one unarmed girl was escorted by three intelligence agents with submachine guns and pistols. She couldn't have gotten away. The thing that troubled us at that moment was not that the girl could get away, or even that she could kill us. It was something else. It seemed that all three of us had the same intuition that she was innocent. If at that moment I had been more hard-line, then surely Lan and Nam would have carried out the orders in silence. War is like that. Carrying out orders is all we do. Who really cares to reason over whether it is just or not? Even if we killed by mistake, it wouldn't jeopardize the common goal."

"And so you set the informer free?"

"It's not as simple as that. This nagging question followed us for dozens of kilometers, and then something happened. Shells began to fall just as our group reached the foot of Tham Hill. This area marked the free-fire zone. When the shelling stopped, everything was completely quiet and thick smoke hung over the brush-covered hill. Then someone moaned, and then cried. Oh God, Nam had been wounded in the stomach and a shell fragment had entered Lan's skull and killed him instantly. The girl was so terrified she was crying, but she was also quick in bandaging Nam's wound and in helping me dig a grave. When we were burying Lan, she couldn't stop sobbing. When we started walking again, it was almost dawn. I secretly removed the rounds from my guns and gave both the two pistols and the AKs to My Huong to hold. Then, with difficulty, I carried Nam until we reached the edge of the forest, where I cut some branches to make a stretcher. My Huong went in front and I went behind. Between us, we carried Nam on our shoulders to the transportation company field hospital, where we almost collapsed from exhaustion. There, My Huong met a former classmate of hers from Hue, who was now a nurse. The two of them chattered like birds and refused to part from each other. I decided we should stay for a night at the hospital in order to regain our strength. The next morning, after we'd finished eating, we asked for a ball of pressed rice and then went on our way. Now there was only My Huong and me. Where would we go? The forests of the Truong Son mountain range are vast, infinite. My Huong asked, 'Do we still have very far to go?'

" 'It's still rather far,' I replied, vaguely.

" 'Is it a large class?' she asked.

" 'Yeah.' Once more, I replied vaguely.

"She asked so many questions, and I answered for the sake of answering. In my mind, I was still debating a certain kind of solution. It was hard to believe this girl was an informer, a person who had wreaked havoc on our unit. If she was an informer, she would have looked for a way to escape. Throughout that long hike, opportunities abounded. Maybe I was missing something? During the Tet Offensive, I had witnessed many cases when people had borrowed the wind to cut their bamboo shoots, borrowed the revolution as a pretext for taking revenge, killing each other. The report from the Khang Xuyen branch committee, which had been compiled by their leader Ton, had not carried any proof. Maybe it was because of a grudge. Besides, was it not an achievement for a branch committee to carry out its security duties by eradicating an informer? I did not want my hand to be stained by the blood of an honest person. I thought I would have to give My Huong her freedom. But in order to make the right decision, I had to check one last time. Stopping by the edge of a stream, after we had finished washing, we sat down to rest. It was only now that I could observe her carefully. She was truly a beautiful and charming girl. I began to talk to her. My voice and expression were neutral but I was following a line of investigation. I asked about her parents, her relatives, her brothers and sisters, her own life, the relationships she'd made in Hue and in Khang Xuyen. Then I switched to the subject of the enemy raid on O Theo's house. My Huong said that although the rest of the village called the old woman 'O Theo', she herself should have called her 'aunt.' My Huong's grandfather and the father of O Theo's husband were brothers. At that time, she was staying in Hue and didn't hear the story until she returned home. By then it was already over. People said that two revolutionary soldiers had been killed in the house and Mr. Thieu's soldiers tied their bodies to the base of an areca palm tree. It wasn't until the afternoon of the next day that they allowed them to be buried. They had no pity. She knew that Aunt Theo had been thrown in jail, but she hadn't had a chance to visit to her yet. And so My Huong's deposition (for now I'll call it her deposition) was completely different from the accusations that had come from Ton. Even though things were clearer to me now, I still kept a serious face. I looked directly into My Huong's eyes and told her that someone had told us the she was involved in the massacre, that she was an informer for the puppet government. What did she think of that? At one moment, My Huong was cheerful and the next her face had turned pale and she'd burst into tears. Oh God, why would they accuse her of something so terrible? When another one of her aunts was sick and hospitalized in Hue, her mother had asked her to take care of her for a week. How could she know anything about the killing of the liberation soldiers at Aunt Theo's house? How could she have the heart to harm the liberation soldiers, and even her Aunt Theo? She wasn't that inhuman!

"I told My Huong the truth, that we hadn't been taking her to a class, that there had never been a class at all, but that we'd received orders to question her about her crime. While crying, suddenly she dried her tears, her lips trembling, and threw into my eyes a challenging look. 'Then go ahead and shoot me!'

" 'No, I'm not going to shoot you. If I had wanted to shoot you, then I would have done so when we were still on the deserted plains, or last night in the free fire zone. I don't believe that you are an informer or a spy. I'll give you back your freedom on one condition—' "

(There was the sound of laughter from Colonel Le Hon.)

"Don't misunderstand me," Hao continued. "At that time I was only 26 years old, still single, healthy, not bad looking, from Hanoi, with a university degree. I could have expressed my love for her without embarrassment. Just like any other young man who looked at the elegant face, charming lips, white neck and throat, and full breasts of My Huong, there were moments when the lustful beast inside of me raised its head. I could either court her or take her by force or beg her to give herself to me. Any of these ways it could have been done. There were only two of us in a very deserted forest. But there was one thing I knew for sure, that after I had satisfied myself, I would have to strangle her. If I had done that, it would have been to my advantage. I would have satisfied myself and achieved something. Plus, I wouldn't have had to worry about the consequences. But I would have lost something important. I would have lost myself. God forbid. I would never allow that to happen. Therefore, the condition that I suggested to My Huong was that she had to disappear, and never return to Khang Xuyen. She could live in Danang, Saigon, or Can Tho, I didn't care. But her presence in Khang Xuyen would be dangerous for both of us. She nodded her head. We continued to walk together until we reached the highpoint at Eo Gio. From there, we could see Highway One. From there, one would only have to walk two more hours before being able to flag down a car. We said good-bye. She hesitated a bit before throwing her arms around me, crying. Truly, at that moment, my heart skipped a beat. I felt short of breath. Without letting my emotions overwhelm me, I carefully untangled her arms. 'Be brave. I wish you a safe trip. Keep your promise.' Later on, when I occasionally remembered that moment, I thought of it as my blue good-bye."

"Okay, let's assume that you believed you were doing the right thing, but why didn't you report to the organization so that they would know the truth?"

"In fact, no one had ever signed the order for me to kill her. The provincial committee only informed us of the situation. The comrade in charge of provincial security assigned its investigation to me as the leader of the intelligence unit. That meant that I had the power to decide the fate of the informer. I set the girl free because I trusted that I was doing the right thing, because I had faith in the truth and in her innocence. And at that time, if I had reported the truth, then the matter would have become extremely complicated. Probably no one would have believed me because at that time the only witness left, Chief Warrant Officer Nam, had already died from his wounds at the Transportation Company's field hospital. Because they wouldn't believe me, they would have picked at everything I told them. To have been disciplined and discharged would have been lucky. They might have killed me—not directly though. Using the enemy to get rid of someone under suspicion was the cleanest way to kill somebody. I understood that very well."

"And so you were afraid of death?"

"I was afraid of death if it was meaningless and absurd, but I wasn't afraid to sacrifice myself for some purpose. As I've already explained, the incident with My Huong, in combination with the haunting memories of my profession, made me determined to be transferred to the sabotage company. Surely you've seen on my background documents that during the three years that I was the sabotage company commander, I received three certificates of heroism and two medals. After being promoted to battalion cadre I asked for a transfer to the infantry. In 1975 I was the captain in command of an infantry battalion attacking Hue, pursuing the enemy down to the mouth of the Thuan An estuary. Among the prisoners of war we rounded up, I happened to come across Ton. He explained that he was drafted into the army immediately after the branch committee at Khang Xuyen had been exposed. The last remaining party member, the old man named Quan, had been caught. What kind of branch leader was Ton if he could take up the enemy's gun and carry it? Seeing him now as a prisoner of war, I felt more assured about my decision to set My Huong free. Ton kept clinging to me, but I avoided him. We didn't say anything about My Huong."

"Have you ever seen My Huong again or do you have any news about her?"

"When I was in Hue I returned to Khang Xuyen to see O Theo. She told me that My Huong was married with children in Saigon. Both of her parents had passed away. That's all I know. I didn't try to contact her. What would have been the point?"

"Did you ever meet Ton again?"

"Ton was sent to reeducation camp and once he came to look for me in Mang Ca, begging me to verify that he had been the branch committee leader in Khang Xuyen and, what's more, that when he was a member of the Southern army he had stayed in contact with the north. He scratched his head and winked cunningly, as if to tell me that he would never forget this favor. I would never have signed something so carelessly like that. I had to hold back my anger and tell him to go back and ask some of the old party members in Khang Xuyen or at the provincial committee. When he kept insisting, I finally exploded and threw him out."

"That was a long story and we've heard enough. We've got your version of it. Now we have to wait for the organization to investigate and draw its own conclusion. Let's leave it for now."

* * *

After reviewing the file named "Y8," Major Can sat in thought. The story wasn't hard to understand, and yet at that time the security office under the command of Colonel Le Hon had been unable to reach a conclusion. The letter supposedly sent by Ton was clearly anonymous. It bore no return address and the content and wording were only meant to draw the unit's attention to a problem that was political, dangerous, and fatal. Was it really Ton? Why would a person like Ton do that? File Y8 bore no conclusion and was shelved in a cabinet marked "Secret," but the suspicion clung to Hao. He was never nominated for promotion to department chief and when it came time for him to be promoted to the rank of colonel, things had gotten stuck there. Colonel Le Hon had called Phan Nhan Hao into his office and persistently tried to persuade him to change or add more information to the story of his relationship with My Huong. Hao responded that there was nothing to change, nothing more to say. Then Colonel Le Hon played his last card: If this matter remained so unclear and inconclusive, then the proposal for Hao's promotion to the rank of Colonel would be difficult. The best course of action would be for Hao to submit a request for early retirement.

"I'm ready!" Hao said. He picked up a pen and paper, quickly wrote the words, and thrust his signature across the page.

That was it. Colonel Le Hon had sighed with relief. It could be said that he had fulfilled his duty and deserved one more pay raise before he retired.

These days Le Hon had been living in retirement for a few years already. He had carried that sigh of relief with him all the way back to his garden in his village in the countryside. As for the Y8 file, it was still gathering mold in the cabinet marked "Secret." Now the office staff was brand new, and none of them knew anything about the file marked Y8 except for Major Can. Filled with doubts, he went to speak with his superiors. They listened attentively, and finally they all said the same thing, "Why dig up old stories like that? Let's put it aside. It would be no simple matter to resolve this case. If the purpose was to restore honor to Hao, no one ever took it from him. Anyway, he retired a while ago. We should be happy for his recovery from his illness. That's it."

Those two words, "That's it," were an order from higher up, and yet Major Can still couldn't resolve the doubts in his mind. Should he let Hao suffer from injustice, even if the only ones who knew the story were a few of the authorities?

Still, it gave him pain and disturbed his peace of mind. Because his conscience kept bothering him, Major Can decided to go visit Hao in order to tell him the truth, hoping that he would forgive. One Sunday morning, Can rode his bicycle there. Hanging from his handlebars was a cloth bag containing a half liter of liquor and a dozen small packages of fried peanuts, all of which he had bought at a drink shop, hoping that they could eat and drink at their leisure and confide in each other comfortably.

That day, Hao was alone in the house. His wife Phuc had gone to the market and both of his children had gone to extra study classes. Hao had shut the door and lay down to reread *The War Between the Three Kingdoms*.

Knock. Knock. Knock. The sudden sound of knocking made him jump up violently. The book fell to the floor.

Knock. Knock. Knock. It grew more urgent and louder. Hao's heart beat wildly. Sweat broke out on his forehead. He breathed heavily and his vision clouded over.

Knock. Knock. Knock. "Is anybody home? Hao! Hao!"

He sat motionless, like a person whose spirit had departed.

"Hao! Are you asleep? It's Can. I've come to visit you."

Knock. Knock. Knock. Major Can held the cloth bag in one hand. In his excitement, he was knocking louder. Then he heard a roar.

"Get lost, you scum!"

Can stepped quickly back. He was puzzling over whether the cry was real or if he had heard it wrong when the door suddenly burst open. Phan Nhan Hao, with a wild look in his blood red eyes, held in his hand the bar that bolted the door and raised it with a scream. Can's mouth opened and emitted meaningless sounds. His face went pale. He only had time to step out of the way and run. Hao swung, cutting the top off the papaya tree by the porch, so that its white sap came streaming out. Neighbors rushed out, held Hao back and helped him back into the house. He was still breathing heavily and refused to say a thing. After he had recovered, Major Can, who still didn't understand what had happened, had to ask a few of the children to bring his bicycle out into the housing project's common yard. His hands were trembling when he opened the lock and his eyes were still glancing in the direction where the bizarre event had just happened.

From that day on, the people of K42 no longer heard the sound of Hao's feet jogging in the morning. The children now played soccer without a referee and so they often quarrelled noisily. Hao slid back into his former illness, only chuckling, his face dazed. He became forgetful, not only about the past, but he also forgot very quickly, even things that had just happened. He told Hang to sleep with her mother while he slept in the bed with Hieu, each of them with a separate blanket. Phuc sighed. Hang and Hieu were also depressed, especially when they saw the bad kids in K42 once again bowing very deeply in front of Hao, yelling "Hello, Uncle Hay!" and bursting out laughing. Once again, Phuc hung out the sign that said, "Please don't knock on the door," which had only been taken down less than a month before. The joy had been so brief, and now her sighs became sadder. Her prayers in front of the incense-covered altar were different now. Not only did she pray to the ancestors to bless the family, but she also prayed that the woman named My Huong would return. Who knows? Perhaps that beautiful woman was a fairy sent to this world from the heavens to save her husband. She had no idea of the origins of what had happened. Many times she thought of going to ask Major Can, but her hesitation held her back. She didn't know that after the bizarre incident and after hearing that Phan Nhan Hao had become ill again, Can had asked for a transfer. No one knew where he had transferred or even if he had continued in the same career.

translated by Bac Hoai Tran and Dana Sachs

Speaking of Courage

Tim O'Brien

The war was over and there was no place in particular to go. Norman Bowker followed the tar road on its seven-mile loop around the lake, then he started all over again, driving slowly, feeling safe inside his father's big Chevy, now and then looking out on the lake to watch the boats and water-skiers and scenery. It was Sunday and it was summer, and the town seemed pretty much the same. The lake lay flat and silvery against the sun. Along the road the houses were all low-slung and split-level and modern, with big porches and picture windows facing the water. The lawns were spacious. On the lake side of the road, where real estate was most valuable, the houses were handsome and set deep in, well kept and brightly painted, with docks jutting out into the lake, and boats moored and covered with canvas, and neat gardens, and sometimes even gardeners, and stone patios with barbecue spits and grills, and wooden shingles saying who lived where. On the other side of the road, to his left, the houses were also handsome, though less expensive and on a smaller scale and with no docks or boats or gardeners. The road was a sort of boundary between the affluent and the almost affluent, and to live on the lake side of the road was one of the few natural privileges in a town of the prairie—the difference between watching the sun set over cornfields or over water.

It was a graceful, good-sized lake. Back in high school, at night, he had driven around and around it with Sally Kramer, wondering if she'd want to pull into the shelter of Sunset Park, or other times with his friends, talking about urgent matters, worrying about the existence of God and theories of causation. Then, there had not been a war. But there had always been the lake, which was the town's first cause of existence, a place for immigrant settlers to put down their loads. Before the settlers were the Sioux, and before the Sioux were the vast open prairies, and before the prairies there was only ice. The lake bed had been dug out by the southernmost advance of the Wisconsin glacier. Fed by neither streams nor springs, the lake was often filthy and algaed, relying on fickle prairie rains for replenishment. Still, it was the only important body of water within forty miles, a source of pride, nice to look at on bright summer days, and later that evening it would color up with fireworks. Now, in the late afternoon, it lay calm and smooth, a good audience for silence, a seven-mile circumference that could be traveled by slow car in twenty-five minutes. It was not such a good lake for swimming. After high school, he'd caught an ear infection that had almost kept him out of the war. And the lake had drowned his friend Max Arnold, keeping him out of the war entirely. Max had been one who liked to talk about the existence of God. "No, I'm not saying *that*," he'd argue against the drone of the engine. "I'm saying it's possible as an *idea*, even necessary as an idea, a final cause in the whole structure of causation." Now he knew, perhaps. Before the war, they'd driven around the lake as friends, but now Max was just an idea, and most of Norman Bowker's other friends were living in Des Moines or Sioux City, or going to school somewhere, or holding down jobs. The high school girls were mostly gone or married. Sally Kramer, whose pictures he had once carried in his wallet, was one who had married. Her name was now Sally Gustafson and she lived in a pleasant blue house on the less expensive side of the lake road. On his third day home he'd seen her out mowing the lawn, still pretty in a lacy red blouse and white shorts. For a moment he'd almost pulled over, just to talk, but instead he'd pushed down hard on the gas pedal. She looked happy. She had her house and her new husband, and there was really nothing he could say to her.

The town seemed remote somehow. Sally was married and Max was drowned and his father was at home watching baseball on national TV.

Norman Bowker shrugged. "No problem," he murmured.

Clockwise, as if in orbit, he took the Chevy on another seven-mile turn around the lake.

Even in late afternoon the day was hot. He turned on the air conditioner, then the radio, and he leaned back and let the cold air and music blow over him. Along the road, kicking stones in front of them, two young boys were hiking with knapsacks and toy rifles and canteens. He honked going by, but neither boy looked up. Already he had passed them six times, forty-two miles, nearly three hours without stop. He watched the boys recede in his rearview mirror. They turned a soft grayish color, like sand, before finally disappearing.

He tapped down lightly on the accelerator.

Out on the lake a man's motorboat had stalled; the man was bent over the engine with a wrench and a frown. Beyond the stalled boat there were other boats, and a few water-skiers, and the smooth July waters, and an immense flatness everywhere. Two mud hens floated stiffly beside a white dock.

The road curved west, where the sun had now dipped low. He figured it was close to five o'clock—twenty after, he guessed. The war had taught him to tell time without clocks, and even at night, waking from sleep, he could usually place it within ten minutes either way. What he should do, he thought, is stop at Sally's house and impress her with this new time-telling trick of his. They'd talk for a while, catching up on things, and then he'd say, "Well, better hit the road, it's five thirty-four," and she'd glance at her wristwatch and say, "Hey! How'd you *do* that?" and he'd give a casual shrug and tell her it was just one of those things you pick up. He'd keep it light. He wouldn't say anything about anything. "How's it being married?" he might ask, and he'd nod at whatever she answered with, and he would not say a word about how he'd almost won the Silver Star for valor.

He drove past Slater Park and across the causeway and past Sunset Park. The radio announcer sounded tired. The temperature in Des Moines was eighty-one degrees, and the time was five thirty-five, and "All you on the road, drive extra careful now on this fine Fourth of July." If Sally had not been married, or if his father were not such a baseball fan, it would have been a good time to talk.

"The Silver Star?" his father might have said.

"Yes, but I didn't get it. Almost, but not quite."

And his father would have nodded, knowing full well that many brave men do not win medals for their bravery, and that others win medals for doing nothing. As a starting point, maybe, Norman Bowker might then have listed the seven medals he did win: the Combat Infantryman's Badge, the Air Medal, the Army Commendation Medal, the Good Conduct Medal, the Vietnam Campaign Medal, the Bronze Star, and the Purple Heart, though it wasn't much of a wound and did not leave a scar and did not hurt and never had. He would've explained to his father that none of these decorations was for uncommon valor. They were for common valor. The routine, daily stuff—just humping, just enduring—but that was worth something, wasn't it? Yes, it was. Worth plenty. The ribbons looked good on the uniform in his closet, and if his father were to ask, he would've explained what each signified and how he was proud of all of them, especially the Combat Infantryman's Badge, because it meant he had been there as a real soldier and had done all the things soldiers do, and therefore it wasn't such a big deal that he could not bring himself to be uncommonly brave.

And then he would have talked about the medal he did not win and why he did not win it.

"I almost won the Silver Star," he would have said.

"How's that?"

"Just a story."

"So tell me," his father would have said.

Slowly then, circling the lake, Norman Bowker would have started by describing the Song Tra Bong. "A river," he would've said, "this slow flat muddy river." He would've explained how during the dry season it was exactly like any other river, nothing special, but how in October the monsoons began and the whole situation changed. For a solid week the rains never stopped, not once, and so after a few days the Song Tra Bong overflowed its banks and the land turned into a deep, thick muck for a half mile on either side. Just muck—no other word for it. Like quicksand, almost, except the stink was incredible. "You couldn't even sleep," he'd tell his father. "At night you'd find a high spot, and you'd doze off, but then later you'd wake up because you'd be buried in all that slime. You'd just sink in. You'd feel it ooze up over your body and sort of suck you down. And the whole time there was that constant rain. I mean, it never stopped, not ever."

"Sounds pretty wet," his father would've said, pausing briefly. "So what happened?"

"You really want to hear this?"

"Hey, I'm your *father*."

Norman Bowker smiled. He looked out across the lake and imagined the feel of his tongue against the truth. "Well, this one time, this one night out by the river....I wasn't very brave."

"You have seven medals."

"Sure."

"Seven. Count 'em. You weren't a coward either."

"Well, maybe not. But I had the chance and I blew it. The stink, that's what got to me. I couldn't take that goddamn awful *smell*."

"If you don't want to say anymore—"

"I do want to."

"All right then. Slow and sweet, take your time."

The road descended into the outskirts of town, turning northwest past the junior college and the tennis courts, then past Chautauqua Park, where the picnic tables were spread with sheets of colored plastic and where picnickers sat in lawn chairs and listened to the high school band playing Sousa marches under the band shell. The music faded after a few blocks. He drove beneath a canopy of elms, then along a stretch of open shore, then past the municipal docks, where a woman in pedal pushers stood casting for bullheads. There were no other fish in the lake except for perch and a few worthless carp. It was a bad lake for swimming and fishing both.

He drove slowly. No hurry, nowhere to go. Inside the Chevy the air was cool and oily-smelling, and he took pleasure in the steady sounds of the engine and air conditioning. A tour bus feeling, in a way, except the town he was touring seemed dead. Through the windows, as if in a stop-motion photograph, the place looked as if it had been hit by nerve gas, everything still and lifeless, even the people. The town could not talk, and would not listen. "How'd you like to hear about the war?" he might have asked, but the place could only blink and shrug. It had no memory, therefore no guilt. The taxes got paid and the votes got counted and the agencies of government did their work briskly and politely. It was a brisk, polite town. It did not know shit about shit, and did not care to know.

Norman Bowker leaned back and considered what he might've said on the subject. He knew shit. It was his specialty. The smell, in particular, but also the numerous varieties of texture and taste. Someday he'd give a lecture on the topic. Put on a suit and tie and stand up in front of the Kiwanis club and tell the fuckers about all the wonderful shit he knew. Pass out samples, maybe.

Smiling at this, he clamped the steering wheel slightly right of center, which produced a smooth clockwise motion against the curve of the road. The Chevy seemed to know its own way.

The sun was lower now. Five fifty-five, he decided—six o'clock, tops.

Along an unused railway spur, four workmen labored in the shadowy red heat, setting up a platform and steel launchers for the evening fireworks. They were dressed alike in khaki trousers, work shirts, visored caps, and brown boots. Their faces were dark and smudgy. "Want to hear about the Silver Star I almost won?" Norman Bowker whispered, but none of the workmen looked up. Later they would blow color into the sky. The lake would sparkle with reds and blues and greens, like a mirror, and the picnickers would make low sounds of appreciation.

"Well, see, it never stopped raining," he would've said. "The muck was everywhere, you couldn't get away from it."

He would have paused a second.

Then he would have told about the night they bivouacked in a field along the Song Tra Bong. A big swampy field beside the river. There was a ville nearby, fifty meters downstream, and right away a dozen old mama-sans ran out and started yelling. A weird scene, he would've said. The mama-sans just stood there in the rain, soaking wet, yapping away about how this field was bad news. Number ten, they said. Evil ground. Not a good spot for good GIs. Finally Lieutenant Jimmy Cross had to get out his pistol and fire off a few rounds just to shoo them away. By then it was almost dark. So they set up a perimeter, ate chow, then crawled under their ponchos and tried to settle in for the night.

But the rain kept getting worse. And by midnight the field turned into soup.

"Just this deep, oozy soup," he would've said. "Like sewage or something. Thick and mushy. You couldn't sleep. You couldn't even lie down, not for long, because you'd start to sink under the soup. Real clammy. You could feel the crud coming up inside your boots and pants."

Here, Norman Bowker would have squinted against the low sun. He would have kept his voice cool, no self-pity.

"But the worst part," he would've said quietly, "was the smell. Partly it was the river—a dead fish smell—but it was something else, too. Finally somebody figured it out. What this was, it was a shit field. The village toilet. No indoor plumbing, right? So they used the field. I mean, we were camped in a goddamn *shit* field."

He imagined Sally Kramer closing her eyes.

If she were here with him, in the car, she would've said, "Stop it. I don't like that word."

"That's what it *was*."

"All right, but you don't have to use that word."

"Fine. What should we call it?"

She would have glared at him. "I don't know. Just stop it."

Clearly, he thought, this was not a story for Sally Kramer. She was Sally Gustafson now. No doubt Max would've liked it, the irony in particular, but Max had become a pure idea, which was its own irony. It was just too bad. If his father were here, riding shotgun around the lake, the old man might have glanced over for a second, understanding perfectly well that it was not a question of offensive language but of fact. His father would have sighed and folded his arms and waited.

"A shit field," Norman Bowker would have said. "And later that night I could've won the Silver Star for valor."

"Right," his father would've murmured, "I hear you."

The Chevy rolled smoothly across a viaduct and up the narrow tar road. To the right was open lake. To the left, across the road, most of the lawns were scorched dry like October corn. Hopelessly, round and round, a rotating sprinkler scattered lake water on Dr. Mason's vegetable garden. Already the prairie had been baked dry, but in August it would get worse. The lake would turn green with algae, and the golf course would burn up, and the dragonflies would crack open for want of good water.

The big Chevy curved past Centennial Beach and the A&W root beer stand.

It was his eighth revolution around the lake.

He followed the road past the handsome houses with their docks and wooden shingles. Back to Slater Park, across the causeway, around to Sunset Park, as though riding on tracks.

The two little boys were still trudging along on their seven-mile hike.

Out on the lake, the man in the stalled motorboat still fiddled with his engine. The pair of mud hens floated like wooden decoys, and the water-skiers looked tanned and athletic, and the high school band was packing up its instruments, and the woman in pedal pushers patiently rebaited her hook for one last try.

Quaint, he thought.

A hot summer day and it was all very quaint and remote. The four workmen had nearly completed their preparations for the evening fireworks.

Facing the sun again, Norman Bowker decided it was nearly seven o'clock. Not much later the tired radio announcer confirmed it, his voice rocking itself into a deep Sunday snooze. If Max Arnold were here, he would say something about the announcer's fatigue, and relate it to the bright pink in the sky, and the war, and courage. A pity that Max was gone. And a pity about his father, who had his own war and who now preferred silence.

Still, there was so much to say.

How the rain never stopped. How the cold worked into your bones. Sometimes the bravest thing on earth was to sit through the night and feel the cold in your bones. Courage was not always a matter of yes or no. Sometimes it came in degrees, like the cold; sometimes you were very brave up to a point and then beyond that point you were not so brave. In certain situations you could do incredible things, you could advance toward enemy fire, but in other situations, which were not nearly so bad, you had trouble keeping your eyes open. Sometimes, like that night in the shit field, the difference between courage and cowardice was something small and stupid.

The way the earth bubbled. And the smell.

In a soft voice, without flourishes, he would have told the exact truth.

"Late in the night," he would've said, "we took some mortar fire."

He would've explained how it was still raining, and how the clouds were pasted to the field, and how the mortar rounds seemed to come right out of the clouds. Everything was black and wet. The field just exploded. Rain and slop and shrapnel, nowhere to run, and all they could do was worm down into slime and cover up and wait. He would've described the crazy things he saw. Weird things. Like how at one point he noticed a guy lying next to him in the sludge, completely buried except for his face, and how after a moment the guy rolled his eyes and winked at him. The noise was fierce. Heavy thunder, and mortar rounds, and people yelling. Some of the men began shooting up flares. Red and green and silver flares, all colors, and the rain came down in Technicolor.

The field was boiling. The shells made deep slushy craters, opening up all those years of waste, centuries worth, and the smell came bubbling out of the earth. Two rounds hit close by. Then a third, even closer, and immediately, off to his left, he heard somebody screaming. It was Kiowa—he knew that. The sound was ragged and clotted up, but even so he knew the voice. A strange gargling noise. Rolling sideways, he crawled toward the screaming in the dark. The rain was hard and steady. Along the perimeter there were quick bursts of gunfire. Another round hit nearby, spraying up shit and water, and for a few moments he ducked down beneath the mud. He heard the valves in his heart. He heard the quick, feathering action of the hinges. Extraordinary, he thought. As he came up, a pair of red flares puffed open, a soft fuzzy glow, and in the glow he saw Kiowa's wide-open eyes settling down into the scum. Briefly, all he could do was watch. He heard himself moan. Then he moved again, crabbing forward, but when he got there Kiowa was almost completely under. There was a knee. There was an arm and a gold wristwatch and part of a boot.

He could not describe what happened next, not ever, but he would've tried anyway. He would've spoken carefully so as to make it real for anyone who would listen.

There were bubbles where Kiowa's head should've been.

The left hand was curled open; the fingernails were filthy; the wristwatch gave off a green phosphorescent shine as it slipped beneath the thick waters.

He would've talked about this, and how he grabbed Kiowa by the boot and tried to pull him out. He pulled hard but Kiowa was gone, and then suddenly he felt himself going too. He could taste it. The shit was in his nose and eyes. There were flares and mortar rounds, and the stink was everywhere—it was inside him, in his lungs—and he could no longer tolerate it. Not here, he thought. Not like this. He released Kiowa's boot and watched it slide away. Slowly, working his way up, he hoisted himself out of the deep mud, and then he lay still and tasted the shit in his mouth and closed his eyes and listened to the rain and explosions and bubbling sounds.

He was alone.

He had lost his weapon but it did not matter. All he wanted was a bath. Nothing else. A hot soapy bath.

Circling the lake, Norman Bowker remembered how his friend Kiowa had disappeared under the waste and water.

"I didn't flip out," he would've said. "I was cool. If things had gone right, if it hadn't been for that smell, I could've won the Silver Star."

A good war story, he thought, but it was not a war for war stories, nor for talk of valor, and nobody in town wanted to know about the terrible stink. They wanted good intentions and good deeds. But the town was not to blame, really. It was a nice little town, very prosperous, with neat houses and all the sanitary conveniences.

Norman Bowker lit a cigarette and cranked open his window. Seven thirty-five, he decided.

The lake had divided into two halves. One half still glistened, the other was caught in shadow. Along the causeway, the two little boys marched on. The man in the stalled motorboat yanked frantically on the cord to his engine, and the two mud hens sought supper at the bottom of the lake, tails bobbing. He passed Sunset Park once again, and more houses, and the junior college and the tennis courts, and the picnickers, who now sat waiting for the evening fireworks. The high school band was gone. The woman in pedal pushers patiently toyed with her line.

Although it was not yet dusk, the A&W was already awash in neon lights.

He maneuvered his father's Chevy into one of the parking slots, let the engine idle, and sat back. The place was doing a good holiday business. Mostly kids, it seemed, and a few farmers in for the day. He did not recognize any of the faces. A slim, hipless young carhop passed by, but when he hit the horn, she did not seem to notice. Her eyes slid sideways. She hooked a tray to the window of a Firebird, laughing lightly, leaning forward to chat with the three boys inside.

He felt invisible in the soft twilight. Straight ahead, over the takeout counter, swarms of mosquitoes electrocuted themselves against an aluminum Pest-Rid machine. It was a calm, quiet summer evening.

He honked again, this time leaning on the horn. The young carhop turned slowly, as if puzzled, then said something to the boys in the Firebird and moved reluctantly toward him. Pinned to her shirt was a badge that said EAT MAMA BURGERS.

When she reached his window, she stood straight up so that all he could see was the badge.

"Mama Burger," he said. "Maybe some fries, too."

The girl sighed, leaned down, and shook her head. Her eyes were as fluffy and airy-light as cotton candy.

"You blind?" she said.

She put out her hand and tapped an intercom attached to a steel post.

"Punch the button and place your order. All I do is carry the dumb trays."

She stared at him for a moment. Briefly, he thought, a question lingered in her fuzzy eyes, but then she turned and punched the button for him and returned to her friends in the Firebird.

The intercom squeaked and said, "Order."

"Mama Burger and fries," Norman Bowker said.

"Affirmative, copy clear. No rootie-tootie?"

"Rootie-tootie?"

"You know, man—*root* beer."

"A small one."

"Roger-dodger. Repeat: one Mama, one fries, one small beer. Fire for effect. Stand by."

The intercom squeaked and went dead.

"Out," said Norman Bowker.

When the girl brought his tray, he ate quickly, without looking up. The tired radio announcer in Des Moines gave the time, almost eight-thirty. Dark was pressing in tight now, and he wished there were somewhere to go. In the morning he'd check out some job possibilities. Shoot a few buckets down at the Y, maybe wash the Chevy. He finished his root beer and pushed the intercom button.

"Order," said the tinny voice.

"All done."

"That's *it*?"

"I guess so."

"Hey, loosen up," the voice said. "What you really need, friend?"

Norman Bowker smiled.

"Well," he said, "how'd you like to hear about—"

He stopped and shook his head.

"Hear *what*, man?"

"Nothing."

"Well, hey," the intercom said, "I'm sure as fuck not *going* anywhere. Screwed to a post, for God sake. Go ahead, try me."

"Nothing."

"You sure?"

"Positive. All done."

The intercom made a light sound of disappointment. "Your choice, I guess. Over an' out."

"Out," said Norman Bowker.

On his tenth turn around the lake he passed the hiking boys for the last time. The man in the stalled motorboat was gone; the mud hens were gone. Beyond the lake, over Sally Gustafson's house, the sun had left a smudge of purple on the horizon. The band shell was deserted, and the woman in pedal pushers quietly reeled in her line, and Dr. Mason's sprinkler went round and round.

On his eleventh revolution he switched off the air conditioning, opened up his window, and rested his elbow comfortably on the sill, driving with one hand.

There was nothing to say.

He could not talk about it and never would. The evening was smooth and warm.

If it had been possible, which it wasn't, he would have explained how his friend Kiowa slipped away that night beneath the dark swampy field. He was folded in with the war; he was part of the waste.

Turning on his headlights, driving slowly, Norman Bowker remembered how he had taken hold of Kiowa's boot and pulled hard, but how the smell was simply too much, and how he'd backed off and in that way had lost the Silver Star.

He wished he could've explained some of this. How he had been braver than he ever thought possible, but how he had not been so brave as he wanted to be. The distinction was important. Max Arnold, who loved fine lines, would've appreciated it. And his father, who already knew, would've nodded.

"The truth," Norman Bowker would've said, "is I let the guy go."

"Maybe he was already gone."

"He wasn't."

"But maybe."

"No, I could feel it. He wasn't. Some things you can feel."

His father would have been quiet for a while, watching the headlights against the narrow tar road.

"Well, anyway," the old man would've said, "there's still the seven medals."

"I suppose."

"Seven honeys."

"Right."

On his twelfth revolution, the sky went crazy with color. He pulled into Sunset Park and stopped in the shadow of a picnic shelter. After a time he got out, walked down to the beach, and waded into the lake without undressing. The water felt warm against his skin. He put his head under. He opened his lips, very slightly, for the taste, then he stood up and folded his arms and watched the fireworks. For a small town, he decided, it was a pretty good show.

The Man Who Stained His Soul

Vu Bao

If everything had gone as we'd planned, I would have nothing now to write about the battle against Che post that year.

Painstakingly accurate plans had been drawn up under the close guidance of the Command Staff. New intelligence about shifts in the enemy's effective strength and weaponry was received every day. The diagram of Che post's defenses was drawn and redrawn so many times it reached a point of absolute perfection. Each enemy fire point was scouted over and over and marked by a different symbol on the diagram. Victory couldn't be more certain.

But war isn't a game in which only one side fires and the other eats bullets. The enemy major in charge of Che post was an experienced soldier. Ignoring the deliberate provocations of our recons-by-fire, he kept the two heavy machine guns he had concealed in the command bunker silent. It wasn't until our company burst through the barbed wire and advanced to the center of the compound in an arrow-shape formation that those guns opened up, catching us in a cross fire.

Our attack was stopped dead. The company was pinned down, with everyone's belly glued to the earth and no one daring to lift his head. It was a miracle we could keep our heads and limbs intact without breathing dirt.

This tactic hadn't been anticipated in the combat plan, and now the commanders couldn't react. Usually, once the company engaged, the Party cell would confer urgently, exchange ideas and make timely decisions. But this time, Luat, the company commander, was stuck with our front unit, the commissar was in the rear of the formation, and the deputy commissar was helping to get the wounded dragged out of the barbed wire and bandaged up. Pulling out his revolver, the commissar fired up into the air and sprang forward, yelling: "Comrades, advance..."

His order was cut short by a bullet.

Luat crawled down the column to me and jerked his chin at the fire point: "Take out the left side and leave the right to me."

We divided the front unit into two V-shaped lines. Half of the men crept after Luat, the other half after me. Only Vinh lay prostrate in his place.

I crawled back to him.

"What the hell are you doing?"

Vinh's voice was strained. "How can we advance—the bullets are pouring in like rain."

"Would you rather lie here waiting for death?"

"Death's waiting up there also."

With the bullets zeroing in on us, this wasn't the time or place to try to turn a coward into a brave soldier. "Give me your cartridge belt and grenades," I yelled at him.

"Then I'll be killed in the enemy's counterattack."

My blood was boiling. I yanked his submachine gun from his hands. "I have to advance. Hang onto the company flag."

I crawled low under the fire, keeping my eyes on the muzzle flashes. Suddenly the fire pecking at us from the bunker's loophole ceased. The enemy gunners must have been changing the belt. I sprang up and rushed the bunker. Someone threw a grenade at me. I snatched it up and tossed it back into the loophole. Then I thrust the barrel of my rifle through the opening and sprayed in a full magazine, sweeping the area inside.

Shouts of joy sounded from all around. Fourth Company had penetrated the base. But what followed was our hardest battle. We struggled to take one fortified position after another, and it was nearly morning before we managed to blow up their headquarters.

Afterwards, the battalion commander ran up to us. "Hurry and scrounge up whatever supplies and equipment you can," he said. "It's nearly dawn—you'll start shitting when the enemy's long range artillery begins firing."

I turned around to see Vinh standing nearby. His left trouser leg was sticking like glue to his thigh. I tore out the bandage I had tucked into my belt.

Luat seized my hand. "Don't bother. He just pissed himself," he said, nodding at Vinh's saturated trouser. "Pissed on his own soul."

We withdrew to Noi hamlet, four kilometers from Che post. Air raid shelters had been dug there by the local militia. Those units that had been held in reserve during the attack were now sent out to guard the perimeter of the hamlet, and huge sauce pans full of chicken gruel were prepared for us in each house. But after our night of shooting, crawling and rolling through the mud, we could only take a few perfunctory mouthfuls. It was better to sleep than to eat. As soon as we lay down on our straw mats, we didn't know if heaven was up or earth was down.

Suddenly I was awakened by someone pulling me to my feet. Still in a daze, my eyes half-sealed, I dimly heard Luat order me to get the unit dressed in full uniform and equipment. "Get everybody over to battalion headquarters—they have a new job for you."

"Yes, commander."

When we arrived at headquarters, the battalion commander told me that a foreign comrade had come to shoot a documentary film. Since the battle was over, it would be necessary to reconstruct the fighting for him. The first shot would be the raising of the company flag over the roof of Che post.

I stood dumbfounded for a moment. "Commander, after the fighting we policed up the battlefield and returned here at once. We didn't have time to raise a flag."

"Then you'll have to raise one now."

"Sir, we don't have a flag."

"What do you mean—what about the Victory flag the regimental commander handed to you before you left? Didn't he give it to you, unit commander, in front of all your men?"

"I passed it to Vinh when the C.O. ordered us to advance. After I took out the heavy machine gun, the rest of the company charged forward. Vinh came along with them, but he forgot to bring the flag."

"Why didn't you look for it?"

"I did, but I couldn't find it. When I went back to that place, all I saw were three mortar craters."

The battalion commander turned to the press liaison officer and told him to get Third Company's Victory flag instead.

The foreign comrade was waiting for us at regimental headquarters. Smiling, he shook our hands. "Glory to Vietnam; of thou I'm proud," he said.

We tightened our lips to keep from bursting into laughter.

The "reconstruction" of the flag-raising didn't go as easily as we thought it would. The machine gun company took positions along the outer perimeter. The heavy artillery company set up four observation posts to watch for air raids. An infantry company deployed inside Che post, ready to take on any enemy parachutists who might try to pounce upon us. And our unit, directed by the foreign comrade, had the task of reenacting the destruction of the command bunker. Unfortunately, when the explosive charges were blown, a piece of concrete from the bunker hurled itself at my knee, knocking me to the ground. I immediately tried to rise, but I couldn't stay on my feet. A medic helped me off the site and stopped my bleeding with a bandage. But I was unable to act in the next scene.

Luat asked the interpreter if the director would like to chose another soldier to raise the flag. The foreign comrade nodded and strolled along our ranks, gazing at us one by one. He turned and coming down the line once again, then stopped in front of Vinh and pointed at his chest.

"All right. This soldier will be the flag bearer."

Before we began the reenactment again, the battalion commander reiterated once again how important making the film was, how it would be seen all over the world. Any idea the director had was to be obeyed as strictly as an order on the battlefield.

Luat raised his hand, as if to object, but dropped it back down. After that, he didn't seem to act out his role with any enthusiasm.

The sappers exploded eight "square cakes" (satchel charges) around the post, allowing the cameraman to shoot the scene through a haze of smoke and fire.

Then came the raising-of-the-flag scene. Under the foreign comrade's direction, Luat waved his revolver and sprang forward, followed by Vinh, raising his flag pole high, and then the rest of the unit. Stop, the director called. Then—action! Vinh scrambled up to the roof of the headquarters bunker and struck the enemy's flag pole with the sole of his foot, sending their flag to the ground. With his legs firmly spread, he stood and waved the Victory flag. The rest of the unit flanked him on both sides. They raised their submachine guns and shouted joyfully.

But the scene had to be reshot three times, as we seemed somewhat sluggish. Taking Che post had been a difficult task, the director explained through the interpreter. Could we please then try a little harder to demonstrate to the whole world how high the morale was in our army?

Finally the filming was over. Staggering with fatigue, we stumbled back to Noi hamlet. Before packing up his equipment, the foreign comrade shook our hands.

"Glory to Vietnam. Of thou I'm proud."

Soon after we were back in battle and had no time to think about that scene. We were happy enough after a fight to simply find that our friends had come through intact. Then the war ended and after a while we turned in our rifles and came home and each of us tried to find ways to make a living. We forgot all about the flag raising at Che post.

One day, not long after the war, I was getting my hair cut and reading a newspaper to pass the time. A large headline flashed up at me. The documentary film, *The Path of Blood and Fire* had just premiered. The words: "Of thou I'm proud" came unbidden into my mind. Under the headline was a photograph of Vinh, spreading his legs on the roof of the headquarters' bunker, waving the Victory flag. He was flanked on both sides by my friends, raising their submachine guns, shouting joyfully.

I knew it was merely a reenactment of the battle. But still my heart beat swiftly in my chest as I read the caption: "A still from *The Path of Blood and Fire*: 'Raising the flag at Che post.'"

I felt it wasn't worth talking about. Like most veterans, my life was taken up with a day by day struggle just to make ends meet. None of us displayed our citations on the wall or pinned our medals on our chests. It was better to spend our energy keeping our plates full. At any rate, the movies were always full of such tricks and gimmicks. When the pig shed in my village cooperative had been filmed, the crew had gathered the biggest pigs from each family and stuck them all together, rubbing crushed garlic on their mouths to keep them from biting each other. And when they'd wanted to shoot our model fish pond, they'd brought baskets full of huge fish and loaded them into the boats so it looked as if the fish had been drawn into the boats with nets.

The victory over Che post had not only been the proudest moment of our battalion, but of the entire division. The division commander had even had the photo of the flag raising enlarged to the size of a double bed sheet and displayed on the center wall of the division museum. The veterans of the engagement knew very well that it was only a reenacted scene. But raw recruits gazed admiringly at Vinh waving the Victory flag and thought the photo had been taken on the spot, under enemy fire.

That still from the film was, admittedly, very beautiful: a People's Army soldier standing dignified and undaunted on top of the enemy's headquarters. One artist used the photograph as a model for a drawing put on a stamp to be distributed on Army Day. It was also featured in calenders, though after the veterans saw that they began to mutter among themselves. Finally, on Division Day, they approached the commissar. He shrugged and said that it was up to the artists to decide what particular images and symbols should be used—it wasn't possible to capture the entire division in one photograph.

Twenty years passed.

One day a director named T. Stevenson came to Vietnam to shoot a film called *Blood and Flowers*. After visiting several studios to view films made during the war, he asked the Minister of Culture to arrange interviews with those people who were in the sequences he wished to buy.

The ministry telephoned the army's political department, which in turn rang up the division. By this time, the old commanders had retired and their replacements believed it had been Vinh who'd advanced through enemy fire to plant the flag on Che post. The division commander ordered his political officers to locate Vinh and bring him to headquarters in order to meet Stevenson.

The original *Blood and Fire* was screened again, all over the country.

And everything Vinh told Stevenson fit the reenactment filmed by the foreign comrade, as if it had all really occurred. He managed to forget that at the time he had been glued to the earth, so filled with fear that he'd pissed on his own soul.

Luat came to see me. "Vinh must have thought we'd all died," he said.

I tried to console him. "What earthly good can the truth of the matter do for us soldiers now?"

"If something that we saw with our own eyes can be distorted this way, then what can happen to other events that happened fifty or a hundred years ago. I've written a letter to the Central Committee confirming that there was no flag raising at Che post. Will you sign it?"

"All right—I'll sign."

"Good. Add your rank, please, and the code word for our unit."

I wrote it all down. Months later, I found out that Luat's wife had had to sell their only pig in order to finance Luat's trips to visit his former comrades-in-arms and get their signatures. He made scores of copies of his letter and sent them all to the appropriate agencies.

The whole division was thrown into an uproar. But no one dared take down the huge photograph hanging in the Division Museum. And no one dared throw away the millions of stamps and thousands of calendars that had been printed.

The division commander arranged a private meeting with us. He asked us not to put everyone into a quandary. The attack against Che post had been the largest battle in the history of the division; it was the pride of the entire unit. Although he couldn't take down the photograph right at the moment, he assured us he would eventually find a substitute.

But I was certain one would never be found, not in a hundred years.

One day, Luat's son rushed to my house.

"Uncle, there's something wrong with my father's stomach. He asked to see you before he went onto the operating table."

I cycled over to the hospital.

Luat signalled to me to approach his bed. He grasped my hand firmly.

"You're a writer. You should never write a half-truth or turn a lie into truth. You have to write what you saw: there was no flag raising at Che post. Write it immediately and read it to me."

"Don't speak so ominously. A lie can't be corrected in a day. But don't worry, of course I'll write about it."

The operation was successful. Luat survived. The photo of Vinh waving the flag still hangs in the Division Museum. And recently, Vinh was invited by Stevenson to visit the director's country and talk about the flag raising as a way of promoting *Blood and Flowers*. He was lucky, that guy. If he'd been so mortified and humiliated when I'd asked him to give me his cartridge belt and grenades that he'd gotten up and charged the loophole and blocked it with his body, he wouldn't have been alive now to brag to foreigners.

Abroad, how can people know that Vinh pissed on his own soul and his trousers were only a prop?

Translated by Ho Ahn Thai
Edited by Wayne Karlin

Dressed Like Summer Leaves

Andre Dubus

Mickey Dolan was eleven years old, walking up Main Street on a spring afternoon, wearing green camouflage-colored trousers and tee shirt with a military web belt. The trousers had large pleated pockets at the front of his thighs; they closed with flaps, and his legs touched the spiral notebook in the left one, and the pen and pencil in the right one, where his coins shifted as he walked. He wore athletic socks and running shoes his mother bought him a week ago, after ten days of warm April, when she believed the winter was finally gone. He carried schoolbooks and a looseleaf binder in his left hand, their weight swinging with his steps. He passed a fish market, a discount shoe store that sold new shoes with nearly invisible defects, a flower shop, then an alley, and he was abreast of Timmy's, a red-painted wooden bar, when the door opened and a man came out. The man was in mid-stride but he turned his face and torso to look at Mickey, so that his lead foot came to the sidewalk pointing ahead, leaving him twisted to the right from the waist up. He shifted his foot toward Mickey, brought the other one near it, pulled the door shut, bent at the waist, and then straightened and lifted his arms in the air, his wrists limp, his palms toward the sidewalk.

"Charlie," he said. "Long time no see." Quickly his hands descended and held Mickey's biceps. "Motherfuckers were no bigger than you. Some of them." His hands squeezed, and Mickey tightened his muscles. "Stronger, though. Doesn't matter though, right? If you can creep like a baby. Crawl like a snake. Be a tree; a vine. Quiet as fucking air. Then *zap:* body bags. Short tour. Marine home for Christmas. Nothing but rice too."

The man wore cutoff jeans and old sneakers, white gone gray in streaks and smears, and a yellow tank shirt with nothing written on it. A box of Marlboros rested in his jeans pocket, two-thirds of it showing, and on his belt at his right hip he wore a Buck folding knife in a sheath; he wore it upside down so the flap pointed to the earth. Behind the knife a chain that looked like chrome hung from his belt and circled his hip to the rear, and Mickey knew it was attached to a wallet. The man was red from a new sunburn, and the hair on his arms and legs and above the shirt's low neck was blond, while the hair under his arms was light brown. He had a beard with a thick mustache that showed little of his upper lip: his beard was brown and slowly becoming sun-bleached, like the hair on his head, around a circle of bald red scalp; the hair was thick on the sides and back of his head, and grew close to his ears and beneath them. A pair of reflecting sunglasses with silver frames rested in the hair in front of the bald spot. On his right biceps was a tattoo, and his eyes were blue, a blue that seemed to glare into focus on Mickey, and Mickey knew the source of the glare was the sour odor the man breathed into the warm exhaust-tinged air between them.

"What's up, anyways? No more school?" The man spread his arms, his eyes left Mickey's and moved skyward, then swept the street to Mickey's right and the buildings on its opposite side, then returned, sharper now, as though Mickey were a blurred television picture becoming clear, distinct. "Did July get here?"

"It's April."

"Ah: AWOL. Your old man'll kick your ass, right?"

"I just got out."

"Just got out." The man looked above Mickey again, his blue eyes roving, as though waiting for something to appear in the sky beyond low buildings, in the air above lines of slow cars. For the first time Mickey knew that the man was not tall; he had only seemed to be. His shoulders were broad and sloping, his chest wide and deep so the yellow tank shirt stretched across it, and his biceps swelled when he bent his arms, and sprang tautly when he straightened them; his belly was wide too, and protruded, but his chest was much wider and thicker. Yet he was not as tall as he had appeared stepping from the bar, turning as he strode, and bowing, then standing upright and raising his arms. Mickey's eyes were level with the soft area just beneath the man's Adam's apple, the place that housed so much pain, where Mickey had deeply pushed his finger against Frankie Archembault's windpipe last month when Frankie's headlock had blurred his eyes with tears and his face scraped the cold March earth. It was not a fight; Frankie simply got too rough, then released Mickey and rolled away, red-faced and gasping and rubbing his throat. When Mickey stood facing his father he looked directly at the two lower ribs, above the solar plexus. His father stood near-motionless, his limbs still, quiet, like his voice; the strength Mickey felt from him was in his eyes.

The man had lit a cigarette and was smoking it fast, looking at the cars passing; Mickey watched the side of his face. Below it, on the reddened biceps of his right arm that brought the cigarette to his mouth and down again, was the tattoo, and Mickey stared at it as he might at a dead animal, a road kill of something wild he had never seen alive, a fox or a fisher, with more than curiosity: fascination and a nuance of baseless horror. The Marine Corps globe and anchor were blue, and permanent as the man's flesh. Beneath the globe was an unfurled rectangular banner that appeared to flap gently in a soft breeze; between its borders, written in script that filled the banner, was *Semper Fidelis*. Under the banner were block letters: USMC. The man still gazed across the street, and Mickey stepped around him, between him and the bar, to walk up the street and over the bridge; he would stop and look down at the moving water and imagine salmon swimming upriver before he walked the final two miles, most of it uphill and steep, to the tree-shaded street and his home. But the man turned and held his shoulder. The man did not tightly grip him; it was the man's quick movement that parted Mickey's lips with fear. They stood facing each other, Mickey's back to the door of the bar, and the man looked at his eyes then drew on his cigarette and flicked it up the sidewalk. Mickey watched it land beyond the corner of the bar, on the exit driveway of McDonald's. The hand was rubbing his shoulder.

"You just got out. Ah. So it's not July. Three fucking something o'clock in April. I believe I have missed a very important appointment." He withdrew his left hand from Mickey's shoulder and turned the wrist between their faces. "No watch, see? Can't wear a wristwatch. Get me the most expensive fucking wristwatch in the world, I can't wear it. Agent Orange, man. I'm walking talking drinking fucking fighting Agent Orange. Know what I mean? My cock is lethal. I put on a watch, zap, it stops."

"You were a Marine?"

"Oh yes. Oh yes, Charlie. See?" He turned and flexed his right arm so the tattoo on muscles faced Mickey. "USMC. Know what that means? Uncle Sam's Misguided Children. So fuck it, Charlie. Come on in."

"Where?"

"Where? The fucking bar, man. Let's go. It's springtime in New England. Crocuses and other shit."

"I can't."

"What do you mean you can't? Charlie goes where Charlie wants to go. Ask anybody that was there." He lowered his face close to Mickey's, so Mickey could see only the mouth in the beard, the nose, the blue eyes that seemed to burn slowly, like a pilot light. His voice was low, conspiratorial: "There's another one in there. From 'Nam. First Air Cav. Pussies. Flying golf carts. Come on. We'll bust his balls."

"I can't go in a bar."

The man straightened, stood erect, his chest out and his stomach pulled in, his fists on his hips. His face moved from left to right, his eyes intent, as though he were speaking to a group, and his voice was firm but without anger or threat, a voice of authority: "Charlie. You are allowed to enter a drinking establishment. Once therein you are allowed to drink non-alcoholic beverages. In this particular establishment there is pizza heated in a microwave. There are also bags of various foods, including potato chips, beer nuts, and nachos. There are also steamed hot dogs. But no fucking rice, Charlie. After you, my man."

The left arm moved quickly as a jab past Mickey's face, and he flinched, then heard the doorknob turn, and the man's right hand touched the side of his waist and turned him to face the door and gently pushed him out of the sun, into the long dark room. First he saw its lights: the yellow and red of a jukebox at the rear wall, and soft yellow lights above and behind the bar. Then he breathed its odors: alcohol and cigarette smoke and the vague and general smell of a closed and occupied room, darkened on a spring afternoon. A man stood behind the bar. He glanced at them, then turned and faced the rear wall. Three men stood at the bar, neither together nor apart; between each of them was room for two more people, yet they looked at each other and talked. The hand was still on Mickey's back, guiding more than pushing, moving him to the near corner of the bar, close to the large window beside the door. Through the glass Mickey looked at the parked and moving cars in the light; he had been only paces from the window when the man had turned and held his shoulder. The pressure on his back stopped when Mickey's chest touched the bar, then the man stepped around its corner, rested his arms on the short leg of its L, his back to the window, so now he looked down the length of the bar at the faces and sides of the three men, and at the bartender's back. There was a long space between Mickey and the first man to his left. He placed his books and binder in a stack on the bar and held its edge and locked at his face in the mirror, and his shirt like green leaves.

"Hey Fletcher," the man said. "I thought you'd hit the deck. When old Charlie came walking in." Mickey looked to his left: the three faces turned to the man and then to him, two looking interested, amused, and the third leaning forward over the bar, looking past the one man separating him from Mickey, looking slowly at Mickey's pants and probably the web belt too and the tee shirt. The man's face was neither angry nor friendly, more like that of a professional ballplayer stepping to the plate or a boxer ducking through the ropes into the ring. He had a brown handlebar mustache and hair that hung to his shoulders and moved, like a girl's, with his head. When his eyes rose from Mickey's clothing to his face, Mickey saw a glimmer of scorn; then the face showed nothing. Fletcher raised his beer mug to the man and, in a deep grating voice, said: "Body count, Duffy."

Then he looked ahead at the bottles behind the bar, finished his half mug with two swallows, and pushed the mug toward the bartender, who turned now and took it and held it slanted under a tap. Mickey watched the rising foam.

Duffy. Somehow knowing the man's name, or at least one of them, the first or last, made him seem less strange. He was Duffy, and he was with men who knew him, and Mickey eased away from his first sight of the man who had stepped onto the sidewalk and held him, a man who had never existed until the moment Mickey drew near the door of Timmy's. Mickey looked down, saw a brass rail, and rested his right foot on it; he pushed his books between him and Duffy, and folded his arms on the bar.

"Hey, Al. You working, or what?"

The bartender was smoking a cigarette. He looked over his shoulder at Duffy.

"Who's the kid?"

"The kid? It's Charlie, man. Fletcher never saw one this close. That's why he's so fucking quiet. Waiting for the choppers to come."

Then Duffy's hand was squeezing Mickey's throat: too suddenly, too tightly. Duffy leaned over the corner between them, his breath on Mickey's face, his eyes close to Mickey's, more threatening than the fingers and thumb pressing the sides of his throat. They seemed to look into his brain, and down into the depths of his heart, and to know him, all eleven years of him, and Mickey felt his being, and whatever strength it had, leaving him as if drawn through his eyes into Duffy's, and down into Duffy's body. The hand left his throat and patted his shoulder and Duffy was grinning.

"For Christ sake, Al, a rum and tonic. And a Coke for Charlie. And something to eat. Chips. And a hot dog. Want a hot dog, Charlie?"

"Mickey."

"What the fuck's a mickey?"

"My name."

"Oh. Jesus: your name."

Mickey watched Al make a rum and tonic and hold a glass of ice under the Coca-Cola tap.

"I never knew a Charlie named Mickey. So how come you're dressed up like a fucking jungle?"

Mickey shrugged. He did not move his eyes from Al, bringing the Coke and Duffy's drink and two paper cocktail napkins and the potato chips. He dropped the napkins in front of Mickey and Duffy, placed the Coke on Mickey's napkin and the potato chips beside it, and then held the drink on Duffy's napkin and said: "Three seventy-five."

"The tab, Al."

Al stood looking at Duffy, and holding the glass. He was taller than Duffy but not as broad, and he seemed to be the oldest man in the bar; but Mickey could not tell whether he was in his forties or fifties or even sixties. Nor could he guess the ages of the other men: he thought he could place them within a decade of their lives, but even about that he was uncertain. College boys seemed old to him. His father was forty-nine, yet his face appeared younger than any of these.

"Hey, Al. If you're going to hold it all fucking day, bring me a straw so I can drink."

"Three seventy-five, Duffy."

"Ah. The gentleman wants cash, Charlie."

He took the chained wallet from his rear pocket, unfolded it, peered in at the bills, and laid four ones on the bar. Then he looked at Al, his unblinking eyes not angry, nearly as calm as his motions and posture and voice, but that light was in them again, and Mickey looked up at the sunglasses on Duffy's hair. Then he watched Al.

"Keep the change, Al. For your courtesy. Your generosity. Your general fucking outstanding attitude."

It seemed that Al had not heard him, and that nothing Mickey saw and felt between the two men was real. Al took the money, went to the cash register against the wall behind the center of the bar, and punched it open, its ringing the only sound in the room. He put the bills in the drawer, slid a quarter up from another one, and dropped it in a beer mug beside the register. It landed softly on dollar bills. Mickey looked at Al's back as he spread mustard on a bun and with tongs took a frankfurter from the steamer, placed it on the bun, and brought it on a napkin to Mickey.

"Duffy." It was Fletcher, the man in the middle. "Don't touch the kid again."

Duffy smiled, nodded at him over his raised glass, then drank. He turned to Mickey, but his eyes were not truly focused on him; they seemed to be listening, waiting for Fletcher.

"Cavalry," he said. "Remember, Charlie Mickey? Fucking guys in blue coming over the hill and kicking shit out of Indians. Twentieth century gets here, they still got horses. No shit. Fucking officers with big boots. Riding crops. No way. Technology, man. Modern fucking war. Bye-bye horsie. Tanks." He stood straight, folded his arms across his chest, and bobbed up and down, his arms rising and falling, and Mickey smiled, seeing Duffy in the turret of a tank, his sunglasses pushed-up goggles. "Which one was your old man in? WW Two or—how did they put it?—the Korean Conflict. Conflict. I have conflict with cunts. Not a million fucking Chinese."

"He wasn't in either of them."

"What the fuck is he? A politician?"

"A landscaper. He's forty-nine. He was too young for those wars."

"Ah."

"He would have gone."

"How do you know? You were out drinking with him or something? When he found out they didn't let first-graders join up?"

Mickey's mouth opened to exclaim surprise, but he did not speak: Duffy was drunk, perhaps even crazy, yet with no sign of calculation in his eyes he had known at once that Mickey's father was six when the Japanese bombed Pearl Harbor.

"He told me."

"He told you."

"That's right."

"And he was too old for 'Nam, right? No wonder he lets you wear that shit."

"I have to go."

"You didn't finish your hot dog. I buy you a hot dog and you don't even taste it."

Mickey lifted the hot dog with both hands, took a large bite, and looked above the bar as he chewed, at a painting high on the center of the wall. A woman lay on a couch, her eyes looking down at the bar. She was from another time, maybe even the last century. She was large and pretty, and he could see her cleavage and the sides of her breasts, and she wore a nightgown that opened up the middle but was closed.

"Duffy."

It was Fletcher, his voice low, perhaps even soft for him; but it came to Mickey like the sound of a steel file on rough wood. Mickey was right about Duffy's eyes; they and his face turned to Fletcher, with the quickness of a man countering a striking fist. Mickey lowered his foot from the bar rail and stood balanced. He looked to his left at Al, his back against a shelf at the rear of the bar, his face as distant as though he were listening to music. Then Mickey glanced at Fletcher and the men Fletcher stood between. Who were these men? Fathers? On a weekday afternoon, a day of work, drinking in a dark bar, the two whose names he had not heard talking past Fletcher about fishing, save when Duffy or Fletcher spoke. He looked at Duffy: his body was relaxed, his hands resting on either side of his drink on the bar. Now his body tautened out of its slump, and he lifted his glass and drank till only the lime wedge and ice touched his teeth; he swung the glass down hard on the bar and said: "Do it again, Al."

But as he pulled out his chained wallet and felt in it for bills and laid two on the bar, he was looking at Fletcher; and when Al brought the drink and took the money to the register and returned with coins, Duffy waved him away, never looking at him, and Al dropped the money into the mug, then moved to his left until he was close to Duffy, and stood with his hands at his sides. He did not lean against the shelf behind him, and he was gazing over Mickey's head. Mickey took a second bite of the hot dog; he could finish it with one more. Chewing the bun and mustard and meat that filled his mouth, he put his right hand on his stack of books. With his tongue he shifted bun and meat to his jaws.

"Fletcher," Duffy said.

Fletcher did not look at him.

"Hey, Fletcher. How many did you kill? Huh? How many kids. From your fucking choppers."

Now Fletcher looked at him. Mickey chewed and swallowed, and drank the last of his Coke; his mouth and throat were still dry, and he chewed ice.

"You fuckers were better on horseback. Had to look at them." Duffy raised his tattooed arm and swung it in a downward arc, as though slashing with a saber. "Wooosh. Whack. Fuckers killed them anyway. Look a Cheyenne kid in the face, then waste him. I'm talking Washita River, pal. Same shit. Maybe they had balls, though. What do you think, Fletcher? Does it take more balls to kill a kid while you're looking at him?"

Fletcher finished his beer, lowered it quietly to the bar, looked away from Duffy and slowly took a cigarette pack from his shirt pocket, shook one out, and lit it. He left the pack and lighter on the bar. Then he took off his wristwatch, slowly still, pulling the silver expansion band over his left hand. He placed the watch beside his cigarettes and lighter, drew on the cigarette, blew smoke straight over the bar, where he was staring; but Mickey knew from the set of his profiled face that his eyes were like Duffy's earlier: they waited. Duffy took the sunglasses from his hair and folded them, lenses up, on the bar.

"You drinking on time, Fletcher? The old lady got your balls in her purse? Only guys worse than you fuckers were pilots. Air Force the worst of all. Cocksucking bus drivers. Couldn't even see the fucking hootch. Just colors, man. Squares on Mother Earth. Drop their big fucking load, go home, good dinner, get drunk. Piece of ass. If they could get it up. After getting off with their fucking bombs. Then nice bed, clean sheets, roof, walls. Fucking windows. The whole shit. Go to sleep like they spent the day—" He glanced at Mickey, or his face shifted to Mickey's; his eyes were seeing something else. Then his voice was soft: a distant tenderness whose source was not Mickey, and Mickey knew it was not in the bar either. "Landscaping." Mickey put the last third of the hot dog into his mouth, and wished for a Coke to help him with it; he looked at Al, who was still gazing above his head, so intently that Mickey nearly turned to look at the wall behind him. The other two men were silent. They drank, looked into their mugs, drank. When they emptied the mugs they did not ask for more, and Al did not move.

"All those fucking pilots," Duffy said, looking again down the bar at the side of Fletcher's face. "Navy. Marines. All the motherfuckers. Go out for a little drive on a sunny day. Barbecue some kids. Their mothers. Farmers about a hundred years old. Skinny old ladies even older. Fly back to the ship. Wardroom. Pat each other on the ass. Sleep. Fucking children. Fletcher used to be a little boy. Al never was. But I was." His arms rose above his head, poised there, his fingers straight, his palms facing Fletcher. Then he shouted, slapping his palms hard on the bar, and Mickey jerked upright: "*Chil*dren, man. You never smelled a napalmed kid. You never even *saw* one, fucking chopper-bound son of a bitch."

Fletcher turned his body so he faced Duffy.

"Take your shit out of here," he said. "God gave me one asshole. I don't need two."

"Fuck you. You never looked. You never saw shit."

"We came down. We got out. We did the job."

"The *job*. Good word, for a pussy from the Air fucking *Cav*."

"There's a sergeant from the First Air Cav's about to kick your ass from here to the river."

"You better bring in help, pal. That's what you guys were good at. All wars—"

He drank, and Mickey watched his uptilted head, his moving throat, till his upper lip stopped the lime, and ice clicked on his teeth. Duffy held the glass in front of him, just above the bar, squeezing it; his fingertips were red. "All fucking wars should be fought on the ground. Man to man. Soldier to soldier. None of this flying shit. I've got dreams. Oh yes, Charlie." But he did not look at Mickey. "I've got them. Because they won't go away." Again, though he looked at Fletcher, that distance was in his eyes, as if he were staring at time itself: the past, the future; and Mickey remembered the tattoo, and looked at the edges of it he could see beyond Duffy's chest: the end of the eagle's left wing, a part of the globe, the hole for line at the anchor's end, and *lis* written on the fluttering banner. He could not see the block letters. "I tell them I'm wasted, gentlemen. The dreams: I tell them to fuck off. They can't live with Agent Orange. They just don't know it yet. But fucking pilots. In clean beds. Sleeping. Like dogs. Like little kids. Girls with the wedding cake. Put a piece under your pillow. Fuckers put dreams under their pillows. Slept on them. Without dreams too. Not nightmares. Charlie Mickey here, he thinks he's had nightmares. Shit. I ate chow with nightmares. Pilots dreamed of pussy. Railroad tracks on their collars. Gold oak leaves. Silver oak leaves. Silver eagles. Eight hours' sleep on the dreams of burning children."

"Jesus Christ. Al, will you shut off that shithead so we can drink in peace?"

Al neither looked nor moved.

"Duffy," Fletcher said. "What's this Agent Orange shit? At Khe Sanh, for Christ sake. You never got near it."

"Fuck do you know? How far did *you* walk in 'Nam, man? You rode taxis, that's all. Did you sit on your helmet, man? Or did your old lady already have your balls stateside?"

"I hear you didn't do much walking at Khe Sanh."

"We took some hills."

"Yeah? What did you do with them?"

"Gave them back. That's what it was about. You'd know that if you were a grunt."

"I heard you assholes never dug in up there."

"Deep enough to hold water."

"And your shit."

Duffy stepped back once from the bar. He was holding the glass and the ice slid in it, but he held it loosely now, the blood receding from his fingertips.

"You want to smell some grunt shit, Fletcher? Come over here. We'll see what a load of yours smells like." "That's it," Al said, and moved toward Duffy as he threw the glass and Mickey heard it strike and break and felt a piece of ice miss his face and cool drops hitting it. Fletcher was pressing a hand to his forehead and a thin line of blood dripped from under his fingers to his eyebrow, where it stayed. Then Fletcher was coming, not running, not even walking fast; but coming with his chin lowered, his arms at his sides, and his hands closed to fists. Mickey swept his books toward him, was gripping them to carry, when two hands slapped his chest so hard he would have fallen if the hands had not held his collar. He was aware of Fletcher coming from his left, and Duffy's face, and the moment would not pass, would not become the next one, and the ones afterward, the ones that would get him home. Then Duffy's two fists, bunching the shirt at its collar, jerked downward, and Mickey's chest was bare. He had sleeves still, and the shirt's back and part of its collar. But the shirt was gone.

"Fucking little asshole. You want jungle? Take your fucking jungle, Charlie."

With both hands Duffy shoved his chest and he went backward, his feet off the floor, then on it, trying to stop his motion, his arms reaching out for balance, waving in the air as he struck the wall, slid down it, and was sitting on the floor. From the pain in his head he saw Duffy and Fletcher. He could see only Fletcher's back, and his arms swinging, and his head jerking when Duffy hit him. He had gone to the far end of the bar, to Mickey's left, and through the opening there, and was striding, nearly running, past the two men who stood watching Duffy and Fletcher. Mickey tried to stand, to push himself up with the palms of his hands. Beneath the pain moving through his head from the rear of his skull, he felt the faint nausea, the weakened legs, of shock. He turned on his side on the floor, then onto his belly, and bent his legs and with them and his hands and arms he pushed himself up, and stood. He was facing the wall. He turned and saw Al holding Duffy from behind, Al's hands clasped in front of Duffy's chest, and Mickey saw the swelling of muscles in Duffy's twisting, pulling arms, and Al's reddened face and gritted teeth, and Fletcher's back and lowered head and shoulders turning with each blow to Duffy's body and bleeding, cursing face.

His weakness and nausea were gone. He was too near the door to run to it; in two steps he had his hand on its knob and remembered his books and binder. They were on the bar, or they had fallen to the floor when Duffy grabbed him. He opened the door, and in the sunlight he still did not run; yet his breath was deep and quick. Walking slowly toward the bridge, he looked down at his pale chest, and the one long piece of shirt hanging before his right leg, moving with it, blending with the colors of his pants. He would never wear the pants again, and he wished they were torn too. He wanted to walk home that way, like a tattered soldier.

The Slope of Life

Nguyen Mong Giac

After the ban on playing prewar songs and disco music had been announced and some of the coffee shop owners on Tran Quang Khai street had been arrested and taken to court for not complying with the law, that part of town became as quiet as a cemetery. Once again, passersby could hear quite clearly the crackling noise of dry tamarind pods tapping against each other in the slightest breeze. At such moments, as yellow leaves were flying in the wind, one could feel the past resurrected. The female sweeper would move her broom hesitantly across the surface of the street. And once in a while the wind would change direction and skitter dead leaves towards an empty coffee shop.

The owner of the shop, a woman as beautiful as Thuy Kieu,[1] cast a glance at the empty swimming pool which was now used as a dump for trash and dead leaves. The furniture inside the shop wasn't the kind that one would normally find in a real coffee-shop: the two dark burgundy sofas with worn-out upholstery had probably been removed from some abandoned house, and a teakwood china cabinet containing some made-in-Japan dishes replaced the usual counter bar. Near the front of the shop, off to one side and close to a cluster of La Nga bamboo, sat two customers. One, a man wearing dark glasses, hardly moved or spoke, and even when he did, his voice was so soft that from afar one would have the impression that the man with salt-and-pepper hair sitting across from him was speaking to a statue. This statue-like person was sitting with both of his legs on the chair, his arms hugging his knees, his face turned towards a bicycle that had been transformed into some sort of carrier and was now leaning against the bamboo hedge. In front of them their two cups of coffee gradually ceased to steam.

When the woman who owned the shop shifted her gaze from the pool, the man with salt-and-pepper hair was still talking:

"No, I was wounded in Operation Lam Son 719."

"...?"

"Seven nineteen? I think you folks called it the battle of Route 9, South Laos."

"...."

"I was still in Cong Hoa Hospital on April 30th;[2] I'd been readmitted because my amputation had become infected again. I wasn't used to walking with a wooden leg—I was in agony. Any time I put my left foot on the ground it was so painful that tears would trickle from my eyes."

"...?"

"Right here. Oh, sorry, I forgot you can't see at all. Just below the knee. That's why I can still ride a bicycle."

"...?"

"An antipersonnel mine, probably one made in Communist China. You'd know it better than I do. I was told it was just this big!"

"...."

"Bigger than that? No wonder I lost consciousness right after the explosion. I was really lucky the helicopter could land and evacuate me to the hospital. As soon as I came to, I asked to see my severed leg. And they showed it to me."

"...?"

"Nothing special. I felt a slight tingling running up my spine. Mostly horror. Or more accurately, a kind of empathy. It was a strange feeling. Even though it had been a part of my body, it looked like a stranger's limb, severed like that. I suppose that an imaginative writer of fiction would say that what you do then is to take it in your hands and burst into tears. But the feeling was more like my memories of my wedding day. Again, a writer would say all kinds of nice things about that day, something about the bride and groom stealing glances at one another or holding hands and walking on the scattered skins of firecrackers, or thrilling at their shared vision of eternal happiness. All lies. I remember I had to take care of every single trivial thing, only to be criticized by my aunts and uncles for minor details. I was dead tired. Anyone who goes through a wedding day once is scared off weddings for the rest of his life—he'll never want to repeat it again."

"...."

"Too cynical? Well, maybe I am. Right now I'm upset about losing money—just before I came upon you I found myself four hundred and fifty dong poorer."

"...."

"No. There's enough thieves swarming in Saigon nowadays, but even a thief still has a heart—no one would deprive a cripple of his meal. I've got a friend who's also disabled, a blind man who earns his living selling lottery tickets. Anyone could fool him. All you need is a crumbled, soiled piece of paper to pass as a fifty dong bill. Yet he never lost a cent! No...I lost my money because of an accident."

"...?"

"Just before I met you. On the other side of Thi Nghe bridge."

"....!"

"You mean I haven't told you how I earn a living yet? How stupid of me—I was speaking as if you could see my bicycle. You'd know what I do if you saw it—I carry goods for hire."

"...?"

"That's it, just like the carriers we used to see when we were going to school in Bong Son. But this one is modified to handle a much heavier road. You remember how, in the past, those carriers were made for tourists or young female vendors who'd sit on a bar between the driver and the handlebar and place their wares in the back on an iron rack? Remember all the stories we used to hear about those drivers? Some of them would take advantage of their position to embrace the girls, or to steal a kiss on their hair or on their sweaty white necks, calling them flowers damp with morning dew. In that situation, you don't mind even if you have to break your back pedaling uphill! But nowadays, all we carry are goods. It's boring."

"....?"

"Take a guess."

"...."

"No, not at all. They're as bulky as they are fragile."

"...."

"I specialize in carrying earthen jars. Those big ones people use to hold rice or water—that's why I said they're as bulky as they are fragile. I broke eight of them this morning."

"....?"

"Yes, eight. Each one costs fifty dong, eight makes four hundred. My fare is five a piece, from Bien Hoa to Saigon. The total..."

"....?"

"When your stomach is flat enough you can figure anything out. The trickiest part is tying all eight of them to the carrier. A really skillful driver can do it all. But I had to hire someone to do the tying since I'm new at this trade. I paid him ten dong for his skill. It all amounted to four hundred and fifty dong."

"....?"

"No, it wasn't a blowout or a broken handle bar. I'm only sorry you can't see the carrier I have parked over at the bamboo hedge. No, you don't need a license to drive it. I salvaged the rear wheel from an old motorcycle, its spokes taken from an old cyclo. Then I cannibalized the handlebar from a French-made Alcyon bike imported during colonial times. The pedals are made of steel tubes seventeen inches in diameter, welded to the sprocket wheel. I use a hard wooden bar with one end cut into a U-shaped groove to support the frame when I park, and the kind of pump people use to inflate automobile tires."

The man in the dark glasses finally raised his voice:

"With your particular handicap, why did you choose this trade?"

The skinny man with salt-and-pepper hair lowered his voice:

"Show me an easier way. I have a wife and four kids to feed. Times have changed—there's no easy way for an honest man to earn his living."

"You're just being cynical again. Why don't you pick a trade where you don't need to use your legs?"

"Like what?"

"Sewing, weaving. Even singing at the bus stations, like many of your soldier friends are doing."

The man with salt-and-pepper hair smiled obliquely:

"What song should I sing that will move people enough to put money into my palm: 'Forward March to Saigon' or 'Ha Noi, My Hope and Love'? Do you know what would happen to me if I sang the kind of songs you hear at the bus stations? Don't forget I was a detainee, released from a reeducation camp."

"It was just a thought. Anyway there have to be plenty of trades you can take up. You're still luckier than I am—you have your sight. You could do sewing, weaving, sculpting—anything!"

The man with the salt-and-pepper hair became pensive for a moment. Then he said, slowly:

"There are many ways, it's true. But I wanted to prove I'm not worthless as a man. Believe me, you have to be in good shape to push a carrier up the hills on both sides of the bridge. I may be skinny and one-legged, but I'm capable of doing the work. The most difficult task in this trade is to be able to handle ten large earthen jars. I was able to handle eight."

"But you failed! You broke all eight of them."

"Sure. But this is the first time in six months at the trade that I ever broke my load. It was all because of an automobile with a green license plate that screeched to a halt in front of me while I was pedaling uphill with my wooden leg. I was so upset that I dragged myself to the curb and just left the whole thing, bicycle and broken jars and all, scattered all over the street. What happened was that the driver suddenly braked when a woman who wanted to buy gas signalled to him. I'm a victim, not a perpetrator. I'm still useful, not useless like they thought when they threw me out of the hospital on April 30th."

The man with the dark glasses hesitated for a moment.

"Look, we couldn't help it. We were so busy with everything we had to do that we didn't have any time for compassion. And besides, we couldn't just leave our own wounded in the hallways of the hospital."

"I'd already lost one leg—I didn't take up that much space."

"At least you were lucky enough to be airlifted to the rear by helicopter so all you lost was one leg, from the knee down. I wish I'd been as lucky..."

The man with the dark glasses couldn't continue. His friend said nothing, but tilted up his face. The two sat in silence for a while. Finally, the man with the salt-and-pepper hair timorously inquired, "You mean your sight could have been saved?"

"Yes, if...."

"Were you too far away from the hospital? Or did you have a mediocre corpsman?"

"Both."

"Did your wife know?"

"I didn't want her to."

"Why?"

"Look, I couldn't even tell her if I wanted. It took about a year, under normal circumstances, to get a message to anyone. You have to understand that communication wasn't easy. Also, information regarding the status of soldiers had to be kept secret so as not to demoralize the rear."

The voice of the man with the dark glasses suddenly became strident, as if he were reciting a lesson.

"Compared to the sacrifices of the revolutionary soldiers who lost their lives in the war, my suffering is nothing."

The bike rider looked at his friend with pity. He pushed the cup of coffee forward.

"Your cup is still full. Enjoy the coffee before it gets too cold."

Embarrassed, the blind man replied:

"Sure. Thanks."

He slowly moved his hand over the table. Since the cup had been shifted, he almost knocked it over. The bike rider waited for his friend to find the cup handle, then changed the subject:

"So your family has moved to the South."

"That was our original plan. But...."

"But what?"

"Have you been back to Bong Song lately?"

"No."

"I didn't feel at ease, returning to our village after liberation. I wouldn't have minded if I'd become somebody, but as you see, I'm just a cripple. I knew I would never again be able to see the cocoanut groves on my mother's land, but I was just as happy to hear the sound of the water conveyors splashing into the River Lai or just to dip my feet into the cool waters of the river of our youth. I'd been wanting to return to the village for so long. I couldn't afford the fare for my entire family, so I just took my youngest with me."

"Why didn't you bring your wife?'

"I would have loved to, but as I said, I couldn't afford it. My youngest child is only seven, so I could get a free fare for her because of my disability. Anyway, it was good that my wife didn't come."

"...."

"My relatives had all been displaced. I couldn't find a single one. I was told they'd moved away, first to Quy Nhon in 1972, then for some other place that I didn't know. I was told that all the tops of the cocoanut trees had been sheared off. I spent the night at the bus station, then left for Thanh Hoa the next morning. I didn't even have time to ask about our school mates at Nguyen Hue. Do you have any information about them?"

"Who do you want to know about?"

"Oh, that whole bunch of old classmates. Let me jog my memory for a moment. How about the guy who sat at the end of the first table in grade seven? That kid who had a habit of blowing his nose all the time."

"Quang. He became a village chief after the Geneva agreement."

"That important, huh! Did he incur a lot of 'blood debt?'"[3]

"I don't know. All I know is that after 1965 his whole family was massacred by a hand grenade tossed into his house while the family was having dinner."

The two friends remained silent for a while. When the blind man continued the conversation, his voice had become soft again.

"What about Luan? The one who took such great pride in his Kaolo fountain pen with its crystal nib."

"He became rich and owned several restaurants in Phu Cat. When the American troops moved into the area, he turned into a real wheeler-dealer in smuggled goods. He practically got rich overnight."

"Ah, a capitalist! Hey, what about that bum who peed on little Ly when he jumped into that trench during an air raid?"

"That was Duc. We used to call him Duc Cong."[4]

"Right. I remember how angry he'd get when we called him that. What became of him?"

"He joined the guerrillas in the early years. Back when we began to outlaw the communists."

"With decree 10/59. How well did he perform?"

"You'd know that better than I would."

"How about yourself?"

"Nothing exciting. I moved to Nha Trang with my uncle after 1955. Went to high school and graduated with a diploma. Then I went to college, but I flunked math two times in a row and got drafted. I was assigned to an artillery unit. I was wounded four times during my ten years of service—lost a leg before I lost everything else. I wasn't as lucky as you."

The blind man turned his face to the other man.

"What do you mean 'lucky as me'? You have to be kidding."

The bike rider stopped and thought for a moment.

"I remember when we were going to school in Bong Song—you had the reputation of being able to memorize everything by heart. I always thought, as long as someone has something to remember...."

The blind man remained motionless and quiet. The statue-like man was still squatting with his arms hugging his knees. His face showed signs of sadness. His friend spoke softly:

"You don't feel well, do you? Do you want to leave?"

"I think we have to. I have some errands to run."

The bike rider stirred his coffee with his spoon. The shop owner approached them.

"Would you like some tea now?"

The bike rider waved his hand.

"No need. How much do I owe you?"

The blind man quickly dropped his feet.

"It's my treat. How much is it?"

"Fourteen dong. Coffee is getting expensive nowadays."

"That much! I was told it would cost a dong a cup."

"Pure coffee is always expensive," the shop keeper explained patiently. "Though back when we were allowed to play music it was only ten dong a cup."

The blind man groped in his pocket.

"Here, let me get that," the bike rider said quietly.

The owner had run out of small change and had to give him four cigarettes instead. He handed them all to his friend. The blind man groped for his aluminum cane.

"Let me give you a ride—I'll take you wherever you want to go," the bike rider offered.

"Thanks, but I wouldn't want to sit on your bike when your legs are like that. I can walk."

"Up to you, friend. See you later."

They parted. The blind man groped his way out of the shop with his aluminum cane. The bike rider limped over to the bamboo hedge to retrieve his bike. Neither of them remembered to get the other's address.

Translated by Le Tho Giao
Edited by Wayne Karlin

---

[1] Thuy Kieu is the main character of Vietnam's most famous epic poem: *The Tale of Kieu* by Nguyen Du.

[2] The day the People's Army took Saigon: the last day of the war.

[3] "Crimes against the people"

[4] Pile of shit

Waiting For Dark

Larry Brown

He was a bro and he was looking at me. Studying me when I opened my eyes. Like he'd been watching me for a long time just to see how long it would take. Somehow, his eyes smiled. But I had to suck in a big breath when I saw the rest of him.

He didn't have any arms or legs, just nubs. Just like *johnny got his gun.*

He winked at me, long and slow. Said Hey man. What's happening? I just shook my head. I didn't know what was happening. Or what had happened. I felt kind of dizzy, and when I tried to raise up, my head felt like it was spinning. I felt like I didn't have any control over my head. So I eased back down on the pillow.

They'd shot me with some kind of shit, evidently, something that would keep me calm and make me be a good boy. I wondered if maybe I hadn't been a good boy already. I wondered if I'd fucked up. I probably had. I do that pretty frequently. Usually about every day. It's how I get by.

I knew I'd just have to lie there until the shit wore off, whatever it was. It wasn't a bad drug. It was sort of nicely numbing. I looked at the guy again. He had his head turned, watching me. He had a very gentle gaze. Not hostile at all. I asked him reckon what kind of shit they had shot me with and he said probably cat tranquilizer. I thought about it for a second, then told him I bet it would really make your old pussy purr. He got to grinning, and then I got to grinning, too. I felt kind of loopy and loose. But I also wondered how he could be in such good spirits. Finally he said he was just kidding me, but they had given me something to cool me out, no shit. I didn't know what he was talking about and he said I'd been a bad boy and didn't want to go along with the program.

I laid there a minute and wondered what I'd done. I didn't know if I wanted to find out or not. So I didn't ask. I didn't ask that, anyway. I asked a real beauty. Asked him how long he'd been like that.

He said twenty-two years.

I closed my eyes. I tried not to concentrate on him. I tried to concentrate on myself, on my situation, and I tried to remember all the things all the doctors had said. What if the scar tissue in my head did cause seizures? How did they know I couldn't live with it for the rest of my life? Haven't people beat cancer? Survived massive heart attacks, and lived through terrible plane crashes? Sure they have. And they'll do it again, too. Just because you get a death sentence, it doesn't mean you have to die. It all depends on the individual person. Everybody's not made alike. Some people can live through what others can't.

I was scared. You wake up in a place like this, a place you've been trying to avoid for years, and you don't know what's happened, or why you're here...it's frightening. And alone. That's the main thing. Alone.

Finally I opened my eyes and looked at him. I told him my name was Walter and that I was from Mississippi. He shook his head and grinned, said his name was Braiden Chaney and that he was from Clarksdale. Said he'd chopped a lot of cotton down at Clarksdale. And he apologized for not being able to shake hands with me.

I didn't know what to say to that. So I just looked at what was left of him. I couldn't quit looking at those four black nubs. His head was peeled slick as an egg. He was kind of like a large baby laid up there on a sheet. But he wasn't a baby. He was about forty-something years old.

I knew I shouldn't get started talking to him. I didn't want to get started talking to anybody. All I wanted was to get back home, away from here. Which here I knew by then was a VA hospital somewhere in the South, probably.

But I knew I had to talk to him. There wasn't any way to keep from it. I told him I lived at London Hill, and that we used to raise cotton on our place a long time ago. Told him I was an old cottonpicking cottonchopper myself, but that not too many people were growing it now.

He nodded and agreed with me. Said everybody he knew was growing that green stuff now. Said that old shit. Said man there was more money in that old shit than a man could shake a stick at. He said he had some friends, and then his eyes went to moving around in his head. He lowered his voice and said he'd give me something but that we had to wait for dark.

I didn't know if he was serious or not. I asked him did he mean wacky tobaccy. Left-handed cigarettes. Boo-shit-tea.

That will make you slap your pappy down, he said. He was grinning like a fiend by then. But it looked like he only had about six or seven teeth scattered around in his mouth. From somebody else having to brush his teeth for him, I figured.

We didn't talk for a while after that. I knew one thing would lead to another. It always does. I wondered what could have eaten him up like that, but I knew. A machine gun, or a mine. Or hell, maybe a claymore. Maybe even one of our own claymores. They loved to slip up on sleeping lookouts and take some white paint and paint the side that said FRONT TOWARD ENEMY white and turn it around and wake the lookouts up, so they'd pull the string and shoot themselves in the face with about three pounds of buckshot.

But I didn't want to talk about that. Or rockets, or machine guns, or fragmentation grenades, or exploding beer cans. Those were the last things in the world I wanted to talk about. I just stayed there and didn't say anything for a while. But he never stopped watching me.

* * *

My man didn't want to talk, I understood that. It was cool. Inside he was probably shaking like a cat shitting peach pits. Hell, come in here, wake up like a duck in a different world quacking. Don't know nobody. I don't think he even knowed his face was all clawed up. Somebody with some fingernails had laid into him. What it looked like. And they had probably give him so much dope since he was so big his mind wasn't right yet. So I knew to lay back, just have patience.

Old patience hard after this long, though. Old patience done flew out the window after this long. Lay in here and lay in here and lay in here. Have to watch all that pussy on TV. Miss America. "Days Of Our Lives."

Oh Lance, won't you please come over here and sniff of my magnificent breasts?

Oh Lance, I believe you is bringing me to the brink of a tremendous organism. Yes. Oh, Lance, dolling, oh, oh, oh no don't put the *root* to me!

Get you some this here love bone.

Wait a minute now, Lance!

You know you been asking for it.

Lance, you get that thing away from me now, that's a *weapon*. Let's talk this thing over.

Shoot. Don't need that. Takes too long just thinking about it. I need to invent me something like a radio show. Go on broadcast every night. Be on FM and be a voice in the little blue lights. Be nice to do something for kids. Have some late show they could stay up and listen to. Have pajamas on and stuff. Cowboy hats. I'da loved to had me some kids. Little old naked babies you could wash in the tub and stuff. Make you so happy you wouldn't know what to do. Little black asses running around all over the house. Wonder if the Lord made the black man at midnight. We know You love us. We love You, too. I mean, six, seven thousand years from now...won't make no difference, will it? Everybody gonna be so mixed up by then that far in the future that they all gonna be the same color by then, ain't they? Whyn't You set me down here five or six thousand years later? They won't even have no damn guns by then probably. And I could move on me some one-sixteenth Polynesian milkmaid from Hamburg with a uncle in New York whose brother was a Jewish guy. Naw, I know, can't do it. Got to keep us all separated. But how come they ain't a word in black language for them bad as they word in white language for us? Why didn't we think us up a bunch of good words instead of picking all their damn cotton? We wasted about two hundred years picking fucking cotton.

I know. I'm a sinner. I have lustuous thoughts every day. Cause they show it on TV. Bob Barker's got them girls on the tube all the time. Who is that...that Janet Pennerton? Naw, that other one. That poody-woody one. She is so fine. One of em done had a baby now she don't look as fine. What'd I do with that *National Enquirer* that had that picture of her in it? I never did finish reading that story about that little space-boy come in them people's window had them two little space-puppydogs with helmets on sticking out his butthole anyway. Hell they done got it over there. All the way across the room. I guess the damn nurses been reading it. Well shit. Muse yo self. Spect yo self. Wawa wawa wa.

All right, motherfucker, where's the damn Percy Sledge album? Getting tired of this shit. Y'all gonna give away *two million dollars* or you gonna show the damn movie? Why hell I done seen that one three times. That's the guy that gets all them kids in that boat and then rows em all the way across the Pacific Ocean with two stale crackers to eat the whole way over there. I don't want to see that shit no more. That's bad as that one the other night where this guy had this rare disease, one of them rare disease movies. Why don't y'all put something good on? Have to watch some old fat-ass white lady trying to win her a car or something. Trip to Mexico. Won't put on nobody good like Humphrey Bogart rolling them little steel balls around in his hand. Old Humphrey could get the damn women. Had them women crawling all over him. He was so swab and debonair with them women. I liked the one where he was pulling old Katherine Hepburn around in that boat and got them leeches on him and got the heebie-jeebies every time she pulled one off. They don't make movies like that no more. If you dumbass Casual Company rejects over there had any culture you'd turn it over there on some National Geographic stuff or something educational. Naw I'm a trump I'm a spade naw you broke the widder what is all that shit about anyway. Play poker like y'all some hot-shit gamblers till it drives me up the wall and bet damn nickels. Bring it over here sometime if you want to gamble. I maybe can't deal but by God I can play if somebody'd hold the cards for me. I got the money. Naw. Y'all can't communicate with me.

Y'all ain't stuck in here. Y'all just got to come in here in the daytime and make a bunch of noise and fuck up my movie watching. Y'all done just smoked too much dope or wrecked your car cause of some dope dependency from some dope habit you picked up overseas and ain't never come down yet. Ain't never smoked no dope cause you had to. You just don't know what it is. Fear. Help you get you some heightened awareness. You know your ass can be blowed off any second, you choose the heightened *perception.* When that trip wire's like a hair, and you on your knees, and everybody behind you trying to be silent and black and invisible, and they don't take a step till *you* say that next six inches is clear....

You boys don't know what it was like. Y'all didn't grow up with the threat of a war hanging over your head. They was drafting then. Couldn't just worry about pussy. Had to worry about going to *war* and getting your *ass* shot *off.* Especially if your ass was black as mine. Yeah. Aw yeah, y'all went out and trained, I know. But you ain't got that threat over you. My mama, Lord, she cried, just took on something awful. Wasn't never gonna see her baby again. Got down on her knees and begged You not to take me. Couldn't stand to see me go. Closer to time it got, more she cried. Every night.

What'd she think, reckon? You's gonna step down between me and the U.S. Government? She prayed enough for it, didn't she? Never saw a woman so heartsick. Looked good then, didn't I, Lord? Two hundred and nineteen pounds of blood and bone and muscle. That old woman raised me on peas and biscuits. Go home that's what she'd feed me. Tell me to eat. Last time I left I know I was laying in there in my bed and I woke up just before it was daylight. Light was on in the kitchen, and I could smell her cooking biscuits. Wasn't nothing but a little old shack. I was gonna build her something better later. I woke up, just wide awake. I was leaving that day. Boarding a plane at Memphis, going for orientation and weapons fire before we jumped off. What we called jumping off. Jumping off the world. I had all that in head of me and I woke up in my mama's house with her cooking biscuits for me. Smelled the same way every morning. Always smelled the same. She never woke me. Didn't have to. Biscuits woke me. I heard her tell people, That child can smell them biscuits in his sleep and when he smells em he wakes up. My mama was so good to me.

I laid in there that morning. Had my uniform hanging up in there. Soldier of the most powerful nation in the world. And all I could think was Why, you know, why? I didn't even understand the whole thing. Just went cause it was my duty. I'm sure there was plenty who went didn't understand the whole thing. Just went cause it was their duty. This my country, I'm gonna fight for my country. Sentiment was strong for God and Country, young boys, listen up. Everybody's daddy had been in World War II. Some daddies, anyway. Now they telling us we won't never be in another one like that one again. That one taught us a lesson.

We ain't having no more futile wars. Till we have one in the Middle East. Or down in Nicaragua. Ain't no need in having a war lessen they just bomb the hell out of you like Pearl Harbor or something. Then all you can do is just bomb the shit out of them right back, and fight, and get a whole bunch of people killed and finally not accomplish a goddamn thing except get your economy ruined forty years later.

Everything just pisses me off. The world gets worse all the time. Had one man one time that would have stopped it. Of course they had to kill him. And then things just went to shit. I don't know what they want to watch this crap like "The Love Connection" for. If all these people so attractive and not married why ain't they out legging down off TV? They seem like they had a good time, though. I guess I sort of like "The Love Connection." I like old Chuck Woodery. But half the time these motherfuckers'll let you get halfway through a program and then switch channels. Fraid they might miss something else. That morning I woke up in my mama's house was the last morning I was whole, and with her. I'd shined my shoes the night before. Me and her had watched some old movie on TV. I'd brought us home a sixpack of Miller. Loved her a cold beer, now. She drank two and I drank three. It was old Jimmy Stewart in something. He was in the Civil War. And he got shot, and he had this beautiful horse, and his arm was almost blowed off, and this doctor said he couldn't save his arm but saw that horse he was riding and remarked over what a fine animal it was. This guy was like a low-down motherfucker on the battlefield of life. Couldn't save his arm, see, just couldn't save it. Then he seen old Silver over there. And old Jimmy Stewart told him, Doc, if you'll save my leg, arm, whatever it was, you can have that horse. Well the old Doc decided he might could save it then. What I'd love to seen after he got through fixing old Jimmy Stewart's arm was about four corporals come in there and get him and march him out to a wall and shoot the sumbitch full of holes. But old Jimmy never did write home again and his mama thought he was dead and finally President Lincoln got him in his office and told him he'd better write his mama if he knew what was good for him. Bunch of years later they (after they got happily reunited) found his old horse pulling a coal wagon in Kansas City or somewhere and bought him back for like five bucks. They was gonna keep him in a warm barn and all for the rest of his life. It was a real heartwarming story. It was a happily ever after.

What you got to do is stay up late at night and check your *TV Guide* for this good stuff. You'll maybe see it once in the next fifty years. I done seen it. Just can't remember the name of it. But me and Mama had a good time that night, watching that movie. We was cooking us some popcorn in between times. She'd run in there and turn the burner on and run back in and set down and I'd run in there and put the popcorn on and she'd run in there and shake it and run back and then I'd run in there and shake it and that way didn't neither of us miss much. And we had butter. REAL butter. Not this fake shit now. My mama still had a churn between her legs every morning.

But it come time to go. That morning it did. She fixed me some coffee, I was smoking for the first time in front of her. She didn't see me leave from Memphis. She just saw me leave from Clarksdale. Cotton was up. Most of them around us had a pretty good stand. Looked like they's gonna make it good that year. I felt better, finally, looking at it, knowing I wasn't going to have to chop no more of the shit. My little sister was standing out there with us. Old boys I knew from Tunica was taking me to Memphis. They was all out there in the car waiting. One of them times, you know. I didn't have to report until the next morning. We was going to Beale Street that night. But there my mama and them having to tell me goodbye. And what a thing for her, me having to go off to something like that. Ain't no words to say, except the ones everybody thinking about but just don't want to say. Don't die.

What you gonna tell em? You can't do nothing but kiss em and hope they right.

I wish they'd put that other movie back on, that one I seen that time. One where that guy had all his arms and legs blowed off and his face too. That guy talked to Jesus a couple of times. I don't think Jesus ever come and set on his bed like He does mine, though.

PART FOUR
Hauntings

4

We want the bones. We want all the bones. You will hear this. Good people will say it. They are all good people. They say it. They say: *We want the bones.* And they mean it, they mean what they say. They carry it into sleep, into their children, into the voting booth. We want the bones. *That's what we want. We don't want the ghosts. You keep the ghosts. We don't want them. Just the bones.*

Your ghosts are driving us out of our minds.

Waiting for a Friend

Ngo Tu Lap

Birds begin to chirp loudly and clearly, a sound that somehow recalls the scent of bone-dry straw to me. The horizon catches fire with a scorching red flame. A new day has begun, a day that I know will be filled with gusting winds and dazzling sunshine.

From somewhere deep in my consciousness I am aware that sunshine and wind used to bring me great pleasure when I was a small child sitting in my father's blacksmith shop, peeping through the crack of the door. Yet nowadays I can't stand either the wind or the sun. They exhaust me. I have no doubt that, with their help, I will slowly turn into dust and vapor and evaporate into the sky. I like only the moon, whose gentle light makes all natural objects glisten strangely. It is on such moonlit nights that I wander over the earth.

Usually I return when the path begins to glitter in the early morning light. My corpse is at the foot of Dun mountain, pinned underneath a gray rock that is shaped like the head of an elephant and covered now with luxuriant foliage. Most of my corpse that is: my feet were burned to ashes under the wrecked tank and my head blown away to the edge of a stream. From there the floodwaters floated it out to the Cai River along with the branches of trees that had been torn off by artillery shells; it was carried along, bobbing and sinking and bobbing up again, almost to the sea. Eventually it came to rest in the mud flats of the Vam Delta where it became stuck between two big roots. These days large prawns make their home in its eye sockets.

My corpse is my home now, and a perfect home it is, peaceful and quiet, even though it is no longer pristine. At first it was only discovered by a flock of hungry crows who swooped down from the rim of the elephant's-head rock and fought one another to get at me. Their noisy battles echoed against the mountain walls. But how could a few crows move such a heavy rock? Frustrated and angry, they abandoned their efforts and left their treasure to the maggots. To be honest I found that group's eating habits to be quite disgusting. Luckily, when they saw there were no more bits and pieces to be stripped from my bones, the whole lot of them wiggled off.

Then the monsoon began. And then the weeds began to sprout and grow.

Nowadays my state of complete oblivion is only interrupted by the crowing of a carefree wild rooster or the cautious pad of an animal that has strayed from its herd or pack.

Oblivion—this is where I find my greatest comfort. Out of all my friends in the squad, only I am so lucky. It was impossible to identify the others' bodies, so people gathered up the corpses—bits of meat and bone were scattered all over the place—threw the pieces together haphazardly, then stuck them into nylon bags and took them to the cemetery outside the city, right where the stream runs into the Cai River.

But to us, you see, words on tombstones, paper tokens and floral wreaths all mean nothing. Nor do we need food or wish to buy things or fear illness or death or feel desire or a need for vengeance. Even our memories of the past don't move us, not a bit.

There is only one regular event for us—once a year we return to this place and gather together. The crater has turned into a pond full of water ferns, complete with schools of tadpoles. The wrecked tank is no longer there. Earlier this year it was removed, dismantled and sold overseas. Along with some of the ash from my feet, it is now on its way to Japan.

We never make appointments with each other to gather here and once here we have no language in which to tell stories to each other. If you hear anyone ever say he has seen us, you will know he is lying. Like time, we have no visual manifestation. We can only sense one another, the nine of us—almost the whole squad. Only Ha, the cripple, is missing.

I remember how, on that dreadful night, he had crawled back to us, unable to speak, still clutching a bunch of wild bananas to his stomach—he'd gone off looking for something to eat and had stepped on a concealed booby trap. Oh, the pangs of hunger that drove our actions in the mortal world, Ha. But don't worry, my friend—hunger no longer tortures us now and someday you'll be beyond its torment also.

In reality, the past has no hold on my emotions, even though I can't forget it. Ten years is three thousand six hundred days. Three thousand six hundred days ago when suddenly I saw the earthen trail shake violently. It was the tank, suddenly appearing around a bend, its trembling searchlight crawling across the valley. Back then, it spread fear among us. Back then, we soldiers realized for the first time that we were still the mortal children of the earth and we fell to our knees and shook like the light on the tank.

With the charge burning my hand, I crawled over the damp earth. Did I grip it tightly like the heavy burden of responsibility or was I acting out of an instinctive self-defense, or was I lusting after glory and medals? No matter— suddenly a pillar of fire arose, an explosion as dazzling as that sunrise I now see...and the elephant's head rock came crashing down.

Bodies fell, piling one upon the other like fruit falling from a tree, all revealed in the flames from the tank. Then the enemy soldiers charged up the slope, their bayonets striking in a frenzy.

But Ha wasn't there. The earth thrown up from the explosion had covered him and saved him.

The fires were still flickering when for the first time we gathered at the edge of the trench. When for the first time we waited for Ha.

No, he doesn't forget us either. Once a year we hear his limping footsteps come around the same bend where the tank had appeared. His knapsack is full of paper tokens: hand grenades, uniforms, nine canteens. He can still discern the elephant's head rock, under the foliage. He weeps as he lights the sticks of incense. His tears are thick with salt and they fall on the leaves of the water ferns.

It isn't until late in the afternoon that Ha leaves. The jungle night swallows his small lonely form. He doesn't know his friends are waiting for him. Waiting, but still hoping he will forget and go on living. Of the whole squad, only he remains.

We have been waiting ten years. We will wait fifteen years, twenty years, more, longing between time and oblivion. But sooner or later Ha will rejoin his squad for—in this world—no one can live forever.

Translated by Jay Scarborough
Edited by Wayne Karlin

Paco's Dreams

Larry Heinemann

It may come as something of a surprise, James, but Paco, for all his trouble, has never asked, Why me?—the dumbest, dipstick question only the most ignorant fucking new guy would ever bother to ask.

Why *you*? Don't you know? It's your turn, Jack!

Not in all the hours that he lay terrifically wounded—the rest of us long gone, Paco as good as left for dead—did he ask. Not on that dust-off chopper with the medics delicately and expertly plucking debris from his wounds, Paco bursting with gratitude, whimpering and shivering from the cold. And not on any of these nights lately, after work, when Paco would sit up in bed, sore and exhausted, gazing down at himself—bitterly confronted with that mosaic of scars—waiting for his nightly doses of Librium and Valium to overwhelm him (like a showering torrent of sparks, some nights, or an avalanche of fluffy, suffocating feathers).

No, James, Paco has never asked, *Why me?* It is we—the ghosts, the dead—who ask, Why him?

So Paco is made to dream and remember, and we make it happen in this way, particularly on those nights when his work—washing the last of the dishes, clearing up and stowing down after closing—goes particularly well with no one to pester him, and he settles into a work rhythm, a trance almost ("I wash and God dries," he'll tell you, James). Even the burgeoning pain in his legs and back—that permanent aggravating condition of his life—blossoms and swells, warming him like a good steady fire of bottom coals. It is at those moments that he is least wary, most receptive and dreamy. So we bestir and descend. We hover around him like an aura, and declare (some of the townsmen have bragged and sworn they have seen us). Paco would finish his work virtually in the dark; Ernest, the boss, long gone to deposit the day's receipts; Paco turning around in his astonished pleasure at discovering the work so agreeable—entranced by the surprising ease of it—reaching around, dipping his hand into the last of the greasy bus pans for the next thing to soak and scrub and rinse clean. But everything is done, and dry; and his work is ended.

He would slip off his apron, soaking wet and sour with sweat, and hang it on a nail, straighten his T-shirt, take up his black hickory cane, and take that droning, warm feeling for the work out the back door and across the street to the Geronimo Hotel, up to his dingy little room overlooking the brick railroad alley at the back of Earl and Myrna's Bar downstairs. He would flop headlong across the bed, with the sore pain of his wounds itching like the burning sting of a good hard slap.

It is at that moment we would slither and sneak, shouldering our way up behind the headboard, emerging like a newborn—head turned and chin tucked, covered head to toe with a slick gray ointment, powdery and moist, like the yolk of a hard-boiled egg, and smelling of petroleum. We come to stand behind him against the wall—we ghosts—as flat and pale as a night-light, easy on the eyes. We reach out as one man and begin to massage the top of his head; his scalp cringes and tingles. We work our way down the warm curve of his neck—so soothing and slack—and apply ourselves most deeply to the solid meat back of his shoulders. And Paco always obliges us; he uncoils and stretches out even more, and eases into our massage bit by bit, leaning into our invigorating touch wholeheartedly. And when Paco is most beguiled, most rested and trusting, at that moment of most luxurious rest, when Paco is all but asleep, *that* is the moment we whisper in his ear, and give him something to think about—a dream or a reverie.

Some nights he dreams escape dreams: being chased, sweating and breathless, into a large and spacious warehouse with a paving-stone floor crisscrossed with narrow ore-cart tracks (like trolley tracks, say), enormous whitewashed skylights overhead, and dusty cobwebs hanging down as thick as Spanish moss. There are huge cranes aloft, bolted fast to the thick cedar rafters, and long, greasy loops of winch chain hanging nearly to the floor. There is the echo-ous ring of Paco's every footfall, and water from burst pipes in distant rooms dripping into shallow puddles. Wandering from room to room, soon enough Paco hears trucks pulling up outside, the rattling of tailgate chains and the solid slamming of many doors. Paco moves on, compelled, and comes to a part of the building that opens out like a cathedral gallery, as spacious as a dirigible hangar (fine and airy). Flimsy ropes as light as felt hang down from the high cross timbers in clusters, like the creosoted ticking plumbers use to pack soil pipe joints with, as sour and overpowering as a bitter narcotic. And never far behind Paco is the grumbling of many voices, the heavy click of many boots, the hard tapping of many ax handles on the rough floor or the pipes that festoon the walls. There always comes a moment when Paco knows that in another instant they will turn the corner, come through a fire-door entrance, and be upon him (Paco twitching in his sleep, his heart pounding), as mad and murderous as a lynch mob. So he reaches up and gathers an armful of those ropes into a loose bundle, like a bouquet, and begins to shinny up—those ropes moist and as hairy as cat fur. And it is *always* slow going, James, an excruciating, dream-speed slow motion. He presses the clinging, greasy ropes so tightly that juice runs down his arms—oily as milkweed fuzz. He pulls himself up, curling his legs and feet around the bundle, then peels away his fingers and hands and arms, freeing himself with prodigious effort, then stretches his whole body upward with a sweeping, calculated lunge, gathering more ropes into a cable and hoisting himself up the next little bit. The higher he climbs, the more suffocating and stuffy is that creosote smell—as pungent as temple incense. By the time he has climbed up among the lowest rafters and narrow, spindly catwalks (with the milky skylights just beyond), Paco is nauseated and pouring sweat, his skin itching like crazy and as sticky as pine tar. But as hard and fast as he climbs, never in the dream does he escape, climbing through the veils of cobwebs and free of the ropes to clamber along the catwalks, and then up and out the open skylight. And always, James, those truckloads of men come to stand beneath him, switching those ax handles against their thighs, muttering and bitching.

Or he dreams of waiting rooms—the passenger lounge of a ferry boat, say: the solid iron floor deeply rumbling with the surging effort of the diesels and propeller screws, aft. The heavy furniture, long couches and wide easy chairs, slides this way and that as the boat rolls and scuds along in the heavy chop, shuddering. The boat makes its way through the contrary currents between high, rugged cliffs of a deep fjord (whitewashed with streaks of guano as thick as candle drippings), and many of the older passengers are plainly ill and troubled. Paco swings around the room, hanging on to the pillars (wrapped in varnished cord) to steady himself while he passes the hat (feeling sheepish and cheap, James), panhandling. "How 'bout it now. How 'bout a bit of change for old times' sake," he hears himself say, beseeching and apologetic at the same time, collecting the coins and bills in a collapsed wool watch cap. Outside, on the open-air deck, where the cars and campers are parked bumper to bumper, stem to stern, flocks of sea gulls soar and hover overhead, like a cloud of gnats, screaming and beckoning. Some of the passengers, desperate for entertainment, fetch loaves of bread and fling slices into the air—Frisbee-fashion—and the gulls dive down, crowing, to nip the slices in midair and then fight for scraps on the wing among themselves, swooping and dodging. And never does so much as a crumb touch the water; there are that many gulls and they are that good at the game. And in the dream, James, Paco always winds up with drooping pocketfuls of change—the money so solid in his pocket he can hardly drive his fingers through it—pressing his face against the cold porthole glass, staring forward, trying to impel the boat onward by the keenness and concentration of his gaze.

And some nights he dreams execution dreams. A group of soldiers, Paco among them, is led down a narrow, well-lit corridor—the hot-water piping overhead plenty warm, humming; the floors painted battleship gray, glistening with wax. The men are escorted into a small room of bare concrete, as crowded as a rush-hour elevator, everyone stuffy, hot and itchy. The group consists of one man from each platoon in three battalions of infantry—chosen by lot, volunteered—to be executed as punishment for some crime never mentioned. Cowardice? Mutiny? A fragging? The men stand bound with leather thongs twisted and looped around their necks and knotted severely around their wrists in back—as if this might be a way-station rest stop on the Bataan Death March, say (as tightly packed as if that basement vault were a death-camp-bound box car—so that if you fainted, James, you could not fall, and once you collapsed, you never came to). Some of the men are pale and woozy already in the claustrophobic air and extreme tension of anticipation. Some are as miserable-looking and stoic as if they're standing at ease, by company, on the Sunday-afternoon regimental drill field, waiting for a rainstorm to let up—"I just want to fucking sit down!" And some men are really pissed off—"I ain't done a goddamned thing, hear me!" Paco, at the back of the room, presses his forehead against the concrete—smelling of dust, with the raw imprint of the birch plywood grain as plain as day—the twisted thong around his neck lathered with sweat and nearly choking him. He can sense how very thick the wall is by how solid and profoundly cold is the concrete (a deep yellow, purple, and black—the colors of a deep bruise). That cold seeps into him, at first a pleasant comfort in that stuffy room, but then he becomes stiffly cold as the warmth is drawn from his body as neatly as a soundless whistle. Two plain-faced medics enter through the riveted steel door, dressed in long lab coats, one carrying a small medical case about the size of a first-aid kit spread open in both hands. The case contains a large glass-and chrome syringe notched off in quarter inches, a set of five large needles, and one big bottle of bluish, pearlescent poison. The two medics efficiently muscle through the crowd, almost rowing with their shoulders. And when the executions begin, the medics stand on either side of a man; the first medic cuts the twisted-up thong with a jackknife, the man drops his arms—his sides relieved of the tension—sighing sharply as though enduring a burn. Then the medic takes up the hypodermic (the plunger with a large thumb ring), pinches a handful of flesh at the arm or the back of the neck, and stabs the needle in and squeezes the plunger home all in one neat motion. The executed man half gasps, as much from the surprise as from the sting of the needle, and suddenly shivers as if he'd been plunged into a cold bath of cracked ice. In that same instant, the executed man rolls his eyes back into his head and droops to the floor. Paco leans against the concrete wall, feeling the sharp pain of the cold spreading through his body—the cold like a nail in his head where his skull touches it. Paco remembers (in the dream now, James) how the city dog pound used to kill its leftover dogs. Someone would hold the animal up by the loose skin at the neck, stretching the eyes, petting and stroking it, while someone else would jab the needle in—at the neck back of the ears—and inject the poison. (Not a breath later the dog would slump in the guy's arms. And if we stood at the door of the city pound loading dock, James, you'd see a pile of dogs, all shapes and sizes and colors, looking like so many ripped-up rugs, but with legs and ears and long black tongues.) The two medics execute first one man, then another, and another, stepping over the corpses. Sometimes they circle; sometimes they make a beeline; sometimes they move obliquely, like chess pieces; sometimes it's one right after another—a cluster fuck, we called it, James. Never in the dream do the executions cease, but never does the crowd thin—Paco standing, cramped, with the cold pouring into the back of his skull like dry-ice vapor spilling over a tabletop. Never do the medics change their flat, benign expressions—eyeing Paco out of the corners of their eyes—and never do they run out of fresh needles or does the bottle run dry of that pearlescent, metallic-tasting poison.

But just as often, James, Paco dreams of what it would have been like to leave Vietnam on his own two feet, the 2nd squad of the 2nd platoon humping along a flat orange road in full battle dress, bristling with guns and ammunition—radios, LAWS, claymores, frags, and all. We come to a large, glazed-brick building in the middle of a broad plain—a theater, say, or a gymnasium with sparkling brown windows that reflect everything darkly. Paco, urged always in the dream by a sudden, excited impulse, turns abruptly aside from us, calling, "Good-bye and take good care!" and we call back, "Take good care and fare thee well." He jumps a deep and narrow ditch, brimful with stagnant, brackish water and creamy with a bubbling scum. He sheds his rifle and bandoleers, his rucksack and flak jacket and pistol, as well as his gray gas-mask bag crammed with spools of black wire, his fillet knife, and other booby-trap makings. He walks on, peeling his T-shirt off his body, and into the thick pastel shade of many tall rubber trees. He jumps up the low steps of the building and comes right to the entrance, feeling that sliver of ice-cold air blowing through the split in the wide double doors—that steady blast burning as though he's being sliced in two. The door springs open, and in he goes, to a low, wide lobby of smooth gray carpet crowded with other homebound troops. A drooping banner at the far end of the lobby is festooned with red, white, and blue bunting, and reads:

WELCOME TO THE
451ST PROCESSING AND TRANSPORT
FACILITY (DET.)

CAPT. OMAR BERRY, CO

ALL INCOMING PERSONNEL
REPORT HERE

Paco makes his way among the tight, in-facing groups of soldiers—everyone decked out in their Class-A khakis, with their traveling gear piled in the middle of each group. Does Paco recognize any of the men?—everyone talking casually with their bulky greatcoats thrown over their arms, their collar brass glittering like 14k gold, their trouser creases as crisp and perfect as stitching; all of them standing tall and robust, faces full of color, healthy and soldierly. Paco—in the dream now, James—feels diminished, achy and rheumy with the sour nausea of heat exhaustion coming over him, his skin much reddened, hot and dry to the touch. He finally makes it through the doors under the welcome banner and into a broad auditorium—the place sloping gently down like an Olympic bleacher, but solid, and upholstered wall-to-wall with the same gray carpet as the lobby. The place is always crammed with more GIs—these decked out in sloppy, baggy fatigues—and so crowded that you have to mind where you step. Men sleep profoundly, curled up against their duffels and seabags, sprawled across footlockers and boxes and other crated luggage ready to ship. They use their shirts and field jackets for pillows and lay their hands nonchalantly over souvenir rifles—everything shipshape, registered, and tagged (French bolt action assault rifles, Chinese SKSs, and Russian AKs with Chinese markings). Paco tiptoes exaggeratedly, like a ballet clown, in his clumsy, filthy boots and baggy, rugged fatigues, over the duffels and bundles and spread-out coats. And all the while a smooth, well-modulated announcer's voice calls over the public-address system an endless roster of names, ranks, and parenthetical service numbers—like a recipe, James—paging the men to be loaded aboard the charter planes that wait outside on the tarmac, bound for home. There is a constant hubbub going on around Paco as he shoulders and urges his way to the exit. But as many times as he has had the dream, James, as many times as he has listened to that voice (always the very air around the speakers throbbing and popping, *crackling* with static; Paco's flesh tingling), never can he make out any of the names, and never does he hear his own, "Paco Sullivan, US 54 800 409, step to the door..."

And the next morning Paco would always waken from these dreams in the full, warm light of day with a start, tangled in the sheets and turned every which way in bed. And we, James—the dead, the ghosts who haunt him—long gone.

Tony D

Le Minh Khue

A grim-faced man came to Old Thien's place and stood by the door. Old Thien looked out and saw a body swollen from a steady diet of starch, a muddy, expressionless face stuck on a small head. Without bothering to stand up, he barked:

—You have something about Than?

—Yes. How'd you know?

—Don't matter. What's up?

—Than's dead. His body's lost—gone.

Old Thien's gigantic Adam's apple jerked up and down like a brick in his throat. His son Than had gone to search for gold in the central highlands almost a year ago, joining the ranks of prospectors from all over the country. This was the third time someone had stopped by to bring news of his death. He'd drowned the first time, been beheaded the next. Now he'd disappeared. The man who'd brought the news stood by the door licking his lips hungrily. Old Thien knew guys like this backwards and forwards. Keeping his face blank, he asked:

—Why can't they find his body?

—The ditch collapsed; they couldn't get down to him.

—Three ways!

—What?

—Three kinds of liars, three kinds of death. All of you can go to hell!

The newsbearer was taken aback. His eyes swept around Old Thien's room, but fell on nothing worth picking up. What a junk heap, he muttered, then said aloud:

—Look, I went through a lot of trouble to get here—the train and bus fares cost me a bundle. I need a little something for my trouble.

Old Thien swung an arm towards a dark corner.

—See what you can find! Grab any damn thing you can.

Desperately, the man stepped around Old Thien and snatched up an electric fan with mouse-eared blades.

—I'll take this!

He put the fan under his arm and walked out. Old Thien shouted after him:

—You better watch out! When that Than of mine comes back, he'll suck out your blood to the last ounce. Now get out of my sight, you lousy bastard.

Old Thien knew that even though his son was stunted as a mouse, he was one of those people who wouldn't die even if struck in the head by lightning. Than was like the wild grass that would be burned away seven times and seven times grow back stronger. Once, while Than was burglarizing a flat, he'd fallen from a third-floor balcony. But thanks to some merit left over from his ancestors' good deeds, he'd landed right on a soft sand heap. Nobody could get the better of his boy.

But Old Thien still felt uneasy, even after he'd gotten rid of the fool with the latest news of Than's death. That night he pulled out the tiny radio he kept carefully hidden among a heap of broken dishes under his bed. Slowly he turned the dial. He took a special comfort in just twisting it, even though he never stayed long enough on the same frequency to catch a complete sentence. Whenever he picked up any noise, even a hiss of static, he'd sit and listen for a few seconds and then spin the knob again. The neighbors would growl, but what did he care? He wasn't pissing on their ancestors' graves, was he? He couldn't imagine why a human being couldn't sleep just because of a little noise. He'd sleep through even if a ton of bombs exploded next to his ears. Nothing bothered him. At each meal he'd bolt down eight bowls of cheap moldy rice mixed with salty fish heads and greasy chicken guts. He ate those delicacies every day even though the whole compound held its nose. What did he care? He was big as a bear and clunky as an old tractor drained of its oil and abandoned to the dogs. People said he was a ghost from hell come to wreak havoc on this terrestrial world. None of his neighbors wanted to come near him. He'd browbeat them with stories about his virtuous family and their support for the revolution, tales that would spew from his mouth without warning, whether anybody was interested or not. For the most part his audience was made up of the neighborhood kids who could make no more sense out of what he was saying than ducks listening to thunder. It didn't matter. If his stories wouldn't impress people, then his size would. He was big and heavy as a heap of steel and strong as a bull. When he'd walk across the courtyard, it would shake as if an earthquake was rumbling through. He did whatever he wanted and had no patience with weak intellectuals and their so-called "consciences." He stepped on everyone.

Old Thien had been a watchman until he'd retired ten years ago; he'd had a house outside the city, with a yard and fish pond. Then one day he suddenly sold the whole lot and moved into town. He used the money from the sale to buy gold which he promptly hid away. Pretending to be poor as a beggar, he forced his family into a windowless hole of barely ten square meters, right next to the public toilet that filled up the whole compound with its generous stench. Directly across from his place was a terrace taken over by people who had partitioned it off with bamboo mats. Each tiny marked-off space was the living area for a family. It was a colorful scene. One couple, singers in a street theatre troupe, would fight with each other all day like cats and dogs, then entwine all night on their narrow cot, laughing loudly and telling jokes through those evenings when the rain diluted the stink of the courtyard and sweetened the air. Then there was a clan of young males who would spread out helter-skelter in the daytime to hustle for work and at night would all pack themselves back into their little hole. There, with no electricity, no fans and barely enough water to cool their sweaty bodies, they'd sleep half-naked, packed together like sardines in a cooking pot. All along that terrace that long ago had been a meeting place for the sons and daughters of the rich there now echoed the musical snores of common human beings, sound asleep under the starry sky of God, protected only by Heaven. They slept like a destitute and dispossessed herd. And when daylight came, they became devils, a pack of animals with the fittest and strongest grabbing the most, no different than thousands of others in the public housing projects where the souls of human beings were forced into the same mold....

Old Thien had sold his house in the country and had enough gold to plate his entire body. Yet he was determined to play the part of a ragged pauper. He too had crawled into one of the holes in the terrace, to live among the animals. And among them, he had become the creature with the sharpest teeth.

* * *

A few days later, Than appeared out of nowhere, carrying a mysteriously bulging knapsack on his back. He strutted into the public courtyard. From every hole and crack in the compound, eyes peered at the knapsack. A voice with a Nghe An accent called to him from the space beneath the staircase.

—Than!

—Yeah? Than turned to look at a heavy-set woman with folds of fat under her chin, her face thick with makeup she'd applied as generously as any of the working girls at the train station. She smiled broadly, revealing a piece of scallion stuck between her teeth.

—Hey there, boy!

—How you doing, big sister Phan.

—What you got in that knapsack that's making you walk with your nose in the air?

—Just my clothes.

—Fuck you, clothes! Look how heavy that sack is—it's gold, ain't it?

Old Thien rushed out to protect his son:

—What gold? It's just twigs.

—Yeah—twigs made out of gold, Than muttered. He continued up the creaking stairs....Catching sight of him, several street urchins who'd been gambling in the courtyard rushed out and began bellowing: —The Prince is home! Now the Great Mandarin must treat us to a feast!

They had nicknamed Old Thien "The Great Mandarin" because even though everybody thought of him as an animal living contentedly in the dank murky den that he and his son called a home, he still put on airs. Sometimes he even liked to have birthday celebrations. Real birthday celebrations! The urchins would hold their breaths whenever they watched him throw himself such a party. Because he'd worked as a watchman for an important municipal agency, Old Thien knew exactly what to do. He'd drag in two helpless old men from down the street. The three would slurp beer, eat peanuts and recite poetry, blasting out poems one right after another—like kids farting. And besides his birthday parties there would be the commemorations of his ancestors' deaths and the lunar-new-year celebrations. His brothers and other relatives would invade the city from their villages far out in the countryside to come celebrate with him. And Old Thien was a genius at finding ways for them to stay in the city. Even though they had no education, he'd managed to get all of them civil service positions. He'd unfold his "Certificate of Support for the Revolution" and brandish it in front of reluctant officials, coming to see them again and again, five, six, seven times. Twenty times. He'd bring no gifts, only his mouth. Still, with that weapon he'd managed to plant two younger brothers, two younger sisters and a dozen other relatives into government agencies. Some sold vegetables at the government shop while others became official security guards. They received official registration cards and ration coupons. When they retired, they'd all get pensions, just like honest people.

At the end of every year, Old Thien would gather the whole gang in his little cave of a house and treat them to a stringy duck cooked in a thin broth and flavored with a bit of spice. His relatives would swarm around and devour the duck, pressed in together but happy to be in the city. Old Thien would be in the center of all of it, solemnly pronouncing words of wisdom as he strode grandly among his nieces and nephews, the gold he'd hidden on his body weighing down his steps. There was no mandarin or king on earth who felt the same satisfaction in his retirement that the old man felt in such moments. The nickname "The Great Mandarin" truly fitted him, for only a mandarin or king could live so grandly and freely in his own kingdom, even when the temperature hit 40 degrees, even when rain leaked through the roof, even when everything stank of dead rats and urine. He did what he wanted and he ate and slept as he pleased.

* * *

Looking exhausted, Than threw down his knapsack and just as quickly snatched it up again and held it tightly against his stomach. He darted his gaze around the room, then he stuffed the sack into the corner where he and his father cooked on a hot plate they powered from a wire they'd stretched to the government agency across the street. Than kept staring at his father. The old man might look clumsy, but when it came to stealing, he was smoother than a cat and had the eyes of an owl, always searching for things he could snatch. And he stole everything. Women's panties, electrical cable from the street near the compound. He'd even swiped a baby's pottie someone left outside in the courtyard. Every once in a while he would shove everything into a big rucksack and take a trip out to the country where his older brother still lived with his ten kids; he'd exchange his sack of stolen junk for some taro and beans. But even though the entire neighborhood knew he was a thief, nobody could ever catch him in the act. Than, though a student of his father's ways, only went for bigger scores.

—Not for small change like you! he'd often scold Old Thien.

Old Thien's wife had died and his daughter had married a husband from the highlands. Now there was only father and son. Than wandered all over with his buddies, wherever he could hustle or scam. Once in a while he gave his father money, but the two never shared a meal together. Either one or the other would eat first. The old man would boil down to a mushy broth the fish heads and pork bones he'd haggled for at the market and drink it. Then smacking his lips, he'd say things like:

—if you're going to steal, you should really do it. Stealing like I do ain't nothing. You can see it all the time in the newspapers and hear it on the radio. People steal billions of dong, nothing happens to them. Me, I'm just a poor little crippled baby chick, eating the grains left around the rice pestle.

* * *

Old Thien paced back and forth in his little room now, sneaking glances at the knapsack. He felt like there were needles pricking his stomach; he'd never seen Than bring home a haul this big. With great generosity, he gave a piece of bread to Than. His son ate in silence. Finally, the old man could stand it no longer.

—This time you struck it big, didn't you?

—Sure.

—So what'd you get?

—Fuck, man! Than cursed, swept up the bread crumbs that had fallen on the mat, wiped his mouth with his hand and went over to the corner. He lifted the lid of the toilet bowl. A putrid urine stench spread through the room. When he was finished, he crawled into the corner where he'd put the sack, stretched out and started snoring like a pig, one of his hands clutching the knapsack straps.

Old Thien sat on embers while his son slept. He racked his brain trying to guess what was in the knapsack, but he couldn't come up with anything. Finally at dark, he felt his way over to Than.

—Get up. I need to talk to you.

—What?

—Look, you've got a gold mine here, right? Well, watch out for Hung. He's been back for over a week now—he escaped.

—Oh yeah? Than sat up, clutching the knapsack to him. Hung was the son of that old woman, Phan, from Nghe An, but he could beat out any of the locals in the tricks of the trade. Only twenty-five, he'd already been in prison five times. Each time he came out, he got more daring. Even Than feared him. This time, his father told him, Hung had gotten five years for rape. But he'd escaped after less than a year.

—Are they after him?

—Probably. He's hiding way up in the attic. No one in this whole neighborhood dares to breathe a word—he'd cut their throats. Look, tell me the truth, tell me what's in here. Then you and I can put our heads together. You're just not going to make it alone.

—OK, but you've got to keep your mouth shut.

Old Man Thien spat in his hand and waved it in front of his face twice, as though performing some secret ritual. The two swore an oath together solemnly. Than moved close to his father.

—They're bones.

—Are you kidding me?

—Listen, these bones are more valuable than gold—they're American bones.

Old Thien snorted and stretched his neck, the way he did when something truly moved him. In a while he whispered:

—You sure? There'd be hell to pay if you're wrong.

—Dao and I dug them up. They're a hundred percent American bones. Dao knows his stuff—he measured them. There was even a chain around the neck, hooked to a name tag. The last few letters had worn out; you could only see part of the name. Tony D. The name of the unit is also faded. Dao's got the tag—he's peddling it now.

—How much can you get?

—Dao said we have to divide it up between the whole gang, but it's still a lot—five million for the two of us who found them. Dao and I are going to split it.

—God damn! That's a lot of money.

—Dao's going down to the port to find a buyer. I'm supposed to take the boat down there tomorrow night—he'll be waiting for me there. We'll sell the bones to the sailors; they'll take them to America, make a bundle. Look, if it all goes down, I'll give you four or five hundred thousand dong, OK?

—It's up to you. But remember—when you take your share, don't get greedy. In the long run, everything goes smoother that way.

—Don't give me any of your lectures, old man—you didn't lose a damned drop of sweat and now you stand to make half a million dong...

—OK, OK...look, you better go back to sleep, get some rest for tomorrow. I'll keep watch.

Old Thien sat next to the bamboo mat door folded like a dog in its den, his arms and legs pressed close to his body. He saw that Than must have felt safe with his old man on guard—soon he was snoring musically. After his first wave of emotion, Old Thien had fallen into the strange state he always experienced whenever he heard his son was about to come into money. Than could never stop bragging anytime he scored. Sometimes he'd even jack up the amount. But sooner or later, he'd lose it all gambling, playing the numbers. Well, what disturbed heaven was paid back on earth. How could Than keep his hands on money like that if he didn't even trust his daddy? Old Thien felt pangs of jealousy and greed. Plots swirled around in his head, but he knew how ferocious his son was and he was afraid to play any of them out. His mind always churned with this jumbled mixture of dark thoughts and sharp fears whenever his boy brought home some loot. His mouth would go as dry as if someone had stuck duckweeds into it, his eyes would glaze over; the whole world would become a blur. That was the state he was in now, swinging back and forth between greed and fear, his ears pricked to catch any noise from outside. He started to doze off when he felt someone pat his shoulder. He raised his head. As clearly as if it was daylight, he saw a face as black as asphalt, teeth as white as lime. A hand that was just bones reached out to caress Old Thien's hair. The old man tried to move, but he couldn't. It was as if his whole body had been painted over with glue. He muttered incomprehensible words to Than. Seeing him so completely helpless, the black man laughed uproariously but didn't make a sound. He stood next to Old Thien, his head intact but his body only the white bones of a skeleton; he was laughing and yet he seemed filled with utter misery. Old Thien was shaken to his own bones. He kicked out against the bamboo mat, and the noise woke him up. The black man was gone. Just awakened also, dazed, Than asked his father:

—Was it Hung?

—Hell, no—it was a black guy.

—A black guy?

—I must have been dreaming. I saw a black man laughing at me.

—You dreamt about a black guy? Damn, I dreamt about him too. I was so scared—I wanted to call out to you, but I couldn't.

Than turned on the light. Father and son, both of them well-known rogues, were discovering for the first time that there existed something mysterious that could interfere with the dreams of man. Something stronger even than man's greed for money, than his stupidity and his thirst for brutality.

—Did he say anything to you?

—No. He only laughed. But I smelled his rotten stench.

—Get rid of these bones! They scare the hell out of me. And get me some joss sticks.

Old Thien lit three incense sticks, filled a cup with water and placed it on the knapsack, stuck the sticks into a can filled with rice and put it on the sack next to them. In his whole life, he had never prayed to anyone. But at this moment, some unimaginable force seemed to get into him and he prostrated himself again and again in front of the knapsack:

—If you are all-powerful and all-wise, please rest in peace. Tomorrow my son will find a way for you to return home. He's doing a good deed, sir—nothing evil. You'll be returned to your father, your mother, your wife and children—it's better than being left in the jungle.

Than listened to his father's prayers in silence. He'd finished seventh grade—he didn't really believe that the spirit of some soldier named Tony D would hold a grudge against him. He understood why Tony was killed; it was just bad karma. Evil begot evil. Tony had killed people so he was killed himself. And he'd been all alone, high up on that mountain and Than had gone through a lot of trouble to find him; now he had to pay Than back. That was all there was to it. Anyway he'd heard that in America people were pretty straightforward in matters of money.

Finished with his prayers, Old Thien pressed his son to get back to sleep. But he didn't dare turn out the lights. He sat motionless by the door, waiting for daylight. Near dawn, he dozed off again. He saw a pair of feet, made only of bones, walking in a circle around him. A putrid odor rose, making him nauseous. Terrified, he shut his eyes, but he could still hear the footsteps circling round and round him like clanging pieces of metal. He dozed fitfully until morning.

Old Thien couldn't close his eyes during the three days Than was away. He kept dreaming of the same black soldier. Sometimes the man's skin and flesh was intact and he would look like a black French soldier Old Thien remembered; the man had been a prisoner and then after the war used to drive by his village. Old Thien had been young then. He remembered how the French soldier had once stopped his car and given him a cigarette. But that black soldier had been so nice compared to the silent Tony. Tony D looked exactly like the old French veteran, but he never uttered a word. Just stood in a corner of the room and stared. And whenever Old Thien dreamed, he smelled again the stinking odor of newly unearthed flesh and bones. Sometimes he'd see a bone-white skeleton clawing and clattering its way around the house. It would climb onto the bed or the window sill, its black mouth gaping at him, its hollowed eye sockets staring at him fiercely. He'd never been frightened of ghosts in his life, but these days his legs would give out whenever he thought about sleep. During the day, he would lock his door and go to the park near the intersection. He'd climb onto a stone bench that still reeked with traces of last night's love affairs and fall asleep. He'd sleep well there, not giving a damn if it rained or if the sun shone or the wind blew. But at night he had to return home. He kept the light on all night and fiddled with the dial on his radio. One day, taking an example from Phan, the old woman, he shook a few grains of salt out of the window and lit joss sticks near the door. He could hear clearly the noises made by the pack of animals sleeping on the balcony.

Next to Old Thien's hole lived a couple who sold dog meat at the market. Xet had abandoned his wife in the village and ran away to the city in order to open a dog meat stand and get himself a piece of this terrace. He'd found a runaway girl to be his wife, a light-skinned highland girl with a soft, undulating voice. To her, washing with Camay soap, wearing Thai panties and using Chinese perfume were like going to heaven. Xet coddled his new wife and brought her all kinds of gifts in expectation of the happy returns he'd get—the pleasures that a healthy and ready female could bestow on an equally eager male full of unrelieved energy thanks to dog meat and alcohol. Xet even bought her a "reporter's" shirt, designer jeans and "bit" shoes. He was proud to see that whatever new style the saleswomen in the market came up with, his wife would already have it...

But for the past few nights, Old Thien's night time pacing and dial fiddling had put a damper on the young couple's activities. Xet's wife lay silently in bed and listened to his movements. But even a lioness begins to melt when she's lying next to a lion. She nudged her face into Xet's smelly armpit, rank with the special sweat-stink that dog-meat eaters get, and then spoke in the sweet soft voice of a highland girl:

—I'm terrified of Old Thien!

Xet caressed his wife's hair just like he'd seen in the bedroom scenes he watched on TV. He wanted to follow up—just like in those movies—with a few tender compliments that would flatter his wife and fill her with love. But it didn't come out right:

—Motherfuck that crazy old goat. Why the fuck should you worry? Come on over here, baby. Damn! How come you got so fat these days? You look like a shaved pig...

The couple's giggling soothed Old Thien. He turned on his radio and fiddled with the dial, then turned on all the lights and hoped morning would come quickly.

* * *

A week later Than finally returned, grinning from ear to ear and lugging a bag filled with money.

—Man, I hit it big!

He'd brought home a bundle of pork intestines wrapped in banana leaves, along with shrimp paste and three kilos of fresh rice noodles. The two of them, father and son devoured the feast in a blink. But afterwards, when Old Thien looked around, he couldn't see the bag of money anywhere.

—Where did you hide it?

—Right here—where else? Look, I'm gonna be gone for the day. As soon as I get back, you'll get your five hundred—you have the word of a "man of virtue."

As soon as Than left, Old Thien didn't sit still. He searched all over the house for the bag of money. He knew every corner and he searched them all. He burrowed into even the most secret places where he'd never failed before to find what was hidden. But he couldn't find a thing. By noon, exhausted, he stretched out in the middle of the floor and racked his brains, trying to think if he'd missed any possible hiding place. He only wanted to pull out a few bills; that goddamned son of his would never even know anything was missing. Thinking of the money, he started to doze off—but bolted up when he saw the skeleton squatting on top of the rafters. He cursed it.

—Fuck your mother! You're on your way home to your country. What the hell else do you want? Why do you want to scare me?

The skeleton stayed where it was, only shaking its skull once in a while. Its bones clicked and tinkled like horse bells. Old Thien was frightened out of his wits. He waved his arms about, signalling the skeleton to stay still, but it gleefully moved even more. The stench from it was choking him. He fought against the ghost all through his fitful sleep. When he woke up, he felt empty and nauseous. His entire body ached as if he'd slept in a draft.

The next day, Old Thien again went back to the park to sleep. That afternoon, Than returned home. Soon after he went to the park and grabbed his father by the neck.

—Come home right now!

Seeing his son's bloodshot eyes, his face blackened with rage, his thin angry lips, Old Thien followed him home quickly. Than entered first. As soon as his father came through the bamboo mat door, Than seized him by the collar.

—Where's the money?

Old Thien was stunned.

—Why ask me?

—I hid it under this brick. What'd you do with it?

The old man could only shake his head, struggling against his son's iron grip. He couldn't form a clear sentence. Looking at his father, Than grew furious.

—Spew it out, old man! That money's my sweat and blood—you're not going to eat it. Three million dong ain't some small shit.

—I didn't take it! Old Thien finally blurted out.

—If you didn't, then what dog fucker did? Come on, spit it out!

—I swear I'm telling the truth. Sure, I looked for it; I was going to steal a few bills. But I couldn't find it. I swear to you, if I'm lying let trains and cars crush me to dust.

—You want me to believe you'll die just because you swear an oath? Dog shit! Do you hear me? Do you understand? Spit it out, puke it all up or I'll strangle you until your tongue squeezes out of your mouth!

He rushed at the old man, seizing that neck with its Adam's apple big as a brick. Old Thien howled like a dog being pushed under water.

—Puke it up. You can't eat it all by yourself. Spit it out—I have to pay off my bets.

—I didn't take it, I swear!

—Swear to a fucking dog, not to me. If you really didn't take it then take that knife and cut your face. Do it. Or I'll strangle you to death. Here—take the knife!

Old Thien shook violently. Holding the sharp knife, he begged:

—Let me go. I didn't take it. Listen, son, I'm your dad—how could I do such an evil thing?

—Cut your face!

—No! Please—I couldn't stand it.

—No? Then cut off a finger. Do it. Right now. I won't believe you unless you do. Do it or I'll strangle you. Do it! Cut it off!

Than lunged at his father, his face swollen with rage. Trying not to think about what he was doing, Old Thien put his left index finger on the plank of the bed. He looked at his son. Than yelled:

—Go ahead, swear to it now, vermin! Cut off your finger or I'll pull out your tongue!

The old man raised the knife. It made a solid thunk as he brought it down. A stream of blood spurted out and the finger fell to the ground. Than looked at it without any emotion. He saw his father's face turn white and his mouth twist to one side in pain. It sobered him up. He stepped outside, careful not to step in the blood. He was burning with the desire to revenge himself on whoever stole his three million. Old Thien's severed finger convinced him his father probably didn't take it. But then who? Who else could it have been? And how was he going to pay off his gambling debts? With this loan shark, if he didn't pay off, he'd get his face washed with acid. Goddamn it, these days, only the most ruthless won. He'd have to skip town now. He began to daydream about the promised land, about Hong Kong...

Mrs. Phan saw Than running down the stairs like a whirlwind. She wanted to smile at him but didn't dare. His face chilled her—it looked as if he'd just drunk human blood. She started to climb up to the balcony, on her way to her room, when she heard Old Thien's agonized cries. Without stopping to find out what happened, she screamed:

—Murder! Someone's been murdered!

Old Thien dropped his head to his chest and sucked on the stump of his finger. Blood spattered all over his chin and dripped onto his shirt. His body— the brutish body of a savage who solved all problems with his muscles—seemed suddenly so shrunken that even a cruel child would feel pity looking at it. He fainted. Through a veil of mist he saw the white-boned skeleton looking at him, its outline only dimly visible. It raised its hand to the top of its head. Thinking it was gesturing to him, he tried to move toward it. It broke into a peal of shrill womanish laughter. He tried to raise his hand to wave back, but he couldn't; his hands seemed tightly tied.

He began to hear human voices.

—He's coming to. Get a cyclo for him—it'll be more comfortable.

A vulgar curse. A woman gave out a sharp laugh. Old Thien realized it was Phan. That pack of animals with whom he shared the balcony for all these years had become human beings, surrounding him, bringing him down the stairs and to the emergency room.

* * *

Since then, Old Thien never again dreamed about the skeleton or the black soldier. He was at peace, except that his boy Than had disappeared without a trace....

One night, not long after, Xet urged his wife to come to bed early. He cradled that heaven-sent soft, plump bundle of flesh in his dog killer's arms and breathed alcohol fumes into her face. It took him a while to think up a line to compliment her:

—Listen, baby, tomorrow I'll buy you an imported fur coat.

—Where you getting the money for all this cool stuff?

She was beginning to use the language of the city.

—Just don't run your mouth off about it or I'll slice out your tongue. Anyone asks, you just say it came from our savings, get it? Do it or I swear I'll cut it off. I got hold of something big, but anyone finds out about it—it's jail time for me, understand?

She laughed loudly, laughed like someone whose throat was being cut. She laughed like that every night, while the whole terrace was submerged in a heavy sleep after another day of fighting for crumbs. Xet and his wife were the noisiest now, the ones who stayed up he latest. They were still beasts, even at night, when beasts became human beings again. On this night it was hot and humid. A storm was coming. Old Thien felt the pain spike through the stump of his finger. He sat at the window, looking out, waiting for the falling rain to soften his pain. Beyond the window was the city. Houses upon houses. The soldier Tony D was no longer bothering him and in general he was content again, except at moments like this when the piercing red-hot pain in his hand made him tired of life's upheavals. A shocking idea suddenly burst into his head—he was stunned he hadn't thought of it before. It must have been that black soldier who'd stolen the bag of money! Fuck his mother! No wonder he hadn't been around again. The fox!

Translated by Nguyen Ba Chung and Nguyen Qui Duc
Edited by Wayne Karlin

The Billion Dollar Skeleton

Phan Huy Duong

Richard Steel, the richest American—that is to say, the richest man in the world—the one they call simply "The Billionaire," leaps into his private jet. Destination: Saigon. His entourage is impressive. More than one hundred people. He isn't taking any chances. Everyone who can contribute to the success of his operation has been included. Mission impossible: To find his son, John, missing in action since 1972 during a bombing raid over the seventeenth parallel. John, his only son. He'll find him, he'll bring his remains back to the United States. The Billionaire promised his wife on her deathbed, one day their little boy would rest next to her in the family plot. The Steel Dynasty. When the Billionaire decides to do something, nothing stops him. In his whole life he's never known an obstacle he couldn't overcome. No one and nothing can stop him. He's a fighter. He *always* wins.

The Billionaire's staff is silent. They've all worked hard to prepare the mission. Everyone is fascinated by the Billionaire's insatiable drive. But no one believes he can succeed.

"Everything in order for tomorrow, Colonel Wood?" said the Billionaire, emptying his glass of whiskey in one swig.

Colonel Wood had been hired as Staff Commander. When he'd worked for the State Department, the MIA/POW problem was his issue. It was the Colonel who had negotiated with the Vietnamese government; he was the one who had personally sifted through the four thousand documents delivered by the Vietnamese before the embargo was lifted. But there had been no trace of John Steel.

"Everything is ready, sir," the Colonel said gruffly. "The warehouses, the buildings, the equipment, the telecommunications network. The entire area has been ready for a week now. You'll have direct satellite links to the rest of the world. You'll be able to follow the operations closely. The command post is located in a wing of your villa. Your wife's Bible is on the altar, in the little chapel next to your bedroom. I've checked everything."

"What about the publicity campaign?"

"Yes, sir. Radio stations, the television networks—the entire national and local press corps will be there for your conference tomorrow morning. Almost a thousand of them. We've bought the front page of every newspaper, a radio spot every hour, and the national television station every night for a hundred days. Prime time. We've got all the publicity spots in the country. There are billboards all over the place. No one will be able to miss the offer. We start tomorrow morning. You just need to choose your service woman."

The Colonel passed a photo album to the Billionaire: "We've already bought them all. There's no risk of AIDS or infection. Your doctor has examined them— they're virgins, healthy girls. Whoever you choose will be brought to your suite tonight. She won't be allowed out for any reason. The villa is well guarded."

The Billionaire flipped through the album. Indeed the girls were young and beautiful. But that didn't really interest him. He had never been particularly attracted to a pretty face. But doctor's orders were doctor's orders: he had been advised to make love once a day to maintain his physical and psychological equilibrium. The Billionaire quickly skimmed through the candidates' resumes, and stopped at the first girl who spoke English fluently.

Colonel Wood coughed. "There's still time to change your mind. The mission is impossible. I've managed this portfolio for more than twenty years. It's absolutely crazy...you've got one chance in a million."

"Well, I'll buy that chance. I've got a budget of a billion dollars for it. The GNP of this country is $164 per head. We've got enough to *buy* that one chance in a million. I'm giving you one hundred days to find it. We're going to win, Colonel. You just leave your bureaucracy, your dossiers, your politics, your strategies, and all your stupid diplomatic tactics in the closet. I don't investigate, I don't negotiate, I act. I buy. I'm going to succeed where your Pentagon has failed."

The next morning, the entire national and local press swarmed into the Billionaire's vast conference room. The Billionaire wasn't a man to waste his time on a long speech. He got right to the point: "I've got a billion dollars to find my son, John Steel. U.S. Air Force. Disappeared in combat on the 24th of December 1972 over the seventeenth parallel. I'll make the person who helps me find him—dead or alive—a millionaire for the rest of his life. What's more, I pay cash: $164 for all unidentified skeletons. And I mean *all* of 'em—whether they're men, women, or children. Find 'em, bring 'em to me, I'll pay. No questions asked. Our offices are open twenty-four hours a day for exactly one hundred days. Everybody's welcome." And he left.

The news spread like wildfire. Every morning, on their front pages, every newspaper in Vietnam published a photo of John Steel, his measurements, his facial traits, the phone, address, and fax number of the Research Center, a map to get there, bus schedules from the surrounding cities, train timetables, planes...the $164 reward for each whole skeleton, and a range of fees for separate bones. The radio stations announced the offer every hour. National television repeated it each evening. In one night, Hanoi, Saigon, all the provincial towns, even the most remote villages, were covered with posters. *A skull...$164 per* *skeleton...public offer to purchase...*repeated millions and millions of times throughout the entire country. The Billionaire's operation was passionately debated, from the highest ranks of the Vietnamese Communist Party to the most squalid slums. Some were for it, others were against it. No one thought of forbidding it. Such an indisputably humanitarian project. The Vietnamese worship their ancestors, the memory of the dead. They couldn't oppose this. And then, the Vietnamese economy had never had such a windfall. A billion dollars for a skeleton! And everyone had a chance—from the most powerful to the most humble. Never had they known such justice, such democracy.

On the first day, no one showed up at the Research Center.

The second day, as night fell, a suspicious-looking man with scruffy hair and a face half-masked by a bushy beard slipped into the reception room, a dirty sack slung over his shoulder. The man unpacked the contents of his sack— a large male skeleton—pocketed the $164 and disappeared.

The Billionaire immediately ordered forensic work on the skeleton. In a specially conceived laboratory, Professor Smith and his team had all the data, all the instruments needed to identify even the smallest bone that might belong to John. They had all the photos, all the X rays of John from the day of his birth to his disappearance. The shape and size of the bones—everything had been photographed, measured, calculated, and cataloged in a precise graphic and numerical data base. A camera scanned images of the skeleton and transmitted them to a neuronic computer, where artificial-intelligence software gave an exact reading on whether or not they belonged to John Steel.

The Professor: "It's not him. But the skeleton is unusual. From its configuration, it could be either Vietnamese or American. According to the computer, it's fifty-fifty. Probably a half-breed. What do we do with it?"

"Put it aside. It's the first. An authentic unknown soldier. When we find John, we're gonna give this boy a coffin cut to the measure of his tragedy."

By the third day, people in rags were swarming up to the counters. They were all well received and paid according to the set rates: $164 for a whole skeleton, $10 dollars for a skull, $5 for a tibia...and ten cents for bone fragments.

Colonel Wood's carefully conceived sorting warehouse bustled. Women's and children's bones were dumped into specially tagged bins. Men's bones were stocked in bins close to the command headquarters and directly linked to the laboratory by remote-control belts. Intelligent robots sorted the bones into their 214 known parts: the skull bone, the vertebrae, the clavicle....They passed them one by one under the eyes of the cameras for the first sort. Vietnamese bones were put into the refuse bins. The American bones were given a final examination by neuronic computer.

In Vietnam, as in all poor countries of the world, the grapevine works wonders. Barely a week had passed, but everyone already knew that the Billionaire kept his word, that he paid cash, no questions asked, for any kind of bones brought to him. The Research Center was besieged. People came bearing skulls, tibiae, ribs, a phalanx, a femur. You just presented your bones at a counter, placed them on a conveyor belt to be scanned by the cameras, and pocketed the money. Only dog, cat, and monkey bones were refused.

Long lines of human beings converged from every province in the country to the Research Center. Never had the land, the rice fields, the forests been scoured so thoroughly. Sometimes men, women, and children stumbled onto long-buried mines, undetonated bombs. The Billionaire generously reimbursed the families of the deceased. He bought their skeletons at twice the normal rate.

Never in human memory had so many human bones been piled up by the square meter. Men women children old people Viets Laos Khmers Thais Koreans Australians New Zealanders French black white red yellow brown Australopithecus, and...even a few Americans. The Billionaire sent the Western bones to their respective national governments, and the prehistoric bones to the museums. He had the rest stacked in warehouses kept for this purpose. Men with men, women with women, children with children, old people with old people, babies with babies. Some of the bones were recent, barely clean, scraped down with knives. Sometimes, bits of nerves, shreds of flesh still stuck to the bones. But that didn't matter. The Billionaire didn't want to discourage anyone. He paid. No questions asked.

By the end of a month, the bins were overflowing.

"What do we do now? Do we put them in the bins with the Americans?" asked Colonel Wood.

"Absolutely not. Buy all the rice paddies in the area, and pile them up there. How are we doing?"

"More than 400,000 so far, sir."

"Terrific. We're ahead of schedule. You'll have more than one chance in a million. If it exists, we're going to find it."

The rice paddies were immediately transformed into stocking areas. Men to the north. Women to the south. Children to the east. Babies to the west. At the beginning, the piles formed tiny hills. But day by day, the bones scattered over the Vietnamese land slid toward the center. Soon the hills formed huge mountains visible from several miles away. A dense network of trains was rapidly extended. The four asphalt roads to the Research Center stretched toward the four horizons. Now, you drove to the Center through a mountain range, at the bottom of a gorge, between two steep walls of bones.

The New York Times published a huge aerial photo with the headline: FOR THE LOVE OF A SON: THE MOST EXTRAVAGANT ENTERPRISE IN HUMAN HISTORY. A few intellectuals from the Old World protested. They hadn't understood a thing about the market economy. A few brighter, hipper young philosophers rapped about the operation on CNN. A handful of Vietnamese artists cried scandal. A lone deputy dared suggest setting up an investigative committee. Alarmed, the Vietnamese government published a convoluted communiqué about human rights and the importance of humanitarian missions. It couldn't have done less. It couldn't have done much more. Thanks to the billion dollars, unemployment had vanished from the province. And, if you took the country as a whole, hunger had been reduced.

By the sixty-sixth day—two-thirds of the way into the Billionaire's schedule—land for stocking bones was scarce. On the last few available acres, he had crematoriums built. The Billionaire led all the operations, assisted with the sorting. He seldom ate, slept only about four hours a day, working nonstop from dawn to dusk. In the evenings, after ten o'clock, he would retire to his villa, shower, gulp down a sandwich, wash it down with a half-bottle of whiskey, make love with the service woman, and then retreat to the chapel to pray and commune with his wife. Every evening he would remember his son. Such a tall, handsome young man. So intelligent. Such blue eyes. A life full of such promise, such a future. That was yesterday, some twenty years ago. Every night, the Billionaire would place his hand on the Bible and renew the vow. And every morning, at four o'clock, he was back at the command post.

By the eightieth day, the tide of bones began to subside. Old bones became rarer and rarer. On the ninetieth day, the supply tapered off completely. The Billionaire stepped up his efforts, encouraging, motivating, tirelessly inspiring his men. "If there's one chance in a million to find him, it's now that it's going to happen."

The fateful day approached. Skeleton sellers were scarce now. At the most a dozen per day. Now they either brought new skeletons, or those over a hundred years old. The next to last day, only an old beggar walked up to one of the counters with a big toe bone. And that was the last ten cents of the billion dollars.

The one hundredth day. No one came. From his armchair, the Billionaire watched the hands of the clock on the wall inch along. The office was aglow in the sunset, the rosewood furniture aflame with its rays. The clock chimed, announcing the end of the day. The Billionaire sighed, pushed aside his glass of whiskey, and stood up to go.

Just then, three discrete knocks on the door. The interpreter slipped into the office, shuffling his way to the Billionaire's desk.

"There's an old man here who would like to speak to you, sir."

"Give him the dollars and throw the bones in the pile. The campaign's over."

"He doesn't have a skeleton to sell. He just wanted to give you this."

The interpreter opened his hand. In his palm lay a tiny black velvet satchel. Irritated, the Billionaire picked it up, and distractedly pulled it open. A tiny platinum cross with a ruby heart encrusted at the intersection of the two branches. The Billionaire shuddered. Now it was certain. John was dead. His son would never have parted with the cross. His mother had it made for him by the best jeweler in Paris. The Billionaire slumped back into his armchair.

"Show him in," he said, in a low voice.

A frail old man with white hair and eyebrows and a long white goatee entered. He seemed to float in his peasant pajamas, the earthy, ocher color of the High Plateaus. He advanced softly, leaning on a bamboo cane. He stopped at the desk. The Billionaire offered him a seat. The old man shook his head.

"Where did you find this cross?"

"It belongs to me."

"Do you know where my son is?"

"Yes."

"Show me the place. I'll cover you in gold to the third generation."

The old man shook his head.

"Tell me what you want then," said the Billionaire.

"You will burn the mountains of bones. You will sow the ashes on the Vietnamese land, from the Gate of Nam Quan to the tip of Ca Mau. When you have done it, come to my house, in the Village of Man, at the foot of the Mountain of Peace. I'll give you back your son's bones."

"I'll be there in seven days."

The old man didn't respond. He turned his head, left the office slowly. His cane resonated on the floor. Sharp, regular taps, as if to announce the beginning of a play.

The Billionaire summoned his staff. He ordered the cremation of the bones within six days. The Colonel paled. "But that's impossible! The furnaces are working at full tilt. The locals are already complaining about the smell and the smoke. We've got enough trouble calming the authorities."

"Shut up! What's impossible? God created the world in seven days. Why can't we burn this lousy pile of bones in less time? Quadruple the teams, double the salaries, but make sure that production continues. If there aren't enough furnaces, bring wood, coal, and gasoline. Light as many bonfires as it takes. In seven days, I want my jets to scatter those damn ashes from Nam Quan to Ca Mau. Execute!"

Never in human memory had so much fire and smoke filled one corner of the earth. A hellish furnace swarming with men, women, and children blackened with soot. Human chains crisscrossed and encircled the furnaces—burning embers in the chaotic links of an immense net. They passed the bones hand to hand down from the mountains to the gaping mouths of the furnaces. A thick, acrid smoke hung in the air. By the third day, you could no longer distinguish night from day. Shadows darted in and out of the murky twilight. For six days and six nights running, the smoke covered the province in a mantle of gloom, searing faces, blinding eyes, scratching throats. People burrowed into their homes, barricading doors and windows. They prayed. Babies stopped crying. The earth became as still as a prayer, a silence broken only by the crackling of the bonfires.

By the evening of the sixth day, the furnaces, the bonfires, the prayers, had all flickered out. A bloodied sun appeared and, for an instant, set the sky aflame, and then night engulfed the earth. A warm wind rose in the east, slowly dispersing the smoke. A few pale stars twinkled. And a chill moon lit the silence.

A cock crowed. In the distance, a dog barked. You could hear a baby cry. The sun emerged, shivering, from the fog. On the horizon, a dull rumbling as a squadron of planes took off, howling across the sky, scattering long gray streaks in their wake. Ashes rained to the earth. Not a single rice paddy was spared. Ash suffused the air, dusting the trees, the plants, the flowers, penetrating every human dwelling. It blinded the eyes, blocked the nose, stuck in the throat. All day, from north to south, a tornado of gray ash against the screeching of jet planes. That evening, the tempest subsided. The night returned the silence.

The next morning, the Billionaire went to the old man's house.

"Old man, I have fulfilled your wish. Now, give me my son's bones."

The old man looked at him with tenderness. "I thank you," he said in a soft, low voice. "Our dead have finally been returned to their ancestors. The dead belong there where men build civilizations. Go find your son. He is in my garden, under the altar."

The Billionaire rushed into the old man's garden. At the foot of an old banyan tree stood a brick altar, a few joss sticks smoldering there. The Billionaire ordered his men to unearth the coffin. The men advanced, shovels and pails in hand.

Nearby, crouched against the root of the banyan tree, a child watched in silence. The Billionaire approached him, and bent down to give him a dollar. The boy pushed his hand away, and as he ran to hide behind the old man, his bamboo-leaf hat fell into the open grave. The Billionaire picked it up, and walked toward the boy. He shuddered. The child's eyes, brimming with tears, were blue with hatred.

The Billionaire sipped his whiskey and gazed at the luxurious coffin where his son lay. He had won. He had fulfilled his duty as a father, his wife's last wish. The Billionaire's jet had been ready to return to the U.S. for over a week. But now he hesitated. He couldn't leave Vietnam without knowing how his son had died. He had the interpreter sent to the Village of Man, at the foot of the Mountain of Peace.

The interpreter slid into the office with a feline step. The Billionaire swiveled around in his armchair. "Well?"

"It worked. I spent a fortune. They finally talked."

"Well done. Go ahead."

"Do you really want to know everything?"

"Yes, everything."

"They killed him. John jumped from his plane before it exploded and broke his left leg. He must have crawled through the jungle for a long time. The old man found him lying unconscious next to a stream and carried him home. We don't know how long he lived with the old man. One night, he snuck out to the stream. A child saw him and alerted the village. They arrested him immediately. The village had been routinely bombed. A lot of people died, there was a lot of hatred. The villagers formed a kangaroo court and condemned your son and the old man's daughter to death. They shot your son on the spot. The girl was pregnant, so she got a reprieve. When the kid was born, they gave him to the old man."

"Thanks. You can go now. Not a word to anyone. That's an order. Understand?"

"Of course."

The Billionaire continued to sip his whiskey, staring at the coffin, overcome by a mixture of pain and tenderness. And he stayed there for hours, without moving. Suddenly, he shook his head, got up, and called the service woman.

"Please, help me."

He opened the coffin. Together they carried the bones to the furnace. While the skeleton burned, they laid the bones of the unknown soldier in the coffin.

The next morning, the Billionaire went to the old man's house. He clutched an urn of ashes to his chest. The old man was seated in the shade of the banyan tree. The boy stood behind him, his skinny arms enlaced the old man's neck. His eyes were intense, blue, full of hate. The Billionaire sighed.

"Old man, I've brought you your son's ashes. This is his final resting place. And now, I must say good-bye."

"Farewell. May peace be with you."

The Billionaire looked over at the boy with the blue eyes one last time. He walked away, his step calm, assured. His heart filled with a strange sense of relief.

He brought the unknown soldier's skeleton back to the United States. He buried it with great pomp and circumstance in the family plot next to his wife's grave. He married the service woman. They had many children. And they lived happily ever after. Among their vast progeny were many learned people, famous women and men of letters, beloved citizens. One of them became the first woman president of the United States.

—*Translated by Nina McPherson and Phan Huy Duong*

PART FIVE
Exiles

5

Thinking of it in terms of your country, I could say I was the son of peasants. We earned or made everything we had. I learned to honor people for what they do, not for their positions. I've never been able to escape the rightness of that. To explain it in terms of my country, it means: if I didn't have enemies here, I would choose to live in exile.

The Autobiography of a Useless Person

Nguyen Xuan Hoang

I was born into a large family, the twelfth child among thirteen. There were so many of us that now I can't even remember all of my siblings very clearly; I can only recount the stories of a few people in my household. But in selecting to breathe life back into those few, I believe I will also be creating a self-portrait.

Let me begin, of course, with my father. He was large, deep-chested, vigorous and strongly-built. But his unusual size was not the first thing you would notice about him. No, it was his eyes that would claim your attention and stick in your mind. They were cold and compelling and hinted of much fierceness and perhaps a touch of cruelty. They were the eyes of a man accustomed to giving orders and commanding obedience. Great orbs of brown surrounded by very little white, they claimed affinity with the eyes of tigers and panthers. Sometimes those eyes were sharp as rapiers, aimed at my fragile nape.

I feared my father. To this day I still can't decide whether I loved him.

My mother often called him a wine-worm. True, he drank like a fish, and yet I never saw him inebriated. "Me drunk? In any contest, you bet I'd win hands-down, even if I was drinking against wine itself," he boasted often and defiantly.

Mother fought him constantly, for to her wine was poison. Father fought back, claiming that wine was the wisteria of the gods. Father hoarded his wine; Mother hid whatever she found. Father became taciturn after he drank. Mother was never a talkative person.

I do not resemble my father in this respect. I do not drink.

Even though my family was large, it was cold and sad. We moved, ate, walked, studied and spoke to each other like new guests in a boarding house, brought together at mealtimes only from necessity.

My mother was taller than most Vietnamese women. She was yin to my father's yang. Fair-skinned, silver-haired, with a high-bridged handsome nose and sparkling, mischievous eyes, she was beautiful, and I loved to watch her. After arriving home from school, I would waste no time before seeking refuge in her kitchen. At times one of my sisters would join us. When prompted, Mother recounted to us bits and pieces of my father's life. Threading together these stories, often told without beginning or end, I managed by embellishing and adding my own interpretation here and there, to piece together a plausible story of his life.

A sailor on merchant ships, my father had floated from one port to the next. One day would find him in Hong Kong, the next in Singapore, then Marseilles, Amsterdam....He was a shark living haphazardly, free to move between sky and earth. The elaborate tattoos I saw carved into his rugged, hairy chest and on his rippling forearms bore testimony to my mother's story. Before marrying my mother, Father had had another wife. Her name was Suzanne; she was a French woman born in Marseilles, a city in which my father thought to settle down and rest from his wandering. But because of a mindless deed, he had to leave that place hastily. One day, when he stopped by his usual bar to have a couple of drinks, he found that everyone, including the waiters, was ignoring him. The owner paced in and out of the door, from time to time throwing contemptuous glances in Father's direction. Irritated, he seized the owner by the collar and demanded a reason. The man replied that there was no room in his establishment for "the yellows." Fury seized my father; he threw the owner to the floor and struck him with a few hard blows. The man died without a word. To escape the web of the law, Father fled with Suzanne to Paris. But there was no safety for him there, and finally he had to return to sea, leaving behind the city of light and the woman who now carried a drop of his blood inside herself. Later, my mother told me, his flesh and blood grew up into a beautiful woman named Marthe. Mother thought to write to Suzanne, but my father stopped her, telling her to stay out of his business. Until now, that was all I ever found out about this half-sister of mine. After he left Paris, father returned to Hong Kong to find another boat, to float yet again from one port to another. It was during this time that he met my mother.

She was half Chinese and half European. In her stories she referred to her father, my grandfather, with the utmost reverence. It was as if he were a God full of power. "Your grandfather was born into the aristocracy," she would remind us often. "As different from your adventurer father as heaven and earth."

"Mommy, what does it mean that he was born into the aristocracy?" I wanted to know.

"The aristocracy is not the common people."

"So why did you marry Father?" Even though I was young, I grasped the contradiction in her words.

"I don't know. Stop being so nosy. Just remember that I want all of you to pay attention to your studies and not to wander aimlessly."

She didn't want us to be adventurous like my father in his youth. But I don't believe her wishes were fulfilled.

My grandfather was from Beijing, born into a well-placed family that sent him to England to study. He subsequently married an English woman, who gave birth to my mother. Then, for a reason forever unknown to us, he left his wife in London and returned home with his daughter. But he didn't keep her with him, either, and instead entrusted her to the care of a Chinese family in Hong Kong, which he periodically supplied with funds.

How the romance between my father and mother grew, none of us knew. Mother remained silent about why the beautiful daughter of a mandarin would give her heart to a wanderer like my father. She was very Vietnamese, from the way she managed the family to the sacrifices she endured to ensure that her children and husband were well taken care of. She worked hard all day, without a break, attending to every need her children had, worrying about every meal, shielding this here, mending that there, determined to make our house a home. She never complained or protested. As for myself, I stole my height from both of them, but I inherited neither her lofty endurance nor his steadfast courage.

For all that, it seemed I was the one my mother spoiled. My father was cold-natured and my siblings were indifferent. Often I thought I would be hard put to find a thread that bound us. My older siblings didn't hate or reject me. But they showed no affection for me either. When I was young I believed I hated my whole family, with the exception of my mother. To hate wasn't difficult: I merely had to absorb the iciness around me and reflect it back like a mirror. All my warmth and love I lavished on my mother.

But I'm not being entirely truthful. Actually my sister Thao, who bore a great resemblance to my mother, was one whom I did love, almost as much as I loved my mother. Yet between us there was an inexplicable barrier. We never exchanged more than a couple of phrases before tempers flared and sparks started to fly. True to her name, she was a wild grass, bursting forth from the dry decayed landscape that was our family. Her wild, untamed beauty worried my mother a great deal, bringing her more unhappiness and alarm than pride. Thao had my mother's beauty, but she also inherited my father's cruelty.

When she was seventeen, she was pursued by a rich young man from the city. He bought her numerous expensive gifts. In the beginning she laughed and waved the matter aside like a joke. Later she threw everything he sent to her out of the door. His name was T, and if my memory serves me, he was not bad-looking. But no matter how he tried, he not only failed to conquer her heart, but faltered miserably while aiming for her pity. Not that he wasn't resourceful; he tried to get to Thao by pleasing everyone in the family. He discreetly brought wine to my father, gave expensive fabrics to my mother, and toys to me. He rounded the whole periphery before fastening on his intended prey, my sister. If she had asked him to kneel down and beg for a morsel of her love, he would have done so willingly, without hesitation. But Thao refused to bend or even reveal any sympathy for him. I don't know whether she was in love with someone else. But she consigned T's passionate, blind and pitiful love to the drain and sewer. In the evenings, I often saw him on the other side of the street, leaning morosely against the trunk of the flowering cassia tree, its brilliant golden blooms contrasting with his wistfulness and humiliation as he stared into our house. He was clearly suffering. And to tell the truth, I felt sorry for him and thought my sister cruel. My father didn't drink a drop of T's wine. And even though our budget was tight and my mother yearned to make us new clothes, she resisted temptation also and returned his gifts. Once my father asked T to drink with him. T said he didn't know how. Father replied, "A man without a drink is like a kite without wind." T's expression was pitiful. My father knocked down one glass. T emptied his in one shot. "Pretty good," Father said and poured out a second glass. Glass after glass after glass. When Father saw fit to release T, he threw up all over the place then fainted into his own puke.

When the French returned to Vietnam after World War II, T joined a small French unit as its translator. His reputation for savagery spread wide and far. Many died under his hands. In his lust for sexual conquest, in each village he raided he left behind at least two or three women victims. One could always find two Moroccans at his side, their faces marred with old scars. Many women, after being raped, had their breasts cut off or were stabbed by these two monsters.

It was during this time, because of the fortunes of war, that my family was shattered to pieces. When it became unsafe to remain in our town, we had to split up and scatter to different parts of the country. I went with my father to Hon Lon, a famous site in Central Vietnam. We lived at the foot of a mountain; houses had been thrown up precipitously on the rough terrain there, giving an impression of impermanence. But the sounds of war were far from that place.

Meanwhile, in a far away region, my mother and sister found themselves in an area within the trajectory of T's raids. My mother recounted what happened later. One evening, T broke into the house, accompanied by his Moroccans. He puffed leisurely on his cigarette, playing spectator as the Moroccans pinned Thao down and tied her to the bed, then tied my mother to a chair in the corner. Mother was terrified. This was the gist of the exchange between T and my sister:

"Will you come to me willingly?" he asked.

"No," she responded calmly.

"Why not?"

"No particular reason."

"When will you change your mind?"

"Never."

"Are you afraid of me?"

"Why should I be afraid?"

T drew the small pistol from his belt, stuck it against her forehead and repeated the same questions. Thao didn't show any emotion; she didn't even bother to look at him. My mother cried out in fear, afraid he would fire. He struck her. Then he tore off Thao's clothes and raped her in front of all those present, like a beast pouncing on an elusive prey. Because she had to witness such an atrocity, my mother fell seriously ill. Afterwards Thao left, leaving behind no indication of where she might be found. The story made a deep impression on me: in my mind I saw T and witnessed his actions.

As for myself, once I became an adult, I realized that one cannot survive without loving and relying on others. To put it simply, when I discovered I needed to love Thao, she was no longer there.

But I came to cherish in my heart two of my other brothers: my eldest and the brother closest to me in age.

Eldest Brother left to travel the world when he was fourteen. I had not yet been born then. Mother told me he had gone to Saigon, then to Ca Mau, Rach Gia, Nam Can, Can Tho, Chau Doc and the other large provinces of Vietnam. Once when we were eating, Mother mentioned that she had just received a letter and some cash from Vientiane. Another time in response to one of Thao's questions, she said he was in Savanakhet. During a time I remember well because my father gave up wine and started drinking tea from an antique Tho Hao Tran cup of which he was very proud (but then quickly went back to wine) Eldest Brother was working on a plantation in Cambodia. We were unclear where he was at any given time. I never met him until much later in my life.

Closest Brother was large, yet very sophisticated. Thus it came as a total surprise to the whole family that as soon as he passed his secondary school final examination, he joined the military and became a professional soldier. He succeeded in being admitted to the military academy in Da Lat and joined the Air Force when he graduated. He loved literature and surrounded himself with writers and poets, even though he had never written a poem or a short story. He also had many girlfriends, mainly cabaret singers who caught his eye. Yet he told me he knew nothing of love.

In 1972, at the end of that bloody summer and just before my mother passed away, he announced he was getting married. She was a biology teacher, someone far removed from his world. His beauty and elegance were the weapons he'd used to seduce his singers, but those were useless with his fiancée. She married him because of his honesty, not his looks, she told me later. The marriage forced him into a tight mold. Household, family and neighbors filled his days, leaving no room for the licentiousness of his past. "It's true love," he confided in me, after he'd had a child. Even so, each time the captive broke free and went to

Saigon, it was as if a fish had found water. He fed on friends and drinks, on dancers and singers, on bars and music. He lived fast, as if the world might turn to dust the next day. Once during one of his visits he stayed sober enough to tell me of his fears about the direction the war was taking. There was much he didn't understand. The political situation was getting worse day by day. The large cities seemed helpless, as if they had drawn themselves into a fetal position. The war was not a matter of battlefields; it was woven into the fabric of every day life, into every corner of the country, into cities and countryside, into farms and orchards, into every household. It was fought with each breath we took, in each fiber of our bodies. Yet there was no despair in his voice when he said this. He began to describe the huts and houses which appeared and disappeared as he flew past, about the forests, the mountains and the rivers over which his plane had carried him. He described the bleached clouds that expanded into billows of cotton in the vastness of the blue sky.

But here let me go back to the story of my eldest brother.

Like my father, Eldest Brother was very tall and robust. He had a square, somewhat flat face, thick eyelashes, a stub nose, large mouth, square chin and a beard so black it almost seemed a shade of blue. A scar ran from his left eye to his ear. His eyes gave an impression of fierceness and stubbornness, like my father's. His curly hair snarled into little fists at the nape of his neck. He had a round, solid neck, broad shoulders and large hands. His face was an extraordinary contradiction in itself, a bizarre fusing of hardness and softness, love and hate, cruelty and sympathy. When I was a four year old child I was suddenly forced to meet this stranger, this creature who materialized out of nowhere. As I clung to my mother's shirt and watched his burly figure advance towards me, I felt, strangely enough, that I had known him for a long time. But I didn't greet him. He still didn't seem real: he wasn't flesh and blood, but an acquaintance of my mind. He didn't stay long then and I don't remember when he left. What remains in my mind of his visit is a picture of a nearly complete family, even though the atmosphere in our household was still one of coldness and reserve. It was as if we understood that something shattering was to happen, as if we were poised on the edge of a storm. In fact I remember my eldest brother was very solicitous towards Thao. He singled her out and as I watched them talk at length to each other, I caught mention of T. One night, as we gathered around the table, my father began a conversation that was clearly meant to draw out stories from Eldest Brother's life. He threw back his head and laughed, his beard giving him a definite Caucasian look. But when he spoke at last, he spoke slowly and carefully. In this he resembled my mother. He told us of the places he had temporarily called home: the rubber plantations, the indentured servants in the North, the autocratic French plantation owners, the inhuman torture of workers for absenteeism by the foremen. He told us anecdotes about the people he had met, the jobs he had held, but he gave us no clues about his inner life. When he stood up, my father made a sudden enigmatic announcement: "This one is like me!" It wasn't until later that I found out he'd killed a foreman in a fit of anger over the latter's cruelty towards a worker.

One year later, the August revolution against the French exploded, enveloping the whole country. Eldest Brother joined the guerillas and was carried away by the events of the time which blew him from one mountain to another, one forest to the next, to battlefield and war zone, leaving no trace of him until after the grievous incident that befell Thao.

That year when the bombs began exploding in our town, it was as if a bee's nest had been smashed and the bees, in panic, scattered in every direction, bewildered and lost. My mother and Thao went one way, other brothers and sisters went another. I accompanied my father past villages tucked away at the bases of mountains, past green rice fields and mango groves and rose apple orchards and their crudely constructed irrigation systems, crossing wide rivers lying drowsy in the sun or flowing lonely in the moonlight. I saw herds of cattle chewing on grass and the water buffalo wallowing in muddy water. The war followed us city folk. At first, as we threaded our way through the countryside, we heard the sound of gunfire from far away. Then, as time went on, it sounded like it was coming from the next bend in the road. One day we came to a crossroad. In front of us were rice fields and villages and behind us stone mountains and verdant forests. Hon Lon was a dead end; there was nowhere left to run. So we settled down and Father became both woodcutter and farmer. He taught me that only through one's own labor and sweat should one be privileged to a bowl of rice. The earth only nourished and protected those who loved it, lived on it, worked with it. Father was very handy. He was familiar with every task performed by a farmer and, best of all, his work yielded results. He told me that in the veins of every Vietnamese coursed the blood of a farmer in touch with the earth. It was at this same time that Father returned to drinking tea out of an earthen pot. He was an early riser and made tea as soon as he woke up. And I became his companion. Our lives in the confines of this world were happy, maybe because our circumstances didn't allow us to feel anything else.

Then one day a man brought news that my eldest brother had come back from the war zone and had asked to see Father. I was very excited, but my father seemed thoughtful and silent. I can see clearly now, as if it were yesterday, our reunion on the front veranda. That evening in the mountains was bitterly cold. My brother stood in the courtyard. I was still struck by his height but I could see he had lost much weight. He had shaved off his beard; however his hair was still curly and tight against his skin. I looked from him to my father. Although he was thinner, Eldest Brother bore an uncanny resemblance to him. The two adults stood very still, staring like two hunters ready to pounce on their prey. The light from the setting sun gleamed in my brother's eyes. At last, my father called his name. That night as we sat around the fire and ate a meal of rice mixed with corn and flavored with fish sauce, its intense saltiness lightened by sugar sticks, I was happy. In the brightness of that fire of thanksgiving, even the monotonous meal tasted good. Eldest Brother gathered me into his lap, drew his gun from his belt, emptied out the bullets and handed it to me. He recited a poem by an author whose name I learned later was Quang Dung:

> ...*Have you seen my mother*
> *among the bodies clogging the rice fields...*

Those verses remain with me until this day and I will never forget them. Sometime later that night he drew close to my father and said in a shaky voice:

"I met T."

"T?" My father asked intently. "Where?"

"In Tan Hung. Near Go Quit. Do you remember?"

"Yes. What happened?"

"I asked him if he knew who I was. He said yes. I asked him if he was scared. He said no..."

He stopped and looked thoughtful. "You should know that I did what needed to be done for Thao."

Silently Father poured out the tea into the earthen cup and drained it in one draught.

My brother in the Air Force reached adulthood when the war in Vietnam entered a different phase. The French had left after losing Dien Bien Phu, the Americans arrived, Emperor Bao Dai was dethroned. President Ngo Dinh Diem took power and the First Republic was born. Of our family of thirteen only my youngest sister remained home with Mother. Eldest Brother and Thao had disappeared. Closest Brother joined the Da Lat Military Academy. I left for Quang Trung, then Thu Duc. Ngo Dinh Diem's presidency fell. Generals vied for power. Father passed away at the time of the Tet Offensive. Four years later Mother died, at about the same time that a French reporter wrote about the Highway of Horror in Quang Tri, where a Marine friend of mine wrote a poem entitled "Old Town" before sacrificing his life. My youngest sister got married. We sold our childhood home. As for myself, my luck held, for I was a soldier who served more in an office than on the battlefield. Once again, I was the spoiled child in a society that didn't indulge many spoiled children. Closest Brother was still handsome, but he was a model father and a good husband. Once when we happened to meet in Saigon, he reminisced about our eldest brother and Thao. We wondered where they were, whether they were alive or dead. He said that war was horrible and asked for my opinion. My opinion? But I really had no opinion. Just an understanding that I loved everyone and harbored no hatred in myself. Closest Brother said the same thing.

April 1975. Saigon fell and within the ranks of the victorious my eldest brother appeared. He searched me out just before I was called to report to a reeducation camp. He had changed. His scar seemed less pronounced, his once muscular body had withered. He was thin and contemplative. He didn't want to see our other brother and didn't want to explain why. Youngest Sister had followed her husband and left the country right before that fateful day in April. Yet my brother in the Air Force, the one with an ideal escape mechanism, stayed behind. Until now I don't understand his motivation. I packed up some clothing and food to take with me on the promised ten days of reeducation. It was three years until I returned; meanwhile Closest Brother remained imprisoned in a camp in the North. After my release I became a jack of all trades. I travelled and worked in numerous places. But however much I searched, I never found Thao or heard anything about her. It was as if she had never existed.

Eldest Brother came to visit me once more, after I was caught trying to escape by boat from Rach Gia. He advised me against trying again, saying that he considered taking to the sea an act of treason. It wasn't until ten years after the fall of Saigon that I found myself arriving safely in Pulau Bidong, after a trip that wasn't as harrowing as that of many others. I was always the lucky one. One year later, thanks to Youngest Sister, I was accepted into the United States.

While waiting at the camp for a country of asylum, I heard of the death of Closest Brother at the reeducation camp. It was a double loss, for almost at the exact same time I received another letter telling me that Eldest Brother had inexplicably taken his own life by putting a bullet into his head. In the same letter I learned that he had done so after he'd visited my closest brother at his deathbed.

I am now a technician earning a basic salary, enough to survive.

Yesterday I received a letter from my sister-in-law in Umbatta, Australia announcing that she had remarried. Her new husband was also Vietnamese and together they had opened a restaurant. They invited me to come and visit and were kind enough to offer to buy me a ticket and arrange a place for me to stay. I telephoned to congratulate her and told her I wanted to bring my nieces and nephews to the United States for a visit. She promised that it would be soon.

Life in America is full of comfort. I am not rich, yet really I don't miss anything. Only on the weekends, as I perform my ritual of strolling in Mile Square Park, am I reminded of that part of my childhood I spent with my father in the mountains of Central Vietnam. As on many autumn mornings in the highlands, the sunrise uncovered a forest thick with white fog. The wind billowed through the cold trees, touching off the melancholic calls of the birds. Walking over ground covered with glittering dew, puffing on a damp cigarette, I had felt old. Now, forty years later, I am just as old as I was then.

Translated by Thai Tuyet Quan
Edited by Wayne Karlin

Coming Down Again
John Balaban

That morning, with the early sun already fierce above the village, Lacey dangled his feet off the edge of a little deck built out from the porch as a drying rack for firewood, for the hundreds of tiny silver fish to be pounded with hot peppers into a paste, and for the strands of cotton to be dyed and woven into the colorful stovepipe leggings that Lawa women wore with their loose shifts. Still wearing his white shirt and white, canvas, rope-soled shoes from Spain, but having discarded his seersucker pants for dark, baggy, drawstring Lawa trousers, Lacey bent his neck to the hot sun and happily wrote in one of Johnson's old Cheyney notebooks. He was writing a poem, an event that in recent years had become rarer for him, and was usually filled with threat of failure, interruption, and corresponding irritability. As he sat here now on the deck near the ripe smells of dead fish and drying wood and penned livestock, assaulted at the ports of all of his senses, he was serenely composed, busy with the poem, alert to the village, and, to use a phrase of his philosophical friend, Vivian Bloodmark, "manifestly aware of his own manifest awareness." A rat rustled in the buffalo straw beneath his feet. Clucking bantams pecked the dirt road, still puddled here and there with yesterday's rain. And while most of the villagers were transplanting rice seedlings in the terraced, flooded fields above and below the village, a few others were still about. Across the way, a man was kneeling on his porch baiting a cone-shaped fish trap with crickets. Down from the mountain to Lacey's left, a kerchiefed woman was waddling home with large bamboo tubes filled with spring water, an awkward and heavy burden of about ten three-foot tubes lashed to a shoulder yoke. She sloshed past a ten-year-old girl flashing a long machete down upon a stob that she was cracking into kindling. Ahead of the water-carrier, a young man was leading a black-and-white, quasi-pinto pig off to the valley market; and near him, across the way and under some house pilings, a water buffalo rose up off its huge knees and tossed its horns when a boy with a switch came to lead it out to pasture. Next door, behind Lacey's house, a bare-chested man and his wife, both smoking pipes, were treadling a rice mill and tossing the chaff to a trio of pigs grunting around their feet and sliding their blubbery noses in the dirt of the threshing shed floor.

At the end of the village, just before the mountain's rounded, tree-shorn brow dropped off in steep ravines, a stream sparkled in the sunlight. Across the stream lay a bridge, and by the bridge a long pole had been planted, and from the pole—to mark a Haw trader's shop—fluttered a bright red banner. Lacey's senses took all this detail in, and let the abundance inform, breathe into, inspire his poem.

"My men in Chiang Rai say your wife beautiful." Chom was on the porch loading shiny, stubby .45 slugs into the long clip for the greasegun slung over his shoulder. He had been watching Lacey from the kitchen and had only come out now that Lacey seemed distracted from his writing. "Don't you like your wife?"

"Sure I do. Why?"

Chom walked across the creaky boards of the drying-deck and sat down next to Lacey. He continued to talk as he slowly took more slugs from a canvas bag and shoved them into the clip, one of a dozen that he intended to load. Each clip held thirty rounds. Chom's fingers moved methodically, automatically, as they had moved the night before when he had played with the palmetto bug. Chom looked about as he fed the magazines. He might have been whittling. He had bathed. He was relaxed. His baseball cap was doffed for once, and his long black hair, still wet, was straight and sleek in the sunlight. "Well," he said, "Why don't you stay home with her?"

Lacey put down the notebook, sticking his pen in the pages to mark his poem. "You should understand that. You went off after a friend," he said, nodding to the house where Pae was still sleeping, "and I went off to look for mine."

"Yes, but you came ten thousand mile. I only trave'd one hundred."

"Your one hundred were hard. Mine were fun."

"Fun to be so fa' from home?"

"Fun *because so* far from home."

Chom held a short, heavy slug up to the sunlight, turning it to study a bevel that his fingers had discovered on the lip of the casing. "I doan understan' that. I think of Baw Luang alla time. My house. The stream that runs in valley. Our fields. Elpha's bringing rice in big baskets. Our lam talking to field spirit."

"My home is not so interesting."

"How so?" Chom laid the questionable bullet beside him.

"It's boring," Lacey said by way of explanation, but realized that he had only confused things more. He tried then to describe what life was like for him: his committee and office obligations, the entertainments in a college town—the three movie theaters, cable TV, the one disco where the kids lined up outside in designer clothes, football weekends, his inert colleagues, two-party politics, owning a mortgaged home, paying income taxes, the ordeal of keeping a car, the *distance* from nature, the distance from other people, from a community where you had real concerns—love, marriage, birth, death. How unreal those concerns had become for him. The endless talk in a world stripped of any real action. He tried to explain Western boredom. Chom was uncomprehending.

"Boring," Chom repeated and paused, as if to see if the word would take on meaning once it passed his lips. None of the English-speakers he had known had ever used the word, not James or Beta or even the Reverend Thompson. "In Lawa we have word for 'idle' which rea'y mean 'sleepy-sad.' Idle is nice, not boring. You are quiet. You think. You get sad maybe." Chom stopped loading for a moment and looked directly at Lacey as they both sat dangling their feet off the deck. "When I get ol' I want to be samang in Baw Luang or maybe even lam. I sit on my por' and decide the lan' for my people or maybe drink whiskey and listen to spirits....What the opposite 'boring?'"

"Excitement."

"You want e'citemen'?"

"Not just excitement. In the West, there's an old saying, 'Judge a man by what he says and does,' and, of course, by the possible discrepancy between the two."

"Discrepa'cy?"

"Difference." Lacey took an extra clip and helped Chom load. "The idea is that you have to see *both* to judge a man's worth. In modern lives, real actions are absent. We just talk."

"Here we no much like action man. So'diers not respected. Poets, maybe. Wise man sees things or makes things happen aroun' him. It is e'citing to be quiet, to listen to spirit. Very e'citing for me, because when I listen to spirit again, they will be many blood spirit. Because I spill blood. Angry spirit."

Wheel and deal, Lacey thought. Get in there and kick ass. None of that "sleepy-sad" shit or letting things happen around you like the eye of a hurricane. Then, as Lacey reached into the bag of bullets, another snippet of Western belief floated up from his memory. "We have another saying: 'Virtuous knowledge results in human action.'" Lacey remembered Sir Philip Sidney, knight, poet, and Christian humanist. "Maybe that is what I am looking for. And it applies to you, too, Chom; I mean, the way you act as opposed to the way Khan Su acts."

Chom took Lacey's finished clip, thumbed the top round, and then smacked the clip up into the submachine gun. He took a two-inch, funnel-shaped flash hider out of the canvas bag and screwed it onto the short muzzle of the greasegun. "Khan Su," he said, "very smart but, like you say, he have no power here. I can beat him." Chom put his hand to his heart, or really to his stomach, the Lawa seat of compassion and the forces of the soul.

Across the road the young girl was still whacking firewood with the machete. She wore baggy pants and a white blouse and smiled at them with very white teeth, her short black hair flying up with each swing. Her fat, naked little brother—his tiny pecker fluttering like a moth as he ran to pick up the pieces after each of his sister's swings.

"You have chi'r'en'?"

"No. We don't want any."

Chom paused from loading clips to look at Lacey, unsure if Lacey weren't teasing him. "Doan want?"

Lacey shook his head 'no' and tried to explain how he and Louise didn't think America in the seventies was much of a place to raise children.

"Lacey," Chom began, "I doan know America, but I think you talk crazy. When was there ri' worl' for chi'r'en'?" He gestured to the surrounding mountains. "You think this is ri' worl' for them? With TB, malaria, cho'ra, plague, worm, fevahs, lep'osy, bad food, no medicine? I afraid to bath in rivah now because of James. Lucky Lawa doan know disease—they think spirit kill James. May be if they know about disease, they think crazy like you. How can a man refuse to live his life? Should those chi'r'en'"—he pointed to the pair of little woodcutters—"not be born?"

Lacey sighed a large sigh of hopelessness.

"You know Nee Chee?"

Lacey shook his head.

"Yes. Yes. You know him. Famous German writer. Johnson give me his book."

Nietzsche! Lacey had thought he was hearing about some Chinese.

"He say, 'Whoever consent to his own return, participates in the divinity of this worl'."

Lacey was smiling.

"You like that?" Chom smiled too.

Lacey was smiling at Chom, not Nietzsche. He felt a little stupid. He would like to set Chom down on an American interstate at night, with a CB walkie-talkie in his hand, and let him listen to the insane, hopeless, disoriented chatter and the reports of random violence. He wanted to tell Chom about what it was like to grow up in the U.S.A.—the inanity of American schools, the drugs (!) and booze, the aimlessness, how everything seemed punctured by impending nuclear war. But all that seemed stupid to talk about. Here there were no schools, and children grew up educated in the complex modalities of their tribes. Here opium was always at hand, and everyone seemed to understand that it was dangerous, that only the weak and those desperate for defeat took it and, moreover, that they would take something else if opium weren't available. And here warfare was never far off, and yet for centuries the power of the mountain peoples to fill up the high valleys with peaceful communities seemed far stronger than the power of death and mayhem to sweep away their upland utopias—the terraced hills, the tiny spirit houses, the shared labors in the fields, the wrists tied in marriage strings. No TV, no "parenting" lectures. Here the kids were live on all channels, and the whole village loved them, taught them, chided them, plotted their marriages, reviewed their sorrows, and called them into the flooded fields, into the common scattering of splayed feet and bending backs, into the unchanging song of the harvest. Lacey felt a little stupid, and very remiss, spiritually remiss. He knew why Chom's beliefs were almost reflex, instinctual, unquestioned, and he envied Chom his instincts. What was Dowson's phrase? "Between the idea and the act, falls the shadow." Chom lived in the sunlight of enterprise informed by tradition—he had *fucking spirits* telling him what to do. Throughout Lacey's world fell the shadow. He wished he could translate Chom's world—perilous to the flesh; empowering to the spirit—into his own life. Instead, he was doing the reverse.

A good-sized lizard with a bright blue head scuttled across the deck, slipslapping its tail as it made a madcap escape from nothing in particular. Lacey jumped and Chom laughed at him, handing him the submachine gun. "Can you shoo' this?"

Lacey took the submachine gun in his hands. It was a heavy mother, weighing about ten pounds with the loaded clip, and it was very ugly. They called it a greasegun because the dull, gray, cheap, stamped parts assembled into something that looked more like a garage tool than a firearm. The U.S. had turned them out by the thousands at the end of the war. And the OSS, the CIA's forerunner, had ordered thousands more for Asia. Lacey's gun had been around a long time. It was slow-firing—about four hundred rounds per minute, comically primitive in comparison to modern light machine guns and assault rifles—and it wasn't very accurate at a distance; but it fired a big slug and was brutal at short ranges. Lacey had never fired one, but he knew all about them, had carried one, even slept with one, for days during the Tet offensive in 1968. For a whole day he had guarded an operating room in a province hospital while the war raged beyond the hospital fence and water splattered the sandy courtyard all about him when the hospital's water tower took a drilling in the cross fire. But he had never fired one. He was proud of that. He had sat there all day near the electrician's shack and the barking generator, looking at the *Playboy* pinups, looking nervously around the hospital grounds and one-story wards for the VC, who were supposed to be prowling for medicines and perhaps to kidnap a surgeon. To Lacey's immense gratitude none ever showed. How could he shoot someone whose cause he supported? Well, he could. He had agreed to. If he wouldn't have, the surgeons would have quit operating, and the hundreds of shredded and bleeding civilians who lay sprawled in the sun about the court would surely have died. Of course, he could. Shoot at me, I shoot at you. He wasn't a nitwit. But he never fired one. He sat there all day, looking at the girly photos, looking around the buildings. Later in the day a Vietnamese nun and nurse came and put a red-cross band, *hong thap tu*, on his left arm. Perhaps she thought he had earned it. He wore it like decoration, the greasegun still across his knees. Nee Chee! "Yes," he said, pressing the metal stock extended against his shoulder. "I know how." The reliable piece of shit in his hands had cost about $22 to make. How many people had it killed? "Will I have to shoot, too?" He tried not to sound afraid.

"May be three."

"No, I mean—"

"Yes, yes. If they chase us through mountain, you may have to shoo'. But I tell you when. Sometimes not shooting get better resul'. We'll see."

"Okay." Lacey sounded overly grave, even to himself.

"Lacey, want to hear a poem?" Chom said this with enthusiasm, as if to perk up their conversation.

"Sure."

Chom's poem was a folk song. He sang it. Each word a syllable so that the notes coincided with each word. Chom translated:

> "*Phoenixes compete; so do sparrows,*
> *They call before the shrine, behind the chedi.*
> *I can use men who are loyal, if not elegant.*"

"Lacey," Chom's tone was serious, "you elegant. You must be loyal or you fuck up everything. You listen me, okay? Carlos, he listen Beta."

Lacey nodded. "Okay," he said.

"Now, tell me your poem." Chom's voice was enthusiastic again. "When I see you writing, you happy. He is writing to his wife, I think, or he is writing poem."

Lacey opened his notebook and read his poem; he did this without fanfare, the first sign of his loyalty.

> *Under the tattered umbrellas, piles of live eels sliding in flat*
> *tin pans. Catfish flip for air. Sunfish, gutted and gilled, cheek*
> *plates snipped. Baskets of ginger roots, ginseng, and garlic*
> *cloves; pails of shallots, chives, green citrons. Rice grain in*
> *pyramids. Pig halves knotted in mushy fat. Beef haunches*
> *hung from fist-size hooks. Sorcerers, palmists, and, under a*
> *tarp, thick incense, candles. Why, a reporter, or a cook, could*
> *write this poem if he had learned dictation. But what if I said,*

simply suggested, that all this blood fleck, muscle rot, earth root
and earth leaf, scraps of glittery scales, fine white grains, fast talk,
gut grime, crab claws, bright light, sweetest smells
—Said: a human self; a mirror held up before.

"That's called 'Chiang Rai River Market.'"
"Market like a mi'ah?" Chom said reflectively.
"Yes."
"I like it. But the English too hard to hear."

The Key

Vo Phien

To say that the first picture in the memories of the wanderings of an unfortunate man who has lost his country and left everything behind is a shower seems ridiculous. What a strange recollection. Perhaps I should say something sorrowful, more poetic. But how can I? None could take refuge the way he wished.

We came to U.S. territory at night. Despite our excited state, darkness prohibited a clear view of part of a country in which we were going to spend the rest of our lives. At that late hour the island of Guam seemed to consist of thousands of lights.

Our ship dropped anchor about 3 A.M., July 5, 1975. We, nine thousand people, gathered on deck, confused at first. Then, one by one, we climbed down the rope ladder. One man led his son by the hand, another carried his old father; one carried his briefcase, another wrapped his property in a blanket and another loosely held a water container in his hand. One was really naked, wearing only underwear. These poor people were warmly received. Not only were U.S. military officers waiting at the port, there were also Red Cross workers, local authorities and some church leaders.

I watched the beginning of the exodus into the foreign land from the deck of the American Challenger. The refugees proceeded slowly into the well-dressed crowd. Everyone, whether Christian or not, was deeply moved by the presence of an old bishop on the deck in the early morning hours.

My fellow countrymen passed by the important persons cautiously. Carrying sleeping mats and blankets, fathers and sons walked together quietly for nearly fifty feet and then they caught sight of the signs to...the showers! Yes, there were the Showers.

The first showers we saw in America stood there in open air. So from the deck I watched people, old and young, quickly undress, rub off the dirt and splash under the showers. Taking a bath so hurriedly at that hour, close to such a solemn setting! I felt lost. "Yes, even in this country, sanitary measures went along with the warmest feelings. Good."

In my country, there is an expression, "rubbing off the dirt." In honor of a friend or relative who just returned from a trip, we might have a party or a dinner "to rub the dirt off from the long journey." The word "dirt" is, of course, used figuratively. And so, I compared the rubbing-off-the-dirt feast in my country with the way people rub off the dirt with soap and water here and could not help but worry for the vast differences between the two cultures.

During our stay in tents on Orote Points, the baths at those open air showers became an important part of our daily activities. From early morning until late afternoon, in the hot sun, people lined up to get to the showers. The gatherings around the showers were quite interesting. With 5, 6 or 7 persons in a small wooden room—four rooms standing next to each other—we could look at the sky above, watch the slowly drifting clouds and make conversation with new friends. We discussed many things: the ceremony of lowering the Vietnamese flag on a warship before entering the Subic Bay; the flavor of the ham we'd just eaten; the last days of the nation; getting milk for the babies, etc. Valuable experiences were exchanged, unexpected stories of the fates of friends and relatives were shared under the showers at Orote Points.

In contrast, we had another kind of bathroom at the Fort Indiantown Gap, Pennsylvania, refugee camp. There, each section had about 100 people with only a small shower, a pitch dark, stifling shower with no window. There was no door either; just a curtain. In that small room, there were three showers so that three people of the same sex could bathe at the same time. There was a cardboard hanging on a curtain with one side reading "Men" and the other "Women". To avoid serious mistakes, one had to check and put out the appropriate side before using the shower.

As the shower was airtight, some people used it as a fumigator. If one caught a cold, he came into the room, then turned on the shower and stepped aside to avoid the hot water. The steam would rise, the man would be soaked with perspiration and eventually would feel much better.

The shower was also used for recording. The refugees were very thirsty for musical tapes. Each family tried to get some familiar songs and favorite voices before they left the camp. Some thought of the shower. About midnight, when most of us had fallen asleep, when all the noises had quieted, one could bring two cassette recorders into the showers. Yes, this was the place for tape recording. With a few borrowed tapes, two recorders together, one as a transmitter, the other as a receiver, the country music lover could continue his work until the next morning.

And it was in the bathroom that I had the chance to listen to the confessions of a man in his mid-fifties.

He was an extremely shy, cautious man. Ordinarily, he seldom talked to anyone in an open manner. Nearly all of us had suffered many heartbreaking losses. Everyday, we moaned, talked on and on while the ladies often cried. Being together for a while, we came to understand the circumstances of others pretty quickly, at least in a general way: this lady, wife of a colonel, could get out but her husband and sons got stuck in Vietnam; that fellow, student of the School of Agriculture, ran for his life from B. to N. province, then from N. to Saigon and met a rescue ship there and now his parents won't know what happened to him; or the family of that wealthy businessman hurriedly climbed on an American ship, leaving behind gold and dollars which could be worth millions of piasters; and so on....

However, I didn't know exactly what had happened to the family of that old man.

His was a complete family of husband and wife, a daughter and two sons. It was good enough, for who could expect to have brothers and sisters, aunts and uncles to go with? Yet, there was grief and apprehension on the couple's faces. That concern overruled their surroundings and even spoiled the liveliness of their young sons.

I'd wanted to ask him many times. But at the same time I found that it was not an easy thing to do. I wondered if it might be too curious or crude, especially to a man like him. Besides, he didn't need us; he seemed to be trying to avoid our friendliness.

In fact, I had hardly ever met such a shy man. He was as shy as a girl who just reached maturity. He spoke good English, and it was rumored that he'd been an English teacher for many years. At the refugee camp's main office, he was sometimes asked to do translation for other people. On such occasions he was even more bashful. If someone said something, he listened and remained quiet for a while. He would look at us questioningly as though it was too bold to say. And perhaps, for him, everything was too bold. He'd hesitate again until someone reminded, "Please translate it for me." And again, his attitude was the same.

Would it be too daring to ask anything from such a man?

And then, one night about 11 o'clock, I went to the shower. As I stood in front of the curtain, I read the sign: "Men" and could hear the sound of splashing water inside. I asked, "Who's in there? May I come in?"

A cheerful voice replied, "Sure. Please come in."

Raising the curtain, I recognized the shy man immediately. He was unusually kind to me.

"Hello! Feel free, please. More people, more fun. Ha, ha."

He was "feeling free" in the shower, indeed. He was naked and covered with soapsuds. Vietnamese laws do not require a person to cover a particular part of his body in front of someone else, but we don't, however, get accustomed to being nude at public baths as the Japanese do. His attitude really encouraged me. I then started "feeling free."

While I was taking off my clothes, my new friend continued to talk, asking question after question: "When did you leave Saigon? Oh, really? April 29? Half a day earlier than us, then. Which street did you live on? H. Street? We had an uncle who lived on that very street. We used to visit them quite frequently....Might have passed by your house, who knows? Ha, ha. When did you come here? Applied for a sponsor yet? Which one?..."

I was amazed and delighted. It seemed to me this man was completely different from the one I had known before. From one topic to another, my friend talked and talked in a cheerful mood while rubbing his body. We treated each other like long time old friends. I soon realized that sometimes displaying human bodies eventually led to displaying human hearts. Once getting rid of all the clumsy clothes, of all artificial relationships, suddenly feeling free, a man in the shower would no longer be afraid of any daring act.

Finally, he talked about his own trip:

"My father is 93 years old now. My wife and I had thought about it over and over since N. province was lost. Surely it was time to run away, but what about my father? He's too old and weak to bear any hazard we might encounter during evacuation. As for us, we ran for our lives, not for any trip, didn't we? On the other hand, we wouldn't have peace of mind leaving him alone! I have a younger sister who lived in D. province. Since the loss of that province, I haven't heard anything from her; she's dead or alive, or where is she living now? I don't know. Oh yes, I still have a few cousins, a few nephews and nieces, but they all planned to go. It's hard to find someone to take care of him. To tell you the truth, it's been six years that my father has become more and more senile. He's absent minded and sometimes behaves like a child. Poor father. Whenever he thought about his own age, he asked me to buy a coffin for him."

"A coffin?"

"Yes. A coffin. Traditionally, old men asked for a coffin ready at any time. But that usually happened more in rural areas. Who dares to put a coffin in his home if he lives in the city? It would look terrible, especially since our children do not accept old customs and habits. That's why we had to keep promising him a coffin, a real good one for when he passed away. Yet people said that if anyone died during the evacuation, the body would be thrown into the sea. As you can see, how could we urge him to throw himself in danger?

"Finally, our relatives met to solve the problem. We concluded that it was almost certain that not all of us would be able to get out. Therefore, anyone who stayed would take care of my father. On the other hand, if we could all get out, then friends and neighbors would be asked for help. All the money and valuables would belong to those who stayed with my father.

"And then, on April 29, with him seated in a big chair in the living room, all of us, one by one, bowed and thanked him, saying goodbye. We knew this would be goodbye forever.

"What the military situation is, what is happening in the country, what his descendants are trying to do, and so on, I'm sure my father is not clear-sighted enough to understand. But, strangely enough, he could feel that something extraordinary, something tragic, was going on. Yes sir, he sat in the chair with tears flowing gently down his cheeks. We tried to comfort him, but he didn't say anything.

"Later, we packed our luggage. We hid all the money and valuables in a wardrobe and locked it up. An ounce of gold was set aside for buying his coffin. Anybody, friend or neighbor, who decided to take care of him, was entitled to all we left. We couldn't put it all in his pockets as it would be too hazardous for him.

"When we had prepared everything, around 8 P.M., he was still sleeping. It was painful to watch him sleep in the bed, his body all curled up like a small child. We hesitated for a while and then walked away. Waking him up at that time would be a heartbreaking thing to do.

"At that time, enemy forces had advanced into some areas of the city, and the situation was critical. We didn't even know if we could make it out.

"A friend of ours organized the evacuation program which would take place at the port of H. The small boat was so overcrowded that many times I thought we would not survive. After three days of struggling for survival, on May 2 we were rescued by an American ship in international territorial waters. We knew then we'd escaped death.

"But sir, it was right at that moment that I was shocked. As I was checking my luggage, I put my hand into my pocket and found that in my hurry I had forgotten to leave the key to the wardrobe for him. My God, I put all the money along with gold and jewelry in the wardrobe, then locked it up!

"I remained silent awhile. Then, gradually, various things appeared in my mind: my father's confusion when he woke up, finding himself alone in the empty house; the scene of our relatives and friends coming in, asking for money we had left; questions about the 'hidden key' would be raised; the scene of smashing the wardrobe would frighten him. And thieves and robbers might come in and assault or beat him up. What made me so stupid, so absent minded like that...hic!"

The man stopped. He was choking on water maybe. I could hear just the sound of running water. Then he continued:

"My friend, since then I have been obsessed by those terrible pictures. From day to day, month to month, I never feel relieved. God has punished us, you see. I'm so stupid. Hic. I brought the key with me. Hic."

The man stopped again. The water stopped running simultaneously. He had finished his shower. His hands were searching for the towel. Having accustomed my eyes to the dark, I could see his shoulders tremble gently. The man wiped the water from his body and the tears from his eyes.

When did he cry? When I thought he had choked on water? But he was dressing hurriedly as though he was trying to run away. As he stretched his hands out to put his shirt on, I saw a key hanging on a string. There, my old friend carried his key where a Christian typically wears a picture of his God.

Remaining alone in the bathroom, I stood motionless for a while. Then I turned off the water, dressed, raised the curtain and left. Most people had gone back to their rooms and were asleep.

It was a quiet night. The moon was bright in a clear sky. I looked at the shiny moon, touching lightly the key in my hand. Yes, I had a key, kept in my pocket, from a situation similar to that of the old man. (In fact, isn't it true that most of the refugees brought a key along? I mean, who did not feel sorry for a certain mistake, a certain shortcoming he had made to his relatives and close friends who were left behind, something he would feel sorry for the rest of his wandering life?)

Later, a few times, I tried to tell my own story to that man, but it was not easy, as he had returned to the attitude he had had before, extremely quiet and shy. Sometimes, I thought he avoided me as though he was avoiding the same mistake or seeing a bad moment in his life again.

I didn't have a chance to meet him again in the shower.

Translated by Phan Phan

The Walls, the House, the Sky

Thanhha Lai

Only balcony seats are left when Mr. Thinh arrives. He sits among teenagers who are hugging, kissing, yelling, hiding. He scans the lower floor for his wife, without luck. The girl beside him swings her hair into his face, then apologizes by offering him a Juicy Fruit; he neither declines nor accepts. Instead he stares at her large pores, curled hair. She shoves the gum into his palm; her red nails pinch him. It then occurs to him that her hair is remarkably soft.

"Are you Tina's dad?"

He knows that is his daughter's American name, self-given. The girl guesses his answer, and rambles on about his daughter's popularity, seeing him before in his greenhouse, the role she didn't get, the prom coming up. He listens, eyes shifting between the piece of gum in his hand and her mouth, lipsticked, swiveling. Music begins. He sees her turn and give the boy next to her a quick kiss.

Actresses appear in old-time European dresses, layered below the waist like a pastry shell. Mr. Thinh thinks he recognizes his daughter in one of three dresses; they stand together, still, it is impossible to tell. Then someone in white dances past the dresses. Her hair, long, bluish black, intertwines with her ballerina skirt, as if she were drowning. His daughter. *She looks just like her.* He wrings the gum into a ball. Sugar leaks from the wrapper, seeps into his palms. His breathing accelerates; he tries holding his breath to calm it.

The last time he saw his girl, when his daughter had barely shown on her mother's belly, she was dancing. She wore white silk; her hair and gown lifted, fell. Her girlish breasts, braless, remained motionless. *She looked drugged.* He avoided her eyes, stared instead at the candle, its wax spread thin across his palm.

Now his daughter spins, then slips, or pretends to. Laughter. He remembers that blond devil had laughed too, watching his girl twirl; drunken, joyous of his luck. Mr. Thinh slaps his sticky palms together. On stage, his daughter and a boy remain; they talk, more laughter, the boy grabs his daughter, hugs her. *Damn.* Mr. Thinh squeezes his lips together; his teeth cut into them. That devil had lunged at her too, every time her scarf flew near him. You *asshole, stop this.* He had not said it.

She had been his, back in those Saigon days when he was important, when such luxury was accepted. He chose her from the heaps of poor, pretty school girls. Her eyes lured him; when she smiled, he saw the tails of a phoenix. It was supposed that he would marry her, although her parents never dared ask and he never mentioned it. He did supply the gifts that would be proper even for one with the most serious intentions.

Then marriage. His family arranged for a pure girl, beautiful, and he thought he loved her. She was pregnant when he returned to his post, to his girl. He thought he loved his girl too. When he went to tell his girl that his marriage should not change her, she had found work, dancing for the highest bidder, usually an American, sweaty, loud, waving his GI dollars for bargains he could not have afforded at home.

His daughter dances to another song. The boy sits on a chair and beams at her. Watching his daughter twirl, Mr. Thinh thinks of his girl's hair around his neck, the beauty mark behind her left ear, her arms, so white against that shiny river of black. He stands up. Sits down. Stands back up. Nothing. He climbs past the gum girl and her boyfriend and walks out.

At home, Mr. Thinh throws away the *pho* noodles and its beef broth. Food his wife always sets out for him at night. He likes watching the white strands swivel in pain before disappearing down the disposal. Then he scatters the magazine pile, turns on the television, makes warm body imprints on the couch, moves from room to room, living in minutes the spaces he would have occupied during the previous hours.

Upstairs, in the dark, he sits by the window. *Don' t think.* Moonlight always calms him. His grandfather had told him the story of a farmer, his wife and a willow tree, why their silhouettes can be seen on a full moon: a man had loved his beautiful wife so much that, at her insistence, he stole the beauty potion of the queen for her. He warned her of rumored consequences; still, under a willow tree, she bathed with the potion. Water splashed onto the tree. It began to float. The tub rocked; she climbed out, sending it tumbling to earth. The farmer, who was clearing a field, heard the crash and saw his wife floating above him, clutching onto the root. He jumped, hung onto her, thinking his weight would drag them down. They drifted up and up and landed on the moon.

Mr. Thinh used to sit with his girl in her room, more her corner, a twin bed with curtains around it, and stare at the moon. He said he was the farmer and she his tormentor. She would shake her head; he knew he was lying too. Life had made her the pursuer. It still seemed unbelievable he had slept with her in her parent's home, always leaving before dawn; they had greeted him like a son-in-law and accepted that war left no time for marriage. This, in a country where virgin girls were protected like gold. *We all have to save face.*

On their first night together, she lit a candle and brought out two rings. They were real; he wondered what gift of his she had sold. He never gave money.

Her story was so familiar that sadness or pity seemed cruel: her father was wounded, her mother sold rice cakes, her soldier brothers had not been heard from in years. They need not wear the rings, she said, just keep them. *We are now married,* so determined in the only act he saw her initiate that he did not have the heart, or the nerve, to contradict her. The ring remained in his wallet, taken out only when he exchanged an old for a new. Even now.

His wife and daughter come home, move softly, voices, suppressed, their way of acknowledging his presence. Yogurt and granola, food he never tasted yet knows they are eating. His wife cooks separately for him the same three or four dishes he has ever requested. Lying on his back, hands behind head, his military sleeping position, he listens. Only whispers. He lies still, except for the uncontrollable part. His toes wiggle, arch, his feet wrestle, contort, a nail jabs his skin. *Stay.*

Mr. Thinh awakens. Moonlight stretches across the room, rests on his bed. He reaches for his iron water mug; the act of drinking, lips against the rim, stirs him. He motions his arm to hurl the mug, yet clutches it at the crucial point. Water spills on the comforter, between his legs.

He thinks of his wife. It has been a long time; a silent agreement has arisen between them. His feet touch the cold floor, jump, finally getting what they want. Fingertips glide along the hallway wall, guiding him to her room.

They sleep with the door open. Inside, it smells pretty; he is not sure why. Two twin beds stand parallel in the center of the room, separated by an end table. He does not recognize the matching bedspreads, colorful and dotted with flowers. The body to his right is his daughter's, from the way the hair hangs off the bed and the S curve of her body. *Every girl must sleep this way.* He stands between the beds, wondering whether to touch the end of his daughter's hair, whether it would be coarse as horse hair or smooth as skin. Long ago, he had learned one could not tell by looking.

Mr. Thinh turns to the left body. He touches her hair. Short, permed. *Ugly as a poodle's.* Her face lies in the shadow, her body still awkward, thin. He had loved protecting it, like on their first night when she squinted in anticipation of pain. He touches her arm, naked outside the covers; an electrical spark, she jumps and ages in front of him, brows twist onto corrugated forehead, mouth screams backwards, sucks in breath. He flees. In bed, eyes shut tightly as his fists, alarmed voices echo, again, again.

Shadows jitter on the wall: a peacock pecks the head of a gorilla, then smashes the fleas between its beak. A pregnant goddess rides on an elephant; she falls when a hummingbird strikes her temple. He imagines yellow and red cranes circling his room, their purple mouths gaping open but no sound comes. They fly faster, creating orange flashes; as their mouths become drier, they begin to drop. One by one they dissolve into his skull, enlarging it, until it bursts to the edges of the walls, the house, the sky.

The next day, Mr. Thinh awakens to the sounds of his wife and daughter in the bathroom. Makeup. *If only they would listen.* Without it I look as green as moss, he could hear his wife answer. His daughter would remain silent. They speak Vietnamese at home. Here, he is still the commander.

He waits until they leave before coming downstairs. The curry is cold. Every morning he eats it, for the smell more than the taste. He stirs it; the smell calms him.

Having gone into work late, he stays late, hums alongside the fluorescent bulb as he reviews life stories. He feels a certain power over the poor. Then a woman phones, asks to see him. Her accent is sharp, northern, his own. She was walking by with her children and noticed his office light.

Her file tells of a young mother of two, husband still in Vietnam, a seamstress, no welfare. The buzzer startles him. He drops the folder; picking it up, he sees he had written *rat dep*—very beautiful.

She nods a greeting, then begins talking without provocation, eyes on a piece of string twisted around a bandaged finger. The older daughter circles one arm around her mother's right thigh and the other arm around the handle of the stroller. She is old enough to have the embarrassed eyes of the poor.

"How long ago?"

"Two weeks."

"You should have come in right away. Nothing to be ashamed of. I have people who would hammer off their own fingers for free money. Now, let's see, I'll change your case to AFDC. It might take two weeks, a month before...."

She is not listening, eyes focused on the string. When she glances up, her lips curl against her will. *She blushed.* She stops talking, now bows or shakes her head to his questions. He offers to take her and the children home, when she can not remember her new phone number. She declines an invitation to dinner.

She stares straight ahead in the car. A clip holds her hair; still, little wisps escape around the temple. The toddler on her lap hides her face. He does not try to talk. He thinks of taking them to the Cape, a day away from the projects. They could eat crabs and lobsters and buy the kind of junk that pleases all children. Perhaps he could ask her to wear a touch of lipstick, light pink.

At her home, he waits on a lopsided gray couch. *No doubt charity from church.* A lamp sits on the floor. The end table is used for a Buddhist altar: fruit, incense, and a portrait, black and white, of an old woman, probably her mother. He takes out a twenty and slides it under the lamp. A photograph is tucked there: she is expressionless, holds the toddler; the older girl's face peeks out at her side. Behind them stands a man, an American. Mr. Thinh pinches the photograph; short nails cut into the meaty tips.

"That's a volunteer at church."

He is silent, watches her mood change from confused to alarmed to defensive.

After leaving her house, he realizes she lives within blocks of his daughter's school, itself miles from his house, too far for his daughter to drive. It bothers him that he just now noticed it.

At a stop light, a man comes to his window; he holds up three fingers and a rose. Mr. Thinh is startled, then annoyed, thinking it is still too cold to deal with peddlers. He wonders if the man is on welfare and pockets the cash he makes. *Don't think that.*

Mr. Thinh gives the peddler a five for a yellow rose. He now feels obligated to stop by the school. When he parks, cars are pulling out of the lot. He heads to the balcony; it is empty. He sits in his old seat. The curtain has closed. Groups of teenagers stand in front of it. He spots his daughter, one of the few Asians in the crowd, giving others armfuls of herself and her hair. *Too much touching.* So different from home, where he rarely hears her voice or sees her face. He thinks of his girl: proper, icy in public, so adorable, so soft when they were alone.

At the bottom of the steps that leads to the stage, he sees his daughter smile. *This must be her night.* He takes the first step, pinching the stem of the rose carefully, avoiding the thorns, but too forcefully. The stem cracks between his fingers. He rehearses saying, You were wonderful, or, You danced beautifully, or, You look so pretty on stage, or, I'm proud. His body was almost on stage when he heard a familiar voice in the sing-song language that seemed out of place amid the raw laughter and affection.

He stares at his wife, confused, as if it were unimaginable that she should be here. She is speaking; a smile stays on her mouth and in her eyes. *She looks lovely.* Out of her blue post office uniform and men's shoes. It has been years; still, he has not gotten used to a working wife. He knows her reasons well: The House, The Food. He wants to hug her and his daughter, everyone. He panics. His wife has stopped talking and now looks at him, head slightly tilted, waiting for an answer. He pushes the rose at her and walks out. From the edge of his vision, he sees that his wife did not catch the rose. It drops to the floor.

During the following week he avoids his family. His wife continues to set out food for him, as if he were an ancestral spirit. He no longer sets an alarm; instead he relies on their whispers. At night, he would be in his room when his wife and daughter return from the play. The noises they make would soothe him to sleep.

One night they come in late. He makes himself stay up; his body tricks itself into thinking it received rest. Their noises stimulate him. When the house becomes quiet again, he is alert. Back then, if he were restless, he would ride his moped to see his girl. Only in those predawn hours could he race down the boulevards of Saigon, devoid of cycles and bodies, and the pungency of sweat.

It seemed she was always ready to receive him, her jasmine scent, her polished face. He liked being her world, she there, waiting for him. Sometimes for weeks he would not visit, yet he was comforted knowing she was there. For years now he had tried to forget the last image he saw of her, imagining instead that she was still there, waiting.

Noises come from the hallway. He pictures his daughter, not his wife. The master bedroom, with its own bathroom, belongs to him. He has thought of offering them the room, but never did. Now he needs to know who is in the hallway, as if solving this would put him to sleep.

He stands in front of his bedroom, waits until the bathroom door opens, then strolls down the hall, knowing he would pass her. Her movements stop, and when he looks up, she has pressed herself against the wall. They are within touching distance. She is wearing a white T-shirt that drops to her thighs; her body, straining against the wall, holds a certain softness that he adores. *You have grown up,* he wants to say. The words stop when he makes out her face, curious, haughty, a narrowing of the eyes that show defiance. He must have stared at her for some time before she whispers her regular greeting, *"Chao Bo,"* and walks away. He lingers in the hallway for some time before letting his fingers glide against the wall, guide him back to his room.

It is Saturday, the one day his daughter would sit through breakfast with him, silent, listening to her mother update him on her school life. By afternoon she would be gone, to shop, to study, to spend the night with friends. Her friends never stay over at his house.

When it is quiet he comes downstairs. Under a bowl is a note, still warm from the heat of the curry. The Cuongs have invited him to a late lunch, which often lasts until dawn. His wife would meet him there later. *Maybe she won't go.*

He goes to his greenhouse. The collard greens are ready for a bigger pot, so are the strawberries. Everything is grown in pots, too much lead in the soil. With pots, he can manipulate the seasons. He wants his strawberries in the spring.

The first time he saw a strawberry, too beautiful, he could not bite into it. It was for the homesick Americans, expensive enough. She was with him. *Held hers as if it were a quail egg.* They must have been in Cho Lon, where every merchant had a scheme to earn dollars. It had become his routine to take her to that market for Chinese pork noodle; she ate what he ate, yet he must have asked. At times he would pick her up right after school, she still in her white *ao dai,* sitting across from him, so lovely, listening to his theories of this or that battle or when the South would win, sitting there as if she were in class, the only alteration being a light touch of pink lipstick.

His friend calls at mid-afternoon. Mr. Thinh is to come over right away, for a poker game that would start a day of cognac and nostalgia. He is not sure if he likes his friend. Admires him, certainly. His friend has profited from the construction business, began as a helper to an American, and now runs his own crew. Mr. Thinh has to admire how easily his friend found a place in this society, never has moments of doubt if he, a Vietnamese, should be doing this or that. He has to admit he laughs more around his friend.

Mr. Thinh is half way there, has passed the pond where a tree grows out of the water, when he remembers his lucky coin. A nickel piece from back home in the shape of a flower, worth one-thousandth of a cent. Poker is unthinkable without it. Passing the pond on the way home, he thinks he sees buds on the limbs of his tree. He feels lucky.

His wife's car is in the driveway. The living room is spotless. A flower arrangement stands on the coffee table. He knows there will be picture taking. The family album is filled with occasions and their designated flowers, unintrusive but always in the background. His wife had traveled to Japan, learned how to make flowers speak, for their wedding. *Always so efficient.*

He hears English from the women's bedroom. He walks towards it.

"Like that, that looks beautiful, like...."

"No, Mom, that makes me look like a Hawaiian. Let's leave the flower out."

He glances in. His daughter stands in front of a mirror, dressed in a long white gown, the kind princesses wear. She looks different, womanly; it seems he has never known her. She lifts a pink orchid from her hair, runs her fingers through it. *She was this age.* He used to comb her hair with his fingers, throw it into the wind and watch it fly. They went to beach resorts just so he could play this game in the breeze.

"Mom!"

She drops the orchid, fingers curl, thumbs scratching against pinkies, tearing off the nail polish. In the mirror, he can see his daughter's eyes, the same look of defiance that now confuses instead of angers him. His wife picks up the flower, balances it in her palm. She approaches him.

"She has a dance at school tonight. Every student does this in the spring. It's all right."

"Why wasn't I told?"

"She didn't want you to see her all dressed up. Still a tomboy, you know. Now go on to your room, you'll embarrass her."

He stares at his daughter. His left fingers wiggle, wanting to touch her hand. His arm, body, become lead. Only his eyes move in a steady gaze that he hopes expressed softness. Someone else takes his hand, his wife, and leads him away. He twists back for a last look. *Should have told her she is beautiful.*

On his bed, he sat on his hands, saw flashes of his girl's smile, never a full laugh, just a smile. When they spent the entire night together, in hotels, never in her home, always in separate beds, sometimes he heard her cry and believed her when she said it was because she was happy. He loved her during those moments, when she forced herself not to sniffle or stir, so as not to disturb him.

The doorbell rings. He hears his wife's quick feet. English spoken.

"Hello Paul, how are you?"

"I'm great, just great. Wow, you look great, Tina."

"Thanks. C'mon, let's go. I think we're late."

"No way, I'm early for once. Your mom told me she wanted to take pictures."

Mr. Thinh stands in the hallway. The boy turns towards him, arms around his daughter's waist. They smile, he, brightly, she, shyly. *I know him, of course, from the play.* The boy gets on one knee, stares up at his daughter, brings her hand to his mouth, roars, his blond hair swings back. The camera clicks. *Jesus.* That devil had caught her sleeve, yanked her near him, laughed; she drew away, he had time to kiss her flowing sleeve. *Don't do that. Say it.* Then, now. *Leave. This is not done.* The boy stares at him, incredulous, then retreats. She runs to him. It is only his imagination. He is motionless. They must have kept talking; he does not hear. They leave. The door cries out. When that devil took his girl into the bedroom, after the dance, the door slammed then, too. He rushes to the window. The boy opens the car door for his daughter, kisses her cheek. They disappear.

Mr. Thinh twists the curtain, thick, ribbed, as if he could tear it in two. His shoulders shake. He senses his mouth opening.

"She's growing up. She needs to have friends."

His wife stands behind him. Her breath lands on his neck, sinks into him, releases him. A scream wiggles from his lungs to his throat, he lets it out, deafening. *She heard it.* Mouth closes. Nothing has sounded. The shaking stops. His wife places her hand on his shoulder.

Twilight

Hoang Khoi Phong

Finally, after three days, my bewilderment faded and I found myself growing accustomed to my new neighborhood. Such a strange concept: a "mobile home" park. This particular one had been designated for people over fifty-five. But the natural instincts of owners to make the best use of an empty property conspired to make me a resident in an area from which—since I didn't meet the simple criteria of age—I should have been excluded.

About a hundred trailers were parked in the complex. As a newcomer I thought I should take some time to introduce myself to my neighbors or at the very least get to know the faces and names of those living on both sides of my fence and in the trailer facing mine.

And that was where I stopped, right in front of a "single-wide" mobile home supported about a yard and a half off the ground by six stone blocks. The house had an air of genteel shabbiness about it, from the exposed wheels that the owner hadn't thought to conceal, to the empty aluminum cans scattered in the shadowed spaces near the base of the trailer. In the garden next to the house, I saw the owner sleeping soundly in a wheelchair, under the shade of several peach trees laden with fruit. A thin blanket covered his legs and lying on his lap was a bag of seeds brought to feed city birds too lazy to forage on their own. As I watched, a bold squirrel snuck up and surreptitiously gathered the corn kernels strewn across the lawn, now and again cautiously standing up on its hind legs and listening for a sound, watching for a movement. I turned back and sat on the rattan chair on my porch, looking at my sleeping neighbor and wondering how much longer it would take before I could go over and perform the small yet obligatory act of greeting that seemed required in my adopted land.

I wondered how old the man was. It seemed as if the color and weight had been leached out of him, leaving him wrinkled and spent. The lines on his face and neck were as pronounced as the carvings on an old sculpture. Yet even though time had atrophied his body, leaving only a layer of skin over a framework of brittle bones, he still managed to fill the entire chair. He must have been a strong and forceful man when he was young.

The old man suddenly stirred and opened his eyes. He seemed dazed. I should give him a couple of minutes to regain his bearings, I thought. But even as I watched, he shifted and went back to sleep. Fifteen minutes later, I saw him wake and grope for the whistle he had around his neck. As soon as he'd found it, he blew long and hard. The sudden noise startled me. The door behind him opened and out came an old woman who quickly asked: "Honey, are you OK?" She bent down to whisper in his ear, then turned and kissed him lightly on the forehead.

Gathering my confidence, I went over and introduced myself, explaining that I was a new arrival to the neighborhood. The old man, incapable of speech, bade me welcome with his eyes. But not his wife. The eyes that a moment before had gazed upon the old man with warmth and pity clouded over into two pools of indescribable darkness when they looked at me. I wondered if it would be wise to greet any of my other neighbors.

The next day was a Saturday, and I decided to do some laundry. I had just put two large bags of dirty clothes into my car when I saw another old man approach, his walk energetic, his eyes mischievous, his voice booming. "Good morning, son!" he called. "You Vietnamese?"

I felt annoyed. If he knew I was Vietnamese, then he should have understood that the diminutive "son" didn't appeal to us, particularly when coming from a foreigner, I was still debating how to reply when the man, nonplussed, continued:

"My name's Bill—I'm your next door neighbor. I was in your country for three years, '69 to '72."

"My name is Nguyen."

"You a vet too? ARVN?"

"I served in the army."

I resigned myself to making the best of his visit—at least it meant one less person to whom I'd have to introduce myself. We exchanged some pleasantries about the weather and then our biographies. Bill had retired from the Air Force; he'd been stationed in many places. He actually knew quite a bit about Vietnam and had a good grasp of the kind of Vietnamese vocabulary not used in polite society. While he'd been in Vietnam, he'd supported a "little wife," he told me. Although he was sixty-five, he seemed to me to have the vigor of a man in his fifties.

After that first meeting Bill would often come by to chat with me through the fence, and even, occasionally, visit my house. He'd appointed himself as the bearer of news about what was happening in the neighborhood for me. For the most part, our conversations were one-sided—I let him do most of the speaking, since I was insecure about my English. Through him I learned about everything that was happening in this little world of ours.

"Hey, Nguyen, you coming to the party at the clubhouse this weekend?"

"What party?"

"Steve and Laura's two year anniversary."

"I don't know them—I wasn't invited."

"Hey, don't sweat it—parties around here are open to everyone. Come on; there'll be free food, music; it'll be fun. Steve and Laura got married right here. They're both in their late eighties. Hell, they both got great-grandchildren."

Changing the subject abruptly, he said: "Listen, do you know that guy White in F8."

"I haven't met anybody except the couple next door and you."

"He's a black guy; a vet—he was in Vietnam too. You know, the first five years he's here, I never even knew he had a son. Then the kid starts coming over, spending his nights here. One night, two AM, he breaks into Mrs. Barbara's trailer, M4, steals about two hundred dollars. Then he rapes the old woman and stabs her to death. Then the nervy little bastard comes back the next week, probably to do in someone else. That's when they got him. Since then White hasn't dared to show his face, case someone thinks he's an accessory."

"Nine out of ten his son just took advantage of him to scope out the area," I said. I felt a twinge of sympathy for White.

"Well, I guess the police thought the same thing—they asked him a few questions, then let him go. But I'll tell you, Nguyen, no matter what, I just don't trust any of those people."

* * *

That night, when I arrived with my bouquet of flowers and a greeting card, the clubhouse was filled to capacity with fifty or sixty elderly couples. Some of them were in wheelchairs, though I saw no sign of the couple next door to me. As soon as he saw me, Bill rushed over and introduced me to everyone. I felt awkward and out of place among this gathering of elders. Steve and Laura, the anniversary couple, denied the passage of time with brightly colored clothing that was too young for them. His hand trembling, Steve took the bouquet I brought and muttered an almost unintelligible thank you. I mumbled my best wishes back, but the atmosphere depressed me. As soon as Bill brought me a paper plate, I took a sandwich and retired to a chair in the corner. Soon after I sat down, a black man entered, carrying a beautifully wrapped gift. His entrance reduced the commotion in the room to soft murmurs of surprise. The man's face was marked with loss and suffering. He brought the gift to the wedding table, put it down and gave his best wishes to the couple. Ignoring the stares of the other people, he settled into the empty chair next to mine and introduced himself.

"Hi. My name's White."

"Nguyen."

I gave him a firm handshake, and I was abruptly conscious of the few furtive glances thrown in our direction. Then someone must have given a sign, for suddenly an old lady sat down at the piano and began to caress the keyboard. Songs about youth and love tumbled from her lips. Bill, full of energy, seemed to grow younger; he was at his most entertaining. He hugged one person, swung another one out on the floor to dance. Some of the dancers were too heavy to even walk; others were fragile and thin as toothpicks. Many of them left the dance floor wheezing or consumed by fits of coughing. As the noise abated, Mr. White got up and went to the piano. He bent and whispered to the pianist, who flipped through her songbook and tested a couple of chords before she started to play. Her music blended with White's voice and an indescribably sad song filled the air. All of the people seemed visibly moved. As the song went on, I got up and snuck out, uncomfortable with all of the signs of mortality around me. My mind was haunted with images of withered bodies, of snowy white hair, of the elegance of the lady pianist. I felt mesmerized by the way clouded eyes were able to shine for a brief moment of happiness before returning to their distant dullness.

* * *

For several days soon after, the guest parking lot outside the complex filled up with cars bearing out of state license plates. Young couples and sometimes even small families complete with chubby, rosy-cheeked babies, roamed the compound. In the morning, I went to the convenience store to pick up a few things and saw Mr. White, paying for a gallon bottle of whiskey. When he saw I'd noticed him, his eyes clouded with uneasiness. I drove back home, haunted by his look. As I stepped out of the car, Bill came over to me.

"Hey, Nguyen, any visitors today?"

"I have many friends, but they were afraid they wouldn't be able to find parking here. Anyway, usually we just meet at Vietnamese restaurants."

"Well, I didn't mean your friends. It's almost Father's Day —everyone's expecting their kids. Except me. I got a card from my son yesterday, says he can't make it this year."

"Where is he?"

"San Francisco. After he finished up at U.C.-Davis he decided to stay up there, on account of his job. Been there about ten years now; he's thirty-two. By the way, that couple next door to you? They haven't had a visitor in the last five years."

"I tried to visit them when I first moved here. But up to now I haven't even been able to find out their name."

"Sarkissian, that's his name. Armenian. He's a doctor, or was a doctor—he came to the states in 1945, when he was thirty-five. So he's what now, close to eighty? I heard he left a wife and son behind back in Armenia; his wife now's a nurse who worked with him in a hospital. They had a son too. But he was killed in your country, in the war."

It was as if he had cleared up a nagging mystery and opened up a whole new line of thought for me. I remembered the dark glance the old woman had given me that first day when I went over to make their acquaintance. In my mind, I heard again that whistle, saw clearly the lazy city birds and squirrels that fed on the old man's sorrows. Even those seeds made perfect sense now. And yet I remembered also, very clearly, how the old man's eyes, when they fell on me, had been much gentler than his wife's.

"Hey, you know why my kid isn't coming up this year?" Bill interrupted my thoughts.

"I imagine he's probably just busy. The holidays are perfect for making money."

"Nothing that exciting," Bill said. "It's because of his worthless new wife. The fat bitch. You know, his first wife wasn't only very pretty—she was real nice. Brought me tons of gifts every time they came up. But the one he has now is not only fat and ugly—she's lazy as hell. She makes me feel like hating my son."

"Well, look, at least we're both luckier than White. I saw him buying a whole gallon of whiskey this morning."

"His son just got sentenced—life in prison. About half this trailer park went to the courtroom the day they announced the verdict."

Soon the excitement of Father's Day passed and the parking lot returned to its usual emptiness. The sight of relatives wheeling their loved ones in the dying light of the sunset became less frequent. Now in the evenings, as the sun moved level with the windows, the old folks searched for companionship at the public beaches near the complex. In this way their lives passed by, a calm seclusion, interrupted only by the periodic need to say farewell to a departing neighbor. There were only two reasons for leaving the trailer park: death or nursing homes for those unfortunate ones who could no longer prepare their own meals or care for their own most basic needs.

* * *

So the days passed until one evening I came home to a great commotion. Police cars, ambulances and fire trucks had filled up the parking lot and my neighbors were clustered around F8, Mr. White's trailer. From the look of them, I knew that something serious had occurred. The lady pianist, her face stained with tears, was being comforted by Bill, who'd put his arm around her and was leading her over into the shade of the peach trees. The police had cordoned off F8 with a yellow tape. Emergency medics entered and exited while the firemen, deprived of an opportunity to ply their trade, squatted down and leisurely puffed at their cigarettes.

It was Veterans' Day, and I knew that Bill and the other veterans had planned to throw a party. Those who had managed to preserve their old uniforms and ribbons had taken them out of their closets to display to one another. As I found out later, the old timers had visited each other all morning, telling their war stories. Bill had been everywhere and had gone to see everyone—except White. Perhaps it had slipped his mind. Finally, just before five in the afternoon, when the party was to have started, he remembered White and decided to go to his trailer and drag him along. He knocked, but there was no answer, so he'd gone to check the car shed. Sure enough, White's Buick was there. Bill went back and knocked again. Still no answer. He circled around to the back door. Noticing a little space where the blind didn't quite meet the bottom of the window, Bill peeked inside. White was hanging in a corner of the bedroom, his face bloated and pale, his tongue sticking out at least an inch. Bill felt faint and had to sit down for a while to regain his composure. After several minutes, he got up and went to the home next door and called the police.

A half an hour later, the party began as scheduled. Bill stood next to the piano, but the pianist sat motionless. No one played, no one sang. All that could be heard was Bill's agonized voice recounting over and over the day's events, reproaching himself. He should have dropped in on White sooner. If he had, if he'd said hi to White, had a drink with the black veteran, he knew he could have stopped him and White would have been here, at the party, singing God Bless America with everyone else.

* * *

Time slipped by and before I knew it I had been at the trailer park for more than a year. White left behind nothing more than a few belongings and his trailer was sold quickly and cheaply in order to pay off his debts. The new owner was Korean. He was about my age and very well-mannered. Soon he made the acquaintance of all the families in the park. He seemed better than me in all ways. He drove a shiny new Hyundai, repainted his house in a bright color and hung a poster of the 1988 Olympics on the wall. Backing him was a country embarked on a successful road to development. Once in a while, I saw Bill stop by the Korean's for a drink.

At that time I was working the second shift. After getting home from a full day of work, I'd clean up, read the newspaper and watch a program or two on TV; by then it would be three in the morning and time to sleep. But whenever I woke up, still cocooned in the comfort of my bed, the first image of the day I'd see through my window would be the old man next door, motionless on his wheelchair, his back supported by an air pillow, his body curved against the chair, his eyes looking up at the sky. Once in a while, one hand would grope for the feeding can fastened on the armrest. With a flicking motion, his hands would direct the birds first to one side, then to the other to snatch their much awaited seeds. I became thoroughly familiar with his system of whistles. A long steady sound signalled his need for water, two shorter ones a wish to be moved into the shade, three and he needed to go inside the house; I imagine to take care of bodily needs. Each time he gave the three whistle sequence, his wife would appear immediately and wheel him inside. At noon he left the peach trees and went inside for his nap, then appeared again after four o'clock in the winter and after five-thirty in summer. That old couple cared for each other with a tender love that was greater than any other love on earth. Often she would sit beside him and whisper into his ear. If she was inside, his whistle invariably brought her smiling face back outside. And when she came, she never failed to kiss his forehead or his cheek.

Since I'd learned he was a refugee from Armenia, I'd felt close to the old man. He had left his country against his will, and then his son had died on the soil of my land. I felt I understood him and I longed to speak to him, but his circumstances prevented me. Even with his wife, he could only whisper, and more often than not he just had to signal his needs. Besides, the woman's coldness towards me hadn't dissipated. Perhaps I was a reminder to her of her present childlessness, her future loneliness. Many times I helped her carry her laundry bags from the car to their trailer, or lifted some heavy articles for her, only to receive a curt and cold thank you. She gave no sign of thawing, of forgiving. But I became used to it and continued to help her without hope of receiving any acknowledgment.

At Christmas I took a ten day vacation. Feeling that I'd been isolated for too long, I decided to visit old friends, many of whom lived around the Washington D.C. area. By coincidence, Gorbachev was visiting the United States and the media was filled with stories about glasnost and the two superpowers bringing peace to the world. But suddenly Heaven was angered and disaster struck Armenia. The same land ravaged by the hands of man, the land oppressed by the Russians for close to half a century, now became the victim of violent earthquakes which claimed hundreds of thousands of lives. Gorbachev cut short his visit and hurried home. But Heaven must have no eyes and the old Earth gods must have no ears, for why did they wait until the exact moment when the Armenians were about to demand their independence to rain such calamities on them? The images I saw on my television and in the newspapers reminded me of my neighbor. Having himself survived intact, was he now thinking about his homeland? My meetings with my friends were bittersweet, as we told each other the old stories and talked about Vietnam. For a while I pushed the images of a distant city covered with debris and rubble out of my mind.

But the minute I returned, even as I was turning my car into the complex, an uneasiness came over me. It was ten o'clock already, yet the old man wasn't in his wheelchair under the peach trees. The door to his trailer was closed tightly. As soon as he spotted me, Bill ran out of his house like a whirlwind.

"Did you hear? Sarkissian dropped dead."

I was stunned to the point of speechlessness. The only person here with whom I'd felt a sense of connection had vanished to the Ninth Cloud. After a long while, I was able to ask Bill when it had happened.

"Three days after Christmas."

"Was it an accident, or did he fall ill?"

"Hell, Nguyen—he was just old."

"Where's his wife?"

"Right after the funeral, she moved to Fresno to live with her sister."

"Has someone else bought the place yet?"

"No, not yet. You know, Nguyen, I helped her pack. She had all of these stacks of books and magazines and photo albums, and a box of old letters she'd hung onto. All this stuff. She told me that towards the end, the old man wanted to hear her read all those old letters from forty or fifty years ago from relatives and friends. He couldn't see a thing, so he'd ask her to flip through the pages in the photo albums one by one, then read him aloud the name in each caption under every picture. I got a look at the album. He was a great-looking guy when he was young, handsome, full of muscles. A veteran, like you and me, only he was a doctor. All those old books and magazines had stuff about his country in them."

"Did you go to his funeral?"

"Sure. Everybody here went, except the people in wheelchairs."

"Where's the cemetery?"

"Down at the corner of Bolsa and Beach."

"Do you know where his grave is located?"

"Naw, I never remember stuff like that. Check in at the cemetery office—they should be able to give you the fine details."

I visited the cemetery that evening and found his resting place. And there I lit some incense, to commemorate a compatriot.

* * *

Finally, I moved out of the "mobile home" park. A friend had bought a small house near the place I worked and asked if I would move in with him, to share expenses and keep him company. The rent was cheaper, so I left. But I miss that place, miss the old couple, the nosy insensitive neighbor with his secret good heart, the elegant pianist, the tragic black man. The man who took over my 1969 model mobile home was yet another Korean, even younger than I, and fresh off the boat. I moved out in the morning and he moved in that afternoon. He too drove a Hyundai and had in his possession a large poster of the 1988 Seoul Olympics. The difference between us was that he always walked with his head high, while for the last ten years it seemed that I had always looked down.

Translated by Thai Tuyet Quan
Edited by Wayne Karlin

PART SIX
Legacies

6

In my country we shift blame. After the war, those who went became pariahs. Not the ones who started it, not the ones who carried it. And because not everyone can overlook rejection or memory, more who went have died by their own hand than by your mines or bullets. There are more suicides among us now than names on our monument in the capital, our broken dash against the landscape, scar that would span the city if it listed the actual dead, black river that would surge across the country if it listed everyone ruined on every side.

I want this remembering to end, yet cannot let it. It's like drinking the ocean, but someone must remember, someone refuse to be tethered.

I visited your country at the wrong time, but if I had not I still would not understand the nature of things, would still think my country is paradise, which in many ways it is, but which it is not. It is built on graves, on bones, on promises broken and nightmares kept, on graves that howl deep in the earth, on skulls crushed with religious objects, on human skin used as rugs, on graves upon graves of graves. And we are always busy conquering ourselves.

Whatever it is holds us in a spell of wonder when we are children, abandoned me when the war began. I don't mean just me or just youth, I mean something about this country. But I don't mean just this country, I mean the world. I've spent my time searching for what it is, like a suicide who refuses to die, an optimist who is empty, a buoy on the sea.

Rashad

John Edgar Wideman

Rashad's home again. Nigger's clean and lean and driving a mean machine. They say he's dealing now, dealing big in the Big D, Deetroit. Rashad's into something, sure nuff. The cat's pushing a Regal and got silver threads to match. Yea, he's home again. Clean as he wants to be. That suit ain't off nobody's rack. One of a kind. New as a baby's behind. Driving a customized Regal with RASHAD on the plate.

It was time for it to go, all of it. Nail and banner both. Time she said as she eased out the nail on which it hung. Past time she thought as she wiggled the nail and plaster trickled behind the banner, spattering the wall, sprinkling the bare floorboards in back of the chair where the rug didn't reach. Like cheese, she thought. All these old walls like rotten cheese. That's why she kept everybody's pictures on the mantelpiece. Crowded as it was now with photos of children and grandchildren and nephews and nieces and the brown oval-framed portraits of people already old when she was just a child, crowded as it was there was no place else to put the pictures of the people she loved because the rotten plaster wouldn't take a nail.

The banner was dry and crinkly. Like a veil as she rolled it in her hands, the black veils on the little black hats her mother had worn to church. The women of Homewood A.M.E Zion used to keep their heads covered in church. Some like her Grandmother Gert and Aunt Aida even hid their faces behind crinkly, black veils. She rolled the banner tighter. Its backside was dusty, an arc of mildew like whitish ash stained the dark cylinder she gripped in both hands. How long had the banner been hanging in the corner? How long had she been in this house on Finance street? How long had the Homewood streets been filling with snow in the winter and leaves in fall and the cries of her children playing in the sunshine? How long since she'd driven in the nail and slipped the gold-tasseled cord over it so the banner hung straight? No way to make the banner stand up on the mantelpiece with the photos so she'd pounded a nail into the wall behind the overstuffed chair, cursing as she had heard the insides of the rotten wall crumbling, praying with each blow of the hammer the nail would catch something solid and hold. Because embroidered in the black silk banner was the likeness of her granddaughter Keesha, her daughter's first baby, and the snapshot from which the likeness on the banner had been made, the only photo anybody had of the baby, was six thousand miles away in her daddy's wallet.

Rashad had taken the picture with him to Vietnam. She had given it up grudgingly. Just before he left, Rashad had come to her wanting to make peace. He looked better than he had in months. I'm clean, Mom. I'm OK now, he'd said. He called her mom and sometimes she liked it and sometimes it made her blood boil. Just because he'd married her daughter, just because there'd been nobody when he was growing up he could call mom, just because he thought he was cute and thought she was such a melon head he could get on her good side by sweet talking and batting his droopy eyelashes and calling her mom, just because of all that, and six thousand miles and a jungle where black boys were dying like flies, just because of all that, if he thought she was going to put the only picture of her granddaughter in his hot, grabby, long-fingered hand, he better think again. But he had knocked at her door wanting to talk peace. Peace was in him the way he'd sat and crossed one leg over his knee, the way he'd cut down that wild bush growing out the top of his head, and trimmed his moustache and shaved the scraggly goat beard, peace was in his hands clasped atop his knees and in the way he leaned toward her and talked soft. I know I been wrong, Mom. Nobody knows better than me how wrong I been. That stuff makes you sick. It's like you ain't yourself. That monkey gets you and you don't care nothing about nobody. But I'm OK now. I ain't sick now. I'm clean. I love my wife and love my baby and I'ma do right now, Mom.

So when he asked she had made peace too. Like a fool she almost cried when she went to the mantelpiece and pulled out the snapshot from the corner of the cardboard frame of Shirley's prom picture. She had had plans for the photo of her granddaughter. A silver frame from the window of the jewelry shop she passed every morning on her way to work. But she freed it from the top corner of the cardboard border where she had tucked it, where it didn't cover anything but the fronds of the fake palm tree behind Shirley and her tuxedoed beau, where it could stay and be seen till she got the money together for the silver frame, freed the snapshot and handed it to her granddaughter's daddy, Rashad, to seal the peace.

Then one day the package came in the mail. The postman rang and she was late as usual for work and missed her bus standing there signing for it and he was mad too because she had kept him waiting while she pulled a housecoat over her slip and buttoned it and tied a scarf around her head.

Sign right there. Right there where it says received by. Right there, lady. And she cut her eyes at him as if to say I don't care how much mail you got in that sack don't be rushing me you already made me miss my bus and I ain't hardly answering my door half naked.

I can read, thank you. And signs her name letter by letter as if maybe she can read but maybe she had forgotten how to write. Taking her own good time because his pounding on the door again after she hollered out, Just a minute, didn't hurry her but slowed her down like maybe she didn't quite know how to button a housecoat or wrap her uncombed hair in a scarf and she took her time remembering.

Thank you when she snatched the package and shut the door louder than she needed to. Not slamming it in the mailman's face but loud enough to let him know he wasn't the only one with business in the morning.

Inside, wrapped in pounds of tissue paper, was the banner. At first she didn't know what it was. She stared again at the rows of brightly colored stamps on the outside of the brown paper. Rashad's name and number were in one corner, "Shirley and Mom" printed with the same little-boy purple crayon letters across the middle of the wrapping paper. Handfuls of white tissue inside a grayish box. Then the black silk banner with colored threads weaving a design into the material. She didn't know what it was at first. She held it in her fingertips at arm's length, righting it, letting it unfurl. It couldn't be a little fancy China doll dress Rashad had sent from overseas for Keesha, she knew that, but that's what she thought of first, letting it dangle there in her outstretched arms, turning it, thinking of how she'll have to iron out the wrinkles and be careful not to let her evil iron get too hot.

Then she recognized a child's face. Puffy-cheeked, smiling, with curly black hair and slightly slanting black eyes, the face of a baby like they have over there in the jungle where Rashad's fighting. A pretty picture with a tiny snowcapped mountain and blue lake worked into the background with the same luminous threads which raise the child's face above the sea of black silk. Though the baby's mouth is curled into a smile and the little mountain scene floating in the background is prettier than anyplace she has ever been, the banner is sad. It's not the deep creases she will have to iron out or the wrinkles it picked up lying in its bed of tissue paper. It's the face, something sad and familiar in the face. She saw her daughter's eyes, Shirley's eyes dripping sadness the way they were in the middle of the night that first time she ran home from Rashad. Pounding at the door. Shirley standing there shaking on the dark porch. Like she might run away again into the night or collapse there in the doorway where she stood trembling in her tracks. He hit me. He hit me, Mama. Shirley in her arms, little girl shudders. You can't fight him. He's a man, baby. You can't fight him like you're another man.

Shirley's eyes in the baby's face. They used to tease her, call Shirley *Chink* because she had that pale yellowish skin and big eyes that seemed turned up at the corners. Then she remembered the picture she had sent away with Rashad. She read the word in the bottom corner of the banner which had been staring at her all this time, the strip of green letters she had taken for part of the design till she saw her daughter's eyes in the baby face and looked closer and read *Keesha*.

How many years now had they been teasing Keesha about that picture hanging in the corner of the living room?

Take it down, Grammy. Please take that ugly thing down.

Can't do that, baby. It's you, baby. It's something special your daddy had made for you.

It's ugly. Don't look nothing like me.

Your daddy paid lots of money for that picture. Someday you'll appreciate it.

Won't never like nothing that ugly. I ain't no chinky-chinky Chinaman. That's what they always be teasing me about. I ain't no chinky baby.

How many years had the banner been there behind the big spaghetti gut chair in the dark corner of her living room? The war was over now. Rashad and the rest of the boys back home again. How long ago had a little yellow man in those black pajamas like they all wear over there held her granddaughter's picture in his little monkey hand and grinned at it and grinned at Rashad and taken the money and started weaving the face in the cloth. He's probably dead now. Probably long gone like so many of them over there they bombed and shot and burned with that gasoline they shot from airplanes. A sad, little old man. Maybe they killed his granddaughter. Maybe he took Rashad's money and put his own little girl's face on the silk. Maybe it's the dead girl he was seeing even with Keesha's picture right there beside him while he's sewing. Maybe that's the sadness she saw when she opened the package and saw again and again till she learned never to look in that corner above the mush-springed chair.

Keesha had to be eleven now, with her long colty legs and high, round, muscley butt. Boys calling her on the phone already. Already getting blood in her cheeks if you say the right little boy's name. Keesha getting grown now and her sister Tammy right behind her. Growing up even faster cause she's afraid her big sister got a head start and she ain't never gonna catch up. That's right. That's how it's always gon be. You'll have to watch that child like a hawk. You think Keesha was fast? Lemme tell you something. You'll be wishing it was still Keesha you chasing when that Tammy goes flying by.

They get to that certain age and you can't tell them nothing. No indeed. You can talk till you're blue in the face and they ain't heard a word. That's the way you were, Miss Ann. Don't be cutting your big China eyes at me because that's just the way you were. Talked myself blue in the face but it was Rashad this and Rashad that and I mize well be talking to myself because you were gonna have him if it killed you.

She unrolls the banner to make sure she didn't pull it too tight. It's still there, the bright threads still intact, the sad, dead child smiling up at her. The dead child across the ocean, her dead granddaughter Kaleesha, her own stillborn son. When you looked at it closely you could see how thicker, colored threads were fastened to the silk with hundreds of barely visible black stitches. Thinner than spider's web the strands of black looped around the cords of gold and bronze and silver which gave the baby's face its mottled, luminous sheen. From a distance the colors and textures of the portrait blended but up close the child's face was a patchwork of glowing scars, as ugly as Keesha said it was. Rashad had paid good money for it sure enough but if the old man had wept when he made it, there must have been times when he laughed too. A slick old yellow man, a sly old dog taking all that good money and laughing cause it didn't matter whose face he stuck on that rag.

She had heard Rashad talk about the war. One of those nights when Shirley had run back home to Mama he had followed her and climbed through a basement window and fallen asleep downstairs in the living room. She heard him before she saw him stretched out on her couch, his stingy brim tipped down over his eyes, his long, knobby-toed shoes propped up on the arm of the couch. His snores filled the room. She had paused on the steps, frightened by the strange rumbling noise till she figured out what it had to be. Standing above him in the darkness she'd wanted to smack his long shoes, knock the hat off his nose. He's the one. This is the nigger messing over my little girl. This the so-called man whipping on my baby. She thought of her sons, how she had to beg, how she just about had to get down on her knees and plead with them not to go to their sister's house and break this scrawny nigger's neck.

He's sick, Mama. He can't help it. He loves me and loves the baby. He came back sick from that filthy war. They made him sick again over there.

She looked down at Rashad sleeping on her couch. Even with the trench coat draped over his body she could see how thin he was. Skin and bones. Junkie thin because they just eat sugar, don't want nothing but sugar, it's all they crave when that poison gets hold to them. Her sons wanted to kill him and would have if she hadn't begged them on her knees.

She has to fight her own battles. Your sister's a grown woman. Stay away from there, please.

She had felt the darkness that night, heavy as wind swirling around her. She had come downstairs for a glass of wine, the sweet Mogen David in the refrigerator which once or twice a month would put her to sleep when nothing else would. She had a headache and her heart had been pounding ever since she opened the door and saw Shirley with Keesha in her arms standing on the porch. There had been calls earlier in the evening, and Keesha howling in the background and Shirley sobbing the second time and then it was midnight and what was she going to do, what could she say this time when the baby was finally asleep and the coffee cups were empty and there were just the two of them, two women alone in the middle of the night in that bright kitchen. Finally Shirley asleep too but then her stomach and her pounding heart turned her out of bed and she checked Shirley and the baby again and tipped down the steps needing that glass of wine to do the trick and there he was, the sound of his snoring before she saw him and then the night swirling like a wind so she was driven a thousand miles away from him, from his frail, dope-smelling bones under that raggedy trench coat, a thousand miles from him and anyone, anything alive.

It was his screaming which broke her sleep again, the last time that night or morning because one had bled into the other and she heard him yell like a man on fire and heard Shirley flying down the stairs and by the time she got herself together and into her robe and downstairs into the living room, Shirley was with him under the trench coat and both were quiet as if no scream had clawed sleep from her eyes and no terror had nearly ripped his skinny body apart.

Sunday morning then, too late and too tired to go to church then so it was the three of them at the table drinking coffee and nodding with that burden of no sleep from the night before, Shirley, Rashad, her own weary self at the table when he talked about the war.

I was a cook. Had me a good job. You know. Something keeps your butt away from the killing. A good job cause you could do a little business. Like, you know. A little hustle on the side. Like be dealing something besides beans to them crazy niggers. Little weed, little smack. You get it from the same gooks sold you the salt and pepper. Had me a nice little hustle going. Been alright too cept some brothers always got to be greedy. Always got to have it all. Motherfucker gon gorilla me and take my little piece of action. Say he's the man and I'm cutting in on his business. Well one thing led to another. Went down on the dude. Showed him he wasn't messing with no punk. Eyes like to pop out his head when I put my iron in his belly. You know like I thought that was that and the nigger was gon leave me alone but he set me up. Him and some of them jive MPs he's paying off they set me up good and I got busted and sent home. Still be in jail if I hadn't copped a plea on possession and took my dishonorable.

Yeah, they be killing and burning and fragging and all that mess but I only heard stories about it, I had me a good job, I was feeding niggers and getting niggers high. Getting them fat for the jungle. And getting my own self as messed up as you see me now, sitting here at this table not worth a good goddamn to nobody.

She knew there was more to tell. She knew he had been in bad fighting once because her daughter was always reading the newspapers and calling her on the phone and crying and saying, He's dead, Mama. I know he's dead and my poor little girl won't never know her daddy. That was before his good job, before the dope he said was as easy to get as turning on a faucet. But he wouldn't talk about the fighting. He'd dream about the fighting and wake up screaming in the night but he wouldn't talk.

Now she had it down, rolled in her hands, and had to put the banner someplace. It was time to take it down, she knew that but didn't know where to put it now it was off her wall. Where the nail had been, a dugout, crumbly looking hole gaped in the plaster. If she touched it, the rotten wall might crack from floor to ceiling, the whole house come tumbling down around her heels. A knuckle-sized chunk of wall gone but she could fix it with patching plaster and in the dark corner nobody would hardly notice. The paint had sweated badly over the chair and a stain spread across the ceiling over the corner so one more little spot a different color than the rest wouldn't matter because the rest wasn't one color, the rest was leaks and patches and coming apart and faded and as tired of standing as she was tired of holding it up.

One day she'd like to tear the walls down. Go round with a hammer and knock them all down. She knew how the hammer would feel in her fist, she knew how good each blow would feel and she could hear herself shouting hallelujah getting it done.

But she needed someplace to put the banner. She was late as usual and Shirley and the girls would be by soon to go to church. Shirley might be driving Rashad's new car. On Sunday morning he sure wouldn't be needing it. Be dinnertime before he was up and around so he might give Shirley the keys so she could drive the girls to church in style. The girls loved their daddy and he loved them. When he came to town it was always a holiday for the girls. Presents and rides and money and a pretty daddy to brag on for months till he appeared again. She wondered how long it would be this time. How long he'd be flying high before somebody shot him or the police caught up with him and then he'd be dead or in jail again and he'd fall in love again with "Shirley and Mom."

Here she was with the banner still in her hand and the kitchen clock saying late, you're late woman and she's still in her robe, hasn't even filled the tub yet but she just had to stop what she was supposed to be doing and take it down. Well, when the girls come knocking at the door, calling and giggling and signifying and Shirley sits behind the wheel honking to rush her, she'll fling open the door and stuff it in their hands. It will be gone then. Someplace else then, because she never really wanted that sad thing in the first place. She didn't understand why she'd left it hanging this long, why she let it move in and take over that dark corner behind the chair. Because it was a sad thing. A picture of somebody wasn't ever in the family. More of Rashad's foolishness. Spending money when he has it like money's going out of style. Rashad living like a king and throwing a handful of money at the old yellow man when the banner is finished. Rashad living fast because he knows he's gonna die fast and the old chink grinning up at the black fool, raking in the dollars Rashad just threw on the floor like he got barrels of money, stacks of money and don't know how to give it away fast enough.

She loves him too. That handful of money he throws over his shoulder would feel like the hammer in her hand. She'll pray for Rashad today. And Tommy. So much alike. A long hard prayer and it will be like hoisting the red bricks of Homewood A.M.E. Zion on her shoulders and trying to lift the whole building or trying to lift all of Homewood. The trees and houses and sidewalks and all the shiny cars parked at the curb. It will be that hard to pray them home, to make them safe.

She starts up the stairs with the rolled banner still in her hand. She'll soak a little in the tub even if it makes her later. They can wait awhile. Won't hurt them to wait a little while. She's been waiting for them all the days of her life and they can just sit tight awhile because she needs to pray for them too. Pray for all of them and needs all her strength so she'll soak in the tub awhile.

At the top of the steps, at the place they turn and her sons have to stoop to get by without bumping their heads on the low ceiling, at that turning where she always stoops too, not because her head would hit if she didn't but because the slight bend forward of her body brings them back, returns her sons to this house where they all grew tall, taller than the ceiling so they had to stoop to get past the turning, at that place near the top of the stairs when she stoops and they are inside her again, babies again, she thinks of the old man sewing in his hut no bigger than a doghouse.

Rashad would lean in and hand him the photo. The peace offering she sent with him all those miles across the ocean. The old man would take the snapshot and look at it and nod when Rashad pointed to the banners and faces hanging in the hut. A little wrinkled old man. A bent old man whose fingers pained him like hers did in the morning. Swollen fingers and crooked joints. Hands like somebody been beating them with a hammer. She had kept it hanging this long because he had sewn it with those crippled fingers. She took it down because the old man was tired, because it was time to rest, because Keesha was almost grown now and her face was with the others decorating the mantel.

She saw him clearly at that turning of the stairs and understood the sadness in the eyes. The lost child she would pray for too.

The Sound of Harness Bells

Nguyen Quang Lap

Over half a human lifetime had passed by the time the couple met again. Their story was not an uncommon one. Even as a twenty-one gun salute ushered in the day of complete victory, thousands of husbands and wives, separated for decades, were searching for each other. Husbands in the North, wives in the South, husbands in the jungle highlands, wives in the coastal lowlands, husbands severed from their wives by the iron bars of the prisons built by the Americans and their puppets, all sought each other and reunited with embraces and tears of joy. These were the lucky ones. Another army of husbands and wives, though only separated by a single meter of earth, remained deaf to each other's cries.

He searched for her in Nha Trang to no avail. He searched for her in Phan Thiet, but still there was no trace. Then, after ten frantic, exhausting days in Da Nang, he spotted her at the living quarters of the Minh Hieu Military Management Committee. She was standing in the courtyard, coddling a two year old child. He stopped abruptly at the gate, his chest beating as if struck by a firing pin. The day he'd left her, they'd been childless.

He approached her slowly, deliberately. "March forward, fear nothing," had been the slogan he'd lived by throughout his thirty-six years in uniform. She didn't recognize him.

Maybe he has a proposal for the Military Management Committee, she thought. Or a contract, or a complaint, or some kind of lawsuit.

He was struck by her stubborn youthfulness and the paleness of her skin.

"Lanh!" He called out.

Her eyes widened. Confusedly, she set the child—not her own—on the ground, straightened her hair and stared up at him. He bent down to fix the strap on his sandal.

What a klutz! he thought to himself. Why am I being so awkward? He stared back at her.

"Oh my God!" she cried.

She covered her face and began to sob. He opened his arms, leapt forward and grabbed her tightly. Caught unaware, she pushed him away. He looked startled.

"Is it really you?" she said, looking up. "Is it really my husband?"

Twenty-one years alone had hardened her. Her passions had sedimented into something fixed and inflexible. But his abrupt appearance jarred something loose.

She flung herself on his chest and sobbed. "Oh my darling, why so long?" On the day they said good-bye, he had promised that he would return to her within two years.

He took her to the Division's Domestic Living Quarters. As they heard the joyous news, scores of cadres and soldiers came to offer congratulations. Division Commander Hung, his comrade in arms for over ten years, visited every day for over a week. He couldn't conceal the inordinate warmth he felt towards the recently reunited couple.

"Answer me truthfully," he said to the husband during one private visit. "I know Lanh's forty-six. Can she still...can she have children?"

The husband smiled. "It's strange, but we're sure she can."

The Division Commander placed his hands firmly on the husband's shoulders and shook him gently. "That's great—really great."

She had remained fertile, but her sixteen years in the jungle had left her stricken with chronic malaria. Her skin was unnaturally pale; her hair had thinned and faded to a sickly yellow. Night after night, he held her in his arms. She listened to his beating heart and wondered if it was still strong. He had aged as well; he was already fifty-seven. Every night she noticed the sweat dripping from his tired, liver-spotted face. In his embrace she felt the dryness of his skin and noticed the layers of deadened cells accumulating daily on his back.

If there's no baby by next year, then it's over, she thought to herself. Few women gave birth after fifty.

Six months passed without a sign. Chi watched her toss and turn at night. She was thin as a piece of paper. One day, after complaining of dizziness and nausea, she vomited. He was both worried and hopeful.

"It's not that," she told him. "In the jungle I was hit by chemical poison six times. Since then I often get these symptoms."

A lump formed in his throat.

Division Commander Hung continued to visit the couple regularly. Often, he'd speak of a therapeutic program of Chinese medicine known by its advertising program "Maintain Your Youth, Slow Down Old Age." He took it upon himself to drive to Institute 17 and request Doctor-Lieutenant Colonel Le Giau to conduct an prenatal examination. Dr. Giau, a comrade from the anti-French resistance and a highly respected obstetrician, was gentle and compassionate. After listening to the Division Commander recount the couple's story, he cheerfully agreed to devote his special attention to the case. He carefully enumerated the medicines currently available in the city, medicines which could possibly improve the wife's condition. With Dr. Giau's prescription and letter of introduction in hand, the husband tracked down each and every medicine listed on the prescription, even the rarest and most precious.

But night after night in his arms, she began to lose hope that their dream would be realized. Often she would pinch his nose to rouse him from sleep. She would have never made such demands on him if he had already given her a child. Just one child. A child which would wipe away the painful memories of their long separation. She lay awake at night haunted by thoughts of the jungle.

Once, while she was working as a cook at a jungle military camp, she had heard a rumor that a man named Chi whose description could fit her husband's had stopped at a neighboring camp. She packed some food and headed off through the jungle. But after two exhausting days of solitary travel, she arrived only to find that this Chi was not her husband. She fainted into his arms. Like her Chi, this Chi was also far from his wife. He spoke to her softly. "It'll be okay. Try to take it easy. You pretend that you really met him and likewise, I'll try to pretend that I met my wife. It'll be all right. In wartime some illusions are necessary."

She'd tried to internalize that illusion during the thirty-nine kilometer trip back. But the jungle had been recently sprayed with chemical poison and leaves were falling down. Finally she started to sprint, desperately, until she fell exhausted alongside a quiet stream. When she awoke, she saw the eyes of her commander staring down at her.

"Did you meet him?" he asked.

Tears came to her eyes. She gently nodded her head. "Yes, I did."

That was eleven years ago. Perhaps her current inability to have children was somehow linked to her exposure to the American poison. The idea suddenly consumed her. She sat up, bathed in sweat.

One night she sensed within her husband a renewed vigor. Afterwards, when she gazed upon him and saw the same old, sweaty face, tears came to her eyes and a chill ran through her body. A cool feeling washed over her, stretching from her toes to her lips. She pulled him to her, kissed him passionately and bust into tears. Ignoring his astonishment, she tucked her head into his armpit and smiled contentedly.

During the following weeks, she observed the telltale signs but dared not inform him immediately. She wanted to wait until no doubt remained. After a month she noticed her nipples turning a dark color. She watched with satisfaction as her breasts became swollen. She grew feverish and suffered vomiting spells. Her husband took a day off to care for her. Her pain and exhaustion confirmed to her that she was with child. When she was feeling a little better, she approached him and whispered haltingly:

"I'm pregnant."

"Is it true?" he cried out. "Let me see!" He hugged her tightly.

"What are you looking at?" She blushed and pushed him aside. Sitting awkwardly beside her, he held her shoulders and rocked her gently.

"Is it true?"

She didn't answer, just quietly kissed his cheek. That night he didn't sleep. Ignoring her urging to get some rest, he sat up and smoked until morning.

He waited until the end of the weekly briefing to break the news of his wife's pregnancy to the Division Commander.

Hung leaned back in his chair. "Really? Are you sure? Have you checked?"

"How can I check? I only know what my wife tells me. But she seems certain. It's been a month and five days already..."

Commander Hung pulled his collar away from his neck, the way he did whenever he felt moved. "Good! Really great!"

He turned to the officers leaving the briefing. "Breaking news, comrades: Colonel Chi is going to have a child!"

The room erupted with cheers, handshakes and laughter. Chi smiled, tears welling in his eyes.

Immediately the Domestic Living Quarters buzzed with the news. Military wives came in droves to congratulate the expectant mother. She listened quietly as all the current mothers dispensed advice. They told her the various activities she should avoid to protect the unborn child: what to eat and how she should walk and sleep. As she listened, she tried to imagine how her child would look. She envisioned him cute and plump, tottering next to the bed, crying out to his father, "Pa! Pa!" Then he would wave his little hands and motion for his father to hug him. The voices around her grew dim and distant, mingling dreamily with her thoughts like a soft melody.

One night she woke around midnight to see her husband rummaging through his suitcase. She wondered what he could be searching for at this hour of the night. He looked up at her, meeting her eyes. "Here it is," he said cheerfully.

In his hands he clutched a picture of himself as a boy. "Our son will look like this, like me."

She smiled at him. "How do you know it will be a boy. Maybe it'll be a girl."

Her response startled him, but he quickly regained his composure. "Of course, you're right," he smiled back at her. "But it'll still look like me."

As the months passed, she grew weaker. Walking became difficult and her already pale skin became paler and more sickly. Her husband tried to improve her diet and Commander Hung offered a medicinal concoction composed of honey, wine and egg yolks. Dr. Giau bicycled to their house regularly to monitor her condition. Then suddenly, during what should have been the happiest period of her life, her condition took a turn for the worse. The Division Commander stayed up all night with her husband as he waited outside the emergency room.

Due to the seriousness of her condition and his own emotional involvement, Dr. Giau insisted on supervising Lahn's treatment himself. While tending to complications linked to her age and extended periods of malnutrition, he felt her wish for a child had put him into an additional and more serious dilemma. His patient had been practically saturated with Agent Orange; every chemical analysis he ran told him that. Without informing the couple, he prescribed medication thought to counteract the deadly effects of dioxin. He was confident in his skills and he never allowed himself to lose hope that she would recover.

Finally she began to show signs of improvement. Although weak and frightfully pallid, she was eventually well enough to return home from the hospital. Still, as her due date approached, she was barely able to walk and her husband had to stay with her constantly, acting literally as her crutch. Despite feeling a chronic, debilitating weakness, she kept her spirits up by recalling how lucky she was to be pregnant at such an advanced age and in spite of all her past difficulties.

At night, her husband pulled her shirt up and listened attentively and patiently to the sound of his child. Then he would lie back down and look at the harness bells hanging from the ceiling. He'd carried these bells with him into battle for over fourteen years. They had been given to him by a fellow soldier, just before he died.

"Shake them whenever we have a victory," the soldier had said. "Then I'll hear them too and be happy."

He'd never forgotten those words. The harness bells had been carved from a goat's horn and their sound reminded him of a child's laugh. After the war and the final victory, he had hung them from his ceiling. He thought of how in the future, when his son (he still imagined the child would be a boy) turned one year old, he would give him the harness bells as a gift. It would then be his son's duty to keep the harness bells the rest of his life. He would instruct the boy that after his mother and father had passed away, he was to shake the bells whenever he met with good fortune. Then they too would be able to hear the bells and share in his joy.

He again tucked up his wife's shirt to listen to the sounds of his child.

"Stop it, please," his wife said. "You're just disturbing him."

"Shh!" he said gently. "Let's hear if he thinks I'm disturbing him or not."

She burst out laughing.

"Well, does he have any opinion?" she asked, feigning curiosity.

"He seems to agree with me," he responded in a deadpan voice. "But what's that noise he's making? Te-e, te-e...it sounds like he's playing the trumpet."

She slapped his shoulder. "Cut it out. You're a foolish old man."

He laughed. "Tomorrow I'm going to give him the harness bells. Then he won't have to play the trumpet. It's too tiring for him."

He hugged her and kissed her on the cheek. "When he's sixteen, this foolish old man will arrange a wife for him."

"Why are you so sure it's a son?"

"It's definitely a son. I already had a dream about introducing him to his father-in-law."

Several days later she went into labor.

Her husband brought her to the hospital and two nurses helped her to the maternity ward. Dr. Giau was waiting at the door. He knew that hers would be a difficult delivery, perhaps requiring special measures. Outside the door to the ward, Chi, Commander Hung and about sixty officers looked in at her excitedly. Dr. Giau told them to sit tight and not worry too much. Then he closed the door.

One hour passed; then two hours, then three. The husband nursed a cup of water as Commander Hung pulled at his collar. Several of the soldiers put their ears to the door, listening for the sound of a child crying. Four hours passed, then five. Finally a nurse opened the door and stepped out.

"How is it?" one soldier asked.

"Sister Lanh has given birth," the nurse said. "It's a boy." She tried to smile, but her voice trembled and cracked.

"Ah! Hooray!"

Everybody jumped up. The Division Commander hugged the husband and rocked him back and forth. Deliriously happy, Chi spun in a circle. Suddenly he remembered the harness bells....

In the maternity room, Dr. Giau informed her it was a boy and she smiled faintly. The baby was brought to the postnatal recovery room where an old nurse was bathing it in "endothermic water." Dr. Giau leaned against the medicine cabinet gasping for breath. His worst fear, a fear he had tried for months to suppress, had finally come to pass. The child was horribly deformed—its left leg stiffly twisted to its buttocks, its face distorted, with the left eyelid so big it covered one cheek and the lower lip drooping grotesquely below the chin. He knew that God was not so cruel as to create something like this. Only a high concentration of Agent Orange poison within that poor woman's body could have caused such disfigurement.

A feeling of intense hatred for the creature welled up in Dr. Giau. He labored in vain to catch his breath.

"Water! Give me some water!" he cried

An orderly entered the room with a cup of water. As she passed in view of the baby, she abruptly stopped and involuntarily jerked back, letting out a small cry...ooang! The cup of water crashed to the floor and shattered. She sat down and looked sadly at Dr. Giau. But he was gazing off into space.

He sighed and went silently over to the window. He tugged it open and stared out into the courtyard where the soldiers had surrounded the new father. He watched him holding aloft the harness bells, shaking them and chatting cheerfully:

"I'll find a wife for him when he turns sixteen," the father was saying.

The harness bells rang like a laughing child.

Translated by Peter Zinoman and Nguyen Nguyet Cam
Edited by Wayne Karlin

Point Lookout

Wayne Karlin

Mary had just gotten to work at midnight when the first gunshot casualty was brought in, the ambulance attendants nearly knocking her over in the corridor. She glanced down briefly and the boy's eyes met hers; he was fluttering somewhere in the pull between panic and unconsciousness. The boy was black, maybe fifteen; the wound was through the left chest wall.

Dr. Sayed grabbed her arm. "Give me a hand here."

She tried to walk past him. "I'm an obstetrics nurse, doctor."

"You're a fucking nurse, give me a fucking hand."

The double doors flung open and she saw another kid being wheeled in, clutching his belly.

She helped cut the rest of the boy's clothing off, got an IV going. The boy's eyes rolled back; he was making gargling noises. "Come on, for fuck's sake," Sayed said. They rolled the boy onto his right side and she tied off the bleeders as Sayed cut, her hands falling into a rhythm she'd thought they'd forgotten. The doors slammed open again. Out of the corner of her eye she saw another child wheeled in, his hand clutching an Orioles' baseball cap. More doctors and nurses had arrived now, but it was a weekday night and they were a small country hospital and she knew she couldn't leave. Sayed removed a bullet from the boy they were working on and held it up for her to see. "7.62 millimeter," he said bitterly. "Where the fuck are we, nurse?" She helped start a saline irrigation. Sayed's hawkish brown face seemed enclosed in a trance, as if the memory of another life had taken him over. She held ribs apart with a retractor. She helped get the chest tubes in to drain the wound, pump up his collapsed lungs; she catheterized the boy with difficulty, his penis shrinking as she tried to hold it. The floor was slippery with blood. "Hardee's restaurant," someone said, "guy just walked in." She wondered if Sayed had treated casualties of the Afghanistan war. She wondered where he'd learned to say fuck. The word, as had the movements of her own hands, called another memory, the way that particular word rolled out like someone screaming a panicky instruction when the death got too thick. She realized she couldn't remember if this observation had been hers from the time she'd worked ER or if she'd heard it from her husband. Sayed closed. She moved over with him, her feet sliding out from under her on the blood, helped debride the other kid's abdominal wound; it was embedded with what looked like pieces of a salt shaker; undigested hamburger and pickles were scattered up from the bowel to the chest. Her husband had been in a helicopter crew in the Vietnam war; he'd told her how during medevacs they'd pack the interior with wounded and dead, how the blood of the dead and living would mingle. At what point had their memories leaked together? Sponging, watching Sayed's skilled hands, his lean fingers squeeze along the length of a bowel, searching for fragments, probing, cutting, suturing skillfully, she felt a wave of lust, a heat that opened like liquid petals inside her body.

She didn't get to obstetrics until three in the morning. At eight o'clock, Margaret Vail, the shift supervisor, looked at her and told her to go home; she was calling in the standby nurse. No babies had been born on Mary's shift before she left. One of the three boys brought into ER had died. A man had walked into the restaurant—it was IHOP not Hardee's—and shot the black teenagers with cool deliberation. There were conflicting stories as to whether the man was black or white, if the shooting was part of a drug war or just the act of a crazy. She didn't ask Margaret if the shooter was a vet.

At home she vacuumed the living room and smoked. She waxed the kitchen floor. She did a load of laundry. Brian was at work and Tim was in school. She couldn't stand the empty house. She made two pastrami on rye sandwiches and put them in a paper bag. When she went back out, the black Labrador, held on a running lead, whined at her piteously and even though she didn't like the dog, she unclipped him and let him jump into the back of the station wagon and she drove south to Point Lookout with him panting like the whole manic night behind her.

During the Civil War there had been a federal prisoner of war camp on the wedge of land between the Chesapeake Bay and the entrance to the Potomac river; her husband was sinking trenches in a mass grave found south of Fort Lincoln, along the river shore. She parked in the recreation area parking lot and leashed Butch—the dog was young, too untrained to let loose at the site. The grass was shaded by tall loblolly pines, evenly spaced; she went under them, Butch pulling her into a half-run, to the sliver of beach, then turned and walked up it to the dig. There were virtually no waves on the Potomac side, though a breeze crinkled the surface of the river and a sparkling, transparent edge of water advanced slightly on the sand beach then drew back to show a glittering strip of pebbles and shells.

Brian was hunched over a sifting tray. As she came up behind him she stood still for a moment, the movement of his fingers probing the sand reminding her of Sayed's.

Her husband looked up and smiled, his face registering confusion at seeing her there, reforming as it did when she'd wake him up from a dream.

"Everything all right?" he asked. "Down, Butch."

The dog was trying to jump up on him, trying to pull her arm from its socket.

"Sure," she said. She put her free arm around his waist. "I just felt like seeing you."

"Are you all right?" he repeated.

Several of the student volunteers were looking at her. One of them was wearing an Orioles' baseball hat. She closed her eyes tightly.

Brian hit the palms of his hands against his trousers. "Look, I need to finish here. Why don't you relax for a while, take a walk. We can do a picnic on the beach afterwards."

"Telepathy," she said. "I brought some sandwiches."

"I have..." he started to say, but something in her face must have stopped him. He squeezed her arm.

Mary nodded at the tray. "How's it going—any surprises?"

He looked distracted again. "Just dem bones."

He looked in fact worried, she thought with a sudden leap of her heart that startled her. The dig was grant funded and nearly finished—if he didn't find more burial sites or a more spectacular discovery, he didn't think there'd be any more money or a chance at a permanent teaching position at the college. Another archaeologist had found three lead coffins at the Historic State Capital site: they were believed to contain the remains of the founders of the state. Brian's dead Confederates couldn't compete. "They aren't politically correct corpses," he'd said bitterly, though, Mary thought, with that archaeologist's pride at finding and using a piece of contemporary language, that archaeologist's ignorance that the phrase was already somewhat dated. Her contempt surprised her. He wanted to buy the house they were renting here, and he thought she did too. She'd gone along with him in applying for the mortgage; it would be messy now if they had to move. But she'd just realized how relieved she'd felt when she'd seen the worry in his face. She didn't want to stay here.

She said she'd see him later.

The dog pulled her up the beach. She jerked sharply at the chain leash. "Heel, damn you." The dog looked back at her, all stupid Labrador affability, all wasted charm as far as she was concerned, and yanked her forward again. She pulled it to her, hand over hand, and at the end pulled up the collar, yanked the dog's forepaws right off the ground in a burst of rage. Butch panted and whined. She unclipped him and let him go. Maybe the idiot animal would get lost. She felt suddenly ashamed of her anger though she recognized, another realization in the clarity of this morning's light, how deeply she disliked the animal. She could hear its panting, the relentless rustle of its pad keeping pace with her now, just behind the curtain of trees. Butch had been one of a litter born in the barn across the country street in front of their house; the puppies had swarmed the yard, Tim and this one finding each other. "It's a pity for the kid to live in the country and not have a dog," Brian had said. But Mary had blown up at her son when she'd first heard him calling the puppy Butch, naming it, creating a responsibility, a living connection to this place, that she didn't want.

She stopped and squinted at the expanse of the river. She could barely see the coastline of Virginia; it was a misty gray line on the other side. On the Maryland side she could see up the green curve of the coast to the point of land which marked the head of the tributary that twisted in near the house: the Brits had sailed up here, turned there, began their settlement nearby, started something.

The dog came back, proudly holding a broken-necked rabbit in its mouth, its eyes gleaming at her over the broken flesh and fur. "You murdering little bastard," she said, and grabbed the hind quarters. The dog backed up, growling, digging its front paws into the sand, then snapping its head around and winning the tug of war, running off, its grinning mouth full of death.

She walked on towards the dig. Near or on this ground her feet pressed prisoners had starved to death or been murdered: Brian had found the pit he was working in an area where no dead were supposed to be; the corpses were thrown in haphazardly, some with shattered skulls, mini-balls buried in their bases; ribs splintered by bayonet thrusts. All of Point Lookout was supposed to be haunted: the locals had many ghost stories. Park rangers had picked up voices on recorders left out at night in deserted areas. She'd seen a photo taken during the sixties inside the Point Lookout lighthouse; when you stared at it long enough, a man in a Confederate uniform emerged from the background. His face angry. His eyes accusing. Nothing went away. During their first year together she'd sometimes held Brian at night when he'd sweated and moaned, half suspecting it was phony, behavior copied from a movie or book; it seemed to her so much of the war was that anyway, but even if so the nightmares were there, the constant unearthing of the dead in his mind. She hadn't minded; they'd pull each other from the pit; whatever had been violated in him would leave a space where the flesh of their hearts could grow together: they would be closer in it than husband and wife, man and woman.

But they were in their twentieth year now and what had changed? One of her neighbors, a counselor of troubled girls, had told her of a half-Vietnamese, half-American girl, brought to the states as a baby on one of the orphan airlifts; she'd grown up in a series of foster and group homes, and now had run away and was hiding in the woods like the veterans Mary had heard of in Oregon or Washington, leftovers from the war, things that would not go away. Earlier in the year she'd miscarried (her mind going smooth and blank over the word) and the girl seemed somehow connected to the ache of loss she felt, she and her husband entwined in a curse whose elaborate intricacies wearied her. Brian suspected the miscarriage (it was a terrible word, truly, as if something inside her hadn't held the child right) might have had to do with his exposure to Agent Orange. But he wasn't sure how much exposure he'd had. That is to say he suspected a curse. Nothing went away. One night she'd come into his office to find him asleep at his desk, his desk light burning. By his hand were notes about the Point Lookout massacre, under his sleeping head were photos and articles about My Lai that he was using as one of his modern references: the tangled and torn bodies of women and children pooled around his head like spilled dreams. Where the fuck are we, nurse?

She realized that her feet were getting wet. The ribbon of sand had gotten narrower: perhaps the tide was coming in. The water was icy. A red, clayey mud bank, maybe ten feet tall, grew up on her right side. The water had lapped and gnawed at it, created a dark cavern under a frozen Medusa spread of exposed and shiny tree roots. Butch was darting around the roots, barking. She saw him nose into the bank, his tail wagging, and begin to dig frantically, mud and water flying.

She called him and to her surprise he jumped into the water and swam over to her, making deep, coughing and choking sounds; he had something gripped in his mouth. He got onto the sand and sat down and dropped it in front of her, a trick Tim had taught him. Mary felt touched in spite of herself, more at seeing her son's efforts than at the dog's action. She reached for the slim brown cylinder, some part of her mind noting the shape, the knobbed ends, the cool, smooth almost plastic feel of it; as she touched it she felt a chill seizing over her skin. The dog growled and snatched it back, twisting it free. Butch ran off down the beach, then stood looking at her warily, the shape in its mouth like a cartoon cliché. From the size she thought it could be a femur.

She went to the umbrella of roots and tried to push herself in through two black, gnarled branches. The space was too narrow. She took off her shoes and waded out into the water, then squatted awkwardly and peered through the roots. At first it was too dim for her to be sure, but a shift of the light reflected off the waves, into the hollow worn in the fleshy clay bank, and in that second she could see a broken outline that she squinted and connected into a human form socketed into the clay: the washboard cage of the ribs, the pelvic cradle, the grin.

Brian, she'd seen him work, would photograph and sketch the site, plot the exact relationships of objects on a finely drawn grid: only then would he delicately brush the earth away, layer by layer. She reached both hands roughly into the opening between the roots and gripped and drew out as if to birth. The first one came loose with a wet, plopping sound, a satisfying release of tension. She placed it carefully on the sand—the dog had disappeared again—waded back and pulled out another, barnacle encrusted, cutting her hands, then another, then another, desecrating the site, leaving it torn and open. She tried to form the outline of a shape, lumping wet sand over the shapes, connecting. The water lapped dangerously close. She stood, feeling dizzy, and looked at what she'd placed on the beach, dem bones. But the form was incomplete, something strange and broken that had come from her. There were too many parts missing; they left gaps, an aching void. And when she turned her head away again, the dog broke from the trees and snatched its trophy from her grasp.

Humping The Boonies

Bobbie Ann Mason

The footsteps on the boardwalk grew louder. Sam closed the zipper on her backpack, inching it along. She intended to leave the path and creep through the jungle back to the car. But it seemed a cheat to have a car for escape. She should have had a foxhole, with broken branches over it, to hide in. But the V.C. would know the jungle, and they would see where she had been. They would see the picnic cooler. The V.C. rapist-terrorist was still at the boardwalk. A bird flew over but she didn't dare glance at it. Its shadow fell on the bushes.

Here she was in a swamp where an old outlaw had died, and someone was stalking her. In her head, the Kinks were singing "There's a little green man in my head," their song about paranoia. But this was real. A curious pleasure stole over her. This terror was what the soldiers had felt every minute. They lived with the possibility of unseen eyes of snipers. They crept along, pointing the way with their rifles, alert to land mines, listening, always listening. They were completely alive, every nerve on edge, and sleep, when it came, was like catnapping. No nightmares in the jungle. Just silent terror. During the night, she had stayed awake in the dark swamp, watching and waiting. She could make out faint rings of lights and winking lightning bugs. She put herself in Moon Pie's place. In Emmett's place. She had fantasized Tom there with her in her sleeping bag, the way her father had tried to imagine her mother. But Tom floated away. She was in her father's place, in a foxhole in the jungle, with a bunch of buddies all breathing quietly, daring to smoke in their quiet holes, eating their C-rations silently, their cold beans. She remembered Emmett eating cold split-pea soup from the can. She felt more like a cat than anything, small and fragile and very alert to movement, her whiskers flicking and her pupils widening in the dark. It was a new way of seeing.

Now she felt no rush of adrenaline, no trembling of knees. She knew it was because she didn't really believe this was real, after all. It couldn't be happening to her. In a few moments, everything would be clear and fine.

Her breathing was silent. Not even her eyes moved. She could see bushes stir as the rapist approached. He had left the boardwalk and was heading down the path in her direction. Her only hope was to remain hidden, with the can of oysters ready to cut his eyes out. The greasy oysters leaked onto her fingers.

A leaf moved, a color flashed. Someone whistled a tune, "Suicide Is Painless." This was a joke, after all, for it was only Emmett, in an old green T-shirt and green fatigues. He was empty-handed. His running shoes were wet with dew and his hair was uncombed. She stood up, feeling like a jack-in the box. In

Vietnam, this scene would never have happened. It would always be the enemy behind a bush.

"Hey, Emmett," she said.

"What are you doing here?"

"How did you know I was here?"

"I saw your car out there."

"I know that. But how did you know my car would be here?"

"Just a guess."

"How'd you get here?"

"Walked."

Her knees still weren't trembling. She hadn't been scared. She marched ahead of him on the path, and he trailed after her. She had her backpack, and he had grabbed the cooler. She said, "It was crazy to walk all the way out here."

"Jesus fuckin'-A Christ, Sam!" Emmett yelled suddenly. "You worried me half to death! Crazy? I'd say it was crazy to camp out here. I thought you'd gone off the deep end. Man, I thought you'd lost it."

Sam reached her car and opened the door and set her stuff in the back seat. The windows had mist on them. The car inside seemed damp and cool. It must not be watertight, after all. Emmett was haggard and unshaved, and his T-shirt was dirty. The smoke from his cigarette flooded the swamp, obliterating the jungle smells.

"You scared me," he said. "I was afraid of what you might do. You might have considered that some people would be worried about you."

"Ha! I'd talk if I's you. At least I left a note."

"I was worried. I was scared you'd get hurt."

"You didn't have to come after me."

Emmett sat on a front fender and put his hands on his face. He was trembling, and his teeth chattered. A bird flew by and Emmett didn't look up. It was a Kentucky cardinal, a brilliant surprise, a flash of red, like a train signal.

"What were you doing out here?" Emmett asked.

"Humping the boonies."

"What?"

"I wanted to know what it was like out in the jungle at night." Sam scraped the dew off the bumper with her boot.

"This ain't a jungle. It's a swamp, and it's dangerous. I thought you aimed to stay at the Hugheses' last night."

"I didn't want to. Where were you?"

"I went over to Jim's. He's back from Lexington. I thought it would be a good time to set off that bomb, with you gone. But I went back to round up Moon Pie at dark and I went in and found your note."

"Did you leave Moon Pie in the house to breathe those fumes?"

"No. I took him to Jim's. He hated riding in Jim's truck."

"When I found that stupid flea bomb, I thought you'd flipped out again."

"I had to get rid of those fleas."

"Those fleas don't even bother Moon Pie, and you know it." He smoked his cigarette down and ground it out on the gravel. He said, "I found out something yesterday morning after you left."

"What?"

"Buddy Mangrum's in the hospital. His liver's real bad."

Sam kicked at the car. "I hate Agent Orange! I hate the Army! What about his little girl?"

"She's home. That operation went O.K., but I don't know how they're going to pay all the bills. If he dies, maybe his wife will collect some benefits, but I doubt it."

Emmett leaned against the VW hood, its prim beige forehead. He said, "Jim and me went up to the hospital for a while, but we didn't see Buddy. We hung around in the waiting room a long time arguing about Geraldine Ferraro." Emmett smiled. "I guess Jim's afraid Sue Ann might decide to run for President or something." Emmett seemed old and worn out. He said, "I know why you were out here. You think you can go through what we went through out in the jungle, but you can't. This place is scary, and things can happen to you, but it's not the same as having snipers and mortar fire and shells and people shooting at you from behind bushes. What have you got to be afraid of? You're afraid somebody'll look at you the wrong way. You're afraid your mama's going to make you go to school in Lexington. Big deal."

"I slept out here in the swamp and I wasn't afraid of anything," she said. "Some people are afraid of snakes, but not me. Some people are even afraid of fleas. I wasn't afraid of snakes or hoot owls or anything."

"Congratulations."

"And when you came, I thought it might be a hunter, or a rapist. But I wasn't scared. I was ready for you." She had left the can of smoked oysters behind, but her hands still smelled.

Emmett lit another cigarette and the sun came up some more. The fog was burning off. Emmett's pimples were crusted with yellow salve. Bile was yellow. Maybe his bile was oozing up from his liver. His liver would go next.

"I wanted to see that bird," she said. "That bird you're looking for." He shrugged, and she went on. "I saw a cardinal. And some raccoons. And a blue jay teasing a squirrel."

"Good for you."

She breathed deeply and kicked at the fender. She was bored with Cawood's Pond. How could that outlaw have stayed out here in hiding? What did he eat? What did he do for recreation? She said, "How did you know I was here?"

"I called around."

"Nobody knew I was here."

"I thought you might have gone to Lexington, but I called Irene this morning and she hadn't seen you."

"You didn't tell her I was missing, did you?"

"No. I just talked about something else. I knew she'd mention it if you were there. I finally figured out you were here from your note. For one thing, I figured you'd go someplace to escape. And also someplace dramatic, because that's like you. Also, you took my poncho and space blanket. When I read that diary I tried to imagine what I would have done, and this is what I would have done. Once when I was little and Daddy gave me a whipping because I didn't feed the calves on time, I ran away from home. I ran to the creek and stayed there till it got dark, and while I was there I thought I was getting revenge, for some reason. It's childish, to go run off to the wilderness to get revenge. It's the most typical thing in the world."

"That explains it, then," Sam said disgustedly. "That's what you were doing in Vietnam. That explains what the whole country was doing over there. The least little threat and America's got to put on its cowboy boots and stomp around and show somebody a thing or two."

Emmett walked down the path to the boardwalk, and Sam followed him. She watched her feet, carefully avoiding a broken plank. He flung his cigarette into the water.

She asked, "What did you think of the diary?"

"I didn't sleep none after I read it."

"He couldn't even spell 'machete'."

"Are you disappointed?"

She fidgeted. "The way he talked about gooks and killing—I hated it." She paused. "I hate him. He was awful, the way he talked about gooks and killing."

Emmett shook her by the shoulders, jostling her until her teeth rattled. "Look here, little girl. He could have been me. All of us, it was the same."

"He loved it, like Pete. He went over there to get some notches on his machete."

"Yeah, and if he hadn't got killed, then he'd have had to live with that."

"It wouldn't have bothered him. He's like Pete."

"It's the same for all of us! Tom and Pete and Jim and Buddy and all of us. You can't do what we did and then be happy about it. And nobody lets you forget it. Goddamn it, Sam!" He slammed the railing of the boardwalk so hard it almost broke. He would have fallen into the murky swamp. Emmett was shuddering again, close to sobbing.

"Oh, Emmett!" cried Sam. She was standing with her arms branched out, like the cypress above, but she was frozen on the spot, unable to reach him. She waited. She thought he was going to come out with some suppressed memories of events as dramatic as that one that caused Hawkeye to crack up in the final episode of *M.A.S.H.* But nothing came.

"Are you going to talk, Emmett? Can you tell about it? Do the way Hawkeye did when he told about that baby on the bus. His memories lied to him. But he got better when he could reach down and get the right memories." Sam was practically yelling at him. She was frantic.

Emmett said, "There ain't no way to tell it. No point. You can't tell it all. Dwayne didn't begin to tell it all."

"Just tell one thing."

"O.K. One thing."

"One thing at a time will be all right."

Emmett lit a cigarette and started slowly, but then he talked faster and faster, as though he were going to pour out everything after all. He said, "There was this patrol I was on and we didn't have enough guys? And we were too close together and this land mine blew us sky-high. We was too close. We had already lost a bunch and we freaked out and huddled together, which you should never do, so we was scrambling to an LZ to meet the chopper. And first we hit this mine and then this grenade come out of nowhere, and I played like I was dead, and I was underneath this big guy about to smother me. The NVA poked around and decided we were all dead and they left, and I laid there about nine hours, and I heard that chopper come and go, but it was too far away and it didn't spot me. I was too scared to signal, because the enemy was there. I could hear 'em. They shot at the chopper. What do you think of that? For hours, then, until the next day, I was all by myself, except for dead bodies. The smell of warm blood in the jungle heat, like soup coming to a boil. Oh, that was awful! They got the radio guy and the radio was smashed. I couldn't use it. I was petrified, and I thought I could hear them for a long time."

"That sounds familiar. I saw something like that in a movie on TV." Sam was shaking, scared.

"I know the one you're thinking about—that movie where the camp got overrun and the guy had to hide in that tunnel. This was completely different. It really happened," he said, dragging on his cigarette. "That smell—the smell of death—was everywhere all the time. Even when you were eating, it was like you were eating death."

"I heard somebody in that documentary we saw say that," Sam said.

"Well, it was true! I wasn't the only one who noticed it. Dwayne smelled it."

"He probably liked it."

"Oh, shit-fire, Sam! We were out there trying to survive. It felt good when you got even. You came out here like a little kid running away from home, for spite. Now didn't it feel good? That's why you weren't afraid. 'Cause it felt good to worry me half to death."

Sam said, "If you ran away when you were little, and you think it's childish to run out here, don't you think you do the same thing? Don't you think it's childish to do what you do, the way you hide and won't get a job, and won't have a girlfriend? Anita's a real pretty woman and it just kills me that you won't go with her."

Emmett's head fell forward with sobs. He cried. Sam hadn't seen him cry like that. The sobs grew louder. He tried to talk and he couldn't. He couldn't even smoke his cigarette.

"Don't talk," she said. He kept crying, his head down—long throaty sobs, heaving helplessly. Sam let him cry. She heard him say "Anita." She was afraid. Now, at last. She went into the woods to pee and when she got back he was still crying. He sounded exactly like a screech owl. She touched his shoulder, and he shoved her hand away and kept crying—louder now, as though now that they were out in the woods, and it was broad daylight, and there were no people, he could just let loose.

His cry grew louder, as loud as the wail of a peacock. She watched in awe. In his diary, her father seemed to whimper, but Emmett's sorrow was full-blown, as though it had grown over the years into something monstrous and fantastic. His cigarette had burned down, and he dropped it over the railing.

They walked back to the car. Sam sat in the car and Emmett, still crying, sat on the hood. His bulk made the car shake with his sobs. Sam reached in her backpack and wormed out a granola bar. She resisted the temptation to turn on the car radio. An old song, "Stranded in the Jungle," went through her mind. A flash from the past. A golden oldie. It would be ironic if the car wouldn't start. But Cawood's Pond was beginning to seem like home. She and Emmett could stay out here. Emmett's ability to repair things would come in handy. He could rig them up a lean-to. He could dig them a foxhole. It still made her angry that she couldn't dig a foxhole. That woman Mondale nominated could probably dig one.

She had left the car door open. Emmett hung on the door and bent down to speak to her through the window. He said, "You ran off. When you ran off I thought you were dead."

"No, I wasn't dead. What made you think that?"

"I thought you'd left me. I thought you must have gone off to die. I was afraid you'd kill yourself."

"Why would you think that?"

"So many kids these days are doing it. On the news the other day, those kids over in Carlisle County that made that suicide pact—that shook me up."

"I wouldn't do that," Sam said.

"But how was I to know? You were gone, and I didn't know what might have happened to you. I thought you'd get hurt. It was like being left by myself and all my buddies dead. I had to find you."

"Thank you." She wadded up the granola wrapper and squeezed it in her hand. She said, "You've done something like that before, Emmett. When you went to Vietnam, you went for Mom's sake—and mine."

He nodded thoughtfully. He said, "It wasn't what you wanted, was it? It wasn't what Irene wanted. Then she got stuck with me because of what I did for her. Ain't life stupid? Fuck a duck!"

"Get in, Emmett," she said, reaching to open the door on the passenger side.

"No. I ain't finished." His face was twisted in pain and his pimples glistened with tears. He said, "There's something wrong with me. I'm damaged. It's like something in the center of my heart is gone and I can't get it back. You know when you cut down a tree sometimes and it's diseased in the middle?"

"I never cut down a tree."

"Well, imagine it."

"Yeah. But what you're saying is you don't care about anybody. But you cared enough about me to come out here. And you cared about Mom enough to go over there."

"But don't you understand—let me explain. This is what I do. I work on staying together, one day at a time. There's no room for anything else. It takes all my energy."

"Emmett, don't you want to get married and have a family like other people? Don't you want to do something with your life?"

He sobbed again. "I want to be a father. But I can't. The closest I can come is with you. And I failed. I should never have let you go so wild. I should have taken care of you."

"You cared," she said. "You felt something for me coming out here." She felt weak. Now her knees felt wobbly. She got out of the car and shut the door.

"I was afraid," he said. "Come here, I want to show you something." He led her to the boardwalk, and they looked out over the swamp. He pointed to a snake sunning on a log. "That sucker's a cottonmouth."

"I wish that bird would come," Sam said.

"You know the reason I want to see that bird?"

"Not really."

"If you can think about something like birds, you can get outside of yourself, and it doesn't hurt as much. That's the whole idea. That's the whole challenge for the human race. Think about that. Put your thinking cap on, Sam. Put that in your pipe and smoke it. But I can barely get to the point where I can be a self to get out of.

Sam picked a big hunk of fungus off a stump and sniffed it. It smelled dead. Emmett said, "I came out here to save you, but maybe I can't. Maybe you have to find out for yourself. Fuck. You can't learn from the past. The main thing you learn from history is that you can't learn from history. That's what history is."

Emmett flung a hand toward the black water beside the boardwalk. "See these little minnows? It looks like they've got one eye on the top of their heads. They're called topwaters. They're good for a pond. Catfish whomp 'em up. See that dead tree? That's a woodpecker hole up there. But a wood duck will build a nest there."

"How do you know all that?"

"I've watched 'em. There are things you can figure out, but most things you can't." He waved at the dark swamp. "There are some things you can never figure out."

He turned and walked ahead of her, walking fast up the path from the boardwalk. She followed. He entered a path into the woods and walked faster. Poison ivy curled around his shoes. From the back, he looked like an old peasant woman hugging a baby. Sam watched as he disappeared into the woods. He seemed to float away, above the poison ivy, like a pond skimmer, beautiful in his flight.

Letters From My Father
Robert Olen Butler

I look through the letters my father sent to me in Saigon and I find this: "Dear Fran. How are you? I wish you and your mother were here with me. The weather here is pretty cold this time of year. I bet you would like the cold weather." At the time I wondered how he would know such a thing. Cold weather sounded very bad. It was freezing, he said, so I touched the tip of my finger to a piece of ice and I held it there for as long as I could. It hurt very bad and that was after only about a minute. I thought, How could you spend hours and days in weather like that?

It makes no difference that I had misunderstood the cold weather. By the time he finally got me and my mother out of Vietnam, he had moved to a place where it almost never got very cold. The point is that in his letters to me he often said this and that about the weather. It is cold today. It is hot today. Today there are clouds in the sky. Today there are no clouds. What did that have to do with me?

He said "Dear Fran" because my name is Fran. That's short for Francine and the sound of Fran is something like a Vietnamese name, but it isn't, really. So I told my friends in Saigon that my name was Tran, which was short for Hon Tran, which means "a kiss on the forehead." My American father lived in America but my Vietnamese mother and me lived in Saigon, so I was still a Saigon girl. My mother called me Francine, too. She was happy for me to have this name. She said it was not just American, it was also French. But I wanted a name for Saigon and Tran was it.

I was a child of dust. When the American fathers all went home, including my father, and the communists took over, that's what we were called, those of us who had faces like those drawings you see in some of the bookstalls on Nguyen Hue Street. You look once and you see a beautiful woman sitting at her mirror, but then you look again and you see the skull of a dead person, no skin on the face, just the wide eyes of the skull and the bared teeth. We were like that, the children of dust in Saigon. At one look we were Vietnamese and at another look we were American and after that you couldn't get your eyes to stay still. When they turned to us, they kept seeing first one thing and then another.

Last night I found a package of letters in a footlocker that belongs to my father. It is in the storage shack at the back of our house here in America. I am living now in Lake Charles, Louisiana, and I found this package of letters out-side—many packages, hundreds of letters—and I opened one, and these are all copies he kept of letters he sent trying to get us out of Vietnam. I look through these letters my father wrote and I find this: "What is this crap that you're trying to give me now? It has been nine years, seven months, and fifteen days since I last saw my daughter, my own flesh-and-blood daughter."

This is an angry voice, a voice with feeling. I have been in this place now for a year. I am seventeen and it took even longer than nine years, seven months, fifteen days to get me out of Vietnam. I wish I could say something about that because I know anyone who listens to my story would expect me right now to say how I felt. My mother and me were left behind in Saigon. My father went on ahead to America, and he thought he could get some paperwork done and prepare a place for us, then my mother and me would be leaving for America very soon. But things happened. A different footlocker was lost and some important papers with it, like their marriage license and my birth certificate. Then the country of South Vietnam fell to the communists, and even those who thought it might happen thought it happened pretty fast, really. Who knew? My father didn't.

I look at a letter he sent me in Saigon after it fell and the letter says: "You can imagine how I feel. The whole world is let down by what happened." But I could not imagine that, if you want to know the truth, how my father felt. And I knew nothing of the world except Saigon, and even that wasn't the way the world was, because when I was very little they gave it a different name, calling it Ho Chi Minh City. Now, those words are a man's name, you know, but the same words have several other meanings, too, and I took the name like everyone took the face of a child of dust: I looked at it one way and it meant one thing and then I looked at it a different way and it meant something else. Ho Chi Minh also can mean "very intelligent starch-paste," and that's what we thought of the new name, me and some friends of mine who also had American fathers. We would meet at the French cemetery on Phan Thanh Gian Street and talk about our city—Ho, for short; starch-paste. We would talk about our lives in Starch-Paste City, and we had this game where we'd hide in the cemetery, each in a separate place, and then we'd keep low and move slowly and see how many of our friends we would find. If you saw the other person first, you would get a point. And if nobody ever saw you, if it was like you were invisible, you'd win.

The cemetery made me sad, but it felt very comfortable there somehow. We all thought that, me and my friends. It was a ragged place and many of the names were like Couchet, Picard, Vernet, Believeau, and these graves never had any flowers on them. Everybody who loved these dead people had gone home to France long ago. Then there was a part of the cemetery that had Vietnamese dead. There were some flowers over there, but not very many. The grave markers had photos, little oval frames built into the stone, and these were faces of the dead, mostly old people, men and women, the wealthy Vietnamese, but there were some young people, too, many of them dead in 1968 when there was much killing in Saigon. I would always hide over in this section and there was one boy, very cute, in sunglasses, leaning on a motorcycle, his hand on his hip. He died in February of 1968, and I probably wouldn't have liked him anyway. He looked cute but very conceited. And there was a girl nearby. The marker said she was fifteen. I found her when I was about ten or so and she was very beautiful, with long black hair and dark eyes and a round face. I would always go to her grave and I wanted to be just like her, though I knew my face was different from hers. Then I went one day—I was almost her age at last—and the rain had gotten into the little picture frame and her face was nearly gone. I could see her hair, but the features of her face had faded until you could not see them, there were only dark streaks of water and the picture was curling at the edges, and I cried over that. It was like she had died.

Sometimes my father sent me pictures with his letters. "Dear Fran," he would say. "Here is a picture of me. Please send me a picture of you." A friend of mine, when she was about seven years old, got a pen pal in Russia. They wrote to each other very simple letters in French. Her pen pal said, "Please send me a picture of you and I will send you one of me." My friend put on her white *ao dai* and went downtown and had her picture taken before the big banyan tree in the park on Le Thanh Ton. She sent it off and in return she got a picture of a fat girl who hadn't combed her hair, standing by a cow on a collective farm.

My mother's father was some government man, I think. And the communists said my mother was an agitator or collaborator. Something like that. It was all mostly before I was born or when I was just a little girl, and whenever my mother tried to explain what all this was about, this father across the sea and us not seeming to ever go there, I just didn't like to listen very much and my mother realized that, and after a while she didn't say any more. I put his picture up on my mirror and he was smiling, I guess. He was outside somewhere and there was a lake or something in the background and he had a T-shirt on and I guess he was really more squinting than smiling. There were several of these photographs of him on my mirror. They were always outdoors and he was always squinting in the sun. He said in one of his letters to me: ":Dear Fran, I got your photo. You are very pretty, like your mother. I have not forgotten you." And I thought: I am not like my mother. I am a child of dust. Has he forgotten that?

One of the girls I used to hang around with at the cemetery told me a story that she knew was true because it happened to her sister's best friend. The best friend was just a very little girl when it began. Her father was a soldier in the South Vietnam Army and he was away fighting somewhere secret, Cambodia or somewhere. It was very secret, so her mother never heard from him and the little girl was so small when he went away that she didn't even remember him, what he looked like or anything. But she knew she was supposed to have a daddy, so every evening, when the mother would put her daughter to bed, the little girl would ask where her father was. She asked with such a sad heart that one night the mother made something up.

There was a terrible storm and the electricity went out in Saigon. So the mother went to the table with the little girl clinging in fright to her, and she lit an oil lamp. When she did, her shadow suddenly was thrown upon the wall and it was very big, and she said, "Don't cry, my baby, see there?" She pointed to the shadow. "There's your daddy. He'll protect you." This made the little girl very happy. She stopped shaking from fright immediately and the mother sang the girl to sleep.

The next evening before going to bed, the little girl asked to see her father. When the mother tried to say no, the little girl was so upset that the mother gave in and lit the oil lamp and cast her shadow on the wall. The little girl went to the wall and held her hands before her with the palms together and she bowed low to the shadow. "Good night, Daddy," she said, and she went to sleep. This happened the next evening and the next and it went on for more than a year.

Then one evening, just before bedtime, the father finally came home. The mother, of course, was very happy. She wept and she kissed him and she said to him, "We will prepare a thanksgiving feast to honor our ancestors. You go in to our daughter. She is almost ready for bed. I will go out to the market and get some food for our celebration."

So the father went in to the little girl and he said to her, "My pretty girl, I am home. I am your father and I have not forgotten you."

But the little girl said, "You're not my daddy. I know my daddy. He'll be here soon. He comes every night to say good night to me before I go to bed."

The man was shocked at his wife's faithlessness, but he was very proud, and he did not say anything to her about it when she got home. He did not say anything at all, but prayed briefly before the shrine of their ancestors and picked up his bag and left. The weeks passed and the mother grieved so badly that one day she threw herself into the Saigon River and drowned.

The father heard news of this and thought that she had killed herself for shame. He returned home to be a father to his daughter, but on the first night, there was a storm and the lights went out and the man lit the oil lamp, throwing his shadow on the wall. His little girl laughed in delight and went and bowed low to the shadow and said, "Good night, Daddy." When the man saw this, he took his little girl to his mother's house, left her, and threw himself into the Saigon River to join his wife in death.

My friend says this story is true. Everyone in the neighborhood of her sister's friend knows about it. But I don't think it's true. I never did say that to my friend, but for me, it doesn't make sense. I can't believe that the little girl would be satisfied with the shadow father. There was this darkness on the wall, just a flatness, and she loved it. I can see how she wouldn't take up with this man who suddenly walks in one night and says, "I'm your father, let me tell you good night." But the other guy, the shadow—he was no father either.

When my father met my mother and me at the airport, there were people with cameras and microphones and my father grabbed my mother with this enormous hug and this sound like a shout and he kissed her hard and all the people with microphones and cameras smiled and nodded. Then he let go of my mother and he looked at me and suddenly he was making this little choking sound, a kind of gacking in the back of his throat like a rabbit makes when you pick him up and he doesn't like it. And my father's hands just fluttered before him and he got stiff-legged coming over to me and the hug he gave me was like I was soaking wet and he had on his Sunday clothes, though he was just wearing some silly T-shirt.

All the letters from my father, the ones I got in Saigon, and the photos, they're in a box in the back of the closet of my room. My closet smells of my perfume, is full of nice clothes so that I can fit in at school. Not everyone can say what they feel in words, especially words on paper. Not everyone can look at a camera and make their face do what it has to do to show a feeling. But years of flat words, grimaces at the sun, these are hard things to forget. So I've been sitting all morning today in the shack behind our house, out here with the tree roaches and the carpenter ants and the smell of mildew and rotting wood and I am sweating so hard that it's dripping off my nose and chin. There are many letters in my lap. In one of them to the U.S. government my father says: "If this was a goddamn white woman, a Russian ballet dancer and her daughter, you people would have them on a plane in twenty-four hours. This is my wife and my daughter. My daughter is so beautiful you can put her face on your dimes and quarters and no one could ever make change again in your goddamn country without stopping and saying, Oh my God, what a beautiful face."

I read this now while I'm hidden in the storage shack, invisible, soaked with sweat like it's that time in Saigon between the dry season and the rainy season, and I know my father will be here soon. The lawn mower is over there in the corner and this morning he got up and said that it was going to be hot today, that there were no clouds in the sky and he was going to have to mow the lawn. When he opens the door, I will let him see me here, and I will ask him to talk to me like in these letters, like when he was so angry with some stranger that he knew what to say.

Above the Woman's House

Da Ngan

When she saw the trembling smile on the lips of her daughter, she immediately felt the loneliness of her own life. She felt as if the only light in the house had gone out in the night.

That was the moment when Thao, only 18 years ago a toddler, cut into the path along which her mother was cutting rice, grabbed two clusters with one dextrous hand, and cut them all in one swift slice, leaving an unusually ragged stubble on the ground.

"It gets dark so quickly at this time of year!"

The girl said it in a timid voice, as if to call her mother's attention to it. Truly, the weather at the end of the year still bore the influence of December, when you didn't even have time to smile before it got dark. But when the girl stood motionless, anxiously looking up at the sky, the afternoon had not come to a close yet.

It was a late afternoon like all the other dry afternoons of the harvest season. Suddenly, the field glowed, intensely golden. The air filled with birds and falling leaves, and the horizon, seen through the coconut leaves on the other side of the river, looked as crimson as burning coal. Everything exuded the eternally pungent smell of hay and stubble. Green from the plants in the field and all the various kinds of grass grew between the rows of rice. The ground felt refreshingly cool beneath their feet. Pulling her checkered scarf down from her head to her neck and feeling the cool breeze blowing across her ears, the mother knew that the river had risen and the water lilies were floating rapidly into the bow-shaped bay next to the village.

Hai Mat looked at the efficient hands of her daughter and recognized in them the motions of anticipation. The girl set one foot into her path and gathered toward herself as many as fifteen clusters of rice. Her old smoke-colored blouse stuck to her back, revealing her solid pink waist. Her slender arms moved quickly and skillfully back and forth as if she were dancing. The sound of the sickle cutting the stalks was as sharp as the sound of a water buffalo grazing. Occasionally she would lift her head to see when her row of rice met the dike, where patches of flowers overflowing with violet grew within the chicken tail grass. The mother had to hurry to keep up with her daughter, although the girl only allowed her to cut one narrow row of rice. She had never seen her daughter as determined and impatient as this. When the girl laid down the final bundle of rice, without forgetting to use her sickle to pull the last few stalks on the dike out of the path of people's feet, she turned and looked at her mother, her eyes waiting and questioning. The mother pretended not to notice. Unable to hide her impatience, the girl blurted out:

"Should we do more or go home, Ma?"

She squinted, discreetly observing her daughter. The girl lowered her head, her mouth chewing a stalk, the tip of her nose dotted with drops of sweat, her whole body tense with the wretchedness of waiting. The mother suddenly understood and felt terrified with the realization that it wouldn't be long before she would become a grandmother. She had prepared herself for every contingency, but when it actually came she was as stunned as if she had never even considered it. How brutal was the passage of time! She herself was still a virgin, and now her daughter would soon no longer be a child. If she had given birth to the girl with her own body then she would have been happy and worried at this revelation. But under the circumstances, her chaste heart was suddenly beating with an exuberant rhythm, empathizing with her daughter as if she were a friend.

"Okay, let's go home!"

As soon as she heard that generous offer, Thao immediately tossed the stalk aside, smiled and took a step past her mother, using the sickle in her hand to brush the tops of the stubble. She couldn't rush because she was with her mother and in her effort to slow herself down her gait seemed strange. Her smile trembled like a night-blooming flower; it was a smile that couldn't hide its virginal happiness, that confessed the sudden transformation from a bud into a flower in the fullest bloom. The girl kept walking and smiling while the mother followed behind, understanding in a way that only a person who has been through it herself could understand.

During every woman's life there is at least one time when she will smile the way that Thao was smiling now. It will happen when she is liberated from her work and her head fills with images of a tryst with a person who is waiting anxiously at a certain meeting place. That first time, and only that first time, the girl is a flower blooming in the last hours of the new year's eve of her life.

Hai Mat remembered the time of her youth, the time that she could feel her own freshness, the time when she let her hair grow until it touched the hem of her blouse, and clipped it with a sparkling three-pronged clip just like all the other girls in the region. She had secretly loved a soldier who had the face of a sensitive student. Whether happy or sad, it always exuded a youthful nobility. She and Cuong always caught themselves looking at each other, not with a glance of passion, but of innocent curiosity, and every time that happened they would both turn away in terror, holding themselves tightly as if they'd been burned.

About once a week, Cuong's unit returned to the station in Hai Mat's hamlet. He was the most muscular man in the squad and so he often took charge of the rowing. She knew this because every time the boat touched the shore he would appear in front of her house with an automatic rifle and knapsack slung over one shoulder and a pair of wooden oars balanced on the other. He only gave her a hesitant glance and then turned to talk and smile without shyness to her mother. If it hadn't been for that hurried afternoon in the rice field then her love would have forever been a sacred secret that only she knew.

That was a tranquil afternoon, when the war was only a blur far outside the feeling of a heart in love. It was the harvest season then, and the dry season attacks from our side and the enemy side had become more frequent. To make the best use of the time when the enemy planes were inactive, the peasants often stayed in the fields until it was pitch black. When the moon was out, they would stay there all night. Pouring the rice she had just threshed into a sack, Hai Mat suddenly felt her whole body fill with anticipation. She knew that Cuong's unit was on the way back to her hamlet.

"Let's go home, Mom!" she called, loosely twisting the fiber tie around the top of the sack.

"Oh, daughter," her mother scolded lightly.

She had spilled the bag of rice onto the cracked ground and then she couldn't even remember where the coconut fiber ties were. Her mother scolded her in earnest.

"Okay, then we'll go home! Are you so starved already?"

Hai Mat broke into a smile, a smile trembling with happiness. Her mother looked at her in surprise, staring until she understood.

"Well, let's go home and cook an early dinner," she said. "What can we find to cook for them, Mat? They row until the sweat comes out of them and still when they come here they have to dig trenches."

Hai Mat easily lifted the sixty-kilo bag of rice onto her shoulder and raced to the edge of the garden. She met Cuong at the dock and in the weak light of dusk and saw in his eyes an expression of timid love. She returned his gaze with a smile like a night-blooming flower that had only at that moment blossomed. From that moment, it was as if she had said good-bye to innocent joys in order to begin a period of misery and happiness.

The following week, Cuong's unit returned again, but this time the person who appeared in front of her house carrying Cuong's rifle and knapsack and his pair of wooden oars was not Cuong.

Out of her experience as a widow, her mother consoled her with just one sentence:

"It's war! It will pass, dear."

Of course the war and all the sorrow would pass. But her memory retained the image of Cuong with his downy chin, awkward smile, and eyes that expressed the freshness of early morning....

Hai Mat watched her daughter bend over the bugle-shaped container used for threshing rice, her arms gathering a bunch of stalks, perhaps to give to the ducks to pick out the remaining rice. She stood up and ran to the edge of the garden by their house, to the place where the coconut trees began to gather the darkness under their disorderly leaves. She was following the path of her mother's state of mind so long ago. Who was waiting for her daughter? There was a strong possibility that it was the teacher who had lost a foot at the battleground near the border. Despite the sad sounds of his guitar, he had a naturally calm disposition and an unusually conscientious attitude toward life. Only recently transferred to this hamlet by the bay in order to replace the old teacher whose back was longer than his legs, the new teacher immediately began to repair the school and put an end to the need for wearing raincoats during teaching hours. But to choose this disabled teacher or some other man was no longer the mother's business. She would sit wherever her daughter wanted her to sit.

Well, even in that kind of decision, the daughter was like the mother. They had been rather alike ever since the mother had adopted her. At that time, there were already three small children in the house. One girl was seven years old, the daughter of a female provincial cadre. Two boys were five, the twins of another woman, a propaganda officer. Thao was the daughter of a nurse who was well-known throughout the province. From the beginning, upon seeing these women trying to carry out their duties with babies in their arms, the members of the Soldiers' Mothers' Club found a way to help by taking in the children. Even though they were reluctant to do so, these women felt it their duty to leave their families behind and accept the arrangement, considering it a humane solution to very difficult circumstances. During those years, the people could still cling to their fields and gardens, so a bite of rice and a piece of fabric weren't impossible to find. Hai Mat and her mother worked in the fields, planted sweet potatoes in any empty patch in the kitchen garden, collected tiny shrimps and crabs, and found work weaving thatch in order to raise all the children. All the families who did this were operating under the same innocent belief that they were contributing to the revolution.

Thao's mother gave her to Hai Mat as soon as she had weaned her. She had to hold back her tears when she left. That very night, while on her way to deliver a baby for a cadre at another base, she stepped into an ambush and was killed. Every night Thao screamed at regular intervals, her anxious eyes looking at Hai Mat, but when Hai Mat picked her up to hold her, the baby refused to put her head on her shoulder. Crying bitterly, she would turn and stare at the darkness just outside the door. Just as Hai Mat's mother predicted, when the baby was able to attach herself to Hai Mat's scent, she finally got over the mysterious shock inside herself. When she began to babble her first few words, without anyone having taught her she was able to pronounce the word "mother" very clearly. When she spoke, she looked right at Hai Mat and her eyes beamed with joy. Feeling both happiness and misfortune, Hai Mat shuddered and accepted her unexpected role of mother. At that moment, a kind of noble joy began to blossom, extinguishing the first strange feelings, and she rushed to hug her, leaving on the baby's face the marks of her hot tears.

Another unit arrived to replace Cuong's, which had just left the region. Again, she fell in love with a soldier. Why she kept choosing that type of man is as difficult to explain as love itself and no one ever intends to explain it. But truly, there is something in that kind of life that makes young women, however carefully they consider the pros and cons, unable to resist its attractiveness. The soldier's life is well-ordered and disciplined, truthful in attitude and behavior, and, most of all, generous in its heroism.

This time, her already ripened heart found an introspective man named Trang. At the beginning of their meeting, for which her mother had given permission, Trang said in all seriousness:

"I understand you, Mat. That matter is of no importance whatsoever. I will treat your daughter Thao as if she were my own."

She wanted to laugh, but standing in the moonlight that broke through the cracks in the leaves of the star apple tree, she was deeply touched by Trang's face, pale from his honest emotions. His words were simple and sincere. He didn't have the attitude of a person who believes he's sacrificing himself or the misery of a person who feels that life has treated him unfairly. She kept silent, saving the truth of Thao's birth as an important surprise for when she married him.

As it turned out, with the passage of time Thao began to look more and more like Hai Mat, as if she were her real mother. Both had dark skin and clear and gentle faces. The quality of their laughter was crystal clear and their gait was fast as the wind. Both of their spirits seemed weighed down with a certain sadness often found in people who have suffered great loss early in life. Hai Mat found another excitement inside herself, in the fact that no one in the hamlet had ever known that Thao was merely her adopted daughter, the child she didn't have the heart to turn away. If she confessed to it, it would have made her devotion less sacred and complete.

The first time she knew the trembling feeling of being touched by a man was when Thao playfully held one of Trang's fingers, which smelled of smoke, and pushed it onto the birthmark along the hairline next to Hai Mat's ear.

"There! Wipe it off. I've wiped it so many times and it's still not clean," Thao laughed loudly, one foot stomping on the wooden bed, while her arm, as round as a reel of thread, held firmly to Trang's finger and pushed back and forth against Hai Mat's head as if she were playing with a brush.

"Hey! Do you know why your mother has this birthmark?" Trang asked, his breath so close that Hai Mat became light-headed. "Because when she was born her mother smeared soot there in order to mark her daughter."

"Grandma, why did you have to mark her?" The child drew Hai Mat's mother into the conversation.

The grandmother smiled contentedly, then quietly returned to her stove.

"She marked your mother to save her for me!" Trang said, laughing happily. His shirt emitted a strange smell that made her dizzy. She made an effort to push him away. He took a few steps backward, then fixed his teasing gaze on her. She stood up, feeling weak, and smiled, nearly crying with joy.

Hai Mat had many evenings of strong emotions that would last a lifetime. During that time the Muddy Water River lapped against the oars of the soldiers who were rowing within the silent and thick shadows of palm trees along the edge of the river. Twilight descended onto the middle of the water and turned it into a violet sash of silk. A few storks rose into the smoky air, their stark whiteness becoming private and romantic points of light in the evening sky. The sound of fruit falling suddenly among the sea of leaves and the calls of birds echoing across the surface of the river sounded like the melancholy beating of drums. Sitting over the water on a pier made of coconut trunks, Hai Mat saw all of them cut across the sash of silk from the shadows on one side to the shadows on the other. They looked so alike, from their firm physiques to the wide brims of their hats to their immobile faces sitting in their camouflaged boats. Any one of them could be her Trang, but only he could easily recognize that it was her waiting for him on the pier. During wartime, simply to be able to see each other like that meant happiness. On those evenings, the sky took on the crimson color of war, and the tragic, epic songs of those times would never disappear from memory. From time to time the boats unexpectedly returned to her hamlet, and her Trang also unexpectedly reappeared with his refreshing smile. Then one morning at daybreak, when the Muddy Water River was covered with mist thick enough to scoop up with a hat, they returned to her hamlet, and all of them smelled of gunsmoke. Trang's boat was empty, and the place where he used to sit was now filled with the mist of death. The moment she saw that vacant space she immediately felt the emptiness that nothing in life could fill, as if a gale had just swept away the tree above her house.

Of course one day it would be over, the war and all the misery.

Using all its force, the enemy waged fierce battle in her region. Into an area of land as small as one's hand, they threw dozens of battalions. Hai Mat and her mother took the four children to find shelter in a coconut grove owned by a relative near the Vi Thanh market. With many mouths to feed, she had to become a vendor and, wearing a sweat-stained conical hat, all alone among the baskets of rice, she chewed on uncooked rice and consoled herself: "Sooner or later, the war will be over." However much hardship she had to bear, she thought she would be able to manage this fragile life so that she could fulfill her promise to the parents of the children, as long as her mother was not arrested. But the enemy had uncovered the movements of the propaganda officer—the mother of the twins—and arrested her and Hai Mat's mother while Hai Mat was away. Once more, with the help she received from her relations, she gathered the four children together and took them to Can Tho to increase their chances of avoiding the enemy and also to be near her mother's prison. In this central city, she did every kind of hired labor, washing and ironing clothes, hauling water, and even washing the dishes in small taverns.

After the Paris Treaty, before the enemy released its prisoners of war, Hai Mat's mother died in prison. She took the four small children home, but now there was not even a single tree left standing. The first thing she had to do was erect a shack on the old foundation of her house, which was now filled with weeds, and build a shaky altar out of whatever wood she could find.

One by one, the parents who had been in the fighting came back to get their children. The provincial cadre arrived to pick up her child from Hai Mat, explaining that the fighting had lessened and now she could keep her baby by her side. Another woman came and was allowed by law to take the twins first to "D" base and then, following the Truong Son Mountain trail, return north for school, where their mother had been released in the first wave of prisoners. As for Thao, her father came to get her from Hai Mat's shack. He had received the news that his wife had died while he was still attending the political academy in the jungles of the Eastern region. After that, he was kept on as an instructor and it was a long time before he learned of the location where his daughter was taking shelter.

After Hai Mat explained to Thao for the third time that this man was her father, the child's astonished eyes bravely accepted it. She hesitantly fell into his lap, and, because of the tickle of his moustache, avoided his kisses. Only a few hours later she already believed that he was her father. But when he fished from his wallet a yellowed photograph of a woman and explained that this was her mother, she immediately pushed him away in denial and tried to escape from his embrace, then stood looking at him, her pitiful eyes filled with doubt.

That night, she was determined not to sleep with her father. When he pulled her under his mosquito net, which was hanging over the dirt floor in the shack, she was so resistant he finally got angry. When she was finally allowed to get under Hai Mat's mosquito net, she laughed out loud.

"If he says he's my father, then why doesn't he come sleep here with me and you, Mom? Does that mean he doesn't love me?"

She asked the second question seriously and so suddenly that it embarrassed the two adults. After that she started to beg him and when it proved to be useless, she burst into tears in order to force him to lie in the bed with her and her mother. Hai Mat still remembered clearly when his nervous hand lifted the mosquito net in order to climb in. She had sat up quickly, her arms wrapped around her knees, her body huddled as if in a devastating fever. But Thao wouldn't leave her alone. She forced the two adults to lie down and arranged them meticulously so that when she lay down between them neither one was too near or too far from her. Within a minute, she was already asleep, lying in the relaxed posture of an angel, and from time to time she would sob quietly, as any child would do after suffering a wrong. Surreptitiously wiping away the tears on the child's face, Hai Mat accidentally touched his hand, which was pale and bore the simple black strap of a watch. A moment later, when she closed her eyes, she felt as if she could see it, moving nervously next to the hem of the mosquito net. This time, he was the one who sat up quickly, and got out of the mosquito net as if he were a fugitive on the run. For the whole night, she could see the glow of a cigarette at the table in the far corner of the shack.

In the morning, before bending to step out from under the thatched roof of the shack, with an anxious look in his eyes, he gazed at her deeply and blurted out some tactful words.

"I was planning to take Thao to my mother in the suburbs of Can Tho. But now I'll leave her here to be a burden on you."

With his head hanging low, he walked away, his shoulders slumped as if they were being pulled by an invisible force in the earth. The mother and daughter clung to each other, following him until he disappeared from sight. Suddenly Thao began to run after him and cried out loud, but he never once dared to stop. Hai Mat sprinted after the child and pulled her back, feeling at the same time happy, as if she'd just escaped from something, and angry, filled with the odd sensation that she wanted to silently curse.

She had waited, but he never returned. One more time, the hurricane of war had swept away the sheltering tree above her house.

Fate had united her with the fate of this girl.

Next to the incense holders of her mother and father, Hai Mat placed a third, for him. Indeed, at first she had placed two sticks of incense inside it, one for each of Thao's parents, but that had made the child miserable with curiosity because Hai Mat was her mother and Hai Mat wasn't dead yet. After that, Thao always fought to be allowed to place the sticks of incense and criticized her mother for counting wrong. Three war heroes, Thao said, would need three sticks of incense, not four. Looking at the child, Hai Mat felt even more strongly that she didn't have the heart to tell Thao the truth. The feeling that one is only half an orphan is very different from the feeling that one is completely an orphan. Naturally, Thao would be able to bear it all, but Hai Mat was an orphan as well, and Thao had become her life. They needed each other like compensation for loss.

But no truth can be kept under wraps forever. One day, after racing home to ask the one necessary question, Thao put her face in her hands and shook her head repeatedly, as if she didn't believe it, as if she couldn't believe it. When she raised her head again, Hai Mat looked at her in fear: Thao's girlish expression had disappeared from her face.

As she got older, Thao's love for Hai Mat grew stronger. Recently, she had asked for permission to visit an old woman who had often come to visit them. Because this woman claimed to have been a close friend of Hai Mat's mother, Thao called her "Grandma."

Now, standing in front of Hai Mat, Thao was completely mature in her neat black blouse and pants. Her hair, in the shape of a leaf, was tied loosely and fell down her back, not with the three-pronged hair pin that Hai Mat had worn in her younger days, but with a plastic hairpin engraved with a virgin rose.

"If you're in a hurry, then go! I'll go ahead and eat first."

Thao would have smiled if she hadn't suddenly noticed on her mother's face a crystallization of the melancholy and ruddiness that comes with twilight. The woman in Thao suddenly understood: that was why her mother often stared at the roof of their house, where every night the war returned. In Thao's mind appeared the faces of the men for whom she had affection. She wondered if she and her mother could rely on any of them. She was deeply touched when she thought of the cruel passage of time and war that had passed over her mother's head, a fact that could be seen beneath the hairpin where, after twenty years, the line of thinning hair now carried the withered trace of autumn. But at that moment the mother turned to go into the kitchen, perhaps to avoid the shock in her daughter's eyes, and urged Thao:

"Why are you dallying? If you're in a hurry, then go, honey!"

At that moment, Hai Mat heard through the darkening evening the rising and falling sound of a guitar.

Translated by Bac Hoai Tran and Dana Sachs

She In a Dance of Frenzy

Andrew Lam

She grew up a tomboy, could swing a bat the way even her younger brothers couldn't, could kick the glasses off a boy's face, and was not, therefore, very close to her mother. Mother with her gossip and her housewifely chores and her hidden gambling debts and her heavy-set body was not very interesting to her, was never outdoorsy, was too much involved in family things to see the world, the ocean, the blue sky.

She, the daughter, the tom boy who laughed and played, on the other hand, liked sports, liked Kung fu movies, liked sparring, liked to be liked, liked men.

She especially liked hanging out with her Papa, once a sergeant in the South Vietnamese Marine Corps, a trained assassin during the war, or something dangerous like that, though she had been too young in that country to remember for sure. It didn't matter really. All she knew was that he was a gentle man. From him she learned how to hook worms, how to cast, how to be silent so the fish would come. She learned to move with the rhythm of the ocean, feeling the boat bobbing this way and that, learned to watch her father in his quietude, like a stone statue, an ancient being perhaps, yet vigorous and alive.

So scrawny and thin and small, who would ever have thought that she, the tomboy, was going to become a beautiful woman?

But then at sixteen she bled. She bled and the blood oozed out of her like a stream of snapdragons and daffodils. A late bloomer, every one commented, and late bloomers last forever. So beautiful she became, so elegant, grew breasts and an ass and grew hair so long and dark and silky and possessed a smile that dazzled and the agility of a gazelle and the breathlessness of a dove in flight.

At a dinner party thrown for her father's 50th birthday all the men were trying hard not to look at her when she served them drinks. That couldn't be her, they kept saying and her father laughed and said, but it is her, it's my little tom boy. Then one man, the youngest among her father's army buddies, now a successful real estate broker flirted openly with her. Marry me, he said, you are the most beautiful thing on earth. Yes, she said, yes, sure, Uncle, and sat on his lap the way she used to when she was younger, and I want you to buy me a castle up in the hills and he said, anything, anything, and they all laughed but she saw her father's disapproving eyes trained on her. She's my little tom boy, he said to his friends again, and she said, of course, daddy, always, and they all laughed. But afterwards when the men were gone, her father slapped her.

But it was his friend's departing whisper—"You're so fuck'n gorgeous!"—that she heard echoing in that slap. So fuck'n gorgeous and curvy in all the right places so that her beauty became a kind of curse for her as she saw herself in the mirror one day, no longer fitting in the way she used to in her own home—how she moved in her crowded house was all different now; so fuck'n gorgeous that tension between her mother, who was not gorgeous, was homely in fact, and her sisters, who were jealous of her beauty, and her, grew; so fuck'n gorgeous that her father and brothers stopped gazing at her directly, and an uncomfortable silence like a gray cloud grew between them; so fuck'n gorgeous that at seventeen she fled.

It was time, in any case, for her to see the world. Quietly she packed her bags and afterwards said good-bye to her family and they protested but she wondered if the females weren't secretly a little happy inside to see her leave, leaving the place where she was once happy and innocent but could, alas, be no more.

She said good-bye to Papa and Mama, to brothers and sisters, and they wept and she wept and away she went. To college, to the North, where she met a man and then another and then another. Men of all sorts and all colors and stripes flocked around her. Men so strong and young and sensual and handsome and intelligent and ambitious, rich and poor men. Men who fell in love with her and she, she thought, with them. She had all the grace in the world. Was intelligent and possessed a vivid imagination, was exciting and fun and also cooked and cleaned and swept and sewed and she could dance the cha-cha-cha and do the passadoble and perform the passionate tango on a whim and she could stretch her legs effortlessly the way a swan stretched snowy wings and smile as a lover entered her and she, when it rained, could sigh with a profundity that made poetry worthwhile, and wouldn't she be a wonderful companion to any man, be an extraordinary wife to the son of a bitch who happened to win her heart?

But where was her heart? Strange but she would always feel unattached to these men afterwards, always feel alone, and the sex and the embrace were only fleeting moments and the men and their beauty and their talents and their futures and their potential evaporated with the wind and were swept away by the melancholy rain and the fog that drifted down from the hills in the early morning.

Her girlfriend would ask, how is it going with so and so? And she'd sigh and say, Oh, it's all right, but....

But it was not all right. She grew bored easily and would find faults in these men, because of course they being only men, even the strong ones, all had faults. But it wasn't because of their faults that her relationship with them didn't last. It was something else deep inside her, something that forced her to close her eyes, or groan aloud, something that made her fear that her relationships would not or would last, which became after a while the same thing and so she left them.

"What's the matter, honey?" one of her men asked, that typical question, "did I do something wrong?"

"Nothing's the matter, sweet," she said, sighing. "Maybe it's just the weather. Maybe it's just us being too comfortable with each other." And soon his heart was broken because she did not want to see him again. "We're just friends," she would say to one, or "Our relationship has changed and now we're brother and sister," to another. And soon another heart was broken. Then another. Then another. So many that she decided to do away with the noise of their hearts shattering in her answering machine. She disconnected the phone and gave away the machine that recorded the sounds of those broken hearts and, while she was at it, cleared away the cobwebs and debris in her apartment, threw out a table, a chair, a futon, and a few other things like jackets and boxer shorts, and finally said to herself: Ah, there now, this peace, this space, this solitude, this is what I crave; from now on it's just me and myself and my work.

And yet the sadness continued. And soon, out of loneliness, out of need and impulse, she had a new lover and reconnected the phone and some of the broken hearts continued to break on the tape and some were done shattering and could be heard no more. But really, who was counting? Not her. She remained unhappy and distant and the fog continued to drift down some mornings past her apartment. And already she wanted to flee from this new lover, a young and tall and handsome light-skinned African American who was somewhat lost himself but she resisted because then the routine would start again and she was beyond tired.

What was the matter with her? What was it that made her feel like fleeing these men, these young satyrs and dancing bucks who constantly brought her gifts and poetry and the promise of love? What else was there in life? Why did she run from them and long for them at the same time? Why was she always so confused about these things and never said what she meant and never meant what she said? Why did she feel this ambiguity, this hurt, this longing and repulsion for these men who danced now in her dreams? Wasn't a good marriage and children what she, in the end, always wanted? She could easily have made a good life with any one of the men she had loved, or thought she had loved. What was the matter with her? Was she cursed by someone, a water witch maybe, to live the rest of her life longing but never having?

But she could not answer these questions for life had become a little blurry now, the way her audience appeared to her when she danced at this upscale strip bar and restaurant. But if she could just work, doing what she did well, a little dancing, a little flirting, a little flaunting of her exquisite flesh to pass the time, a little extra money, maybe something else would emerge. Maybe if she went away again to some far off place. Maybe if she changed her apartment and had a place with more sunlight. Maybe if she took up the offer of the rich young customer and flew to Paris on his Lear jet or consented to go to Hollywood with the fat one and ride in his limousine and watch how he made fantasies come true, maybe it would soothe some of her personal angst. Maybe if she could hold onto what she was doing a little bit longer—dancing, flirting—that something—but what?—she had lost and could not find again would somehow be restored to her, floating back to her on the crest of the evening tide. Maybe....

Then late one night after work when she sat alone, a quiet time when everything seemed to slow down and she had herself to herself, she started remembering. She had stepped out of a long hot bath and her feet were not hurting so terribly anymore from the dancing and her skin felt supple and soft and her hair cool and wet. On her bed, piled with down pillows, she tried to recount the moments of her young life and the people she had known and the affairs and the things that had moved and touched her. What and who made her most happy, she thought, and who and what made her most sad?

She did not know at first. There were too many faces now and it felt as if she were drowning in a very small room and so she tried in vain to usher them out. But just when she was near suffocation, she heard her name called, her Vietnamese name, beautiful and sweet, and she tried to locate that voice from those faces in that crowded room. A face slowly appeared from a distance, blurry at first. But it was not an unfamiliar face. It was a face from the time before she knew these men and before she became a beautiful woman, before she spoke English and before America was real to her. It was a face of wisdom and compassion, a face she always knew and loved and it came to her as she slept on a mat in the hold of a boat full of Vietnamese refugees in the middle of the Pacific and she was a tiny dot and dying of thirst and wasting away. Her family was around her and the air was humid and farty and a strange drowsiness was the curse on everyone's eyes. Drifting in and out of sleep she saw that face looming closer and she recognized it. Weathered and sad and concerned and full of love, her father said quietly, "Wake up, sweet, wake up and drink this milk before you die."

She remembered how the sun was beating down on her and how the wind was blowing stronger now and remembered seeing out of the corner of her eyes how blue the ocean was, how vast. She felt her father lifting her to him and she tasted again that sticky warm liquid and then through those few gulps the world had entered her and she looked up to her father and blinked and tried to smile for she knew she would survive, if only for him.

And now in her bed, a young beauty weeping, she knew that she was most happy then and not now. For there could be nothing truer than her father's gesture at that moment and everything else—America, the men who loved her, who cared, who wept, who danced, whose hearts shattered like crystals in her answering machine, even the happy home from which she'd fled, even Paris and Hollywood and limousines and cold hard cash were not enough, were never enough. She desired that fleeting gesture now more than ever, felt that frenzied thirst of so long ago on that ocean welling up from deep inside her, a thirst so potent, so exquisitely all-consuming, a thirst that nothing in this world, not even love, could ever hope to quench.

Marine Corps Issue

David McLean

My father used to keep three wooden locker boxes stacked in the tool shed behind our garage. This was at our house in southern Illinois, where I grew up. The boxes, big heavy chests with an iron handle on each end, were fatigue green, but had splintered in places. Chips of paint and wood had broken off during the miles of travel, and a shiny splayed pine showed underneath. Each box was padlocked with an oily bronze lock, the keys to which my father kept on his key ring, along with his house keys and car keys. I knew that because I saw him open the top box once, when a friend of his came to visit. My father lifted the lid of the top chest, and then a tray within, and pulled out an album or a yearbook of some kind, something to do with the war. The visitor was an old Marine Corps buddy, still active and in uniform. They laughed over photographs and drank whiskey, a whole bottle. I crouched in the hallway around the corner from the kitchen and listened as long as I dared. I don't remember much of the talk, names and places I had never heard of, but I do recall the man's calling my father "gunny," and commenting on his hands. My father had damaged hands. "Look at your hands, gunny—goddamn it, look at them!" And I think they cried, or maybe it was just drunken giggles. I don't know. That was the only time I ever saw my father drink. That was 1974. I was ten years old.

My original name was Charles Michael, and for the first ten months of my life, my mother tells me, I was called Charlie. I had no father then—that is, he had never seen me. But when he returned from Vietnam the first time, in early 1965, within a week he began the legal proceedings to change my name. Soon after, I was Jonathan Allen; I still am. I learned all this from my mother when I was twenty and needed my birth certificate for a passport application. My father was three months dead then, when my mother explained to me about Charlie, and how I had been renamed for a dead corporal from a small town in Georgia.

I see my father most often in two ways: playing handball or, years later, sitting on the edge of our elevated garden, black ashes from a distant fire falling lightly like snow around him. As I said, my father had damaged hands—a degenerative arthritis, we were told. They were large, leprous hands, thick with scar tissue and slightly curled. He could neither make a fist nor straighten them completely. Normally they hung limp at his sides or were stashed in his pockets. To grip things he had to use a lot of wrist movement, giving him a grotesque bird-on-a-perch appearance. He rarely touched anyone with them, though he did hit me once, a well-deserved blow I know now, and knew even then in the vague way of an innocent.

My older brother, Joe, and I would watch him from the walkway above and behind the handball courts while our mother waited outside. I was six years old, but can still see him clearly, playing alone, as always. He wears olive-green shorts, plain white canvas shoes and long white socks, a gray sweatshirt, the neck ripped loose down the front, and a fatigue-green headband wrapped tightly around his bony forehead. Black thinning hair dipped in gray rises up like tufts of crabgrass around the headband. He wears dirty white leather gloves. He swings at the hard black ball forcefully, as though he held paddles of thick oak. I hear the amplified slap of his hand and then a huge explosion booming through the court as the ball ricochets back. He runs after it, catches up to it, and slaps it again, driving it powerfully into the corner. His tall thin figure jerks across the court and off the wall, his slaps alternating with the hollow explosions, his shoes squeaking, his controlled breaths bursting out of him as he tries, it seems to me, to break the ball, or maybe rid himself of it forever.

But it always returns, somehow, even dribbling, to the center of the court. Exhausted, he sits against the wall, breathing heavily, his court gone suddenly quiet, though the booming echoes from nearby courts can still be heard. He watches the ball bounce off its final wall and then slowly roll to a stop. I watch it with him, until it again becomes an inert black ball on the wooden floor.

I said that my father had hit me one; it was at our second meeting. The first had been on that six-month home leave when he changed my name. I remember nothing of that, of course. I do remember his second return home, though, when I was five years old. To my new consciousness, Daddy was simply a figure in a photograph, a steely, strong-looking man in dress blues. I remember the disjunction I felt upon seeing him for the first time, how I had trouble believing that this man was the same man as in the photograph. He was thin and gaunt and silent, with deeper eyes and a higher forehead than I had expected to see. He looked at me strangely. He hadn't seen me grow up. I could have been any child, an adopted son, were it not for my resemblance to him.

What I learned shortly after that first real meeting was the necessity of being a noisy child. Noise alerted him to my presence and prevented his being surprised and reacting on instinct. I began to knock on the walls or shuffle my feet or sing to myself as I walked through the house.

I discovered this survival technique one Saturday morning shortly after his return. I had awakened early and had rolled off the lower bunk, my blanket under my arms, a sleepy animal child going to look for his mother. I walked down the hall and into the living room, where my father sat reading. He had not heard me come in. I wanted to play a game. I crept around an end table near his chair, suppressing a giggle, and watched him for a minute. I looked at the back of his head, smelled his sharp aftershave smell, stared freely, for the first time, at his gnarled left hand holding the book in that rolled-wrist way, and then I leaped out from the table and shouted *Boo!*

I saw a white flash—I was airborne, backwards, on my shoulders and over my head. I landed hard on my face and knees, bleeding from the nose and mouth. I looked up and saw him crouched and rigid, eyes on fire, palms flat, fingers as stiff as he could make them.

Then he melted, right there before me, his body slumping down like warm wax, and he began shouting, and crying, "Goddamn it! Goddamn it, Diane! Come and get this God-damned child away from me!" He wouldn't look at me. His hands were in his pockets. He walked out of the house and into the back yard. I didn't see him again until breakfast the following morning. My mother arrived and swooped me into her arms. Only then did I begin to cry.

My mother's life intrigues me. Her strength, well hidden when I was younger, becomes obvious upon reflection. I spend a lot of time reading about the Marine Corps and Vietnam; it is a way of knowing my father. And yet I often find my mother in the books. I cannot read of Khe Sanh or Da Nang without imagining my mother at home with two children under the age of seven and a husband across the world fighting in a war, what I think of as a stupid war at that. She has never spoken about that time, not even about the four continuous years of my father's absence, when, my grandmother told me, she would spend at least two hours every night weeping alone, the children already asleep, and when she could hardly sleep herself. Even after my father's return tension and distance continued for some time. Our family was different from others. I can best describe it as being composed of opposing camps—not camps at war with each other but survival camps: my mother and I in one, my father and Joe in the other. We had no open animosity toward each other, only distance.

My father was in the Marine Corps for seventeen years before beginning his second career in the offices of the Stone City Steel Mill. He was a decorated soldier, a career man forced to retire disabled because of his hands. He had been a drill instructor, a fact that always widens the eyes of those I tell. I can see them reassessing me as soon as I say it—Marine Corps drill instructor—and they look at me in a shifted way that is hard to define. A pity, perhaps, sometimes a fear. I do have a temper comparable to my father's, which usually shows itself in short, explosive bursts of expletives that roll out of my mouth naturally, as if I were a polyglot switching tongues. The violence is verbal only, though I can still see my father, if I make the effort, at my brother's throat. Joe has been caught smoking in the garage a second time. He is fourteen and has been warned. He is pinned to the wall of the garage by my father's crooked paw, his feet dangling, toes groping for solid ground as though he will fall upward and off the earth if he can't find a grip. His eyes are wide and swollen with tears. My father's voice is a slow burn, his nostrils wide. He finishes speaking, drops Joe onto the concrete floor, and strides quickly away.

Despite my father's years of service, our house was devoid of memorabilia. A visitor would have no idea about my father's military career were it not evident in his walk and demeanor. Civilians might miss even these clues. Our house was not a family museum like other houses. We had few family photographs; the décor consisted chiefly of landscape paintings and small ceramic collectibles, dolls and Norman Rockwell scenes and wooden elephants from around the world.

At sixteen I saw the movie *Apocalypse Now*. I had no interest in Vietnam then; I knew nothing of it. The film left me enthralled and fascinated, even a little horrified in an abstract way. I came home agitated but still had not made any connection. The epiphany came when I walked in the front door. My father was sitting quietly in his recliner, sipping coffee and watching the Cardinals play the Reds on television. My mother sat on the couch crocheting under a lamp, humming a hymn to herself, our Labrador, Casey, resting on the floor at her feet. I stared at them for a long twenty seconds before my father snapped the spell. "Hey, Johnny," he said, "come in here and watch the game. Redbirds are up five to three in the seventh."

"Yeah?" I moved into the room and turned to face the television.

"What'd you go see, hon?" my mother asked.

"What?"

"What movie'd you see?"

I lied. I quickly named some comedy that was showing in the same complex. "It was awful," I added, to cut off the questioning.

I saw the movie again a few days later, and I saw it anew. My father was in there somewhere, dug into a bunker, behind a wall of foliage, there amid the ragged poor and the dripping trees and the sounds of gunfire and explosions. And when I returned home from the movie that night, he was reading a John Le Carré novel, sipping coffee, the silky voice of Jack Buck in the background describing the Cardinals game in Atlanta. The evening was hot and dry. It would be a hard summer of drought in southern Illinois.

The next day I walked to the library and borrowed three books about the Vietnam War. My summer project would be to learn about the war and my father's place there. Under a hot midmorning sun I skimmed the thinnest of the three on the way home, anxious, as though poised to turn the knob of a mysterious door. At home I hid two of the books in my safest place, above the loose tiles of the lowered ceiling in my bedroom, and took the third book and my copy of *The Pickwick Papers* into the back yard.

We had a large yard behind the house, enclosed by a fence of pointed wooden slats five feet high. Against the back fence stood a terraced flower garden, built long before by a previous owner. It ran the length of the fence and was fronted by a red brick wall about two feet high. The three levels were separated by stacked railroad ties. My parents loved the garden and would labor all summer to keep it lush. Even that summer of drought, as the grass was browning under a merciless sun, my parents kept the garden well watered. From April to September we had cut flowers on the dinner table every night.

I kept a private place in the upper left corner of the garden. It was known to everyone; if I was nowhere to be found, my family would always check to see if I was there reading. Before watering, my parents would always shout a warning lest I be rained on. Although known, it was still quiet and just isolated enough. I would lie down on the ground behind a thick wall of day lilies, my back against the fence, and read, or think while staring up at the sky.

That is where I learned about the Vietnam War. I lay on my side and read for at least three hours every day, softly repeating the names of places and operations, marking pages with thin weeds. If called or found, I would rise from the flowers with *The Pickwick Papers* in hand, leaving the history book in a plastic bag among the day lilies, to be collected later. In the evenings, while listening to baseball games, I transferred notes from the weed-marked pages into a notebook that I kept hidden in my sock-and-underwear drawer.

Within two weeks I had finished those first three books. Upon completion of the third I emerged from the day lilies feeling expert. My knowledge of the war—dates, places, names—had zoomed up from zero. I was ready to ask my mother some questions. I approached her one afternoon before my father had returned from work. She was peeling potatoes over the kitchen sink when I padded in nervously.

"Mom?"

"Yes, Johnny?"

"Mom, where was Dad stationed in Vietnam?" My throat was dry. I had never before uttered the word to my parents. My mother stopped working and turned to face me, potato peeler held upright in her hand. She looked puzzled.

"I don't remember, Johnny. Lord, that was over ten years ago. I don't remember those funny foreign names. He was stationed in more than one place anyway. Why?"

I felt ashamed, flushed. "Just curious. We learned a little about it at school and I was just curious. That's all."

"I wish I could tell you, but I don't remember. You know me. I have trouble remembering what I did last week." She laughed an unhumorous laugh.

"Should I ask Dad?"

She suddenly looked very tired and thoughtful. "Oh, Johnny, please don't," she whispered. "Don't bring it up with him. It took him so long to forget all of that. Don't ask him to start remembering again." Then she looked directly at me, and I could see that she was pleading with me, and I thought that she was going to cry. But she turned back to the sink and ran her hands and a potato under the tap. She began working again.

"Okay, Momma. I won't. I'm sorry."

"Don't be sorry, honey. You've a right to be curious."

The next day I was with Joe. We were returning from the shopping mall in Fairview Heights, twenty miles away. We were in the old pickup truck he used on construction jobs, trying to cool ourselves with wide-open windows, though even the rushing air was warm and uncomfortable. Joe was eighteen then, and worked nearly every day. I was enjoying the trip all the more because he allowed himself so few days off.

We were speeding down an empty two-lane road through the farmland south of Stone City. It was sickening to see. The corn, usually head-high by the end of June, was barely up to my waist. The ground was cracked and broken in places. Some farmers had recently given up. You could see by the dry brown stalks, standing packed closely together, that they had stopped watering.

"Look at it," Joe said, shaking his head and poking his thumb out the window. He had to shout to be heard over the sound of rushing air. "I've never seen anything like this before. Even Grandma says it's the worst she's seen." I nodded and looked around at the dying fields.

"What'd you buy?" he shouted, pointing at my bag. I pulled out *Great Expectations* and showed it to him. He gave it only half a look and a nod. Then he shouted, "What's the other?" pointing again at the bag. I hesitated, but pulled out *Dispatches,* by Michael Herr. Joe grabbed it and began reading the back cover, completely ignoring the road. We began to drift across the center line into the oncoming lane. I reached over and gave the wheel a slight pull to the right. Joe looked up and grinned. He continued reading, now flicking his eyes up every few seconds.

"Vietnam?" he shouted. "What'd you buy this for?" I shrugged. Joe rolled up his window and motioned for me to do the same. The cab was suddenly very quiet. I looked over and watched a red-winged blackbird light upon a fence post. Joe nearly whispered, "What'd you buy this for?"

"Just curious. I've been reading some history of the war."

"Does Dad know?"

"No."

"Mom?"

"Only a little. Not about my reading." Joe looked down the road. We were already baking in the closed, quiet cabin. "Just watch out. Keep it to yourself." He threw the book into my lap.

"What do you remember about the war?"

"Hell, not much. I remember Dad coming home, hands all screwed up. Quiet, but I hadn't seen him in so long that I don't remember him being different or anything. Maybe quieter. I don't know. I was only seven. And I remember the POW-MIA sticker. Never understood that until I was in high school. We had a bumper sticker on the old green Impala. Remember?"

"No."

"Well, that's all I remember, really. I never took too much interest. I figured he'd tell us if he wanted to."

"Weren't you ever curious?"

"No, not too much. It seemed all bad and ancient history. Water under the bridge and all that. Jesus, I got to roll this window down!"

I considered asking Joe what he thought about my plan, but didn't. I had decided after talking to my mother that I was going to get into the locker boxes, though I had yet to figure out how. My father was in the garden nearly every day after work, and saw the boxes while getting tools or the hose. Obviously, I needed the keys.

I examined the boxes the next morning. They were stacked in a corner next to a small worktable. Coffee cans full of paintbrushes and nails and loose nuts and bolts stood on top of them. As far as I knew, they hadn't been opened in six years. Spider webs were constructed with a confident permanence between the sides of the boxes and the shed walls. I gave a cursory tug at the three locks, each of which had been scratched with a number.

The locks were the common hardware-store variety that always comes with two keys. I began searching for the extras in the drawers in the tool shed. In the days that followed, I rummaged through boxes and cleaned the attic over the garage. I carefully went through my father's dresser, with no luck. I did find one loose key at the bottom of a toolbox, and raced out to the shed to try it, but it wouldn't even slide into the core of the locks. I would have to take the risky route for the operation. The useless old key would help.

I spent three scorching days in the garden reading *Dispatches* and an oral history of the war while I looked for the courage necessary to put the plan into effect. The plan was simple, but I wasn't certain it was safe. I would switch the old key I'd found for one from the key ring, rummage a box and switch the key for a second the following day, and then switch the one after that, for a three-day operation.

The next morning I rose as early as my father, much to his and my mother's surprise. My mother was in the kitchen scrambling eggs, and my father was in the shower, as I'd hoped. I slipped into their bedroom and with nervous, fumbling fingers forced the key numbered one off the key ring, replacing it with my found key. The key ring was tight, and I slipped in my haste, gouging my index finger in doing so. I left the bedroom with my slightly bleeding finger in my mouth, jamming it into my pocket as I passed my mother in the kitchen.

Later, quietly, with an archaeologist's caution, I removed the coffee cans from the top box and set them on the worktable. I then slipped in the key and flicked open the lock. Despite the heat, I felt a shiver through my back and shoulders, my body reminding me that I was crossing some line of knowledge, transgressing some boundary of my father's. My hands shook and I held my breath as I lifted the lid.

The first thing I saw was a yellowed newspaper clipping: the death of James Dean, carefully cut to keep the date intact. I read the whole article with interest. I knew nothing of his death. Then I saw my mother's high school diploma, class of 1955. Stacks of old photographs. Family snapshots, black and-white with wavy white borders. I found my old report cards from early grade school and all of my brother's report cards up to the sixth grade. I found a baked-clay saucer with a tiny hand print pressed into it, and "Johnny 1968" scratched on the back. It was all interesting, but not my reason for the risk, so I lifted out the tray full of family memorabilia and set it to one side.

Underneath I found uniforms. Dress blues neatly pressed and folded. A shoeshine kit. A drill instructor's Smokey the Bear hat. Little plastic bags full of Marine Corps emblem pins like the one on the hat. A tan uniform. And the yearbook my father had pulled out six years before for his visitor. It was a thin platoon book dated 1964, San Diego. I flipped slowly through the black-and-white photos, looking for pictures of my father. The photos were mostly head shots of similar-looking boys in dress blues and white hats. I found action shots of boot training, of the mess hall, of track-and-field competitions. I saw my father here and there, leading a parade, demonstrating a hand-to-hand hold. He was still youthful and very muscular, stern-looking but not weary. The picture of him in his dress blues was the same I'd learned to call Daddy before I'd met him. His hands looked normal in the photographs, the vulnerability gone, his arms strong and well shaped, like solid tree limbs. Upon looking through again, I noticed small notations next to a few of the photos: "KIA," followed by a date. I was looking at dead men. I didn't know it then, but I would go back years later and find a picture of my namesake, Jonathan Allen Whitney, of Hinesville, Georgia, in that book.

But that was all, and it amounted to little. I replaced the tray and closed the lid, reconstructing the tool shed as well as I could.

That night at dinner I waited for the explosion, the accusation, my father holding up the key ring, his tight voice burning through me. I saw it all, but it never came. Later, in my room, I sorted through what I'd seen and made notes in my journal. I hadn't learned much, except that my mother loved James Dean and was a curator of her young sons' lives. As for my father, I'd found little new except the images of a younger, stronger man.

I opened the second box with less trepidation, half expecting to see my mother's junior-prom dress folded neatly inside, a dry corsage still pinned to the front. Instead, I found the memorabilia that probably should have been hanging on the walls inside the house. In the top tray were three wooden plaques commemorating different things my father had done, all before the war. They were homely little plaques given to him by platoons or friends. His dog tags lay wrapped in a green handkerchief underneath the plaques, "Joseph D Bowen" pressed into the thin aluminum. The tags read "Methodist," which surprised me, since he never went to church and mentioned God only as a prefix to "damn it." I found a pile of old letters written by my mother which had been mailed to an address in San Francisco. I couldn't bring myself to read them. I did, however, find three letters dated shortly after my birthday, and opened them. One contained the expected photograph, the usual hideous newborn, with the words "Hi, Daddy! Love, Charlie" written on the back. There was another photo, of my mother with Joe and me. Joe was two, and I was just weeks old. The picture was taken at my grandmother's house and dated June 30, 1964.

Beneath the tray I found more uniforms. Khakis this time, combat-style fatigues with "Bowen" stenciled onto them. There was also a pair of worn black boots, a canteen, two thick belts, and a cigar box full of uniform ribbons and their matching medals. Vietnam service, the crossed rifles for marksmanship, and others. There was an unexpected find: a Purple Heart. He'd been wounded. I wondered where. His hands, perhaps, or the fairly large scar on his left thigh— a childhood farming accident, he'd told us. I was staring at the medal, trying to open my imagination, when I heard the back door of the house swing out and bang against the siding. I threw the medal back into the box, and the box into the locker, and hurriedly shoved everything else inside. I pushed on the lock as the footsteps left the patio, and heaved the first box back on top. I was arranging the coffee cans when Joe walked in. "Hey, what are you doing?" he said. I was sweating, but felt a twitching relief that it was only Joe.

"Looking for a nut. I need one for my bicycle." I dumped one can over and began sifting through the dirty nuts and bolts. Joe walked around me, glanced down at the wall, and began sifting through the pile with me. "I need one for the seat," I told him. He quickly handed me a nut. "That'll do it," he said, and then added, "Hear what happened?"

"What?"

"Some old farmer set his fields on fire this morning. Acres and acres are burning like hell."

"Where?"

"Just east of town, off one-eleven. You can see smoke from the front yard. I thought we could drive out and see it."

"Why'd he do it?"

"I don't know. Just mad, probably. Wasn't doing him any good, dying there in front of him."

It wasn't much to see, really. The flames weren't huge, just crawling slowly across the field of dry stalks, crackling softly. Large glowing leaves swirled into the sky and became flocks of black birds in erratic flight. A few other people had pulled over to watch from the highway before a patrolman came slowly by and moved them along. Joe asked him if the fire department would put it out, and he said no, that it was no real danger, though the farmer would be fined or something. He said it would burn itself out in a day or so. We saw a man near the farmhouse, about a hundred yards from the road. He was old, wearing a red baseball cap, sitting on a tractor watching the wall of black smoke rise from the field. "Probably him," Joe said.

That night my father came home with two tickets to a Cardinals game against the Mets. "Box seats," he said, dropping them onto the table. He was as excited as we ever saw him, shining eyes and a slight smile, nothing showy or too expressive. "Let's go, Johnny."

From the car I watched the thin sheet of black smoke rising harmlessly like a veil on the horizon, not the ominous black plume that comes from a single house burning. I told my father about Joe and me driving out to see the fire and about the old man on the tractor. My father just shook his head. We were driving by his office at the steel mill, a different kind of fire and smoke shooting from the stacks. "Poor old man" was all he said.

I kept looking at the keys hanging from the steering column, expecting a wave of recognition to light up his face any second. I couldn't imagine how he would react, though I considered anger to be the best guess. What I was doing was wrong; I knew that and felt bad about it, especially since he was in such a good mood. His face was relaxed and peaceful, and he was smiling. He'd fought in a war; he'd been wounded in some unknown place; his hands gripped the steering wheel like arthritic talons; his friends had been killed and his sons had grown without him. I imagined him weathering bitter nights; he was driving us to a baseball game, sliding easily through traffic. I kept glancing at his profile, the thinning hair touched with gray, the deep circles under his eyes, the rounded nose my nose. We were crossing the Mississippi River on the Poplar Street Bridge. The Arch was a bright filament in the afternoon sun. The river was remarkably low, looking as though you could simply wade across the once unswimmable, strong-currented distance. I considered telling my father everything right then. I was consumed by guilt, tapping my fingers on my leg. "What happened to your finger?" he asked.

"Nothing. Caught it on a nail in the tool shed. I was looking for a key to my old bike lock." I'd had that excuse saved for two days. I couldn't look at him. I watched people in the streets. He began talking baseball. It had always been the bridge between us. There had always been the gap and one bridge, a love of the game.

The game that night was exciting, a pitchers' duel with outstanding defensive plays. We had never sat together in box seats before, and we marveled at seeing everything so close up, how quickly the game really moves. We talked baseball all night. I kept score; I marked every pitch on the card, like a memory. The game went into extra innings. I didn't want it to end. I knew even then that this was the first time I had ever felt really close to my father. We shared a soul that night, and then, in the bottom of the twelfth, the game ended suddenly with one swing by Ted Simmons, a crack, and a long home run disappearing over the left-field wall. We drove home happy, though quiet from fatigue.

Strangely, he passed our exit and continued around town to the east. "You missed our exit," I said.

"I didn't miss it" was all he said. He was pensive. I was puzzled, but only for a few minutes. We turned onto Route 111 and headed south on the dark highway. Suddenly the land to our left was a glowing pile of embers. We could see little smoke, but the field was alive with orange fires, flickering and rising like fireflies. My father clicked on his hazard lights and pulled onto the shoulder. He stepped out of the car and walked across the still road, with me trailing behind. The unseen smoke was too thick. I coughed and my eyes burned. "I just wanted to see it," he said quietly, and we stood in silence watching for ten minutes before driving home.

I didn't notice the ashes falling until after I'd changed the second key for the third. I was walking back through the kitchen when I saw, out of the corner of my eye, a leaf fall against the window screen, break into pieces, and then disappear. I looked up and out the window. The wind had shifted in the night, and the ashes from the cornfield were swirling above like elm leaves in autumn, some falling gently to earth like a light November flurry, except that the flakes were black. In the back yard I held out my hand to catch one, and it disintegrated in my grasp. The temperature was already over ninety degrees. It was a wonderful and hellish sight. Ashes blew across the patio and collected in the corner against the house.

After my father left for work, I went into the garden to read. Ashes drifted down, breaking between the pages of my book and landing in the day lilies and roses along the fence. I felt strangely uninterested in the third box. The previous night had left me content with my knowledge of my father's past. A new understanding had come to our relationship. I felt guilty opening the third box, as though I were breaking some new agreement between us.

The top tray contained nothing of interest. I found shoe polish, dried and cracked, two more plaques, socks, two dungaree hats. I sifted through these things mechanically and quickly, wanting to be done with it all. The compartment beneath was only half full. A musty smell rose out of the box. It came from the clothing—an old khaki uniform tattered and worn, filthy but neatly folded—that lay on top of the items inside. Also within sight was an old pair of combat boots, unpolished and ragged. They, too, smelled musty. I lifted out the uniform and found a small box made of dried palm fronds. It was poorly woven around narrow sticks with an ill-fitting lid on top. Inside it were yellow newspaper clippings folded up into squares, and a small paper ring box. I unfolded one of the clippings carefully, so as not to tear its tightly creased edges. The headline read LOCAL PRISONER OF WAR TO COME HOME," and was accompanied by that same photograph of my father in his dress blues. The clipping was dated July 13, 1969. I read the article slowly, trying not to miss any details. It explained that my father had been a prisoner for just over three years, that he was to be released July 30, and that he would be returning to the base in San Diego within days. He was being held in a prison camp in the North, just above the DMZ, and had been captured while on patrol near Khe Sanh in 1966. It gave details about the family in Stone City.

I set the clipping aside and quickly unfolded the others. They all told the same story. One was from the Stone City paper, dated the day of his release. I read them all twice, almost uncomprehendingly, before carefully folding them and returning them to the homemade box. I was a little afraid to go further, but I picked up the small paperboard box, felt it rattle, and opened it. Inside were teeth, all molars, yellowed and with black spots in places. I picked one up. On closer inspection the black blemishes became legible: painted on the side of the molar in tiny letters was "N.V. 3.3.66." I picked up a second. It read "N.V. 5.12.66." All six of them had dates, three from March third, one each from three other days. I was breathing through my nose in a deep, mechanical way, sweating heavily in the hot late morning. I put the teeth back in the box and set the box aside. I was shaking and didn't want to continue. There was more to see, a few letters, some folders, a small book.

The book was a paperback, a Marine Corps field manual bound with a manila cover. It was titled *Escape and Torture*. I began flicking through the pages. There were some small, meaningless diagrams, a dull text about techniques for escaping from some generalized prison camp. Then there was a section on Vietnamese torture techniques. I began reading the clinical, distant descriptions of various forms of torture. Naked men in small, cold concrete cells, sleep deprivation, swelling legs, tied hands, beatings. A few pages into the text the notations began. They were written in black ink, always the single word "this" in the margin next to an underlined passage. The first, as I recall, described something with the feet. Then beating on the legs, "this." Then the hands. "This" was a beating of the knuckles. "This" was being strung up by the wrists. I felt my stomach go hollow and my comprehension numb as I stared at that awkward, childlike scrawl in the margin of each page.

I didn't hear my father walk into the tool shed. He appeared suddenly, as though he'd sprung from the ground. I felt a presence and turned to see him standing there in the doorway of the shed, holding his key ring in his right hand and my useless bronze key in his left. I have never seen such confusion on a man's face. He was startlingly angry, I could see, his body stiff, his nostrils flared, his breathing heavy, his jaw muscles rolling beneath his skin. But his eyes were weary, even desperate. We stared at each other while he decided what to do. I didn't move. I said nothing, only watched him. His eyes welled, and bright molten tears ran down his cheeks. Then he dropped the single key and walked away.

I rose and walked out of the dark shed into the hot sun and falling ashes. He was sitting on the edge of the garden with his head down and his eyes closed as if in prayer, his hands lying loose and unattached in his lap. He then moved them to his sides and began clawing at the dry dirt in the garden until he had dug two holes and half buried each hand under the loose dirt. He sat as still as a memorial statue, and I realized that I didn't belong there. I left him with his head down and eyes closed, and walked into the house. I see him there every day.

In the four years that he lived beyond that moment he told me a little about the war. It was a topic I could never raise. On occasion, if we were alone, he would begin talking about some aspect of the war or of his service. These were heavily guarded moments, slow monologues as he groped for the correct words to tell me. It is another way I remember him, speaking the things that he knew he wasn't capable of saying. This is how I love him the most, this great man. Semper Fi.

Mother and Daughter

Ma Van Khang

Duyen was standing in front of the mirror, cocking her head, admiring herself. In her small, pretty room there was a wardrobe made of thinly layered wood and on the left-hand door was a full-length mirror which reflected perfectly. The mirror was objective, impartial, an accurate judge that announced every imperfection and reflected every harmonious details of a person's face and appearance. The whole family had looked at themselves in that mirror. Thuan, in his flight jacket, pulled up the zipper, looking dazed by his youthful and well-toned beauty. Hoa, who had already passed her innocent childhood, remembered every time she looked at herself in the mirror the tale of the queen who was jealous of the princess: "Queen, you used to be the most beautiful on earth, but now the princess is so much more." She had reached the age when girls often preen themselves, looking in the mirror and adjusting every fold, the shape of the eyebrow, and the form of every lock of hair.

Duyen was the one who looked in the mirror the least, compared to her two children. Inadvertently, the mirror reflected her appearance while she was really busy: at quarter to five in the morning she had to climb out of bed to cook rice. After a small breakfast, she would scoop out the rice, divide the food into three small containers, and then hurriedly take out the bike and ride off to work. In the cold weather, it was only when she arrived at the empty stretch of road, and the wind cut into her face that she remembered that she hadn't put on her scarf and gloves. Her house was far from the hospital where she worked so she could never slow down.

But during these days, Duyen suddenly found herself looking in the mirror. And today was so strange. She stood in front of the mirror for a very long time, looking at herself intensely, judging every feature on her oval face. Oh! She wasn't as old as she tended to think. The mirror secretly told her that. The room turned dreamy because of the sunlight that came through the ventilating holes, reflected off the ceiling and back down to the green tile floor, creating a soft and undefined atmosphere. It was exactly because of that atmosphere that, standing in front of the mirror, she had startled herself. What young girl is that? Is that the Duyen of twenty years ago, a nurse of slender build, rather fragile, city-born and raised, with pitch black eyes that were so bright and sweet? "Your eyes take my breath away," Phuc confessed when he fell in love with her during those days he was lying in the hospital that served his regiment. Oh! The military hospital. Those days were so far away already. The sick and wounded soldiers sitting in front of her made her face turn red with embarrassment. "Take a deep breath!" She reminded him. In her stethoscope, she could hear the sound of her own excited breath, filled with love. The next day, the soldiers would have to return to their regiment, and so on this night they sang by the campfire as a present to her.

> *After rainy days, the weather is sunny again,*
> *The sky will be fresh and pink again.*
> *After those days of sickness, now we are well again,*
> *We will go, but we leave our hearts behind.*

The verses had a three-beat rhythm. They were soft and floated somewhere between happiness and sorrow. That was also how she felt. She loved all the soldiers in that hospital.

But standing in front of that mirror a while longer, after her eyes adjusted to the green-tinted light, escaping from the illusion created by her reminiscence, she realized that she had changed a lot through the passage of time. Twenty years had passed and she was 42 already. Forty-two years old and whenever she wanted to read a book she had to put on 0.75 glasses. Her hair had lost its gloss. Her complexion had lost its freshness. Forty-two years old and she had entered a new phase of life. But 42 still wasn't old, at least not with her. Beautiful women can retain their youth a long time. She belonged to that set. The typists at the hospital called her "sister," while they called other women her age "aunt" or even "mother." Other women of the same age would say, "Duyen, when you go out with Thuan or Hoa it's a foregone conclusion that people will assume the three of you are sisters and brother." And one day when she wore a pink wool coat to the hospital, the typists surrounded her: "If you'd just put on some high heels, bell-bottoms, powder and mascara, you'd look perfect!" She laughed and flushed, which made her look even younger. She was like many mothers whose children are about to marry—she remained very young in demeanor, appearance, character, and temperament.

Looking in the mirror, she realized that she had lost the magnificence of her youth. From now on she would be like a picture that had settled. Completely settled. After many transformations and selections, she would always keep those aspects and remain unchanged. As with her eyes, her prominent, slightly snub nose would stay young the longest. It seemed that time had never touched her full, pretty lips and her hair still didn't know the meaning of old age. During Tet, the women of her age at the hospital suddenly started a "movement" to urge each other to go get their hair done. She was a bit hesitant. "I'm middle-aged already...and my hair is...thinning!"

"Oh! Your hair is thick and so pretty. If you get a perm, it'll be fantastic!"

The young girls urged her as well and now her permed hair was full of big, soft curls. Her new hairdo made her look smaller, thinner, and younger. But not really. Leaning to one side in front of the mirror, she realized that she looked younger and more elegant mostly because of her high heels and European-style stretch pants, with bottoms that flared discreetly.

There are times when a woman suddenly becomes so much more beautiful. Today, was she enjoying one of those rare, magic moments? She threw her hair back with a gesture like a schoolgirl and her lips suddenly hummed that line:

> *After rainy days, the weather is sunny again,*
> *The sky will be fresh and pink again…*

But she didn't finish the song. Her lips were silent. She turned and looked into the front room, through the bamboo curtain which was moving slightly in the breeze. Hoa, her daughter, was lying on the small bed, her face turned toward her mother. Hoa was fast asleep, her eyes closed.

She walked away from the mirror and lightly sat down on the bed. She kept her eyes on her daughter, and her heart was full of strange emotions: Hoa had become a young woman already.

Her little girl was now a young woman. That fact was marked by their division of the room when her older child, Thuan, had joined the army. The room divided in two, two separate lives. Things that were once common were divided now, starting from the blankets and mosquito nets. "Okay, this photo of me and father, it belongs to me." That was the innocent language Hoa spoke when she was ten years old. She realized that her young daughter had abandoned her innocence very quickly: she already wanted to treasure the precious things from her father, Phuc, the husband that Duyen had lost twelve years before. And this beloved man now seemed to be divided in two. Her greedy daughter had demanded to keep almost everything that carried the mark of the father. As for Duyen, she could only keep the beautiful and tranquil thoughts of him she could never stop remembering.

Hoa separated from her at the age of sixteen, when she suddenly grew up. Oh! There was one day when she came home from work and called out, and when her daughter opened the door, Duyen was so startled she had to step back. The girl who came to greet her was a gorgeous young woman. Suddenly, Duyen was overwhelmed with happiness.

"Mother, drink some hot tea to warm up. Why do you look so pale?"

She accepted a bowl of tea from her daughter and trembled. Her daughter had begun to observe her. She had already separated, was beyond reach, and from there she could make judgements. A relationship that had once been natural became difficult, and they had to use their will to adjust to it. Hoa began a life that was more private. They couldn't live that old life anymore, that period in which they had often confided in each other about everything from cooking, eating, and sewing to friendship and schooling. "Is this the disposition of a child from a family that's no longer intact?" Duyen thought of her deceased husband. Even though there was good food at mealtime and the mother and daughter had each other, they were still sad. Duyen often took the initiative to open the conversation. Once, she asked her daughter directly, "What's troubling you, Hoa? Let me know." But the girl only looked at Duyen and quietly said, "Trust me, mother. Whatever I can't solve for myself, I'll ask you." Duyen sighed with relief, but while assured, she still had doubts: daughter, you're already a woman, but has your character fully developed?

In the other room, Hoa had just woken up. Brushing aside the bamboo curtain, Duyen stepped out and saw that her daughter was busy writing at her desk.

"Hoa, let's go to a concert tonight, okay?"

Hearing the voice of her mother, the girl put down her pen and turned.

"Have you bought tickets? Where is it, Mother?"

"I have an invitation. It's at the Hong Ha theater. Let's eat early and then we can go."

Replying to those intimate and happy words of her mother, the daughter picked up her pen, her eyes looking down at the paper.

"Tonight I'm busy, mother."

"What are you busy with? But it's Saturday night. Go with me, Hoa."

The girl looked up, sensing something unusual in her mother's voice. What had happened that had suddenly made her mother's warm, beautiful eyes so empty and distant, so full of pleading?

"I really am busy, Mother! I have a whole pile of physics exercises over there."

"If you really have to study, then I'll understand."

"Why do you speak like that?" The girl raised her face and looked at her mother, her eyes full of sympathy and worry. Then she hurriedly looked down again and softly said, "And I also have to go to Grandmother's when I finish studying. She asked that we both come by tonight. She has something to tell us."

* * *

Only five years earlier, Doctor Duyen had transferred from a town in the mountains to the capital in Hanoi. She had struggled up in that small town for more than twenty years. In their decision to transfer her, the authorities had noted this point very clearly and added that they were transferring her to Hanoi to allow her to be near her family. "Family" meant the mother of Duyen's husband, a woman who was all alone and dependent on the money allotted to her after the death of her soldier son and whatever she received from her three other children who were working far away.

Back in Hanoi, the doctor was close to her mother-in-law, and the lonely woman truly had someone to lean on during her sad old age. But deep down, the doctor understood herself better than anyone else: the real reason for her transfer was brought about by her own emotional needs. The memory of her husband, of whose death she had only just learned, kept haunting her. And every day she felt more lonely in her lonely life. Especially when she witnessed her friends seeing their children off to university—when would small towns have the same number of universities as the capital?—and returning home to live alone with their shadows.

The whole family was excited when they heard of the transfer decision. Thuan was fifteen and Hoa was thirteen. Thinking about the capital with its crowded, happy streets, the doctor conjured up an image of a stable family, the three of them living together for the remainder of their lives. But when, seeing her off at the train station, a female friend whispered with a soft giggle in her ear: "Duyen, they say that when you return to Hanoi you'll have a chance to marry again. As for here, in this small town, there's no way. And you're still young and just as beautiful as when you first married Phuc." Duyen's face flushed, frightened. Luckily, her two children were so absorbed in admiring the locomotive that they didn't hear her friend's words—words that terrified her but sounded like the opening bars of a song that would repeat again and again in this new stage of her life.

The doctor said good-bye to her life in the small province. She terribly missed the peaceful life of the town, the friendly homes and loving faces. In a small town, life was at the same time easy-going and narrow-minded, where everyone knew everyone else as if they were members of the same family, where life was tranquil, with nothing standing out or going beyond the ordinary, where every move echoed and was twisted out of shape by daily life. In a small town, your character, disposition, and family circumstances were exposed beneath the blue sky in the transparent and intimate atmosphere of early morning. That was both the beauty and the trouble of it.

People had known her ever since she was eighteen years old, shaking her pigtails coquettishly as she followed the horse that hauled medical supplies for Regiment 246. They had known her husband Phuc very well. He was the youngest company commander in the regiment. They still remembered the year that she had married him. And they also remembered the day he died and the military funeral at the health department, where she had fainted.

In a small town, every individual life blends with other lives.

As for life in a big city, people suddenly become nameless to everyone else. Life there is bustling. Events happen at a fast pace. And anyone's private life seems buried beneath the disorder of so many plans and worries.

For her first few years in the city, the doctor lived exactly like that. Nobody knew anything about her very clearly. She had also very quickly abandoned the life-style of a small town. She folded into herself, shutting herself off in her private life and thus feeling comfortable, less dependent on the outside world.

A life like that is pleasant. She did her work meticulously, conscientiously, earning the trust of her colleagues and the love of her patients. Her two children excelled in school and were well mannered. At twenty, while studying medicine, Thuan volunteered to join the army. Hoa was in the tenth grade, already past that unpredictable stage and more mature. No one could wish for anything more.

Time passed quietly and was the doctor's good friend.

But as for this tranquility, even she could feel how fragile it was. The loud suggestions that came from friends her age and the teasing, bold, and well-intended words of the young girls—all this created a plot of land for seedlings.

One seed accidentally found its way to this fertile land.

That was the day the doctor examined an eight-year-old child. She had rheumatism and symptoms of a bad liver. The child's father was a man who bore the rank of major. His hair had turned grey and the marks of many years of hardship were printed very clearly in his rather long, pale face.

"She'll have to be admitted to the hospital, I'm afraid."

The doctor spoke unemotionally, as if she were talking to anyone with whom she had a business relationship. But she realized that he was looking at her with special interest, although discreet. After thanking her, and promising that he would prepare the child to be hospitalized on the date requested, he suddenly looked at her very carefully and spoke hesitantly:

"You know, you look sort of familiar....It seems like I've met you somewhere before."

"Maybe you're mistaken." Duyen removed her stethoscope from her shoulders and held it in her hand.

"Did you ever work for Regiment 246?"

The doctor shook her head, smiling politely. She lied. However, she could see that the major wasn't offended. He furrowed his forehead, doubting his memory.

It turned out that that incident kept tormenting her. Every time she thought of his pitiful furrowed brow and the sight of him carrying his sick daughter out of the examination room, she felt she had done something wrong.

The doctor waited for the major to return for a chat. Meeting an old friend from her former station would be delightful. But she didn't see him on the day he'd promised to bring his daughter to the hospital. Her remorse urged her to do something she'd never done before. Using the address, she went to look for the family of the child, in order to remind them that the girl had to be hospitalized. She found the family, a family that had only one child and one old, blind woman. The old woman told the doctor that the major had gone off to the front on the border. He was her oldest son, the one who had borne the most hardship in the family. He had fought in the Northwest, in Laos, and also in Cambodia. He was always present in the area of the fiercest fighting. His private life wasn't at all lucky. He had gotten married and only after ten years had they been able to have a child. A few years before, his wife had died of a terrible disease, liver cancer.

The doctor carried the child back to the hospital. She carried her on her back, just as the major had done. And after that, what had to happen had happened. The major wrote to her continuously, thanking her for her motherly kindness. She answered his letters, at first writing only about the condition of his daughter, but after that asking him about his life. In that way, they slowly opened their hearts, without ever realizing that they'd done so.

Then the day came that the child recovered and left the hospital. The major returned from the border and came to get his daughter. That was a happy day for the doctor. She went home very late that night and it was the first time in many years that a man had walked with her to her door.

But entering her house she was startled. Her two children had gone to bed, but weren't asleep yet. Hearing her lift the cover off the tray of food, Thuan sat up.

"Mother, why did you come home so late tonight? Hoa made spring rolls and waited so long for you. Today's her…birthday."

She shivered. Thuan went to his sister's bedside and patted the top of her mosquito net.

"Get up, Hoa," he said. "Mother's home. She was busy and came home only a little late and you're behaving like this?"

"Busy!"

The girl let out the sound of someone horribly wronged. The mother shivered, terrified. Hoa was in that age between childhood and growing up.

* * *

From then on, the relationship between the mother and daughter began to have a small crack in it. In the days that followed, things did not improve. Now, not only the two children took time from her life. A new element had invaded her private life.

The doctor suddenly became unpredictable. She was often in a state of anticipation. When happy, she would return home to find herself lonely. Her daughter had separated from her completely. That was the year that Hoa was in the ninth grade. The girl fell into the normal state of unpredictability for someone at that age. Her studies became very bad. Her head teacher invited the doctor to come to the school. "She's not as good as before, but the thing that troubles me more…there are many times she looks lost and sad for some reason."

The doctor was shocked, but after that something happened that was even more painful. When she went home, she brought up the head teacher's observations and asked her daughter about it. The girl retorted, "That's the way I am. You should ask yourself about it!"

Angry and pained by the insult, she slapped her daughter's face. That was the first time she'd ever hit one of her children. Immediately afterwards, she was filled with remorse. The two of them hugged each other and cried the whole night. How sad! She realized that she had neglected her duty to her children. She had abandoned the real happiness of a mother. She wasn't young anymore, so why had she gotten so wrapped up in such superficial emotions? God! Those moments when she had let herself be carried away were so foolish!

And now was she letting herself be carried away so foolishly again?

The concert was over. There was a power outage in the city. The moon was rising above the tops of the tallest houses. One could hear the clip-clop of the thongs and wooden sandals of the audience as people dispersed into the streets.

"Step onto the sidewalk, dear." The major reminded her lovingly, lightly touching her arm, and the two of them stepped up together. A street cleaning truck turned into the small street and its high beams swept over them. She was moved. He had just called her "dear." The sound of her footsteps echoed loudly on the sidewalk, sounding young and so strange.

They walked beside each other.

When they reached the Temple of Literature, they slowed down beneath the old flame trees and both of them realized that this was the moment when they could say the things they needed to say after hesitating and keeping their emotions to themselves for so long.

"Duyen," the major paused. In the moonlight shining through the sparse leaves of the trees, his face became so white that it seemed drained. "I think you understand without my having to say anything—"

"Don't say it—"

The doctor shook her head lightly. She didn't want him to say it. This was not the excitement of first love between people who were still young. He understood that. But it seemed that he had already prepared what he was going to say and he couldn't stop now.

"We are no longer young," the major spoke slowly, weighing his words. "And it's possible that people's opinions will be very complicated, particularly for you."

She stopped and looked at him. He was trying to remain calm.

"You don't understand everything," she said. "At my office, there's a man who remarried. His four children objected. They went over to that woman's house and cursed her without mercy. The day of the wedding, they packed up all his clothes and belongings in a suitcase and showed him to the door. No, I'm not worried about your family. But my children..."

She trembled. Her breathing was louder than her words. He saw tears in her eyes. He was quiet. They started walking again, then stopped once more at the foot of the Khue Van in the darkness that enveloped the ancient tower.

"Today...I wanted Hoa to come with us," she spoke between gasps, " so that she could get to know you. But she refused. It seems like...she knows. She doesn't approve."

The major sighed quietly.

"Tomorrow I have to return to the border. The situation there is very tense these days. Is your son Thuan still with his old unit there?"

"Yes."

"Let's walk a bit longer, okay?"

"I'm sorry, but I can't. I still have to drop by my mother-in-law's."

"I'll write to you like before."

She was quiet. When he asked, "Is that all right, Duyen?" she shook her head and replied:

"Don't send letters to my house."

* * *

"Mother, did you go to Grandmother's house last night?"

"I did. She gave me some dried carambola to cook with sour soup for you. She knows how much you like sour soup."

"She didn't talk about anything else?"

"She did. She asked how the efforts to find your father's grave are going. Because the anniversary of his death is coming up, she asked if we'd begun to prepare anything yet."

Hoa looked up at her mother and the doctor recognized the questioning look in her daughter's eyes. She felt hurt, especially because the girl had not gone to visit her grandmother as she had said she would when she refused to go to the concert with her mother the night before.

"So, you lied to me, Hoa."

"I didn't lie to you. When I was about to leave, my friend Hien from school came over and asked me to go to Thuy's because it was urgent."

"What was so urgent?"

"She dropped out of school…" Hoa hesitated, looking down with determination. "Her father was a martyr at the liberation of Buon Me Thuot. Now her mother got married again. My friend is so sad she can't study."

Duyen felt like she couldn't breathe and her face became hot. She felt feverish. Hoa looked up at her mother. Why had she told that story? Was it by accident or on purpose? Was it true or did she make up the story in order to gauge her mother's reaction? If it was such a sad story, then why was her face so cold and cruel? It was exactly like the face of her mother-in-law last night. The old woman had also had that cold and cruel expression. Then she had sobbed and wept while talking about her son, using the same lines Duyen had heard so many times already. The happy childhood he had passed. How bright he had been in school. How he had excelled in the army and been promoted every year. How he had received the highest medals. And finally, the infinite sorrow for his mother and children: now this idiot could enjoy all his property, all the fruits of his labor.

This was the first time she ever heard the old woman talk about property. Duyen had to control herself so that she wouldn't explode.

* * *

Those were painful days for the doctor. Once a week, she received a letter from the major. He expressed his love toward her with great feeling. His tone was measured. He approached the issue calmly, appropriately for his age and her circumstances. He didn't expect her to help him take care of his blind mother or his fragile daughter. He and his younger siblings would worry about that. He only said that the two of them needed each other at this age, and particularly when they grew older.

She always wrote him the same answer: the beginning of the letter was a refusal, the middle expressed her wish for having a family life, and the end spoke of a mountain of difficulties. And…none of these letters was ever sent. She burned them all. How sad! She still longed for life. The remainder of her life was still long. But she understood that after thirty years of war, sacrifice was not a personal thing and her circumstances were not at all special. In addition, at that moment, apart from the love of the major, she still had to think of her love and duty toward her children. She loved them. That love deserved to be nourished and her children did not want to share it with anyone. How sad that this love was an obstacle to that love, and that these beloved were obstacles to that beloved. Is it true that happiness, once lost, cannot be found again?

"There is no tranquility without sacrifice." She suppressed her emotions with that thought and tried to forget the image of the major.

In the absence of her replies, the major's letters to the doctor came with less frequency.

Then came the time when Hoa entered the second semester of 10th grade. The doctor spent a lot of time taking care of her daughter. Hoa was busier with her lessons. Even though their circumstances had brought them closer, however, between the student and her young mother there was still an implied distance. The only obvious sign of this fact was that the young girl often went to her grandmother's and the two of them formed a relationship that was intimate and…secretive.

While they were eating one day, Hoa suddenly put down her bowl and looked at her mother:

"Mother, why don't you bring Grandmother here to live?"

Taken aback, the young mother looked at her daughter and felt like crying. She thought, "They'll go to these lengths to keep tabs on me."

She said, as if choking, "I've invited her several times already but she didn't want to come. She's gotten used to her neighbors over there and she said it's more convenient."

"I feel sorry for her living all alone like that. Sometimes when I see her bent over cooking her tiny pot of rice, eating alone, I can't stand it."

Duyen decided that she had misunderstood her daughter. Now she looked at the girl tenderly and said, "I've already told her, 'Please come and live with us. It'll be good for the whole family and you won't have to work so hard around the house. Your granddaughter is grown already.'"

"Mother, yesterday Grandmother told me that Grandfather died when she was only 28 years old. She never remarried and raised three children by herself— Uncle Dam, Aunt Loc, and Aunt Lan. Now she's 78. Fifty years of living such a lonely life. I love her so much more for that!"

"You get used to living that way after a while, dear," she replied for the sake of saying something. Her voice was shaking.

But Hoa picked up her bowl of rice, pursed her lips, and said with authority, "Nam Cao said: 'Bearing misery is like that.'"

"What are you talking about?"

"Nam Cao. Our country's famous writer, Mother. He wrote that—"

"Oh, that was a long time ago…Generally speaking, people can adapt to any circumstances."

The doctor had lived up to her own words: adapt to any circumstances. Time was testing her.

The end of Hoa's school year had come. Duyen forgot her own life, taking care of her daughter and worrying about the examinations. Every meal was rushed and full of stories about the tests. Only twice did the conversation digress. Once, Hoa said that she had just received a letter that Thuan had sent from the front. Thuan said that a major had come to visit him. He said he knew their family. Thuan said that he had really liked the man. Another time, Hoa repeated the story of her friend Thuy, the girl who couldn't study because her mother remarried. Both times, Duyen tried to change the subject, because deep in her heart she really didn't want to cause any emotional disruption either for herself or her daughter.

The efforts of the mother and daughter weren't wasted. After the high school graduation tests were over, Hoa passed the entrance exam for admittance to university. Hoa's happiness was double. A new and beautiful life awaited her. And as for the doctor, after those days of exertion and those happy moments she'd been able to enjoy as a mother, she felt as if she was overcome by fatigue and a sense that in front of her lay a debilitating emptiness. Hoa, her daughter, would soon be far away from her!

That was a September afternoon of golden sunshine. When Hoa was packing her books to take with her to school the next day, to start her new life as a university student, the doctor returned from the hospital.

The girl ran to the door to greet her.

"Mother! You'll be so happy for me. Hien and Thuy and I are all in the same class. You know Hien, the class president, already. And Thuy—"

"Didn't you tell me that Thuy—"

"She went back to school, Mother. We had to encourage her a lot."

Duyen heaved a long sigh, her brow sweating. Although she wanted to, she didn't have the courage to ask, "Well then, how is Thuy's mother?"

Hoa turned on the fan, poured some water for her mother, and then went back to tidying up her desk. She was so happy she was singing. She fished in her suitcase until she found her *ao dai* and put it on. Then she went and stood in front of the mirror, singing softly to herself, "Queen, you used to be the most beautiful on earth, but now the princess is so much more." Suddenly, she rushed through the bamboo curtain.

"Mother!"

"Oh God! You startled me. I almost choked." Duyen set her glass of water on the table.

Hoa giggled and sat down next to her mother. Turning her face away, her voice was tender, "Mother, yesterday, I went by Grandmother's house. I don't know why, but she asked me—" The girl hesitated "—She asked me, 'If your mother ever takes the next step, then you'll come and live with me, won't you?'"

The mother's face clouded over. She was dizzy. The room, the bookshelves, the wardrobe with the mirror on it, all of them were spinning. She held on tightly to the back of her chair, as if she were afraid of falling off, and exerted all her will to keep herself calm. Her voice was breathless and instead of asking her daughter, "What do you think?" she said as if in reproach, "Why did your grandmother say that?"

"I don't know," Hoa turned and looked at her mother. Her two elbows were leaning on the table and suddenly her hands went up and into her thick hair. She looked down, almost sobbing. "I don't know what you think. I told Grandmother that I would only live with you. Mother...please don't hide it from me, poor Mother. Thuan wrote to me and enclosed a letter for you from the major. Mother, Mother please forgive me."

The doctor sat silently in her chair. Tears streamed down her cheeks. She cried without hiding it from her daughter. The girl had grown up.

Translated by Bac Hoai Tran and Dana Sachs

Heat

Richard Bausch

In the newspaper that morning, a political cartoon depicted a book which was labeled *LBJ*, sandwiched between bookends labeled *JFK* and *RFK*. At breakfast, Penny said something about getting back to normal at last when Bobby Kennedy became president, and I saw Father shake his head. Even for what he had been through, he was still a military man. He carried himself that way. When Mother said she wished McCarthy would get the nomination, since McCarthy had gone against Johnson on the war before Kennedy had, Father looked at her almost sadly.

"What?" she said to him.

"I can't believe that's you talking," he said.

"It's me."

"You didn't talk that way before," he said.

"What way?" Penny said, flustered. "What's he mean?"

"They sent you over there," Mother said, "and they let you get caught. And it meant nothing. It meant less than nothing."

"It's a war," he said. "I've always been with my country when there was war."

"I thought he was against the war," Penny murmured.

"Let's talk about something else," said Mother. "Let's get off the subject."

"Listen," my father said, rising, "nobody wants a war."

He went up to his room. He was still there when we left for school, and he didn't come down when we got home. Mrs. Wilson was already preparing for the cookout. "I, for one, am going to celebrate the finished porch—a job well done," she said. She got Russell and me to take the folding card table out to the front yard and set it up. We did this without saying much to each other. And then we helped put the plastic tablecloth on it, the jars of pickles, mustard, and relish, and the chopped onions.

When we came in, Mrs. Wilson called to us from the kitchen. She was making potato salad while Lisa sat at the table cutting carrots.

"Open those cans of baked beans," Mrs. Wilson said to Russell.

He started on one, and I helped Lisa cut the vegetables. I could hear my father moving around in the room above our heads. I imagined him pacing, though the sounds weren't of the rhythmic kind that would indicate pacing. It was as if he were rearranging things, except that there was no sound of furniture being moved.

Presently Lisa pushed the rest of the vegetables toward me and stepped away from the table. "I'm through," she said.

"They're home," Russell said without looking up from his slow work on the cans of beans.

"I'll go see," Lisa said. "Thomas can finish."

Mother and Penny had indeed pulled up. We heard Lisa call to them, and then the screen door slammed.

Mrs. Wilson turned to me: "Go tell your father I need him to start cooking the hamburgers and hot dogs."

I went up the back steps and knocked on his door. Silence. I knocked again. From downstairs came the racket of Mother and Penny entering the house, their shoes on the hardwood floor and the reverberation of their voices in the tall foyer. They were laughing about something. They passed on into the kitchen, still laughing. My father's door opened. "What," he said. His hair was combed and wet. He was wearing a white shirt. There was no emotion in his voice at all.

I told him what Mrs. Wilson sent me to tell him, but found myself with the familiar sense that I couldn't look directly at him as I spoke.

"Come in here," he said.

I stepped inside the room. I had noticed before that it looked exactly the way it had his first day in the house: he had done nothing to make himself at home. This never failed to leave me with a sense of reassurance, since to me it was a sign that he would soon be moving into our part of the house. He closed the door and went to the chair by the bed, offering me the bed. I sat down, experiencing that queasy, butterflies feeling in my stomach: this was going to be something I would have to contend with—some revelation I wasn't ready for—and I received a passing intimation that he was planning to leave.

"It's a tough thing to ask," he began, studying the ends of the fingers of one hand. He bit the cuticle of a nail, looked out the window. "But I want a straight answer."

"Yes, sir," I said.

He looked at me. "Thomas."

"Yes," I said.

"It's hard to have any respect for me, right?"

For the moment I was unable to utter a sound.

"Well?"

"That's not true," I said. But it came too late, with the faltering voice of someone caught.

"No," he said. "Admit it, son. I'm hollowed out where it counts. That's what you think."

"No, sir."

"You can muster enough common respect for me to tell the goddam truth," he said through his teeth.

I was silent.

"Right?"

"Yes, sir."

"I know respect is something that has to be earned," he said. "I always believed that."

I nodded. I didn't know what else was required; I felt the immense anxiety of needing to find out.

"I don't have your mother's respect," he said. "I know that." He breathed out and muttered to himself: "Lost it before all this happened." Then he leaned back, as if saying this had given him some satisfaction. "You know when I lost it?"

"I respect you, sir," I said, and felt my mouth twist with the effort not to break down. I looked at the wall where Mr. Egan's spear had hung. A bare wall; the room was like a cell.

"I'm asking you something," he said.

"I do respect you," I persisted.

He nodded impatiently. "Do you know when I lost it, son?"

I said, "No."

"I lost it in Vietnam."

"No," I said.

He was shaking his head. "She was never quite the same...never the same after that."

I couldn't speak, but my expression refuted him.

"Well," he said. "You don't know. I know."

"She loves you," I told him.

"Jesus," he said. "I'm not looking for reassurance from you."

"Why—" I said, meaning to go on and ask why he was telling me these things now, and finding myself unable to continue.

He shrugged. "I came home pretty scared, boy."

Again, I couldn't look at him.

"I had a lot of trouble going to sleep in the nights. I had awful dreams. She had problems with that. She's—she's not very good about weakness, you see. She has never been very good about it. She's a lot more like her father than she realizes."

I didn't want to hear more. I didn't want to hear about his weakness.

"We kept a lot of it from you and Lisa," he went on. "But the whole thing started from there. My fault, kid. I made the mistake of thinking I could win her back, and things got a little extravagant. I was trying for that feeling we had when we were young—a recklessness, you know. Back when we were going to score big in the oil business and get out from under the old bastard's thumb."

"Don't," I said. "Don't—don't—please."

"Listen—I'm not telling you out of weakness now. That's the difference now."

I had no idea how he wanted me to respond to this.

"She doesn't know she does this to people," he said. "I'm not saying she does it intentionally or with any meanness. It's something she can't help."

"What, then," I said. I couldn't help myself. I wanted him to tell me what he expected me to do with this information.

He said, "I just want you to know I didn't take those things for any personal gain—not for anything I wanted to buy. It was to show her, and it was stupid. And I paid for it."

"Yes, sir."

"I'm tired of still having to pay for it."

"Yes," I said.

"I don't want you to take it wrong when the time comes."

I stared at him, at the cold light of resolution in his eyes.

"I still love her, son. Just like I did when I was twenty-two years old." His eyes brimmed.

"Yes, sir."

"Stop sirring me. I'm talking to you like a man."

"Yes, s—" I stopped myself.

"I still love her and I'm going to fight to keep her, if I have to."

For an instant I had the sensation that he was enlisting my help in whatever he was deciding to attempt, and it was then that I felt the hopelessness of it. The full weight of the knowledge came down upon me that my mother was in the process of finding a way to leave him. It was all I could do to keep from showing him my distress.

"I want you to know," he was saying, "because it's liable to seem kind of harsh for a while."

"Yes, sir," I said, unable to help myself.

"I have to stand up," he said. "It's time to stand up a little. You probably understand what I mean, don't you."

I did, but I shook my head no.

"Well, you will, in time," he said.

"Yes, sir."

"I'm afraid I've let you down enough."

"No." This seemed too absurd to acknowledge. Mercifully he didn't seem to have heard me.

He said, "Are we straight?"

"Yes," I said, this time remembering to leave out the "Sir."

"All right," he said, rising. He offered me his hand. "We buddies?"

The word almost made me wince. "Yes."

"You won't say anything?"

"No, sir."

He shook his head. "She's been riding over me, son. And you can't let that sort of thing happen. I let it go for a while in the interest of peace, you know. This house being what it is. There's not much room for having things out in the open with the woman you love."

"No, sir."

"Okay," he said. "Go tell Mrs. Wilson I'll be down in a minute or two."

So it was afternoon now, and we were all out in front of the house. My father tended to the smoking grill, standing in the mottled, shifting shade of the big oak tree while Lisa and Russell watched him.

Penny Holt and Mother were in the foreground in the bright sun. Penny held a can of beer and Mother sipped from a glass of lemonade. Penny's immaculate skin was lightly tanned where she had been sunning herself, and I sat on the top porch step, watching her as I always was, actually feeling some small glimmer of hope in the fact that she had spoken to me about liking picnics as we started out into the yard—and vaguely tense, too, with that feeling of everything being in doubt.

Mrs. Wilson lounged in the metal porch chair behind me, her stockings rolled down to her big ankles. She called to my father, "I like my hamburgers charred, young man."

"Coming right along," he called back, a false note in his voice now, a fake heartiness.

The smell of charbroiled meat was on the air. Mother walked over to the table and, taking a pickle from a jar, popped it in her mouth. Penny had followed her. I saw Father keeping track of them. He was drinking beer. He was on his fourth can. He finished it and came up onto the porch to get another out of the cooler. From the table in the yard, Mother shielded her eyes with one hand and said, "Get me one too, Daniel."

"Why don't you come up here and get it yourself," he said. But he reached in and brought out one more in a shower of ice, and then stepped down off the porch, holding it out to her.

"Thank you," she said, and gave him a small puzzled smile. He walked away from her, back to the grill, where he had left Russell holding the metal turner. He opened his beer and drank down half of it in a gulp, then raised the can as if to offer a toast to Mother.

She raised her own can, and watched him drink. Penny watched him, too.

"Who wants a hamburger?" he said. "They're ready."

We all moved to the table to take up our paper plates, and one by one we filed by him for our choice of meat. Everything was festive and lighthearted. Mother strolled over to the base of the big oak and sat down in the shade, and Penny joined her. Mrs. Wilson brought her chair down from the porch, and Russell brought one, too.

"You'll want chairs," Mrs. Wilson said. "Russell, get the other chairs."

He did so, complaining to himself. I had not been asked to, but I helped him. Soon we were all seated in a semicircle under the tree, in the spotted shade. We ate, and talked about the food, the way the street was when it was buried in snow. We remarked about the cool weather, and how it was in summer.

"Sometimes in July, you'd swear you were in the tropics," Mrs. Wilson said. "The humidity comes in from that creek, and you can't find any relief from it. It's not the temperature, though. It's the awful humidity."

"It gets up over a hundred," Russell said.

"That's true. It's done that here."

"It was a hundred in Virginia when we were there," Lisa said.

"Not quite," I said. "Ninety-nine."

"It was a hundred and four here," said Mrs. Wilson.

"I don't remember it getting that hot," Father said. And it blew through me again that he had lived a summer here—a season doing hard labor, in fact. He went on to say he remembered the humidity, that he was not looking forward to experiencing that again. As he talked, Mother and Penny were shoulder to shoulder, engaged in their own conversation about other matters, and when Penny laughed at something Mother said, my father turned his attention to them.

"Hey," he said, "how about letting us in on the joke?"

Mother hesitated. "I'm sorry?" she said.

"How about letting us in on it?"

She glanced around at the rest of us. "What," she said. "You mean what we were talking about?"

Penny said, "It was personal."

"Well, yes—all right. It was personal," Mother said.

"Personal?" Father said.

The two women regarded him.

"Personal."

"Yes," said Mother. "It really didn't have anything to do with anything."

"But it was personal."

She said nothing.

"Isn't that a little off, Connie? Trading little personal secrets like that with people around?"

"I didn't say it was a personal secret," Mother said.

"Well, if it's not a secret—"

"I don't think it's your place to worry about it right now, do you?"

"Oh, well—I see. It's about me being in my place."

No one said anything for a time. Then Lisa asked for another hot dog.

"Coming right up," Father said, rising. "Anything for my little girl." There was something pointed about the way he said this. At the grill he asked if anyone else wanted one. No one did. He walked over and handed the hot dog to Lisa, then sat down again.

Penny was saying something to Mother.

He looked over at them. "More personal secrets?"

"No," Penny said quickly.

"Well, tell us all, then."

"It's nothing," she said.

"I'm sure we'd all like to hear it."

"Daniel," Mother said, "please. This is not a schoolroom."

"No, really?"

Mrs. Wilson said, "I'd like to know how you'd feel about painting the eaves of the house, Mr. Boudreaux."

"I don't have any feeling about that," he said.

"You wouldn't be interested?"

"He's afraid of heights," Mother joked.

"No," said Father, shaking his head and looking down into his lap.

Mrs. Wilson hurried to change the subject. "Do you really think Bobby can be President?"

"Looks like it," he said.

"At least he came out against the war," said Mother.

Mrs. Wilson looked at Father. "You went over there—you saw it all firsthand. And you went to prison because you—well, you were against something they were doing...." She trailed off. It seemed to have come to her that she didn't really know anything about why my father had been in Wilson Creek. Perhaps something Mr. Egan tried to tell her, and that she hadn't believed, went through her mind. "Do you think Kennedy's right about it?"

He left a pause. He might have been considering telling her everything about himself. Then he said, "Like most military people, I hate war. But there are tigers in the world, you know."

"Yes," said Penny. "But who's the one with the stripes?" This seemed to have surprised her.

Mrs. Wilson said, "That's communist talk."

"No," said Penny, "it's not. I didn't mean it that way. It's loyal—the loyal—opposition."

"It may not be communist," Father said, "but it sure sounds disloyal."

Mother said, "What do we have to be loyal to? The Air Force?"

He gave her a look.

"Well, really, Daniel."

"I was talking about the country," he said.

"Okay, the country."

"You don't mean that, Connie. I don't know who you've been talking to."

"What is *that* supposed to mean?"

"I just mean that's not you talking."

"It's me," Mother said. "Whether you can hear me or not."

"Are you saying you're not loyal to your own country?"

"I'm loyal to my children. My loyalty stops there."

"What about me?" Father said.

Mother frowned, but said nothing.

"No," Father said, "really. What *about* me, Connie?"

She returned his look.

"I meant my family," she said in a low voice.

"All right. Am I included in that?"

Penny said, "This is getting too personal."

"I was just asking my wife a question."

"Please," said Mrs. Wilson. "This is supposed to be a happy occasion. We're supposed to be celebrating a job well done here, and if you—"

Father interrupted, still staring at Mother. "Am I included in that lucky group, Connie? Your family?"

Mother had pulled up some grass, and was watching it drop from her fingers.

"Penny is," he said. "Right?"

She looked at him. "What're you saying?"

Penny stood. "Let's all stop this and play some croquet or something." Her voice quavered. "You must have some lawn games, Mrs. Wilson."

"There's a volleyball net somewhere," said Russell.

"Volleyball. Okay."

"Just making conversation," Father said to no one in particular. "Just wondering about the future."

"Be quiet," Mother told him. "You've had too much beer."

For a few seconds no one did or said anything. It was as if we were all waiting to see what would happen next. But then Mrs. Wilson stirred, got to her feet, talking about where she had put the volleyball net, and the inertia of the moment was broken; everyone was moving.

"Volleyball," Lisa said. Mrs. Wilson carried her chair back to the porch. Russell had run across the sunny yard to the falling-down shed against the side fence, and began working the combination lock on it. Lisa and Penny stood a few feet away, talking about where the game's boundaries would be. And I saw Penny exchange a look with Mother: a little furtive smirk of collusion at Father's expense. Then Penny turned her attention to Lisa again, and I watched her motions, feeling an abrupt stab of rage, still aching for her even as part of me had begun to wish she would go away. I was in a sort of wintry fever, a secret delirium, wanting to hold her and smash her at the same time. It was a very strange moment.

My mother and father were sitting under the tree, not looking at each other. He ate the last of his hamburger, and she said something to him. I knew what it was; I needed only to see the displeased expression of her face: *You ever do that again. Who do you think you are—*

And he spoke over her, still chewing the hamburger. He was almost cheerful: *It's over, Connie. All over. I've begged and sniveled and bowed my head for the last time. Do you understand, my darling? I'm through being the victim and the sad sack.*

And she: *Our private life is nobody's business—*

And he: *What private life? We have no private life.*

She: *I'm not going to have you parading everything before the others, and especially in front of the children.*

You're not listening to me, Connie.

I'm listening. I hear you.

All right. Good, then. Maybe you can hear this. I'm through being the beggar here, all right? That's what you need to know.

Nobody's asking you to beg.

You were.

No.

You didn't know it, and maybe you didn't want it. It's my fault, maybe—the whole thing. But it's over now. It's done and it's not going to come between us anymore.

That isn't what's between us.

Yes it is. All the way. The whole time.

No.

Well, whatever. I'm through with it.

I wish it was just that.

People generally get what they want in situations like this.

I've told you.

Yes, and I'm telling you now.

It won't change anything.

I'm moving my family out of here, Connie.

Stop this.

Soon. I'm taking my family where they can have some kind of a life.

Back to my father, I suppose.

Maybe. I understand how you meant to hurt me with that, but until I get on my feet—just maybe. And he'll take us in, too.

You're not taking anybody anywhere.

You talk tough. Where'd you learn to talk so tough?

Stop this—

And you came all this way.

I won't listen to this.

I think I'm going to move back in with my kids tonight, too.

What are you saying?

You know. And if you feel you've got to be separate, maybe you'll have to be the one who moves out.

Oh, watch me.

Not interested.

He rose, walked to the grill, and closed it. Then he began clearing the debris from the table, stacking the plastic cups and the soiled paper plates and putting them in a big bag. His hands shook. Russell, Lisa, and Penny were working to put the volleyball net up. Mother strode to the porch and up the steps, on into the house. Mrs. Wilson, sitting in the shade by the front door, watched her go in, then looked at me with a question in her face, which I did not respond to. I walked over to where my father had begun to gather all the jars of condiments and sauce.

"Well," he said, without looking at me, "the battle is joined."

I could think of nothing in the way of a response.

"Here," he said, handing me a tin tray with glasses and silverware on it. "Take this inside."

"Yes, sir."

He began shakily folding the tablecloth.

When I came up the porch steps, Mrs. Wilson got out of her chair and opened the door for me, murmuring, "She went upstairs."

I put the tray down in the kitchen and then climbed the back stairs, making my way along the hall to the partition, the little stoop. She was just on the other side. I heard bureau drawers opening and closing. When I stepped up and looked in at her she turned, startled.

"What."

She was standing by the sofa with her small suitcase open before her. There were several pieces of clothing already folded in it, though haphazardly.

I said, "What're you doing?"

"Don't sneak up on people, for God's sake."

I repeated the question.

She hesitated. "Nothing."

"You're doing something," I said.

"Leave me alone, Thomas. It has nothing to do with you."

"Where are you going?"

This stopped her. She sat down on the sofa and put her hands to her face. "Please leave me alone."

"What is it with Penny?" I said.

She regarded me a moment. "Nothing."

"Penny's doing this," I said, "isn't she?"

"Doing what?"

"Making you act like this."

"Don't be ridiculous," she muttered. "What the—who the hell do you think you are—"

"He loves you," I told her. "Why can't you let him love you?"

She shouted at me. "Get out!"

I went down to the open front door and out onto the porch. Russell and Penny had put the volleyball net up and Father was tossing the ball at Lisa to let her try to hit it. He watched the house, too. Mrs. Wilson had joined them. I moved to the end of the porch and leaned on the railing to watch. My hands were shaking; I felt weak.

"Thomas," my father said. He looked calm now. "Aren't you going to play?"

I couldn't get my mind around what was happening, and I knew that whatever it was, it was only beginning. When Penny looked at me from the brightness and said, "Come on, Thomas," I climbed the rail and made a show of jumping down. (No trouble quite overtakes the vanity of obsessive infatuation.)

We chose sides: Father, Lisa, and Mrs. Wilson against Penny, Russell, and me. It was a very slow game, and very tentative, for Penny had all the difficulty one might expect, trying to play a game that required some peripheral vision. For a long time we were merely trying to keep the ball in the air. Now and again I saw her looking at the house, and I did so, too. Father was into the game, laughing at his failure to hit the ball, helping Lisa serve it, and trying to spike it when it wandered in my direction. We all knew something bad was under way, but we played on, into the beginning of twilight. Finally Mother emerged from the house, and moved to the railing. She called to Penny.

"Come play volleyball," Penny said with a sort of hysterical brightness.

"I'm moving in with you," Mother told her.

We all stood still in the dimness of the yard, waiting for her to say something else.

"Did you hear me?"

"Yes."

"I need the key to your room so I can put my things away."

"All right."

No one stirred.

"It's in my purse," Penny said. "In the dining room."

Mother left the railing. We heard the front door open and slap shut. Then it opened again, and she called from the dark: "Mrs. Wilson, Daniel will be moving out of his room and into our apartment with Thomas and Lisa."

"Mom?" Lisa said. Then: "Mom-eeeee." It was much like the scream she'd emitted the night they arrested Father. He took her hand and started toward the house. We all followed, Russell and Mrs. Wilson trailing behind, clearly uncertain what was expected of them. Penny ran ahead. She was in the house before anyone, and when I got there, just behind Father, I saw her standing at the entrance of the dining room, her hands working at her waist, talking to Mother.

"—I don't think this is the—I don't think—"

And Mother's voice: "Yes it is. It is. When did you think I'd do it?"

"Not like this, though. No, not—I thought we'd get a place."

"We have a place."

"Let me go," Lisa moaned.

Father held her tight, and turned away from Mother as she came into the room and tried to take Lisa. "Will you please give her to me, Daniel. She wants me."

He let Lisa down, and she immediately put her arms around Mother's middle.

"All right," my father said. "Leave us alone, please."

"You stay here, Penny."

"We have to talk this out," he said, "and we have to talk it out now."

"There's nothing to talk about. If you're moving into the apartment, I'm moving in with Penny. We already agreed to it."

He looked at Penny, then at Mother. "You agreed to it? What was it, a contingency plan?"

"We were talking about getting a place together," Penny said quietly.

Father turned to me. "Thomas, take Lisa out of here."

"I will not," Lisa said, holding on to Mother.

"Go on and take her, Thomas!"

"Yes, sir."

"Lisa," Mother said, "go with Thomas. I'm right here. We're right here."

Lisa screamed and fought, and it took all the strength I possessed to get her out to the porch, where Russell and his mother were waiting, like bystanders at an accident.

"Lisa," I said, "be still."

"I don't want them to gooooooo," she wailed.

"Nobody's going anywhere. Will you stop it? Stop it."

Gradually she calmed down. Or else she simply ran out of the energy to continue. She sobbed, caught her breath, and then she stared at the lighted window of the room where she had been dragged away from her parents. It was as if the light reminded her of this, and she started building up to another scream.

"Everybody's here," I said to her. "Be quiet and listen."

Then she seemed to realize what was happening. She gained control of herself and became very quiet. We were all straining to hear. The three of them were still inside, and the muffled, emphatic turmoil of their voices reached us in a jumble, without distinguishable words.

At last Penny emerged, walked to the top of the steps, and gazed out at the night.

"Well?" Mrs. Wilson said.

"Oh, I'm waiting for the sky to fall," said Penny. "I always am."

"What?"

"Dial the number and it rings," Penny said. "Every time."

"I won't have this kind of trouble," Mrs. Wilson said. "I really can't—" She frowned, watched Penny go down the steps and out into the dark of the yard. "What in the world—" She turned to me. "Do you know what that was about?"

"I don't know anything," I said as Penny's slender shape disappeared beyond the pools of light from the house.

"Everybody's gone crazy," Mrs. Wilson said.

A few moments later, Father came out. The door slapped behind him. He put his hands to his head and ran them roughly through his hair. Lisa hurried to his side, and he gathered her in. "Sorry for the commotion," he said to Mrs. Wilson.

She said, "I won't have this sort of squabbling."

He didn't answer for a space. "I'll be moving in with my family."

"And Mrs. Boudreaux?"

"I'm going to sleep on the sofa for now. I got her to see that I ought to be with our children more."

I went down the steps and around the house, looking for Penny. Russell walked with me.

"Go back," I said to him.

"Jesus," he said. "Everybody's gone totally nuts."

"Go on back, Russell."

"I just want to see where she went."

"Get out of here," I said. "Now."

"I didn't do anything." He stormed off in the direction of the back door. I heard it slam. But I was already walking on, toward the creek. Penny had gone to the back edge of the lawn, and she stood there picking a wildflower apart. The petals were white; they were what I saw as I approached her.

"What do you want," she said in an expressionless voice.

I said, "I wanted to be sure you're all right." It was a lie. I had gone there purely out of the need to know what we were going to be to each other now.

She tore the petals and dropped them. "You felt worried about me."

"Yes," I said. I almost went on to say, "I love you." I was barely able to keep it back. It was a reflex I controlled. I said, "What were you talking about back there?"

"Nothing."

"You scared Mrs. Wilson."

"I didn't scare you?"

"You always scare me," I said, trying to tease her back to something of our recent friendliness.

She tore the petals and dropped them. Nothing stirred anywhere.

"I think they've resolved it," I said.

She said, "I knew it would be like this."

"Like what?"

"Lonely."

"We're still friends."

"You were worried about me?" she said.

"Yes."

"Me?"

"Yes," I said.

"Not me." She sighed. "Something in your head."

"I don't get you," I said.

"You don't even see me. None of you do."

"I see you."

"No. You see what you think. I gave you what to think, too."

"I don't understand you."

"Don't you?"

"No," I told her. "I *was* worried about you."

"Well," she said, "I'm glad *somebody* was worried about me."

I couldn't explain it, but I heard the sound in her voice of a disapproving lover, someone feeling ill used and lied to. I thought of this, and then dismissed it.

Presently she said, "Leave me alone. Can't you please leave me alone?"

Walking away from her, I was half hoping she'd call me back. She didn't. On the porch everyone was still gathered—everyone except Mother.

Mrs. Wilson said, "There's still the problem of the rent for your room."

"We'll keep paying it," said Father, "until you can get someone else. We're going to be moving out soon anyway."

"When?"

"We're going back to North Dakota. Connie's father."

"We are?" I said.

"When?" Mrs. Wilson wanted to know. "I've got to make up the income from these rooms."

"We'll wait until you can find other renters."

Penny had come to the base of the porch stairs, and now she started up. "Other renters?" she said. "You're leaving?"

"That's right," my father told her.

She looked beyond him, at the screen door, where Mother was now standing. "Is that true, Connie? You're leaving?"

"It's true," said Father.

"Let her answer."

"I don't have to take instructions from you," Father said.

"Now stop this," said Mrs. Wilson." I won't have it in my house."

"Well?" Penny Holt said, still looking at my mother. "Is it, Connie?"

"I have to think of my children," Mother said. "It doesn't have to mean we don't see you again."

Penny turned to Father. "You simply exercise your power, is that it? You and her father." All her jitteriness was gone now, and in its place was a kind of heat. Her skin gleamed. She opened the screen door, stepped up into its frame, and turned to give my mother a look. Then she went on to the stairs, ascending them slowly as if she expected to be overtaken.

"I want this stopped," Mrs. Wilson said, standing with her back to us, supporting herself on the newly painted porch railing and trying to get her breath. "I want it stopped right now. Enough's enough. This is not right. I want peace. You agreed to peace."

We all moved separately into the house. It was as if no one was quite *with* anyone; even Lisa kept to herself, mincing into the living room and turning to watch us. It grew very quiet. For a few moments the only sound was the racket the insects made out in the night. Mrs. Wilson was shaking, doubtless from the effort of worrying about what might happen. She paid an almost frantic attention to the details of getting the house back to normal from the cookout, listing the tasks in a breathless voice for poor Russell, who seemed vaguely sorrowful, standing there with his hands on his hips, listening to her.

Mother said, "I'll help."

"Well," said Mrs. Wilson, with an air of having been rushed at, "you needn't."

"You put such a nice party together."

"Thank you."

They stared at each other.

Father said, "I'm going upstairs."

No one answered. When he was gone, we all spent a few minutes putting things away in the kitchen. The windows were black. The night bugs made an incessant hum and ruckus, and bullet-sized moths kept butting against the screens. Russell turned the television on, and Lisa joined him. Soon Mother and Mrs. Wilson were there, too. I went out onto the porch in the dark and sat on the top step. The night air was fragrant; it was a beautiful summery night. Behind me, I heard the noise of the television. Other houses on the street showed light in the windows, and somewhere children were playing. Their voices came to me on the breezes. The moon shone bright. It made a shade where the oak stretched its thick branches to the eaves of the house. The wind stirred the leaves. A moment later I heard Father on the stairs. He came straight to the door and out, without even glancing into the living room. He came to where I sat, looked out at the stars, drew a breath, then sat down.

"Nice night," he said.

I made a murmuring sound of agreement. I wondered what he wanted of me now, and I felt crowded by his presence. He was sitting too close.

"Anybody say anything?" he said.

"No, sir."

"There you go with that 'sir' business again."

"I'm sorry."

"Your mother didn't say anything?"

"No."

"She's up to something."

I kept silent.

"She caved in too quick. She's up to something, I'll tell you. I know her."

It was as if I had argued the point.

"The way she looked at me, boy. You don't know—"

It came to me that I didn't want to know. I felt that we had gone over some invisible line and entered a dark area where all the usual customs and applications no longer held sway.

"I know what she'll do now," he said. "She'll give me the passive treatment. The robot going through the motions."

"Don't," I told him. "Stop it, please."

He was quiet. He shifted his weight, then rose, walked down the steps to the sidewalk. He was in the moonlight, splashed with the shade of the oak branches. Out by the street, a couple walked by, talking softly. We heard the tripping syllables of a phrase, and laughter. They walked on, enjoying their quiet joke, whatever it was. "Be back," Father said, and headed out in the opposite direction, across the lawn, as though he were off to search for the place from which those strangers had stolen their lightheartedness and their comfort with each other, the magical source for it all somewhere in the night.

I watched him until he disappeared at the end of the street.

In the house, Mrs. Wilson and Russell were sitting in front of the television. Mother and Lisa had gone upstairs. I made my way up there, and found them sitting on Mother's bed.

"Well," Mother said in the tone of someone addressing the enemy.

"What did I do?" I said.

"Have you been talking with him?"

"Not much."

"What does he have to say?"

"He loves you," I told her. "He's hurt."

"That's what he said to you?"

"In so many words."

She shook her head, looking away. The light in the room was harsh, and made her skin appear sallow.

"So," I said, "is he moving back in?"

"You heard him."

"Are we going back to North Dakota?"

"Thomas, you were there when he told Mabel—Mrs. Wilson."

"Well," I said. "Isn't that—all right?"

She stroked Lisa's hair. "It's what we have to do. You want to go back, don't you."

It was not a question.

"Well?"

"Yes," I said.

"Of course you do."

"It's not a crime to want that," I told her. And I couldn't keep the anger out of my voice.

"Yes," she said, "well—it's just the way Penny says it is. He gets to use his power."

"He just got out of prison," I said, as coldly as I could. "I don't think he cares about using any power."

She said, "You don't know what you're saying."

"Yes," I said. "I do."

And she began crying. The tears just started running down her cheeks. There was no sobbing, no sound at all for a moment. Then she said, "I've tried. I've really, really, tried."

"Why're you doing this?" I said.

"Please, go to bed. Go down and watch television. Do something besides hectoring me."

I went into my room and climbed into bed. I didn't even know what time it was. I lay there trying to put it all together in my mind. The house made its sounds, and I heard the television set downstairs, and then I dreamed that I was hearing it. I'd fallen off into a sort of exhausted sleep—like a lapse, a failure. Or at least that was how it felt when I woke up. In that instant I was breathless, startled. I had the feeling that I had let time get away from me, and that something awful would follow from this dereliction. In the quiet, I got down from the bed and saw that Lisa lay asleep in hers. The apartment was dark. Father was not on the sofa. Out in the hall, I saw that his door was closed. Downstairs, the television still made its small racket, and Russell sat in the silver shifting light of it, the only one awake.

"Hey," I said.

He jumped. "Oh."

"Did my father come back?"

"I wouldn't know." He was still angry with me, and turned back to the television.

I didn't have the energy to deal with him now, so I went outside, to the top step of the porch. The night felt cooler. I was beginning to believe that Father had come back and gone into his room, when he appeared from one of the little ponds of light under the street lamps. Seeing him, I had a sense that he'd been waiting for me to come out. He crossed the lawn again and stopped at the base of the steps.

"You're up late."

"Yes, sir."

He shook his head. Oddly, he had the demeanor of a man who has been locked out. "Well," he said, and looked off.

"Where did you go?" I asked.

He shrugged. "Walked, mostly."

We said nothing for a time.

"It's nice to just walk and keep going, you know? Be able to keep going. I walked through a lot of imaginary lines, son, and it felt good."

"Yes, sir."

"Everybody asleep inside?"

"I guess so," I said. "Russell's watching TV." But then the screen door opened behind me, and Mother stepped out in a robe and slippers.

"Connie," he said.

She padded across to where I was sitting, and said nothing.

"Nice night," Father said.

"A little chilly," she said.

"I've been walking."

She let this go by.

"I was telling Thomas, here, how it felt to be able to cross all those imaginary lines. Just keep right on going and no walls to stop me."

"So," Mother said, "what stopped you?"

He gave forth a small sighing laugh. "Right. Well, you know, that's—there's my family to think of."

"I didn't mean that the way it sounded," Mother said.

"Well," he said. Then he was quiet.

"How—" she began. "How far did you walk?"

He looked off in the direction he had taken. "Oh, on into town and out the other end. Past the train station." He paused, ran his hand through his hair. "I remember when they brought me in there. Right at sunset—a pretty day. What a thought to have at a time like that, but I remember thinking it was a pretty day. Everything was gold, you know, in the light. Way the light gets at sundown on a clear day. The grass, what there was of it. Just—gold. The—the windows. And—and I saw how everybody else seemed so much at home. You know—the people in the station. Ah. So much at home. Guys who were delivering me. The guy behind the counter. Everybody so comfortable, and—at home. That was the awful thing, I guess. They were all so—and you know none of them seemed to appreciate that they were home and could go around like they wanted. And I was coming here to be an inmate. I'll tell you, I sweated that first few days, really sweated. And it was tied up with what was going on in my mind, I guess. This—this trapped feeling. I just sweated worse than anything. Worse than Nam, even. I couldn't wear anything without getting it clammy with sweat. Without even lifting a finger. I don't know what it was. The strain, I guess." He put one foot on the bottom step, his hand on that knee, then swayed forward a little. "My clothes—everything. Just soaked all the time."

"You were always so careful of how you dressed," Mother said.

"Yeah, they—they cured me of that." Again he looked off into the night. A slight breeze moved his dark hair, made it stand up. "I'd count off time in my head." He laughed softly. "Adding and subtracting all day. Just like in Nam, really. In Nam there wasn't any time to think. Someone was always haranguing you. Here, I had plenty of time to think."

"You've been through a lot," Mother said. "I know."

"It wasn't easy for me to say all that," he said. "I think it deserves something more than that kind of polite observation."

"I'm sorry," Mother said.

"Yeah," he said, looking down at the hand on his knee. "Well, we've all been through a lot."

It was almost as if we had come through it now and were on the other side of it: we could be philosophical.

"I guess you can't help what you feel," he said, shifting, standing back a step. He put his hands in his pockets. "I'm aware of it."

"Thomas, why don't you go inside,," she said.

"Ah," he said. It was almost like a cough. Then: "Let him stay."

She was silent. She stood there with her arms folded tight.

"When I was a kid," he said, not looking at either of us, "my father used to talk about my mother's—troubles. He'd get himself into one scrape or another with her—he didn't have much patience with people who gave her grief about her drinking. At least that was the way he was in the beginning. He'd get tangled up in some brawl or other, defending her. And then he'd bring her home, and he'd explain it to me. He'd say, 'Son, there's a kind of person who just can't make his own soul behave, and your mother's—like that. She wants life to be bright and good, and she spends everything of herself trying to make it that way—only her spirit won't let her rest. It does things inside her that she has no control over.' He was trying to tell me about all that spending and wasting and scrabbling after things to make the something inside a person stop driving, stop hungering all the time for more. Once you give in to it, well, it just never quits."

"I'm going in," Mother said.

"I'm just explaining to you that I understand," he said.

"I'm chilly, Daniel. I'm shivering. I thought you were talking to Thomas."

"I deserve better than that, too."

"All right," she said.

He muttered, "It is getting cooler."

She bent down and kissed me on the cheek. For some reason this surprised me. "Good night, son."

"Good night," I said.

She stood and faced him. "Good night."

"Sleep well," he said.

"Will you be sleeping in the sitting room?"

He said, "Maybe that can wait a day."

When she was gone, he cleared his throat and put one foot on the bottom step again. Then he stepped down, turned, and settled there. He had something in his hand, and he put it to his mouth and seemed to chew. Somewhere far off there was a siren, and behind us I heard Penny's voice. Father heard it, too. He threw whatever he was chewing out into the yard, then leaned back on his elbows and sighed, a long slow expiration of breath, almost like a gasp. "Your mother's strong," he said. "That's what she has." His voice was empty; it unnerved me.

"What're you going to do?" I said.

He looked back at me a moment. "Try to make things work some way."

"I don't understand."

He paused. "She never had anything apart—just hers. You see?"

I didn't see.

"She's the one who's strong," he said. "All those times I was gone, you know, I sort of wanted to be gone. Away from the whole responsibility."

"Stop it," I said.

Now the screen door opened and Russell leaned out, looking dazed, only half awake. "They shot Kennedy," he said.

We stared at him.

"Kennedy's been shot."

"Are you awake, son?" my father asked him. "Kennedy was shot five years ago."

"I'm awake. That's not the—"

"What's your name? Can you say your name?"

"I'm not dreaming or sleepwalking. They shot *this* Kennedy. Just now. Five minutes ago."

We were silent.

"I'm telling you they shot Kennedy. Bobby Kennedy."

"Bobby."

"In California," Russell said. "Five minutes ago."

I stood, and Father came, up the steps. We filed into the house. On the television screen, newsmen were recapping the latest catastrophe in the national life. Russell and I, Mother and Father and Penny gathered in a semicircle before the hectic, surreal glow. Before long, Mrs. Wilson walked in from her rooms, having heard the urgent sound of the voices. She started to question us, then was still while the voices went on talking—the speculation and the horrified reactions. I glanced at Penny; she was wearing those pajamas I remembered from the train. She had her hands over her mouth. No one spoke. Once I saw my father reach over and touch Mother's elbow; she turned, looked at him, and then looked away. A moment later, when Lisa stirred, she hurried back upstairs. Mrs. Wilson sat at the edge of her big easy chair and wept, holding a white handkerchief in one fist over her mouth, looking as though she were about to stand again, but not moving to do so.

Russell kept saying "Jesus, Jesus" over and over, and the aggrieved sound of his voice was profoundly irritating to me, like fingernails being scraped across a blackboard. Presently Mother came down again, having soothed Lisa back to sleep.

"I didn't like him," Mrs. Wilson said about Kennedy. "But my God. What are we coming to? What are we coming to?" She seemed to realize then that she had addressed this to my father, and she stiffened, holding the handkerchief to her mouth.

"Maybe he'll be all right," I said.

"He's a goner," said Russell.

"You be quiet, Russell," his mother told him. "You don't know what you're talking about."

"They shot him in the head."

"Stop it."

"Well, even if he lives he'll be crippled, probably," my father said. Penny sobbed.

"But I'm afraid the boy's right," Father said. "He won't live. Not shot in the head like that."

Penny turned and started upstairs. "I can't watch this." She was crying. Mother followed her.

"Why didn't the Secret Service—" Mrs. Wilson began, then fell silent.

"He went back through the kitchen," Russell said. "It wasn't even planned."

"What're we coming to—oh, my Lord, what're we coming to, what're we coming to...."

"This has been a terrible, terrible day," Father said.

But the day was far from over.

The news grew worse in the next hour or so, and finally Mrs. Wilson struggled out of her chair. "Russell, you'll never make it up for school in the morning."

"It's the end of the year," he said. "They're not doing anything anyway. All the exams are over."

"Russell."

"Whole world's falling apart anyway," he muttered.

"Please keep it down," Mrs. Wilson said to us.

Father turned the television off. Mrs. Wilson sobbed again, and started through the hallway to her rooms, Russell following her.

"Jesus," Father said.

We climbed the stairs slowly, almost side by side. On the landing he stopped us by putting his hand on my shoulder. "It's going to be tough for a while."

"Yes, sir."

"There's no love lost in Minot."

"Grandfather Tinan wants us to move back there," I said.

He nodded. Then smiled. "Nevertheless." He followed me into the apartment, and I was aware of the strangeness of having him there.

"I'll just look in on Lisa."

We went quietly across the sitting room and into where she lay in a fold of sheets, looking tossed and forlorn. The moon shone through the window and limned her face. Her hair was matted to her forehead; she was glowing with some riot in her dreams, and she looked feverish. "Is she all right?" I said.

He kissed her forehead. "Yes, cool as a cucumber." He adjusted the sheet at her neck, then kissed her again. I stood watching this, and then suddenly I put my arms around him. I hadn't known I would do so. It hadn't been our habit to be very demonstrative, and I think I surprised him a little.

"Hey," he said. He patted my shoulder blades.

I turned from him clumsily, pulling the blankets back from my bunk.

"You all right?" he said.

"Yes, sir," I managed.

"I know," he said gently. "I know, son."

Somehow, out of the tatters of what this day had been, I was gathering the sense that things might improve for us at last: we could return to Minot and start again as a family. This passage in our lives was finally ending. It occurred to me that more than anything else I wanted to go back to Minot, away from the bad feelings of this house.

"Well," he said. "Night."

"Night," I said.

He moved to the doorway of the room, and apparently he saw Penny emerge from Mother's room. Perhaps Penny seemed like a ghost to him at first, in those white pajamas. I heard the small sound of alarm and consternation that rose in his throat at the sight of her. And then I heard Penny's voice: "Oh, you scared me."

There comes a moment in the pathology of a night like this, with death in the air and all the long built-up suspicions and angers working in the soul; the world has conspired to seem just as chaotic and frightening as the poor lone spirit's own little history, and something snaps.

"What the hell is this?" Father said. "What're you doing in there, anyway? Don't you understand it's over?" And he started toward her. "Goddammit, you don't belong here anymore. You're the one causing all this mess. Get out—get out of here."

From the doorway of my room I saw her, a silver-white shape in the dimness, edging toward the entrance of the apartment, her back to the partition. He was a darkness, coiled, moving slowly at an angle to cut her off.

"Don't you touch me," she said. "You stay away from me. Connie, tell him to leave me alone."

"Daniel," Mother said from the doorway of her room.

"Don't you remember where you live?" Father said. "Get out. Get out!"

"You can't order me around," Penny said. "You're the one who doesn't belong here."

Father jerked a small table out of his way, and the lamp there fell and shattered. She screamed, and Mother shouted, "Daniel!"

For a brittle instant, no one moved or spoke or even quite breathed, and then Lisa woke, crying. It was as though we were all listening to Lisa, who moaned and then said, "Penny?"

This seemed to strike something through my father. He said, "You —goddam you—"

Penny bolted to the entrance of the hall and out, and he started after her in the sound of Mother's shouting: "Daniel, no! Stop! Stop it!" They scrabbled up the stairs to her room, and Mother followed them. The whole house was quaking with noise now—shouts, screams, more breaking glass. The floor shook from the force of the struggle, and I made my way up to where they were, realizing with a sick-feeling swoon that part of me wanted to see Penny hurt, wanted to watch as she was humiliated or beaten. I felt the thrill and recoiled from it, reaching the top step and somehow managing to propel myself into the room. What I found there sent a roar up out of my throat. Mother lay on her side by the open closet door with her hands to her face, crying. Penny had fallen across her bed, and Father loomed above her. He had torn the pajama top open and now held her arms down, his knee pressing against the fleshy outside of her thigh where she'd crossed one leg over the other to protect herself. "Thomas!" Mother shouted from the floor. "Stop him!"

All this in a single flashing instant. And then I was grappling with him, my father, moving with him in a terrible staggering dance, our shadows pitching crazily on the walls under the single wildly swinging ceiling light, my hands on the hard bones of his shoulders, and all around us the cries and shouts of the others, as now he surged upward, seemed to lift out of my grip, something inside me spilling over, and suddenly I was in a weird floating space, looking through gauze, hearing another kind of roaring. I couldn't focus my eyes and I was astonished to realize that I was no longer standing—the floor was punishing my back, and across the span of it I saw Mother rise, still crying. She scrambled to me, kneeled, and lifted my head. I looked into her face, and briefly I believed that I had spoken to her, but no words had come.

And then it was over, whatever it had been. I saw my father in the doorway, breathing like a runner; I observed the light on his gleaming arms, the tight musculature there. He hesitated, then stepped over Russell, who was on his stomach in the doorway, having tripped running up the stairs. I stood and moved with Mother to where Russell was also standing now.

Father descended without looking back. Penny remained on her bed, the blanket thrown over her, crying but without much sound, her face into the pillow.

"Are you all right?" Mother said to me.

"Yes, I think so."

"Your nose is bleeding. You're bleeding."

"I'm okay."

She turned and reached for Penny's hand, sitting on the edge of the bed.

"Get away," Penny said. "All of you. Please."

"Go on," Mother said to Russell and me.

"All of you," Penny said.

We made our way down to the landing, where Mrs. Wilson stood with her arm around Lisa. "I won't have this," she kept saying. "I won't have this."

"Where is he?" I said to Mother.

Russell started down to the living room.

"I don't want any more, please," Mrs. Wilson said, following him. "I want everybody out—everybody. I'll get a job at the prison."

Mother knelt and put her arms around Lisa, who seemed too dazed to notice.

I started down the hall to Father's room.

"Thomas. Leave it alone now. Stop it—you're bleeding."

So I came back and went into the apartment and tended to myself. The bleeding had mostly stopped. My shirt front was covered; it was as if someone had splashed the blood on me. I combed my hair, put a clean shirt on, and then went past Mother and Lisa, who had lain down together on the couch in the sitting room.

"Where are you going?"

"I don't know," I said.

"Leave it alone, Thomas."

"I can't sleep," I said. "I'm going downstairs."

"It's the middle of the night."

"There's the assassination coverage." I said this with a kind of brutal evenness of tone.

"Thomas, for God's sake."

"Please," I said. "I'm all right."

Downstairs, I found Mrs. Wilson sitting at the dining room table, staring into space. Russell had turned on the television, which showed five people discussing the sick society. The phrase was used two or three times by one of them—a thin, reedy man in a black suit whose lower lip drooped while he waited to speak, as if pulled down by some invisible weight in the skin.

"Kennedy's still hanging on," Russell said.

I went out onto the porch, where Father was sitting alone on the top step, his hands resting on his knees. He stared at the street, as though waiting for someone to pull up.

"I know how you feel about her," he said without turning around.

I said nothing.

Now he did turn. He studied me a moment, then went back to watching the dark street.

"Anybody could see it. I didn't mean to pop you."

We could hear Mother's voice now as she tried to get Penny to open her door and talk. Penny asked to be let alone.

"Goddam you," I said to my father's back. And in an odd way my anger was for two things: what he had done, and what the fact of it had made me feel in that harrowing minute before I got to the top of the stairs. I said the words, but it felt all wrong. It felt like something I'd been given to recite.

"You're an upstanding boy," he said. "So was I."

I was silent.

"Well, I was once. Christ—I didn't mean to hit you like that."

I was standing just outside the door. "God," I said, starting to cry.

"Go on inside, son. Nobody's that bad hurt."

I left him there and went back up to our rooms, where I found Mother sitting on her bed with Lisa. We had come so far, we three. We had been through so much together.

"Come here," my mother said.

And I went to her. I sat down and allowed her to put her arm around me. We were quiet. Now and again Lisa made a small sobbing sound. We heard the house settling down, and at last Father's footsteps on the hall floor and the stairs. He came to the landing and hesitated, then went to his room; the door there opened and closed. Mother leaned back, adjusted the pillow behind her, and I lay back with her. Lisa had begun to snore, but this was not restful sleep. "Turn the light out, Thomas."

I did so.

"Try to sleep," she murmured.

The day ended this way.

The General Retires

Nguyen Huy Thiep

ONE

When I wrote these lines I stirred up some emotions which time had effaced in a few friends of mine, and went as far as to disturb the peace of my father's grave. I was forced to do this by a feeling that I had to defend my father's memory, and it is for this reason that I ask my readers to forgive my inadequate pen.

My father, Thuan, was the oldest child of the Nguyen family. The Nguyen family was a very large one, and its male descendants outnumbered those of all the other families in the village, except possibly for the Vu. My grandfather had left the village to become a Confucian scholar and later returned to teach. He had two wives. His first wife died a few days after giving birth to my father, and so he remarried. His second wife was a cloth dyer. I never set eyes on her. All that I heard about her was that she was a very cruel woman. Living with his stepmother, my father had such a bitter childhood that he ran away from home when he was twelve. He joined the army and rarely came home.

Of course, after several years, he came back to the village to get married. But this marriage was certainly not a love match. He had ten days' leave and a great deal of business to attend to. Love has certain requirements, and among these is time.

As I grew up, I didn't know anything about my father at all. I'm sure my mother knew just as little about him, for his whole life had been devoted to war.

I got a job, married, had children. My mother aged. My father was still away on far-flung campaigns. Now and then, he passed by, but his visits were always short. His letters were also short, although reading between the lines I felt they contained a lot of love and concern.

I was the first child, and I have to thank my father for everything. I was able to study and to travel overseas. The material well-being of the family was also due to the arrangements he made. My house is on the outskirts of Hanoi. It was built eight years before my father retired. It's a handsome, but rather uncomfortable country house. I built it from the plans of a well-known architect who was a friend of my father. He was a colonel whose only experience was in building barracks.

At the age of seventy, my father retired with the rank of Major-General.

Even though I knew he was about to retire, I was still amazed when he came home. My mother was already senile (she was six years older than my father), and so I was the only one with special feelings about his return. The children were still young, and my wife knew very little about him because we married when he was out of contact with us for a long time during the war. Nevertheless, my father always had a position of honor and pride in the family. All the relatives and everyone else in the village placed great store on his reputation.

My father returned home with very few belongings. He was in good health. He said: "My life's work is over." I said: "Yes." He laughed. A mood of excitement spread throughout the house, and the long drawn-out welcome home left everyone overwrought for a couple of weeks. With our life in disorder, there were days when we didn't eat the evening meal until midnight. Visitors flocked to the house. My wife said: "This can't go on." I had a pig slaughtered and went to invite everyone in the village to share in the excitement. Although my village is near the city, the customs of the countryside are still very strong.

It wasn't until a month later that I finally had the opportunity to sit down and have a family discussion with my father.

TWO

Before I continue with the story, permit me to say something about my family.

I am thirty-seven years old, and I work as an engineer at the Physics Institute. My wife, Thuy, is a doctor at the Maternity Hospital. We have two daughters, one fourteen, one twelve. As I've indicated, my old mother is muddled and spends her time sitting in the same place all day.

Apart from this, the household includes Mr. Co and Miss Lai, his dotty daughter.

Mr. Co is sixty years old and comes from Thanh Hoa. My wife met him and his daughter after a fire had burnt down their house and left them destitute. Because my wife felt they were good people, she took pity on them and arranged for them to live with us. They live separately down in the outbuilding and keep to themselves, but my wife provides for them. They are not registered inhabitants of the household, and so, like other people in the city, they aren't eligible for the provision of basic rations and necessities from the state.

Mr. Co is gentle and patient. He takes responsibility for the garden, the pigs, the chickens, and the dogs. My wife has a business raising Alsatian dogs. At the beginning, I didn't suspect that this business would be so profitable. However, it has become our main source of income. Although Miss Lai is simple, she is still able to work hard and is good at household chores. My wife taught her how to cook pork crackling and mushrooms and braised chicken. Miss Lai said: "I never eat that kind of food." It's true, she doesn't either.

Neither my wife and I nor the children have to worry about housework. Everything from the cooking to the washing is given to Mr. Co and his daughter to attend to. My wife keeps a tight rein on our expenses. I'm always busy with something and I'm presently devoting myself to an engineering project that involves the application of electrolysis.

There is something else I should say: the relationship between my wife and me is amicable. Thuy is well educated and lives the life of a modern woman. We each have our own way of thinking, and our views on life are relatively simple. Thuy is as well in control of the family economy as she is of the children's education. As for me, it seems to me that I'm old-fashioned, awkward, and full of contradictions.

THREE

To return to the family discussion I was having with my father. He said: "Now that I'm retired, what shall I do?" "Write your memoirs," I suggested. "No!" he replied. "Breed parrots," said my wife. Around town, many people were breeding parrots and nightingales. "Breed them to make money?" my father asked. My wife didn't answer. "We'll see!" said my father.

He gave everyone in the house, including Mr. Co and Miss Lai, four metres of military cloth. "You are very egalitarian," I joked. "That's my rule of life," he replied. My wife said: "With everyone in a uniform the house will become ؛ barracks." Everyone burst out laughing.

My father wanted to live in a room in the outbuilding like my mother, bu my wife wouldn't hear of it. This saddened my father. It troubled him that my mother lived and ate by herself. "This is because she is disturbed," my wife explained. My father brooded.

I couldn't understand why my two daughters rarely went near their grandfather. I let them study foreign languages and music. They were always busy. On one occasion my father said: "What books have you girls got for me to read?" Mi smiled and Vi said: "What do you like to read, Grandfather?" "Whatever's easy," replied my father. "We haven't got any books like that," the girls said in unison. I took out a subscription to the daily paper for him. He didn't like literature—he found today's literary styles difficult to appreciate.

One day when I got home from work, my father was standing near the row of kennels and chicken coops my wife had set up for her business. I could see he was not happy and said: "What's the matter?" "Mr. Co and Miss Lai have a very hard life," he answered. "Their work is never finished. I want to give them a hand, if it's all right." "Let me ask Thuy," I said. "Father was a general," replied my wife. "Now that he has retired he is still a general. Father is a commander; if he acts like an ordinary soldier, everything will be thrown into disorder." My father said nothing.

Although my father was retired, he had many visitors. This surprised and pleased me. But my wife said: "Don't be so glad, Father. They are only relying on you for help. Don't tire yourself." My father laughed: "It's nothing at all. I'm only writing letters like this one: "Dear N, Commander in Chief of Military District....I'm writing this letter to you, etc....in over fifty years this is the first time I have celebrated the third day of the third month under my own roof. When we were out on the battlefield, we often dreamed, etc....Do you remember the village on the side of the road where Miss Hue made some dumplings with moldy flour? She got it all over her, even her back....There is a person here I know named M. who wants to work under your command, etc...." Can't I write letters like that?" I said: "Yes." My wife said: "No, you can't!" My father scratched his chin. "It's only a small request they're asking of me," he said.

My father usually put his letters in stiff official envelopes, 20 cm by 30 cm, marked "Ministry of National Defense," and gave them to someone reliable to deliver. After three months, he was out of official envelopes. He then made his own with exercise book covers of the same size, 20 cm by 30 cm. A year later, he put his letters into the ordinary envelopes that are on sale at the post office counter at ten for five dong.

In July of that year, that is three months after my father retired, one of my uncles, Mr. Bong, held a wedding for his son.

FOUR

Mr. Bong and my father are half-brothers. Bong's son, Tuan, works an ox-cart. Both Bong and his son are alarming characters: they're as big as giants and they talk like daredevils. This was Tuan's second marriage. His first wife wouldn't take his beatings any more and left him. In court he testified that she had left him for someone else, and the court was forced to release him. His wife-to-be, Kim Chi, taught at a kindergarten. She was from a well-educated family, but had somehow got involved with him. It was said he'd made her pregnant. Kim Chi is a beautiful girl, and as Tuan's wife it was certainly a case of "a sprig of jasmine in a field of buffalo shit." Basically, we aren't fond of Mr. Bong and his son. The trouble is that blood is thicker than water, and we can't avoid them on important anniversaries and festivals. Nevertheless, we ignore them most of the time.

Bong likes to say: "Damn these intellectuals! They despise working people! It's only because I have respect for their father that I haven't kept clear of their house." Even though he spoke like this, Bong still came to borrow money. My wife was strict and always forced him to sign a security note. This made him very indignant. He'd say: "I'm their uncle, yet if I overlook a debt they behave just like landlords." He still overlooked many of his debts.

Bong talked with my father about his son's wedding: "You must act as the Master of Ceremonies. Kim Chi's father is a Deputy Chief of a Department, you are a General, you two are of "the same social class". The bride and groom need to have your blessing. What value am I as an ox-cart coolie?" My father consented. The wedding on the edge of the city was a ridiculous vulgar affair. Three cars. Filtered cigarettes that were replaced by roll-your-owns towards the end of the dinner. There were fifty trays of food but twelve were left untouched. The bridegroom wore a black suit and a red tie. I had to lend him the best tie in my wardrobe. I say "lend," but I wasn't sure I'd ever get it back. The best men were six youths wearing identical khaki outfits and wild beards. At the beginning of the wedding the orchestra played "Ave Maria." One fellow from the same ox-cart cooperative as Tuan jumped up and sang a frightful solo:

> O...eh...my poor little roasted chicken
> I've wandered all over the world
> Looking to find some money
> O money, fall into my pocket
> O...eh...my sad little roasted chicken.

After that it was my father's turn. He was bewildered and miserable. He had over-prepared his speech. A clarinet punctuated each sentence by blaring stupidly after each full stop. Firecrackers went off noisily. Young children provided a nonsensical commentary. My father held the paper so tightly his body trembled, and he skipped over a number of paragraphs. He was hurt and frightened by the motley mob that milled around and was rudely indifferent to his speech. His new relative, the Deputy Department Chief, also became frightened, and spilt wine all over the bride's dress. You couldn't hear a thing. The raw band drowned everything out with happy songs from the Beatles and Abba.

After that, my father became involved in something the likes of which he had never experienced before. This was when Kim Chi had a baby only a few days after the wedding. Mr. Bong's family was thrown into chaos. Bong got drunk and threw the bride out of the house. Tuan took a knife and stabbed at his father who fortuitously slipped over and avoided the attack. As she didn't have any way of keeping herself, my father had to take in his brother's daughter in-law. My family had two extra mouths to feed. My wife didn't say anything. Miss Lai had more duties. It was fortunate that, as well as being simple, she also liked children.

FIVE

One night I was reading the Russian magazine, *Sputnik,* when my father came in quietly. "I want to discuss something with you," he said. I made some coffee which my father didn't drink. "Have you been paying attention to what Thuy's been doing?" he asked. "It gives me the creeps."

The Maternity Hospital where my wife worked carried out abortions. Every day, she put the aborted fetuses into a Thermos flask and brought them home. Mr. Co cooked them for the dogs and pigs. I had in fact known about this, but overlooked it as something of no importance. My father led me out to the kitchen and pointed to a pot full of mash in which there were small lumps of fetus. I kept silent. My father cried. He picked up the Thermos flask and hurled it at the pack of Alsatians: "Vile! I don't need wealth that's made of this!" The dogs barked. My father went off up to the house. My wife came in and spoke to Mr. Co: "Why didn't you put it through the meat grinder? Why did you let Father see it?" Mr. Co stammered: "I forgot, I'm sorry, Aunt."

In December, my wife called someone and sold the whole pack of Alsatians. She said: "Stop smoking those imported Galang cigarettes. This year our income is down by 27,000 dong and our expenditure is up by 18,000, leaving us 45,000 out of pocket."

Kim Chi recovered from the birth of the child and went to work. "I'm grateful to everyone here," she said, "but now I must leave." "Where will you go?" I asked, for Tuan had been thrown into prison for being a hoodlum. Kim Chi took her child back to her parents' house. My father accompanied her and went as far as hiring a private taxi for the trip. He also took advantage of the occasion to spend the day with Kim Chi's father, the Deputy Department Chief. He had just come back from a mission to India and gave my father a piece of printed silk and fifty grams of tiger balm. My father gave the silk to Miss Lai and the tiger balm to Mr. Co.

SIX

Before New Year's Day, Mr. Co said to my wife and me: "I wish to ask you both a favor." "What is it?" asked my wife. Mr. Co broached the subject in a roundabout way. Basically, he wanted to visit his home village. While living with us for six years, he had made an effort to put some money aside, and, in accordance with custom, he wanted to go back to exhume his wife's remains and rebury them in a new grave. After so long away, he was sure the price of coffins would have fallen. "Fidelity to the dead is our first duty," he said, quoting an ancient aphorism. After living so long in the city, he also wanted to visit his village to make his relatives feel happy that he remembered them. He had been away a long time now, but even after it's been dead three years "a fox looks back to the mountain." My wife cut in: "So when do you want to go?" Mr. Co scratched his head: "I want to go for ten days and return to Hanoi on the 23rd, before the New Year." My wife made a calculation: "All right. Thuan (Thuan is my name), do you think you can get some time off work?" "I think so," I said. Mr. Co continued, "We would like to invite your father to come with us for the trip," he said. "I don't like that idea. What would he say?" my wife responded. "He's already agreed," said Mr. Co. "Without him, I wouldn't have thought of moving my wife's grave." "How much money do you have?" inquired my wife. Mr. Co replied: "I have 3,000 dong, your father gave me 2,000, that makes 5,000." My wife said: "All right. Don't take the 2,000 from Father. I'll make it up and give you 5,000 more. That means the three of you will have 10,000. You'll be able to go."

Before they left, my wife cooked a big dinner. The entire family, including Mr. Co and Miss Lai, sat down to eat. Miss Lai was very happy, wearing a new dress that was made from the military material my father had given her when he returned home. Mi and Vi teased her: "You're the prettiest, Lai." Miss Lai laughed gently: "No, I'm not. Your mother is the prettiest." My wife said to her: "When you go, make sure you look after my father-in-law on the trip." My father said: "Perhaps I shouldn't go?" Mr. Co was concerned by this comment. "Oh dear," he cried, "I've already sent a telegram to say you're coming. It would tarnish your reputation." My father sighed: "What reputation have I got to lose?"

SEVEN

My father went to Thanh Hoa with Mr. Co and Miss Lai on a Sunday morning. On the Monday night, I was watching television, when I heard a "thump" and ran quickly outside to find that my mother had collapsed in a corner of the garden. She had been helpless for the last four years; she had to be fed and taken outside. Each day, Miss Lai had attended to her without any trouble. But this day, with Miss Lai gone, I had given her her meals, but forgotten to take her to the toilet. I helped my mother inside with her head slumped down on her chest. I couldn't see any sign of an injury. I stayed awake half the night watching her. Her body was very cold and her eyes were wild. I was afraid and called my wife. Thuy said: "Mother is old." Next day, my mother wouldn't eat. The day after that, she still wouldn't eat and made no attempt to go outside. I washed her underwear and changed her sleeping mat. Some days this happened a dozen times. I knew that Thuy and my two daughters couldn't stand filth, so I always washed and changed her clothes—not in the house, but down at the canal. She continued to bring up the medicine she took.

On the Saturday, my mother suddenly stood up. She went by herself for a stroll around the garden. She was able to eat. I said: "That makes me happy." My wife didn't say anything, and, that afternoon, I saw her put away ten metres of white cloth and heard her call the carpenter. "Prepared, were you?" I asked. My wife replied: "No."

Two days later, my mother fell ill again. She rejected food and had to be helped out to the toilet as before. She went into a rapid decline, excreting a stinking thick brown liquid. I poured her some ginseng. My wife said: "Don't give Mother any ginseng. It'll only make her worse." I cried. It had been a very long time since I'd cried like that. My wife was silent, then she said: "It's up to you."

Mr. Bong came over to visit. He said: "The way she writhes around on the bed is terrible." He then asked my mother: "Hey there, do you recognize me, Sister?" My mother said: "Yes." "So who am I?" Bong asked again. "A person," said my mother. Mr. Bong cried out: "So you care for me the most. The whole village treats me like a dog. My wife calls me an oaf. My son, Tuan, calls me a scoundrel. Only you call me a person."

This was the first time I'd seen this ill-mannered, venturesome ox-cart driver turn into a child before my eyes.

EIGHT

My father returned home six hours after my mother died. Mr. Co and Miss Lai were distraught. "It's our fault. If we'd been at home, Grandmother wouldn't have died." "Nonsense," said my wife. "Oh Grandma," Miss Lai cried, "you've cheated me! Why didn't you let me look after you?" Mr. Bong laughed. "You want to look after her, but you went away. I'll close the coffin." As he prepared my mother's body for the shroud, my father cried and asked Mr. Bong: "Why did she leave us so soon? Do all old people die as wretchedly as this?" "You don't know what you are saying," Mr. Bong replied. "Everyday, thousands of people in our country die in shame and pain and sorrow. For you soldiers, its different: one shot—bang—that's a sweet way to go."

I had a temporary shelter built and told the carpenter to make a coffin. Mr. Co busied himself around the pile of timber my wife had cut the day before. "Are you afraid we'll steal the wood?" the carpenter yelled out. Mr. Bong asked: "How thick are these boards?" "Four centimeters," I replied. "What!" exclaimed Mr. Bong. "You could furnish a whole lounge with this. When has anyone ever made a coffin with such good wood? When you move the grave, make sure you give me these boards." My father sat silently and looked deeply pained.

Mr. Bong called out: "Hey, Thuy, boil me a chicken and cook me a pot of steamed rice." "How many measures of rice, Uncle?" said my wife. "Good heavens," said Mr. Bong, "will you continue to speak so sweetly after today? Three measures." My wife turned to me and said: "Oh, your relatives are dreadful."

Mr. Bong asked me: "Who controls the finances in this house?" "My wife," I answered. Mr. Bong said: "That's the everyday expenses. I'm asking about who's looking after the funeral expenses." "My wife," I answered. Mr. Bong said "Good heavens, my boy! That can't be. She's of different flesh and blood. I'll speak to your father." "Let me," I said. Mr. Bong said: "Give me 4,000. How many trays of food do you intend to serve at the funeral feast?" "Ten trays," I answered. "That's not enough to touch the insides of the coffin bearers," said Mr. Bong. "Go and talk to your wife. You need forty." I gave him 4,000 dong and went into the house. My wife said: "I've already heard. I'm counting on thirty trays at 800 dong each—three eights are twenty-four, 24,000. Other expenses, 6,000. I'll worry about getting the food. Miss Lai can arrange the banquet. Don't listen to Bong. He's an uncouth old man." "Mr. Bong has already taken 4,000," I said. "You disappoint me so much," complained my wife. "I'll ask for it back, all right?" I said. "Let it go," she said. "Regard it as a payment for his services. The old man's good enough, but he's poor."

A traditional orchestra of four musicians arrived. My father went out to meet them just before my mother's body was placed in the coffin at four in the afternoon. Mr. Bong pried her mouth open and placed nine dong inside it with a coin bearing the Emperor Khai Dinh's seal and an aluminum dime. "To take you on the ferry," he said. He then placed a pack of assorted playing cards inside the coffin: "She always used to play cards," Mr. Bong added for good measure.

That night, I kept vigil over my mother's coffin, with my mind wandering in aimless thoughts. Death will come to us all, to each and every one of us.

Out in the courtyard, Mr. Bong sat playing cards with the coffin bearers. Whenever he got a bad hand he ran in and bent low in prayer before my mother's coffin: "I beg you, Sister, please help me clean out their pockets."

My daughters Mi and Vi kept vigil with me. Mi asked: "Why must you pay to go on death's ferry? And why put money in Grandmother's mouth?" Vi said: "You have to keep it in your mouth to eat, don't you, Father?" "You children don't understand," I said through my tears. "I don't understand either. It's a superstition." Vi said: "I understand. In life people don't know how much money they'll need. In death it's the same."

I felt very lonely. So did my daughters. So did the whole crowd of gamblers. So did my father too.

NINE

It was only 500 metres in a direct line from my house to the cemetery, but the main path to it through the village gate ran for two kilometers. The path was too narrow for a hearse, and so the coffin had to be carried. Thirty bearers took it in turns to carry the coffin, many of whom I didn't know. They carried the coffin without any sense of the occasion, much as though they were carrying a house post. They chewed betel, smoked, and chatted as they went. When they rested, they stood and sat willy-nilly around the coffin. One of them stretched out on the ground and said with satisfaction: "It's really cool. If we weren't so busy, I could nap here till nightfall." Mr. Bong urged them on: "Hey there," he said, "let's get going, we've still got to get back for the banquet."

So the procession moved on. Supported by a walking stick, I moved backwards in front of the coffin in accordance with the proper custom. Mr. Bong said: "When I die, my coffin bearers will all be gamblers, and pork won't be served at the funeral feast. Dog meat will." "Oh Brother, you are not joking at a time like this, are you?" my father said sadly. Mr. Bong fell silent, then cried: "Dear Sister! You've cheated me by going like this....You've abandoned me...." I thought "Why cheat? Is it really possible for the dead to cheat the living? Is this cemetery full of cheats?"

After the burial everyone returned to the house. Twenty-eight trays of food had been placed out for the guests. As I looked at them, I was full of admiration for Miss Lai's work. Each table called out: "Where's Miss Lai?" "Here....Here," she twittered, running out with trays of wine and meat. When evening came, she had a bath and changed into fresh clothes. She went to the family altar and cried: "Oh, Grandmother, please forgive me, for not being able to accompany you to your last resting place....The other day you wanted to eat crab soup, but I was too lazy to cook it for you. When I go to the market, for whom can I buy food now?..." I felt very bitter. Thinking back over the previous ten years, I realized I'd never bought Mother a bread roll or a packet of sweets. Miss Lai cried: "Would you be dead now, Grandmother, if I'd stayed at home?" My wife said: "Stop crying." "Let her cry," I retorted angrily. "A funeral without the sound of sobbing would be very sad indeed. Who else in our family cries for Mother?" My wife did not seem to hear me and said: "Thirty-two trays. Are you impressed by my exact calculations?" "Exactly," I answered.

"I'm going to have a look at the horoscope," said Mr. Bong. "Your mother was not buried at an auspicious time. She will have "one change of grave, two funerals, one migration". Does she have a magic charm to ward off demons?" It was my father who answered: "Magic charms are monkey business. In my life I've buried 3,000 people and not one of them with a magic charm." Mr. Bong said: "They had a happy end: "bang", one shot." He raised his index finger in the air and squeezed an imaginary trigger.

TEN

That New Year, my family neither bought any peach blossoms nor wrapped any rice cakes. On the afternoon of the second day, my father's old unit sent people to visit my mother's grave. They made a gift of 500 dong. Mr. Chuong, a former deputy of my father's who had risen to the rank of General, went to the grave and lit incense. Captain Thanh, his aide, drew his pistol and fired three shots into the air. The children in the village would then spread the story that the army had fired a twenty-one gun salute on its visit to Madame Thuan's tomb. Anyway, after he had paid his respects, Mr. Chuong asked my father: "Would you like to come and visit your old unit? There'll be some maneuvers in May, and we'll send a car for you." "Good," said my father, "I would like to come."

Mr. Chuong visited my family's estate and was guided around by Mr. Co. "Your estate is really something: a garden full of trees, a pond full of fish, pig pens, and a chicken coop, a country house. That certainly is reassuring for your retirement," Mr. Chuong said to my father. "My son did it all," replied my father. "Your son's wife did it all," I said. "What about Miss Lai," added my wife. Miss Lai smiled with embarrassment and nodded her head repeatedly as though she was having a fit. "Not so," she said. My father quipped: "Thanks to her, we have a model household with gardens, ponds, and pens."

On the third day, Kim Chi came in a pedicab to visit with her child. My wife gave her 1,000 dong for good luck in the New Year. "Have you had any letters from Tuan?" inquired my father. "No," replied Kim Chi. "It was all my fault," he went on, "I didn't know you were pregnant." "What's so unusual about that?" said my wife. "These days, virgins don't exist. I work at the Maternity Hospital, I know." Kim Chi was embarrassed. I cut in: "Don't talk like that. These days, it really is difficult for a young girl to keep her virginity." Kim Chi cried: "Oh, Thuan, it's so shameful for us women. To give birth to a daughter tears me apart even more." "I've got two daughters too," said my wife. "So you think there's no shame in being a man, do you?" I asked. "Men who have a heart feel shame," said my father. "The bigger the heart, the bigger the shame." "You all talk as though you've gone crazy," said my wife. "That's enough. Eat up. Kim Chi is with us today. I've treated everyone to steamed chicken with lotus hearts. That's what comes from my heart. Eating comes before everything else."

ELEVEN

Not far from our house there lived a young man named Con, whom the children called Confucius. He worked for a fish sauce company. But he also liked poetry and sent some of his poems to the prestigious journal *Literature and Art*. Con frequently came over to visit. He said: "Surrealist poetry is the best." He read me some poems by Lorca and Whitman. I didn't like Con and suspected that our friend visited for reasons that were more adventuresome than anything else. One day, I noticed my wife had a handwritten manuscript on the bed. "They're Con's poems," she said. "Do you want to have a look at them?" I shook my head. "You're getting old," said my wife. An involuntary quiver flickered through my body.

One day I was busy at work and came home late. My father met me at the gate and said: "Young Con has been over here since nightfall. He and your wife have been giggling in there, and he still hasn't gone. This is intolerable." "Go to bed, Father," I said. "What's the use of paying attention?" My father shook his head and went to his room. I pushed my motor bike out on to the road and sped aimlessly around the streets until it ran out of petrol. I pushed my bike to the corner of a park and sat down like a vagabond with nowhere to go. A girl with a powdered face walked past and said: "Hey, there, do you want to come with me?" I shook my head.

Con avoided me. Mr. Co hated him and said to me one day: "Why don't you just go and give him a hiding?" I almost nodded my head, but then thought, "Leave it."

I went to the library and borrowed a few books. Reading Lorca and Whitman I had the vague feeling that great artists are the loneliest people. Suddenly, I saw Con was right. I was just furious at him for being so ill-bred. Why didn't he give his poems to someone other than my wife to read?

My father said: "You are weak. You put up with this because you can't live alone." "No, it's not that. Life is full of jokes," I said. "So you think life is a farce?" asked my father. "Not a farce," I said, "but it's not very serious either." "Why do I feel as though I'm lost?" my father muttered.

My Institute decided to send me down to the south to do some work. I said to my wife: "It's OK if I go, isn't it?" "No. Don't go," she answered. "Will you fix the bathroom door tomorrow?" she then asked. "It's broken. The other day Mi was having a bath, and Con went through on some rotten pretext and scared her out of her wits. I've already barred the door to that vile fellow," she explained, before bursting into tears. "I really have failed you and the children," she cried. I couldn't bear it and went out. If Vi had been there, she would have asked me: "Hey, Father, they are crocodile tears, aren't they?"

TWELVE

In May, my father's old unit sent a car to pick him up. Captain Thanh carried a letter from General Chuong. My father trembled as he opened it. It read: "...we very much hope you can come...but only come if you are free, we won't press you." I thought my father shouldn't go, but it was an awkward moment to say anything. My father had aged a great deal since he retired. But, holding the letter that day, he looked so young and sprightly. I was happy too. My wife prepared some food and clothes and said to put them into a travel-case. My father said: "Put them in my pack."

My father went out and said good-bye to everyone in the village, then went out to my mother's grave and told Captain Thanh to fire three shots into the air. That night he called Mr. Co in to give him 2,000 dong and told him to have a tombstone engraved and sent back to Thanh Hoa to mark his wife's grave. Next, my father called Miss Lai in and said: "Make sure you get married." Miss Lai burst into tears: "I'm so ugly, nobody will marry me. I'm also simple." "My dear child, don't you understand that simplicity gives us the strength to live," said my father, choked with emotion. I didn't realize these words were an omen that he would not return from this trip.

Before he got into the car, my father took a small exercise book out of his pack and gave it to me. "I've written a few things in here," he said, "take a look at them, my son." Mi and Vi said good-bye to their grandfather. Mi asked: "Are you going off to battle, Grandfather?" "Yes," he answered. Vi sang the first line of the song which went "The road that leads to battle is very beautiful in this season," then added, "isn't it, Grandfather?" "You cheeky girl!" my father scolded affectionately.

THIRTEEN

A few days after my father had left there was a hilarious incident at home. It happened that Mr. Co and Mr. Bong were cleaning the mud out of the pond (my wife paid Mr. Bong 200 dong a day and provided him food), when they suddenly saw the bottom of a waterjar that had risen to the surface. The two men dug eagerly, then found another waterjar. Mr. Bong was sure that people in the old days had used the jars to bury their jewelry. The two men told my wife. Thuy went out and had a look and also waded into the pond. Then Miss Lai, Mi, and Vi followed her. The whole family was covered in mud. My wife had the pond partitioned off and hired a Kholer water pump to empty it. The atmosphere was very serious. Mr. Bong was pleased with himself: "Since I saw it first, you'll have to divide the booty up so that I get one jar." After digging eagerly for a day and turning up two cracked jars with nothing inside them, Mr. Bong said: "There are sure to be more."

The digging went on. Another jar was discovered. It was also broken. The whole household was exhausted. With everyone starving, my wife ordered some bread so that they could regain their strength. The digging continued, and, at a depth of almost ten metres they seized on a porcelain vase. Everyone was overjoyed and thought that they had finally struck gold. When they opened it, they found a string of rusted bronze coins from the Bao Dai era and a pitted medal. Mr. Bong said: "That's enough, I'm dead. I remember now. Many years ago, I robbed Han Tin's house with that gangster, Nhan. We were chased away and Nhan threw the vase into the pond." Everyone burst out laughing. Nhan had been a notorious thief on the outskirts of the city, and Han Tin had joined the French colonial army. He had participated in an anti-German movement during the First World War known as the "southern, silver spitting dragon campaign to expel the German rebels". Both of them had been dead for ages. Mr. Bong said: "It doesn't matter, even if this whole village dies, I'll still have enough ferry money to stuff into their mouths."

The next morning, I heard someone calling at the gate as I woke up. I went out and saw Con standing outside. "The bastard," I thought. "There could be no worse omen for me than this vile lout." Con said: "Thuan, you have a telegram. Your father has died."

FOURTEEN

The telegram was from General Chuong: "Major-General Nguyen Thuan died while on duty at...on....He will be buried at the War Cemetery at...on...." I was stunned. My wife made all the arrangements very quickly. I went out and hired a car and saw that everything was ready when I returned. "Lock the house," my wife said. "Mr. Co is staying behind."

We took the most direct route to Cao Bang along Route One. But when we arrived, my father's funeral rites had been over for two hours.

"We owe your family an apology," said General Chuong. "Not at all. It was his destiny," I replied. "Your father was worthy of great honors," emphasized General Chuong. "So you buried him with military honors did you?" asked. "Yes," he replied. "Thank you, Sir," I said. General Chuong said. "When your father was on the battlefield, he was always where the fighting was." "I know that," I said, "you don't have to tell me more."

I cried like I had never cried before. I now knew what it was like to cry for the death of a father. It seemed to me that this was the biggest lament in the life of a human being. My father's tomb was located in the war cemetery reserved for heroes. My wife brought a camera and took some photos. The next day, we took our leave, even though General Chuong wanted us to stay.

On the way back, my wife told me to drive slowly. For Mr. Bong, it was his first car ride, and he liked it very much. "Our country really is as pretty as a picture," he said joyfully. "Now I understand why we should love the country. Back at home, even though we live near the capital, I don't feel there's anything at all to love." "That's because you know it," said my wife. "Elsewhere people are the same; they then love Hanoi."

"So around we go, turning like the figures on a magic lantern," said Mr. Bong. "People here love it there, and people there love it here; put it all together and that's our country, our people. The homeland forever! The people forever! Hurrah for magic lanterns!"

FIFTEEN

Perhaps I should end my story here. After my father's death, the life of the family returned to what it had been before he retired. My wife went about her work as usual. I completed my electrolysis research. Mr. Co grew quieter, partly because Miss Lai's condition worsened. In idle moments I read over the thoughts my father had noted in the exercise book he gave me before he departed. I feel I understand him better.

What I have written down is an account of the disordered events that took place in our lives during the year or so my father was in retirement. I regard these lines as the incense of incense sticks lit in remembrance of him. If anyone has had the heart to read them, I beg your pardon.

Translated by Greg Lockhart

PART SEVEN

A Walk in the Garden of Heaven

7

In the dry garden where we walked, where stone represents water as well as itself, the Chinese characters for which mean the center or heart of heaven (天 for heaven, 心 for center or heart), there is a mountain represented, Mount Sumeru, the highest peak of every world, every world a Bodhisattva holds in its hands, every world in the universe, and every world we live in, but it also represents the center of infinity, and because infinity has only centers, we were standing everywhere at once, and exchanged what could not be stated except in language which could never be spoken.

But we must speak it. The question is, how many heads do we have and how many arms and how many worlds do we hold, and just how far will we go to end our war.

8

The order of the universe is that there may be none, not like glasses lined up, each dish upon its shelf. And what we think is wild is not.

I want to be reasonable, it is something that interests, even haunts me, but given certain knowledge, how to be is more hellish.

The room here is small, and at times the way wind kicks up over the fence lip reminds me of animal howling and that in turn of an even smaller room, a box of sorts within a building stilted off the ground beneath a tin washboard roof hammered by rain in your country.

Our rooms there were like boxes really, perimeters not unlike the skin, and came to mean everything for each one, for each had the need to live in containment where there was none, to confine ourselves, as one might a crazed dog until it calms.

Perhaps it is not the past I should concern myself with, but not to speak of it and face what is still happening is not possible.

The double bonds of living for something and dying for something are ribbons that trail from us, drag behind or flap from us, and if I could understand it now or ever this business would be done.

I want to be reasonable, it is something I crave and wish I knew how to pray for but cannot pray, not having the faith of it, having seen.

We have friends, then we do not have them because we reach some border across which words cannot manage, across which silence will not bridge, and in the manner of children we stand without explanation or understanding, and there is no necessity that we question it. We learn to ignore those events which remove things in the way that we know of as "Before their time." It's another weapon we aim at our heads.

9

When we stood in the garden and looked at the stone bridges connecting islands on the gravel ocean, I felt the war lift from us in flames, inch by inch flowing into stone like a river on fire.

We ended something walking together, and started something.

I've read the war is over for you, but have never believed it. Victory is no balm for loss. Any of us may celebrate a moment, but we live a long time, and finality is not what we need, compassion is what we need. Let the future think about the war being over, because then it will be.

We can't afford to heal. If we do, we'll forget, and if we forget, it will start again. When you're thrown off a cliff from a horse, it's best to limp around horses.

We've destroyed too much to be sentimental. We know that those above and those below the jungle canopy killed anything that got in the way, and we're all guilty of something. Wars are always lost. Even if you win.

10

I returned to San Francisco sorry about some things I was not able to explain. For example, the army of beggars in our streets, and how badly we treat the poor. The coldness of it, you see, is a symptom of killing nations at a distance, or even up against their breaths. It has also to do with how freedom can be like the end of a rope. It pollutes all notions of beauty, this living in the streets. My wife pointed out that Americans do help one another during floods, earthquakes, and conflagrations. "That's not compassion," I said, "it's convenience—only generosity when there is no disaster counts." I've become so wise, righteous anger makes me happy. We sat in silence after that. Actually, one was washing dishes and one was peeling potatoes, we could hear the rattle of a bottle gleaner digging through the recycle bin on our sidewalk, a jet was passing over, John Lee Hooker was singing on the radio, the neighbors were having a horrible fight, there was a crash in the intersection, one of our cats spit at the other, and the phone rang but we ignored it, so it wasn't really silent. Then she said, "We would all be wealthy if people were born honest." So. Not all understanding comes from the barrel of a gun.

11

Stretched flat in deep grass   resolute about the sickness of pursuits   watching a moth on a beer can lip swing its curled tongue like an elephant trunk across the water dots.   The only thing I know about fame and success is that they are stumbling blocks when they commandeer my attention.   My real function is to think about things and listen, drunk and lazy, to the buzz in the grass, the millions of insects who do not care what I think.   I'm tired of the world of people—they're not to be trusted on the whole because they don't understand death.   It's not that they're unhappy, it's just that they don't understand death. I'm not above or beneath them, I'm just sometimes not one of them.   I've seen too much to be fooled into thinking we know what we are doing.   Maybe I'm getting too arrogant for my own good, but even that sounds stupid in the face of death.   I understand the insects in the deep grass, even if I can't repeat what they say.

12

I've come out to the cliffs above the Pacific Ocean before sunset. I told you my childhood friends were all killed in the war, and you told me similar things. It wasn't difficult for me to also tell you I was never angry at your country. What was difficult, was to tell you how angry I am at my own.

Pelicans overhead. The rose-colored hood of a finch in the bushes. I sit on a railroad tie post on a high cliff at the edge of America.

Tourists drive up, take pictures, go home.

A cormorant. A sailboat. An Army gunship choppers over the beach.

Behind me, an Army base. In front of me, the sea.

I'm waiting for the sun to set, but it will not.

Epilogue

Gloria Emerson

That day in the Danang airport, the great aorta of the U.S. military in southern Vietnam, we saw something so startling that all speech stopped and a great hush took hold. Two American soldiers were rushing two Vietnamese prisoners through the crowded terminal to an exit where they would be taken to their doom. The sight of the Vietnamese with those milk-white blindfolds of double thickness, quick-stepping in paper slippers used in the hospitals, stunned the G.I.'s who rarely saw the enemy so close. Sprawled on the floor talking to a boy from North Carolina I suddenly hoped to see a mutiny among the troops, as if the soldiers with their love beads and peace symbols and Fuck the Army on their helmet covers might rise up in disgust and stop the war. One of the captives had a ribbon of black hair down her back and I would help her get away. But no one moved and all stayed mute. I could see the prisoners being lifted into the truck but the guards forgot how light they were and hoisted them too hard so the Vietnamese almost fell forward.

There are many worse stories and I know it but all these years I have wondered how it went for the two of them and if they made it through interrogation. Honoring this small memory is the only way to pay homage when there is little else to do. In this remarkable anthology the "enemy" at last shares memories with us that we have never heard before and lets Americans come very close to the men and women who would not submit to our fearful technology and firepower, artillery and better equipped, better-fed troops. Bring the coonskin back and nail it on the wall, President Lyndon Johnson once said, meaning kill them all. *The Other Side of Heaven* dispels at last an American conviction that the old war was only our tragedy, or a ghastly muddle, when it was something so much larger and deeper, so much more ruinous and absurd and heroic as well. Much has been written, and beautifully too—as one sees on the pages of this anthology—about Americans who were rendered unfit by fighting that war. But so little is known by us about the Vietnamese, both opponents and allies, their wounds within, and the memories they carry like huge satchels filled with stone. You have only to read the excerpt from *The Sorrow of War* by Bao Ninh to understand. The narrator is sewn to ghosts, the dead who did not die at all. His job as a soldier was to locate and identify corpses. Bao Ninh writes: "To Kien dead soldiers were fuzzier yet sometimes more significant than the living. They were lonely, tranquil and hopeful, like illusions." Sometimes the men in Kien's group heard the dead playing musical instruments and singing.

Kien and the others are told that they must identify the dead or they will be burdened by their deaths for the rest of their lives. But they are already sentenced men no matter how hard they work.

I have never been back to Vietnam because I am afraid of the ghosts I might conjure, although many friends, who fought there and fought very hard, have gone back and found a peacefulness that they did not think they would ever find. There is a pilgrimage I should make to a village outside of Hanoi for a reunion with a man now in his forties who once sat in my hotel room in Saigon telling me about the war from the other side. He was still so weak from malaria that the interpreter helped him up the stairs. His unit had marched down the Ho Chi Minh trail eleven hours a day and when the malaria attacks came his two closest friends carried him. He missed them grievously and regretted the loss of his diary—each man had one—and the walking stick he carved to be his "third leg." Captured in Quang Nam province in the South he was released when an influential relative in Saigon intervened, possibly with a huge bribe to various province officials. Once, on the trail, his unit passed a group of wounded Southerners in the National Liberation Front, or Viet Cong as the Americans called it, who told them to hurry or the war of liberation would be over. That was upsetting. Another Southerner said not to worry about fighting the Americans. "They have very weak eyes," he said. "If it is sunny they cannot see well." All armies find ways to comfort themselves.

In the South during the war there were so many capricious spirits and phantoms, fortune tellers and astrologers, so many superstitions, that the macabre seemed only what you might expect. The men in an American armored unit would not eat the apricots in their C-rations after the deaths of those who had and they did not want to see you touch them either. On the Saigon-Bien Hoa highway, at the entrance to a huge military cemetery, there was a statue over thirteen feet tall called "Sorrow" who had supernatural powers. Women prayed to him and left joss sticks and incense at his huge boots. The statue was of an ARVN soldier, slumping a little as he sat, his face tired and sad and shut. Some Vietnamese told me the statue walked at night, asking for water or warning people. Others heard him sigh. The sculptor used as his model a corporal who had visited the grave of a friend and then went to a cafe where he ordered two beers. As he drank his beer he talked to the dead man as old friends might. There were some Vietnamese who swore that during Operations Lam Son 719 the statue wept, for they saw the tears. The army trained and equipped and paid for by the Americans had been sent into Laos to cut enemy supply trails, their first large encounter with forces from the North, and suffered an unspeakable defeat. It was a rout, worse than anything the U.S. command imagined in its darkest days.

A survivor of Lam Son 719, who lost a leg and in the hospital saw that severed limb, meets an old friend at a cafe in the lovely story, "The Slope of Life" by Nguyen Mong Giac. They were schoolboys together in the South. The other man has been blinded; he fought with the army that was victorious but both men are wrecked and their lives hang by a thread. There is no bitterness between them, only a sweetness that makes this a different kind of war story, one you do not often read.

Many of the stories here can be described so; there are women in some, and children, Vietnamese and American, those deep inside the war and those way out on the most distant rim until it comes rushing at them full tilt in their own houses. To the young, of course, here and over there, the war is such an old story, a little bit boring perhaps. But there is always a chance they will read these pages and move back in time to understand the suffering, how it took place and how so many were caught.

CONTRIBUTORS

WAYNE KARLIN (editor, contributor) served in the Marine Corps in Vietnam. In 1973 he co-edited and contributed short stories to the first anthology of Vietnam veterans' fiction, *Free Fire Zone*. He has written four novels: *Crossover, Lost Armies, The Extras* and *Us*, and his short fiction has appeared in magazines and has been anthologized in *Swords Into Ploughshares, New Stories from the South,* the upcoming *The Vietnam War in American Songs, Poems and Stories* and *Writing Between the Lines*. He has also worked as a journalist and his non-fiction and reviews have been published in *Gannett Newspapers, The Baltimore Sun* and the *Washington Post*. He has received the *Prairie Schooner* Readers' Choice Award, three Individual Awards in Fiction from the State of Maryland and a fellowship from the National Endowment for the Arts.

LE MINH KHUE (consulting editor, contributor) was born in Thanh Hoa Province. She joined the People's Army of Vietnam at the age of fifteen and spent much of her youth on the Ho Chi Minh (Song My) Trails serving as a member of the Youth Volunteers Brigade (sappers corps) on Routes 15 and 20. From 1969 to 1975 she was a war reporter for *Tien Phong (Vanguard)* and *Giai Phong* (Liberation) Radio. A short story writer and novelist, her works include *Summer's Peak, Distant Stars, Conclusion, An Afternoon Away From the City* and *A Girl in a Green Gown*. She won the Writers' Association national award for best short stories in 1987. Her most recent collections of short stories are *Small Tragedies* (1993) and *Collected Works* (1994). She is an editor at the Writers' Association Publishing House in Hanoi.

TRUONG VU (Truong Hong Son) (consulting editor), an essayist, literary scholar and translator, sits on the editorial boards of some of the major Vietnamese language journals in the United States. A former college physics teacher and an ARVN veteran who left Vietnam in 1976, he lived for a time in the refugee center in the Philippines and then moved to the United States where he earned his advanced degrees in Nuclear Physics and Electrical Engineering. In addition to his literary and artistic life, he makes his living as an Aerospace Engineer for NASA in Greenbelt, Maryland. He is the editor-in-chief of *Doai Thoai, (Dialogue)*, a forum for Vietnamese intellectuals in Vietnam and abroad, and is on the editorial boards of the literary magazines *Hop Luu* and *Van Hoc*. His essays have been published in many anthologies including *A Hundred Flowers Still Bloom in the Homeland*.

JOHN BALABAN, a conscientious objector, served in Vietnam with the International Voluntary Services from 1967 to 1975. Currently the director of the MFA program at the University of Miami, he has been nominated for a National Book Award and is the author of three books of poetry: *After Our War, Blue Mountain* and *Words for My Daughter;* two novels: *Coming Down Again* and *The Hawk's Tale*, and a book of photographs: *Vietnam: The Land We Never Knew*. He has also translated and edited *Ca Dao Vietnam: A Bilingual Anthology of Vietnamese Folk Poetry*.

BAO NINH was born in Hanoi in 1952. He served during the war with the 27th Youth Brigade. His novel, *The Sorrow of War*, about a writer trying to come to grips with his memories of the war and his own ability to love, won the Writers' Association award for best novel in 1990. It has also been published in Great Britain and the United States.

RICHARD BAUSCH was born in 1945 and served during the Vietnam war as an Air Force survival instructor. He is the author of six novels: *Real Presence, Take Me Back, The Last Good Time, Mr. Field's Daughter, Violence* and *Rebel Powers*, and three volumes of short stories: *Spirits, The Fireman's Wife and Other Stories*, and *Rare and Endangered Species*. *The Last Good Time* has been made into a film. His short stories have been anthologized several times in *The O. Henry Awards, The Best American Short Stories* and *New Stories from the South*. He won the National Magazine Award in 1988 and 1990 and was twice nominated for the PEN/Faulkner Award.

LARRY BROWN was born in 1951 in Mississippi and served in the Marine Corps from 1971 to 1973. A former fire captain, he has written the novels *Dirty Work* and *Joe*, and is a widely published short story writer. His first collection of short stories, *Facing the Music* received the Mississippi Institute of Arts and Letters 1989 Award for Literature, and his work has been anthologized in *Best American Short Stories*, and *New Stories From the South*. His latest fiction collection, *Big Bad Love*, was published in 1993, and *On Fire*, a book of essays, was published in 1994.

ROBERT OLEN BUTLER served with the U.S. Army in Vietnam in 1971. He has published a number of novels including *The Alleys of Eden, Sun Dogs, Countrymen of Bones, On Distant Ground, The Deuce*, and *They Whisper*. His short stories have appeared in the anthologies *Best American Short Stories* and *New Stories From the South*. *A Good Scent From A Strange Mountain* received the 1993 Pulitzer prize for fiction.

PHILIP CAPUTO was born in 1943 and served as a Marine platoon leader in Vietnam, later returning to that country in 1975 as a correspondent. Winner of a Pulitzer Prize for his reporting, Caputo has written two memoirs: *A Rumor of War* and *Means of Escape*, and three novels: *Horn of Africa, Delcorso's Gallery* and *Indian Country*.

JUDITH ORTIZ COFER was born in Hormigueros, Puerto Rico. While her father was on sea duty with the U.S. Navy, she spent half of the year living in Puerto Rico and the other half in Paterson, New Jersey throughout her childhood. She has written a collection of prose and poetry, *The Latin Deli*, and her fiction was selected for the *O.Henry Awards* anthology.

DA NGAN (Le Hong Nga) was born in 1952 in Can Tho, Hau Giang Province. She served in the Southern Liberation Force (NLF) during the American War, then in the Hau Giang Literature Center. She is currently an editor in Hanoi, and has written a number of novels and short story collections including *The Warmth of Life, One Day in Life, The Dog's Divorce, Above the Roof of the Widow's House, Her Life Cut Short* and more.

ANDRE DUBUS, who lives in Haverhill, Massahusetts, served in the Marine Corps. He is the author of *The Lieutenant, The Times Are Never So Bad, Finding a Girl in America, Adultery & Other Choices, Seperate Flights, We Don't Live Here Anymore, Voices from the Moon*, and *The Last Worthless Evening*. He has received Fellowships from the Guggenheim Foundation and the National Endowment for the Arts.

GLORIA EMERSON was a foreign correspondent for *The New York Times* in Vietnam from 1970 to 1972. Her articles about Vietnam and other subjects have appeared in *Esquire, Harper's, Saturday Review, Rolling Stone* and *Newsweek*, which chose her as the writer to chronicle the decade of the Seventies in its Sixtieth Anniversary issue. Winner of the George Polk Award for excellence in foreign reporting, she has written three books: *Gaza, Some American Men* and *Winners and Losers: Battles, Retreats, Gains, Losses and Ruins From a Long War*, which won the National Book Award.

GEORGE EVANS, an Air Force medic in Vietnam, is the author of three critically acclaimed books of poetry: *Nightvision, Eye Blade* and *Sudden Dreams*. His poetry has been anthologized in Carolyn Forché's *Against Forgetting; Twentieth Century Poetry of Witness*. He has received two fellowships from the National Endowment for the Arts, a Lannan Literary Fellowship, a California Arts Council Fellowship and a Japanese government Monbusho Fellowship to study the poetry of Japan, where he lived for two years. He lives in San Francisco where he edits *Streetfare Journal*, a program which puts poetry and art on posters in buses nationwide.

LARRY HEINEMANN was born in 1944 in Chicago. In 1966 he served as a combat infantryman with the 25th Division in Vietnam. His short fiction and essays have appeared in many national magazines and he is the author of three novels: *Close Quarters, Paco's Story* and *Cooler by the Lake*. He has been awarded fellowships by the Illinois Arts Council, the National Endowment for the Arts and the John Simon Guggenheim Memorial Foundation. His novel *Paco's Story* won the National Book Award for fiction in 1986 and is currently being made into a film.

HO ANH THAI was born in 1960 in Nghe Tinh. He currently lives in Hanoi. A novelist and short story writer best known for his novel *The Women on the Island* and his short story collection *A Fragment of a Man*, he is a veteran of the fighting against China in 1979 and is currently a columnist for the foreign service magazine *Bao Quoc Te*. His other books include *Men and Vehicles in the Moonlight, The Other Side of the Horizon, Winter Has Come,* and *Out of the Red Fog*. He has won the Hanoi Writers' Association award for best novel written in a five year period. He is also an award winning translator.

HOANG KHOI PHONG (Nguyen Vinh Hien) was born in Hai Duong in 1943. He served in the Army of the Republic of Vietnam. His first major work, *The Rising Sun* was published in 1967 in Vietnam. In 1975 he left Vietnam and is currently living in Southern California. He co-founded the publishing company *Bo Cai* in 1977. Since his arrival in the United States his published work includes *Days N+*, a war memoir, the short story collection *Letters Without Destination*, and *Men of a Hundred Years Ago*, a novel.

THOM JONES served in the Marine Corps. His fiction has appeared in *Harper's, Esquire, The New Yorker* and other magazines, and his stories have been selected for both *Best American Short Stories* and *Prize Stories 1993: The O. Henry Awards*, in which the title story from his collection *The Pugilist at Rest* took first place. The collection was also nominated for the National Book Award in 1994.

WARD JUST was born in Indiana and worked as a correspondent in Vietnam. He has been a staff writer at *Newsweek, The Reporter*, and *The Washington Post* and an editor of *The Atlantic*. A novelist and short story writer, he is the author of two works of nonfiction and ten works of fiction: *A Soldier of the Revolution, The Congressman Who Loved Flaubert, Stringer, Nicholson At Large, A Family Trust; Honor, Power, Riches, Fame, and the Love of Women; In the City of Fear, The American Blues, The American Ambassador*, and *Jack Gance*.

THANHHA LAI was born in 1965 in Saigon and came to the United States with her family in 1975. She covered the Vietnamese community in Orange County, California as a reporter, and in 1990 attended the MFA program at the University of Massachusetts, Amherst, where she began writing fiction. She is one of the new generation of Vietnamese-American writers working in English. Her stories have been published in *The Threepenny Review* and in *The North American Review*.

ANDREW LAM was born in Saigon in 1963 and came to the United States with his family in 1975. Initially a medical student, he discovered a talent for writing both fiction and nonfiction; his subject matter is the tragedies and comedies of Vietnamese-American life and the painful contradictions of exile and adjustment. He is an associate editor at *Pacific News Service* and the winner of the Thomas More Storke International Journalism Award.

LE LUU was born in 1942 in Hai Hung Province. During the American War, he worked as an Army signal man and correspondent on the Ho Chi Minh Trail in the Troung Son Range. He is currently an editor at *Van Nghe Quan Doi* in Hanoi. A novelist, his main works include *Those Who Carry Guns, Near the Sun, Forest Clearing, Border Line, Echoes of Time Past*, and most recently *Stories From the Village of Cuoi* (1993). He won the national award for fiction in 1987.

MA VAN KHANG was born in Hanoi in 1936 and served as a correspondent during the American War. In 1976 he became editor-in-chief of *Lao Dong* Publishing House. He has written three collections of short stories: *Xa Phu, Song of the Moon*, and *A Fine Day*, and five novels: *The Silver Coin, Summer Rain, Borderlands, Leafshedding Season in the Garden*, and *An Unofficial Marriage*. He has won the first prize in *Van Nghe's* short story competittion and the Best Novel prize of the Vietnamese Writers' Association in 1985.

BOBBIE ANN MASON was born in Kentucky. Her first book of fiction, *Shiloh and Other Stories*, won the PEN/Hemingway Award. She is also the author of *The Girl Sleuth, Nabokov's Garden, Spence & Lila, Love Life, Feather Crown* and *In Country*, which was made into a motion picture.

DAVID MCLEAN was born in Granite City, Illinois and curently lives in Brookline, Massachusetts. His father, a career marine, served in Vietnam. "Marine Corps Issue," his first published story, appeared in *The Atlantic* and was selected for the 1993 O. Henry Awards.

NGO TU LAP was the commander of a Naval patrol ship and a military judge before becoming a writer. He has since published two collections of short stories: *Farewell to the Island* and *The Fifteen Day Month*, and is currently an editor at the People's Army Publishing House in Hanoi.

NGUYEN MONG GIAC was born in 1940 in Phu Yen. He began publishing novels, literary essays and criticisms in 1971. His novels included *Residue of a Storm, Bird Songs in an Old Garden, Crosswinds on the Bridge*, and *One Way Street*. In 1981 he left Vietnam and lived in a refugee camp in Indonesia for a year before being granted asylum in the United States in 1982. He currently lives in California and is the editor-in-chief of the *Van Hoc* journal and often contributes to other Vietnamese literary journals. His most recent novels include *The Con River in Deluge, The Horse with Weary Legs, Drifting*, and *A Season of Rough Seas*.

NGUYEN HUY THIEP, born in Hanoi in 1950, spent much of his youth in the rural provinces of Vietnam, where his mother worked as an agricultural laborer. After graduating from the Teacher's College in 1970, during the American bombing campaign, he moved to a remote province where he taught history, wrote and painted. By 1987 he began to be published in the major journals in Vietnam, and in 1988 over twenty of his stories were published. "The General Retires" which appears in this collection is the title story of a collection of Thiep's stories published in England and made into a film in Vietnam.

NGUYEN QUANG LAP was born in 1956 in Quang Binh Province. A People's Army veteran of the American War he is currently secretary of the Quang Tri Writers' Union. He is the author of two short story collections: *An Hour Before Dawn* and *The Call of Sunset*, and a novel, *The Pattern of Black and White Sky*.

NGUYEN QUANG THIEU was born in 1957 in Ha Tay Province. He is a poet and fiction writer, and an editor of *Van Nghe*. In 1993 he won the national prize for poetry for his collection *The Insomnia of Fire*. His other books include *The House of Green Age, The White-haired Woman*, and three novels. His story "Two Village Women" was recently made into a film.

NGUYEN XUAN HOANG was born in Nha Trang in 1940. He taught Philosophy at the Lycee Petrus Ky in Saigon: his first novel *Fogged* was published in 1972, and he edited the Saigon literary magazine *Van*. After coming to the United States in 1985 he became managing editor of the *Nguoi Daily News*, the best known newspaper in the Vietnamese community in the United States. His other works include the novels *Birthday, Scorching Forest, Anytime, Anywhere, The Man with His Head in the Clouds, Desert, Dust and Rags*, and *The Red Roof House*, a collection of stories and poems.

TIM O'BRIEN was born in Minnesota and served in the U.S. Army in Vietnam as a radio man in an infantry company. He is the author of the memoir *If I Die in a Combat Zone* and five books of fiction: *Northern Lights, Going After Cacciato, The Nuclear Age, The Things They Carried*, and *In the Lake of the Woods*. His short fiction has appeared widely and he has been anthologized in the *O. Henry Awards* and *The Best American Short Stories. Going After Cacciato* is the winner of the National Book Award, and the title chapter from *The Things They Carried* won the National Magazine Award in fiction.

BREECE D'J PANCAKE was born in West Virginia. A writer of great talent, he took his own life in 1979 at the age of twenty-six.

PHAN HUY DUONG was born in May of 1945 in South Vietnam. He left the country in 1955 and settled in France in 1965. He is the author of *A Metic Love*, a collection of short stories written in French, and is a translator, with Nina McPherson, of contemporary Vietnamese fiction.

ROBERT STONE served in the U.S. Navy and worked as a correspondent in Vietnam. His first novel, *A Hall of Mirrors*, won the Faulkner Award for a first novel, his second, *Dog Soldiers*, won the National Book Award in 1975, and his third, *A Flag for Sunrise* won both the Los Angeles Times Book prize and the PEN/Faulkner Award. He has also written the novels *Children of Light* and *Outerbridge Reach*. Stone's other honors include a Guggenheim fellowship, a National Endowment for the Arts fellowship, a grant from the National Institute of Arts and Letters, an award from the American Academy and Institute of Arts and Letters, and the John Dos Passos prize for Literature. His first two novels were made into motion pictures.

TRAN VU (Luu Linh Vu) was born in Saigon in 1962. He left Vietnam in 1979 and now lives in France. His works include short stories and essays that have appeared in numerous Vietnamese language magazines in the United States and Europe. He has published two collections of short stories, *The House Behind the Temple of Literature* and *The Deaths of the Past*.

VO PHIEN (Doan The Nhon) was born in 1925 in Binh Dinh, Central Vietnam. He has published 29 works over a quarter of a century. In 1960 he was awarded Vietnam's National Literature Prize: he was (and is) a well known writer in Vietnam before coming to this country, via a refugee camp, in 1976. Since emigrating, he founded and edited the literary journal *Van Hoc Nghe Thuat* and has continued to write and publish fiction and essays in Vietnamese, often about the adjustment of a people in exile to their new country.

VU BAO was born in 1931 in Thai Binh Province is a highly decorated combat veteran of both the French and the American War. His works include the short story collections *To Be God, Our Tanks, Your Father Was a Woman* and *The Eldest and the Youngest*, the novels *Getting Married* and *Time Doesn't Wait*, and the film scripts for *The Starlets, The 89th Minute, Birthday Celebration* and *Late Tears*. He is the Editor-in-Chief of the Vietnam Cinema Committee and Vice-Chairman of the Hanoi Writers' Association. He was awarded Best Short Story prize by the Army Literature and Arts Magazine in 1988 and 1989 and received the Best Novel prize for 1991 from the Hanoi Writers' Association.

JOHN EDGAR WIDEMAN of Amherst, Massachusetts, is the author of *A Glance Away, Hurry Home, The Lynchers, Damballah, Hiding Place, Sent for You Yesterday, Brothers and Keepers, Reuben, Fever*, and *Philadelphia Fire*.

XUAN THIEU, born in 1930 in Ha Tinh Province, was the former Deputy Editor in-Chief of the People's Army Literature and Arts Magazine and Chairman of the Vietnam Writers' Association. An army veteran of both the French and American wars, his main works include the short story collections: *Shoulders, The River, Wind from the Sandy Land, The Guilty Mother, The Blue Sky, The Legend of the Fairies' Inn,* and *Don't Knock on My Door* and the novels *A Call From the Front, A Village by the Highway, Hai Van Pass—Spring 1975, The Prelude* and *Hue in the Season of the Red Apricot.*

TRANSLATORS of stories originally translated for THE OTHER SIDE OF HEAVEN:

BAC HOAI TRAN is an instructor of Vietnamese at the University of California, Berkeley. He was educated in Ho Chi Minh City and Dalat University. An Associate Editor of *The Tenderloin Times,* he had written the textbook *Anh Ngu Bao Chi; Introductory Vietnamese; Intermediate Vietnamese,* and served as a consultant on the documentary film *Which Way is East.* He immigrated from Vietnam under the orderly departure program in 1991.

NGUYEN BA CHUNG, a poet and writer on East-West cultural issues, resides in Boston, Massachusetts.

NGUYEN NGUYET CAM teaches at the Nguyen Du School for Creative Writing in Hanoi. Her translation into Vietnamese of E.B. White's *Trumpet of the Swan* was published by Kim Dong Publishing House in 1994. Her Vietnamese language version of *Charlotte's Web* will also be published by Kim Dong, in 1995. She is currently working on several translation projects including an edited collection of contemporary Vietnamese literature in English translation.

NGUYEN QUI DUC was born in Dalat and came to the United States in 1975. He has been a radio producer and writer since 1979, working for the British Broadcast Corporation in London and KALW-FM in San Francisco and as a commentator for National Public Radio. His work has appeared in *The Asian Wall Street Journal Weekly, The New York Times Magazine, The San Francisco Examiner, The San Jose Mercury News* and other publications, and he has published essays in *Zyzzyva, City Lights Review* and *Salamander.* He is the author of *Where the Ashes Are: The Odyssey of a Vietnamese Family.*

DANA SACHS is a journalist specializing in topics related to Vietnam. Her work has appeared in *The Far Eastern Economic Review, Mother Jones, Sierra,* and *The San Francisco Examiner.* In collaboration with her sister Lynne Sachs, she made the award-winning documentary film about contemporary Vietnam, *Which Way is East,* which was screened at the Sundance Film Festival and the Museum of Modern Art in New York. She is currently writing a book about Hanoi.

JAY SCARBOROUGH left for Vietnam to work with International Voluntary Services in 1967 on his 21st birthday and lived there until the end of 1975. He taught English at a high school in Phan Rang and at Dalat University, and spent a year working for Pan American Airways in Can Tho. In March of 1975, while working on a manuscript preservation project on a Ford Foundation grant, he was captured in the Central Highlands by the People's Army, during their final push of the war. He was interned for eight months in both the South and the North. He now lives in San Francisco where he is a lawyer for Jardine Matheson.

THAI TUYET QUAN was born in Saigon in 1965 and came to the United States in 1979. She received her undergraduate degree in acounting from the University of Washington and her graduate degree in Public Policy from Princeton University in 1991. She presently works for the General Accounting Office in Seattle.

PETER ZINOMAN, a doctoral candidate in Vietnamese History at Cornell University is currently Resident Director of the Council on International Educational Exchange's Study Center in Hanoi. His essays and translations of short fiction by contemporary Vietnamese writers Nguyen Huy Thiep and Pham Thi Hoai have appeared in *Grand Street, The Vietnam Forum* and *Vietnam Generation.*

CURBSTONE PRESS, INC.
is a non-profit publishing house dedicated to literature
that reflects a commitment to social change, with an emphasis
on contemporary writing from Latin America and Latino
communities in the United States. Curbstone presents writers who
give voice to the unheard in a language that goes beyond
denunciation to celebrate, honor and teach. Curbstone builds
bridges between its writers and the public – from inner-city to
rural areas, colleges to community centers, children to adults.
Curbstone seeks out the highest aesthetic expression of the
dedication to human rights and intercultural understanding:
poetry, testimonials, novels, stories, photography.

This mission requires more than just producing books.
It requires ensuring that as many people as possible know about
these books and read them. To achieve this, a large portion of
Curbstone's schedule is dedicated to arranging tours and programs
for its authors, working with public school and university teachers
to enrich curricula, reaching out to underserved audiences by
donating books and conducting readings and community programs,
and promoting discussion in the media. It is only through these
combined efforts that literature can truly make a difference.

Curbstone Press, like all non-profit presses, depends on
the support of individuals, foundations, and government agencies
to bring you, the reader, works of literary merit and social
significance which might not find a place in profit-driven publishing
channels. Our sincere thanks to the many individuals who support
this endeavor and to the following foundations and government
agencies: ADCO Foundation, J. Walton Bissell Foundation, Inc.,
Witter Bynner Foundation for Poetry, Inc., Connecticut
Commission on the Arts, Connecticut Arts Endowment Fund,
Lannan Foundation, LEF Foundation, Lila Wallace-Reader's Digest
Fund, The Andrew W. Mellon Foundation, National Endowment
for the Arts, and The Plumsock Fund.

Please support Curbstone's efforts to present
the diverse voices and views that make our culture richer.
Tax-deductible donations can be made to
Curbstone Press, 321 Jackson Street, Willimantic, CT 06226.